HIDE

Darlington Academy, Book 1

D.V. EEDEN

Julia!
Thank You for Everything
you do!!
Love DV

Written by D.V. EEDEN

Edited and proofread by J Rose and Stanley Editing

Cover design by Maria Spada

❀ Created with Vellum

This book isn't dedicated to anyone in particular, but this book started out as a little daydream I had once, my wild imagination creating another world which seemed better than life itself. I must admit, I hated reading whilst growing up, never knew why people loved books so much, but my friend once recommended a series, which I read from start to finish, and that was the first time my imagination - I like to say ' Ignited'. Now reading is a form of an escape from my depression, my anxiety, and every day that I struggled. I would lay in my bed creating worlds in my mind. So, I thought, why not write down the stories and share with the world. This book is dark, but it represents a lot of hurdles I had to face whilst growing up. I come from South Africa, and a lot of comments mentioned - be warned they are rather nasty - are what were said to me, but I faced those challenges. I take this time to thank you for the time you are investing in reading my story. A story I slightly relate to, even though this is greatly exaggerated for effect!

Enjoy the book, but please be warned if you do have trigger warnings, I wouldn't recommend reading beyond this page, but if you do, I hope you enjoy reading it as much as I did writing it.

Disclaimer

This book is a reverse harem, which means the FMC will end up with three or more partners.

This book also has trigger warnings for emotional/physical bullying, eating disorders, suicide attempts/references, abuse, mature content/ swearing and drug use. So please do not read this book if you are easily offended.

As this book involves bullying, that does not mean I condone any form of bullying, and there will be a happy ending in book 3.

Also this book is written by a South African/British author so references may be used that the reader may not understand.

This book is intended for the ages of 18 and older due to mature content.

Unofficial Playlist

Ghost of You by My Chemical Romance
    Call out my name by The Weeknd
    Messed up by Fredrik Ferrier,
    Bad Girlfriend by Theory of a Deadman
    Pyotr Ilyich Tchaikovsky 'Swan Lake',
    I Don't Care by Apocolyptica
    Heart shaped Glasses by Marilyn Manson
    Pour it Up by Rihanna
    Haunted by Beyoncé
    The Dope Show by Marilyn Manson
    Greatness by Don Broco
    Popular Monster by Falling in Reverse
    The Drug in me is you by Falling in Reverse
    The Kill by 30 seconds to Mars
    Mr. Brightside by The Killers
    Scream by Avenged Sevenfold
    To Be Loved by Papa Roach.
    Smells Like Teen Spirit by Nirvana
    Bloody Valentine by Machine Gun Kelly

Prologue

"*A*re you all set to go, hon?" Paul shouts from the bottom of the stairs as I pack the final bits in my suitcase, ready to leave for him to drive me to the airport. As I zip my suitcase shut a tear escapes, staining my already red cheeks. I haven't been able to stop crying since realization hit me last night- I'm leaving today.

Wiping away the tears, I pull the suitcase down from my bed and then roll it through the corridor to the top of the stairs. Taking in a deep breath, I lift the twenty-three-kilogram suitcase, and step by step I carry it down, trying not to stumble and fall flat on my face.

"There you are, are you all set?"

Paul comes into view, grabbing the handle when I reach the last few steps. I haven't been able to stop thinking about how he must feel. Right now, he's acting as happy as can be, but the look on his face says it all. The corners of his lips are unable to reach his eyes when he smiles, and the sadness fills his deep brown eyes when he looks in my direction.

"Yup, all good," I respond, my body shaking from anxiety.

The nerves are riveting through my veins. I keep replaying the same questions in my head, on repeat like a broken record – was this the right decision to make? Is this now my future? And will I regret this?

Paul places his warm hands on my bare shoulders. He takes in a deep breath before speaking.

"Look, I know this is hard, but England will be an amazing opportunity for you. It's not every day you get invited to attend a privileged college, and it will be a great time to reconnect with your father."

My breath hitches as another tear escapes and falls to the ground. Why did my life have to drastically change within a few days? The few days where my mum died, and I received a call from my father who then offered an amazing opportunity for me to attend Darlington Academy. I was stunned when father called, considering the last time I heard from him was on my birthday, and even then, it was rare. But why now? Why does he want to build a relationship after eighteen years of no effort? When he offered for me to move to England and attend Darlington, my emotions were all over the place. I had a serious conversation with Paul, because he has been a father to me since my mum married him. I couldn't wish for a better father, but he agreed that letting this opportunity slip was stupid and I would regret it in the long run.

Unfortunately, I have no future here in South Africa, and in order to broaden my horizons, England is the best option - I was born in England after all.

Wiping away the tears that fall, I nod in response to Paul, who unclasps his hand from my shoulder and already I feel the warmth deteriorating. He picks up my suitcase and carries it out to the car.

Meanwhile, I walk into the living room, taking it in for the last time. The small room is only able to host two cream leather sofas, both facing the open brick fireplace, and just above it is our fixed forty-inch television. The magnolia painted walls are scattered with golden frames filled with family portraits.

I step in front of one where my mum, Paul and I are sitting in a safari jeep, admiring the view of the animals with no care in the world. My finger involuntarily brushes against the panes of my mum's face, admiring how beautiful and happy she was – how happy I was.

Taking in a deep breath, I fight the urge to cry again. I can't spend my last moments here crying as I have been these past few days. I want Paul to remember me with a smile on my face at least.

Walking out of the room, I make my way outside to where Paul is checking up on the car, a routine he has always completed before driving. He checks the oil, the water and the tyres, making sure the vehicle is safe to drive. My heart strings pull knowing this is the last time I will ever witness such a routine. Before, I thought it was a tedious job but now, I am admiring him. Admiring the fact that he has always put safety first, ensuring I am protected in his care.

"Hey, are you ready?" he asks, his voice slightly breaking as he approaches me. The smile on his face does not reach his eyes. Unknown to him, I'm studying his features, taking in the wrinkles around his eyes as he smiles, his light brown shaggy hair with a few scattered greys blowing in the wind. He is always wearing a goddamn checkered shirt. He has them in every single colour.

"I am ready" I say, my voice sounding raspy.

I clear my throat and turn to look at my home for one last time. The little townhouse which has been my home since I can remember, but now it's time to move on.

The drive to the airport is silent, no words spoken between us, so I turn the radio on to break the sadness. There doesn't seem to be anything left to be said. Paul looks brave on the outside, but during the evenings he locks himself in his room and I can hear him shed his tears. Some nights I can hear his night terrors, with him shouting out my mum's name. I never bring this up to him, knowing he won't be able to confide in me. He leaves his burdens before the threshold of the bedroom, a smile replacing the frown as soon as he exits the enclosed room. He always ensures that I am taken care of, with breakfast on the table for when I wake up.

When we arrive at the airport, Paul drives through to the parking lots, grabbing a ticket from the machine so that he can pay later. He parks the car in a visitors parking bay and shuts the engine off.

"Adelaide, your mum would be so proud of you, I hope you know that…" he whispers without eye contact, and he rushes to climb out of the car before I can say a thing. My hands start to shake, the nerves getting the better of me. It takes a while to compose myself before I climb out of the car, whilst Paul grabs my luggage out of the boot. The fresh air hits me, and I take in a deep breath, appreciating the African atmosphere and heat. This is something I will definitely miss.

Paul escorts me all the way to the check in desk, where I collect my tickets and I notice that father has upgraded me to the first-class experience, which should be a lot more comfortable than economy. Once I have checked in my suitcase and watched it disappear into the baggage hold, I turn around and walk away.

It's too late now.

Without a word, I crush into Paul's chest, wrapping my arms around his neck and squeezing him tightly.

I don't want to let go.

I can't let go.

Tears appear in the corner of my eyes, staining my cheeks red as they fall onto the blue checkered shirt that Paul wears. His arms wrap around me tightly, giving me a reassuring squeeze before I let go. His scent of tobacco and cloves lingers in the air.

This is a moment I don't want to forget.

"It's time, Adelaide," he whispers with a faint smile.

I nod in response, the words not leaving my lips.

"This is not goodbye Adelaide, you know that. This is your chance to make a life for yourself. Enjoy what's to come, and you never know, you might prefer it in England. You know you can always come back home if you decide to. I will always be here for you," he says, looking me dead in the eye, and I know he's right. I can always come back home if things don't work out.

Letting go, I brush the stray tears away from my cheeks, a faint smile ghosting my lips as I watch Paul smile down at me. It truly is infectious.

Turning to leave, I walk towards the escalators to make my way through to security. As my feet land on the first step, I turn and look over my shoulder, finally seeing the tears escape from Paul's eyes and the strings pull around my heart.

"This isn't goodbye," I shout before I reach the top. I hope he can hear me.

Inhaling a heavy breath, I look towards the metal detectors and decide that I won't turn around again. I can't face seeing him destroyed once more.

The one piece of advice I would always give another would be to spend as much time with someone you love as possible. You never know when it will be the last time you see someone or be able to tell them you love them.

One moment of happiness can always turn into a lifetime of sadness, but we learn to live with it rather than let it burden our lives.

It's what makes us who we are…

Chapter One

*W*alking through passport control and collecting my baggage has filled me with a bundle of nerves. I haven't been to England since I was ten years old and the memories are flooding back. I can remember when we were a normal family, before my mum and I moved to South Africa, and my father stayed behind to run his business. My childhood was great, I loved how hot the climate was and enjoyed surfing, seeing wildlife, and not having a care in the world. That is, until a week ago when one incident changed my life.

My mum was murdered.

I haven't seen my father since the divorce and our move to South Africa. Mum quickly found a new husband who was a local, and she decided that it was best that we start a new life. She was incredibly happy with my stepdad.

Paul was a great man. Since my mum married him, he really stepped into the fatherly role, brought me up as if I were his own daughter. During my mother's passing, Paul was there for me. He consoled me and really stepped up in being both a mum and dad.

Holding back my tears, I picture Paul's face when he had to tell me the news of my father moving me back to England. Paul was so distraught, one moment he loses my mum and now me. My father never once visited because of his business commitments. I was lucky if I received a phone call, but we are not close, so it didn't really bother me until now. My great old dad has always put his business before family, so it was unsurprising that he's decided to send me to a boarding school a few miles away from Stonewall Cove

After entering the arrivals terminal, I notice a tall, stocky man wearing a sharp black suit and holding a sign with my name on it. "Adelaide," he calls. "My name is Steve; your father has sent me to pick you up. He has a last-minute meeting but said that he will see you before I take you to the Academy."

"Thank you, Steve," I say with disappointment. I shouldn't be surprised my father hasn't even bothered to pick me up from the airport. He is full of empty promises, I am not surprised by another one.

Steve takes my bags and escorts me to the car- a Bentley - which is parked literally outside the airport doors. Just this small walk is refreshing after a ten-hour flight without stretching my legs. Father was nice enough to book me a first-class ticket, so I spent most of my time in the makeshift bed watching movies to pass the time. Steve opens the car door for me right behind the passenger seat and waits for me to get in whilst putting my luggage in the boot.

I climb into the plush vehicle, the fresh new car smell hitting me in the face, the leather seats hugging me into safety. Between me and the front seats is a black box and when I open it, I find a mini bar, filled with tiny alcoholic drinks and two champagne glasses. This must be an added feature for posh people. Steve climbs into the driver's seat, turns over the engine and drives us out of the airport. As we get onto the main road, I plug in my earphones, leaning my head back against the leather headrest to take a little nap. I haven't slept for nearly twenty-three hours; exhaustion is taking over.

"Miss, we are five minutes away from your father's house," his monotone voice jolts me from my nap. Steve is a really intimidating guy, reminding me of a hitman from action films. He's wearing an all-black suit, aviator glasses and an earpiece; all he's missing is a gun.

It has taken nearly a three-hour drive to arrive at Stonewoll Cove, a town I vaguely recognise. We take a left turn down a single lane road, which seems to be in the middle of nowhere. I am guessing my father has decided to move to a more remote location. We come up to a large black electrical gate which Steve has to intercom through for the gates to open. The whole property is surrounded by ten feet brick walls, obscuring the view of the mansion he resides in. We drive down a gravel road which is decorated with beautiful rose bushes along the side. Upon the horizon I can see the mansion my father has built.

"Wow," I whisper, my eyes wide as I take in the view.

From the outside, the house looks grandiose, built with white bricks and marble decorations. Large French windows brighten up the house, symmetrically placed. The roof is high, triangular, and layered with stone slabs. The house itself is surrounded by a well-kept garden. Bright green grass, colourful flower patches and trees have been placed in a stylish way, making the whole scenery extravagant.

We pull up in the courtyard, the driveway circular with a magnificent water fountain placed in the middle, a naked lady holding a serpent around her neck. She looks like Eve from the Bible, with the snake in one hand and an apple in the other. My father – the great Victor Vaughn- stands proud, hands placed in his grey suit trousers and wearing a crisp white button up shirt, matching grey suit jacket, and finished with a royal blue tie. He hasn't aged a day since I last saw him, considering he has always looked rather old for his age. Salt and pepper coloured grey hair, cleanly cut on the sides and the top gelled back. The scowl on his face is no change, wrinkles etched into his forehead from where he frowns too much. He doesn't look too pleased about my arrival, staring down at his watch as if this is a waste of his precious time. As Steve walks round the car to open the door, I inhale a deep breath to try and calm my nerves. I plaster on a fake smile before the door opens so that I look a little excited to see my father.

"Adelaide, my darling daughter," his words drip with sarcasm. He doesn't move an inch from where he stands. His dark eyes scrutinize my form, his lips pressed into a thin line as they move back to my face. I take a step closer, unsure if I should go in for a hug or shake his hand. A whiff of his scent blows in the surrounding air, the leather and cigar aroma which I always hated.

"Daddy," I reply, standing before him, my palms getting sweaty from the nerves. We walk into the mansion, where he leads me straight to his study, my heart beating against my chest as my anxiety peeks - I guess I won't be receiving a tour.

He takes a seat behind the large mahogany desk stationed in the middle of the room. To my left is a large bookshelf, filled to the brim with leather covered books. In the far-right corner is a little bar where crystal decanters sit in perfect size order, filled with golden brown liquids and two crystal glasses. He gestures for me to take a seat directly in front of him and I automatically obey. I rub my sweaty palms on my jeans, waiting in anticipation, as I feel breathless as my chest tightens for what he wants to talk about. As if knowing that I'm waiting for him to speak, he takes his time, lighting a cigar and takes a few puffs, before taking a sip of his whiskey already sitting on the desk.

"Darling, how have you been? I haven't spoken to you since the day of the funeral," he asks, concern edging his voice, but also a hint of irony.

"I have been coping, but I am glad to be here," I say, my voice raspy from the lack of hydration. I clear my throat, trying to get rid of ashy feeling as the little white lie rolls off my tongue. Am I happy to be here? I think to myself as a sudden feeling of nostalgia hums through me. A mere few hours ago I was home, now I am sitting in a mansion looking into the eyes of my father.

"Yes, about that. You will be a resident at Darlington Academy, but you can come home on weekends and holidays. I do have one condition which you must obey though," he says, sounding more serious as his eyes meet mine.

"Well, I don't want anyone to know who you really are you see, so you will be joining the school with a different last name. I hope you understand."

He takes another puff of his cigar, waiting for me to respond.

My pulse quickens, the harsh words offending me. I stuff my anger deep down, feeling sceptical. Clearing my throat again, I nod before questioning him. "Can I ask why?"

"Let's just say…" He starts, but pauses before carrying on. "I don't want my reputation damaged. You know my world revolves around business and if you misbehave, it will reflect badly on me. I hope we are clear?"

I nod to my father's order, my lips pressing together, slightly taken aback by his demands. Clearly, we will not be building a relationship anytime soon. I deflate, disappointed as bile rises up my throat, feeling rejected once again by my father. My heart sinks, and I have to hold onto the cry that wants to burst free from its cage. I need to be strong.

"Now, Steve will escort you to your bedroom where you will go change into your uniform and then he will take you to your new college. This is a very prestigious college, Adelaide. You will keep your head down and study." His tone becomes more serious and he looks up from the whiskey in his hand. "I do not want any trouble. Do you understand me?" he barks, the order sounding a lot like a threat. The grey in his eyes turn dark as he stares at me, waiting for me to comply.

I hold back my anger, forcing a smile.

"Of course, what will my last name be whilst I am there?"

"You will be going as Adelaide Adams, your mother's maiden name. It's easier for you to remember." He doesn't even meet my eyes whilst telling me this.

I leave and shut the door to his study before taking a deep breath, tears forming in the corner of my eyes. My chest aches at the thought of using my mother's maiden name, and my body starts to tremble at the thought. My mind feels hazy, as if a dark cloud has just formed and the sadness takes over with the shock, he decided to go with my mum's maiden name. Is he doing this on purpose to hurt my feelings?

Steve rounds the corner, just as I manage to wipe away a tear from my cheek. He escorts me to the grand wooden staircase which leads to two other stories. The steps are covered in plush cream carpets, and the walls are painted in a sage green matching the style of the foyer. Pearly white skirting boards run along the bottom, matching the staircase. A large French window the size of two floors brightens up the area, the sunlight hitting the crystal chandelier above us. Steve takes me to the first floor, where the same style filters through. The hallways screaming elegance and style but simplicity. We end up at the last white wooden door on the right.

"Miss, this is your bedroom. It has an en-suite and a walk-in wardrobe too," Steve says as he opens the door and gestures me in. My mouth forms the perfect 'O' shape as I take in the large room. In front of me to the right is a queen size bed facing an amazing view of the rear garden. The room is rather plain, with everything decorated in neutral colours. My mind formulates how to make it better. I'm sure I can add my own twist to it. To my far left is a beautiful dressing table, with a few expensive perfumes and make-up. Next to it are double doors which I am guessing is the walk-in wardrobe. Seeing the doorway straight ahead, parallel to the entrance, I go straight to the bathroom which has a massive shower and luxurious whirlpool bath, all fitted in expensive marble.

I could get used to this.

As I take in my surroundings, a hard knock on the bedroom door startles me. I turn around as a lovely looking old woman enters the room, a clothing bag hung on her arm.

"Miss Adams, I am Mrs. Blossom, the housekeeper. I brought your uniform all ironed and ready for you." She smiles at me, her dimples showing, and lays the bag on the bed ready for me.

"Please Mrs. Blossom, call me Adelaide. I am not into formal names, especially if it is a fake one." I smile back at her, trying not to bite at the fact that she called me by my new last name. Apparently, father is even getting the staff around here to use it. Shaking my head, I draw my attention to the bed and stare at the clothing bag the nerves tremble through my veins. Well, I suppose I better get used to it too.

"Sorry dear, Mr. Vaughn wants us to start to use that name. He said it was so that you could get used to it," she says, her cheeks tinting into a soft red from embarrassment.

"That's okay, I understand you are under my father's orders. So am I." I scoff, rolling my eyes.

''So, tell me what the college is like," I say in an attempt to make small talk. She seems nice and I'd love to get to know her. I also want to make sure she doesn't think I'm like my father.

"Well, Darlington Academy was actually originally Darlington Castle. Duke Darlington transformed his home into a college over a hundred years ago. He was obsessed with education and had a vision that all privileged children should attend his prestigious academy," she starts whilst patting down the non-existent creases in the duvet.

''Nowadays, it's the only college made into a university in the United Kingdom that educates students up to twenty-two years of age. They say that it's to prepare the elite for the real world. It's an amazing place, I'm sure you will love it," she smiles.

"Well, I hope you settle in quickly dear. You are expected to leave in twenty minutes, so I would get a move on if I were you," she says with a stricter tone, waggling her finger at me. Before she closes the bedroom door, she gives me one last pitying look and then leaves.

I unzip the bag to reveal my uniform. I'm facing four years at the prestigious school that my father is shipping me off to. He has always been strict when it comes to education and ensured that I receive the best tuition possible. That was the deal my parents made. If I left with my mum, I still had to go to private school.

I discard the outfit that I've been wearing for nearly two days whilst traveling and change into my new identity. My hands smooth over the fabric. I kind-of like this uniform. A blue and black tartan skirt, white button shirt with a black pussybow tie, finished with a black blazer with blue trimming on the collar and the academy crest adorning the right breast. To finish it off, a pair of black knee-high socks and shiny black loafers. The academy even provided a black satchel bag to complete the look.

I stare at myself in the mirror, eyes wide in trepidation. This is my life now. One week and my life changes completely.

I snap a quick photo of myself to send to the group chat with all my old friends, showing off my new look. Before I put my phone down, I stare at my screen saver.

It's a picture of my mother and me. I look like her twin, both with dark brown hair that softly curls. Although, mine is rather long and she always had hers cut short. We also shared the same big blue eyes, so when I stare at myself in the mirror, I see her looking back at me. I choke on my tears, as my hand hovers over my mouth to silence the gasp so no one hears. Tears start to stream down my cheeks, staining them red. I quickly put my phone on my dressing table and wipe away the tears before someone comes up and notices the emotional wreck that I am.

I can't imagine what it's like for my father when he looks at me. I still wonder if he is upset by all this. He has shown no emotion towards her death and now I'm here, a constant reminder.

Chapter Two

The car stops in the courtyard of Darlington Academy. My mouth gapes open as I stare out the window. This place is huge. Plain fields of bright green, well-kept grass cover most of the fields outside of the castle, which is situated on a hill and adds to the overall aesthetic.

People aren't kidding when they say this place is a castle. Four broad, square towers are situated on all four corners, clearly built at the time for defence, connected by high strong walls in a stone so light it must be limestone. Large tracery gothic windows adorn the light stone, placed evenly on every floor level. The entrance is raised, and stone steps surround the large wooden gothic door, which has been renovated but still sticks to the theme.

As I climb out of the car, I rub my sweaty palms against my plaid skirt, biting my lip as I spot an older gentleman wearing a horrid dark brown suit, with a young girl who looks like she is a student here. Maybe she's my guide for the day?

I slam the car door shut and the man turns around, a bright smile on his face.

He rushes down the few steps to meet me. "Miss Adams, welcome to Darlington Academy. I am Headmaster Valentine," he takes my hand and gives it a shake before introducing me to the girl standing behind him.

"Please let me introduce you to Blaire, she will be your student guide and will assist you with anything you need. I need to head back inside for a meeting, but I assure you that you're in good hands." He gestures towards Blaire.

Headmaster Valentine seems to be full of cheer, which is unlike any headmaster I have met. In my old school they were strict as hell. As the headmaster leaves, Blaire strides towards me, inspecting me with big brown eyes. She is stunning; mid length wavy black hair resting on her shoulders, pale skin paired with big brown eyes, and the most immaculate bushy eyebrows I have ever seen. Most girls would pay for eyebrows like hers.

"Adelaide, it's so good to finally meet you. I must admit you are not quite what I was expecting." She chuckles to herself.

My eyebrows raise. I'm not sure whether to take that as a compliment or an insult. "Oh really, well what were you expecting?" I snort with a wry grin.

"I just mean that for a foreign exchange student, you seem so… English?" she says with a question.

Hm, okay then.

What did Blaire expect? That I was going to be a dumb bitch because I wasn't raised here? Already I can tell that it's going to be tough to blend in here. In my old school, I was the popular girl and had many friends. I pretty much ruled my school, but I doubt I'll be fitting in that easily here.

"I'll give you a tour of the grounds, but first let's head over to your dorm room and put all your bags away!" she says cheerfully, grabbing my hand and dragging me up the stone stairs. I am slightly taken back by how friendly Blaire is as she grabs my hand as if we have been friends for ever, but I am sure I could get used to this.

As we enter the building, I can't hide my surprise. My eyes go wide as I stare at the ornate furnishings. The ceilings are so high that I'm left wondering how on earth they manage to clean up there. The walls are original brick work decorated with massive portraits of which I am assuming previous headmasters. As we walk down a corridor towards the dorms, shining suits of armour are placed on either side, proudly holding their swords. Red carpet runs down the hall in all directions and original chandeliers hang from the ceiling, dimly lighting the area.

"This place is amazing, I can't believe it's a college," I say to Blaire, still dumbfounded.

She turns to face me, chuckling. "It's amazing, you'll have a lot of fun here I'm sure. I can show you the ropes" she says excitedly. We reach an old, dark wooden staircase that goes up to the three main floors. Sconces, spaced evenly on the walls, dimly lit the way.

"Sorry, there are no elevators here. You better get used to the stairs; all girls are on the top floor." she shrugs her shoulders.

We finally make it up to the third floor and walk through rustic wooden double doors. As soon as they open there are girls everywhere. They all have their doors open, gossiping and showing each other their phones. I'm quickly spotted by some of them and given weird looks. They stare at me like I'm invading their space, like I don't belong here.

"Don't worry about them, I'll show you the ones you need to avoid if you want your time here to be easy. If you stick with me, the others won't do shit." Blaire gives me a wink before stopping in front of the only closed door in this hallway.

"I forgot to mention, I'm your roommate!" she squeals in my ear, and gestures for me to walk in. I feel pleased that I get to share a room with Blaire, as she is technically the first alliance I have, and I couldn't think of anything worse than sharing with someone other than her right now. For once, I feel content.

"Wow, this room is huge," I reply in awe, my eyes widening at the huge open space. I walk around to my side of the room. There's a double bed, a chest of drawers with a matching wardrobe, and a cute little bed side table. All I need to do is decorate it to my liking.

As I survey the room, another girl strides in with a massive grin on her face. She isn't as pretty as Blaire, but still has that cute girl next door vibe. Beautiful, long auburn hair, flowing past her shoulders, freckles covering her cheeks, and hazel eyes that go wide when she stands in front of me.

"Oh, my goodness, Adelaide! I'm so excited to meet you. We haven't had a foreign exchange student in forever!" she screeches before grabbing me and giving me a tight hug.

"I'm confused though, aren't you from Africa?"

I nod and hum in response.

"But you're white? Is that normal?" she asks, cocking her eyebrow at me while she waits for an answer.

"Wow Maisie, not everyone who lives in Africa is black, you know." Blaire turns to me. "I am so sorry about her; she doesn't think before she speaks." She rolls her eyes and tries to kick Maisie out of the room. "It's fine, it was nice to meet you Maisie," I assure her.

"Come on, let's get on with the tour and show you the rest of the University" Blaire links her arm with mine after I dump my bags at the end of my bed, escorting me out of the girl's hallway. We end up downstairs again and through another corridor. Hanging on the walls are ancient shields that look battered and used. I spot one that has the academy coat of arms emblazoned on the front.

Blaire takes me through the academy and finally decides to show me the dining hall. Thank god, I'm starving. We walk through the double doors and I am in astonishment and my eyes go wide at the opulent atmosphere. This place does not look like a typical dining hall, but rather like a five-star restaurant. All the tables are decorated with royal blue tablecloths that match the academy colours, and in the centre are vases with freshly arranged flowers.

"Our table is over there," Blaire states, pointing to a round table near the far end, right next to a giant window. We take our seats and within a few minutes a waiter comes over to hand us a menu and take our drink orders. Wow, I honestly feel like I am on holiday, going in for the buffet.

"So, tell me about yourself Adelaide, why have you transferred over from South Africa to England?" she politely asks, seeming sincere.

I fight back tears that instantly rise to the surface at her words. I'm rather sensitive when it comes to questions like this, the memory of my mom still fresh from only a week ago. "Well, it seemed like a great opportunity to not miss, I got sponsored to come over here and attend this college." I shrug, holding back the truth.

Steve gave me a lecture in the car on our way up here, reminding me that my father does not want anyone to know who he is. The only reason why I'm being enrolled into Darlington is through a sponsor. For some reason, I just can't fathom as to why he doesn't want anyone to know about it. Especially since it has only been a week since losing my mum.

Blaire grabs my hand and squeezes tight. "Oh honey, I'm sure you will love it here," she smiles, her words warming me.

I return her smile, feeling relieved that I have managed to make an ally. I still have reservations, my heart holds back from trusting anyone just yet; no one is this nice to someone they just met.

The waiter comes over with our drinks and takes our food order. I settle for a simple vegetable soup with homemade bread.

"Where is everyone? It seems really empty in here," I ask, noticing that hardly anyone is eating lunch. I assumed it would be heaving with students.

"Oh, everyone is outside watching the Darlington Academy field hockey team. After lunch we will head over there and watch. My brother is playing," she says as our lunch arrives in record time.

We finish up quickly and Blaire takes me over to the hockey game where all the students have disappeared to. As we walk outside at the rear of the academy, on my right I see a large rose garden with a massive lake, a few swans paddling in the water. There are a few tennis courts with a gravel path through the middle, leading to a field where the game is taking place. The academy is located on a hill, and you can see the horizon in the distance, revealing that we are surrounded by forest and nothing else.

I am literally in the middle of nowhere.

Great.

We walk along the gravel path and all of a sudden there is a sea of students surrounding the field.

"Come on, I know exactly where to stand so that we get a good view. I want to support my brother." Blaire grabs my hand and we filter through the crowd. We stand on the outskirts of the field and Blaire calls out to someone.

Before I register who it is, he turns around and rakes a hand through his ruffled, thick chestnut brown hair, a smile adorning his perfectly sculpted face and then he's walking in our direction.

This must be her brother... a very handsome brother.

"Hey Blaire," he greets her, giving her a kiss on the cheek. He turns to look at me but not with the same soft expression he gave Blaire. Large ocean blue eyes stare at me as he scans my body, starting at my feet and moving all the way up until he meets my eyes. I shiver slightly. He wears a dark expression, a scowl taking over his sculpted features.

"You must be the African girl."

"My name is Adelaide, and yes I am new here," I state as I purse my lips and cross my arms over my chest, refusing to show any emotion, although I can't help but gaze at him.. He does not look eighteen.

The corner of his lips turns into a slight smile. "Good luck Africa, you're going to need it," he warns before turning away.

"Blake honey," a girl shouts from behind me. She pushes her way through to reach the guy and wraps her arms around his neck, practically hanging off him.

"Who's that?" I whisper to Blaire, as the posh, blonde girl starts kissing Blake, basically claiming him in front of everyone.

"That's Ruby Lockhart. She believes that she's my brother's girlfriend but really, she's just another notch on his bedpost." We both share a giggle at her comment and finally Ruby let's go of Blake, letting him get back to the hockey game.

"Oh look, it's the new girl." Ruby comes to stand in front of me, a hand resting on her hip. Her skirt is pulled up so high, if the wind blew, we would get an eyeful of her underwear. Her shirt is unbuttoned up until the point her cleavage is on show for everyone to see, and her cat eyes glare at me as she pouts her pink painted lips.

"Her name is Adelaide. Leave her alone Ruby." Blaire links our arms together as she stands up to this Ruby girl. I have already gathered that Ruby is the popular girl and Blake must be the popular guy, explaining their apparent relationship.

"Oh Blaire." Ruby tuts before continuing. "I see you are protecting the runt of the school. How sweet of you." Ruby flicks her bleached blonde hair over her shoulder as she insults me.

Who the fuck does she think she is?

I frown in confusion, biting the inside of my cheek before losing my cool. "Excuse me, who the hell do you think you are, insulting me? You don't even know me," I snap back without hesitation. I am not letting some girl talk to me like that, especially when she doesn't even know me.

"Cute, the girl from Africa speaks English. How quaint," she snarls in my face. "You will never talk to Blake again, or I will personally make sure you leave this academy. Understood?" she gives me a sinister smile before shoving my shoulder and leaving.

"I do apologize about her. She's a class A bitch and thinks she's better than everyone else. But be warned. She can play dirty, so try and stay out of her way. I do," Blaire shrugs as we carry on watching the game.

The school's team is called 'The Stags' and I must admit, it really suits them. The boys are hunky as hell with their royal blue hockey tops as part of their uniform. Blake's number is 66 which I find unusual, as I thought all the numbers are meant to be numerical for the number of members in the team.

Chapter Three

*A*fter the game, Blaire and I head back to our dorm room to get a bit of studying in. I had received my syllabus and class timetable so I can get a head start and prepare before officially starting. I chose business and dance as my two main subjects. Business, to keep my father happy, but my real passion lies with dancing.

"So...." Blaire says, dragging out the word whilst biting on her pen. "There's a party tonight to start the year, and I think you should come." She raises her dark eyebrows, waiting for me to answer.

"That sounds like fun, I haven't been to a party in ages," I say to her and she shrieks with excitement. This will be the first time in a while that I attend a party, so I'm looking forward to it. Hopefully, it will take my mind off of things, and I can meet new people.

"I have got the perfect dress for you to wear." She gets up and rummages through her closet, pulling out a little black dress. "Here, try it on," she says handing it over to me.

Taking in a deep breath, I take the dress and head over to the bathroom to try it on. It's a bandage style dress with a sweetheart neckline, and it only just covers my ass. I head back into the bedroom to show Blaire and she shows me her appreciation with a grin.

"You look so hot. Your ass looks amazing in that dress," she twirls me around in front of the mirror, inspecting it from pretty much every angle.

"You know I do have my own dresses I could wear. This would look so much better on you," I slouch my shoulders, not feeling all that confident in myself. I know that I have an okay body, I keep fit with my dancing, but I have no confidence to wear dresses that are clearly made for Victoria Secret models.

"Nonsense, I like it better on you. Plus, I have loads of dresses, lending you one isn't a big deal. Here try on these shoes." She hands me a pair of black Louboutin's, and I'm so shocked I gape at her in surprise. I know my parents have money and my father is a billionaire, but I was never showered with loads of gifts and didn't always get what I wanted. Father always said I had to work for what I wanted and to be honest, I never really thought about owning a two-thousand-pound pair of shoes.

I gasp in shock. "You're joking right?"

Blaire shakes her head at me, giggling, and goes back to rummaging in her closet.

"Honey, not to brag but my parents are rich as hell, so it doesn't bother me," she says, and I almost forgot that I googled her family earlier. She's telling the truth; her family is worth billions. They own Crawford Industries, who invest in financial companies and take them over. Not only that, but they also develop large properties around the world.

I get dressed back into my uniform, ready to head back down to the canteen for dinner. It's only six in the evening and the party doesn't start until eleven. "Just to let you know the part is off campus, but it is only half an hour away" Blaire says, and I immediately turn my attention to her.

"Are we allowed off campus?" I ask, my stomach clenching at the thought. I suddenly feel more anxious about going, not knowing the area very well and I am not entirely sure if I trust these people yet. But I guess I have to take the chance and just enjoy myself. I can't keep living life in a bubble.

I need to line my stomach for tonight so that I don't get too drunk. I don't want to make a fool out of myself. I order a chicken and mushroom cream pasta, which sounds to die for. Maisie comes and joins us for dinner, taking a seat directly in front of me.

"How was your trip to America, Mais?" Blaire questions as she stares down at her phone. I bring my gaze up to Maisie, also interested to know about her trip as I've never been to America.

"It was cool, America is so dreamy, but we didn't do much as my father had to work so it was mainly attending charity events or brunches," Maisie sighs, and she looks down at her plate, looking rather deflated. I can sense the disappointment radiating off her, and it honestly pulls my heart strings. It must be awful living in your parent's shadow.

"Adelaide are you excited for the party tonight?" she asks, pushing her risotto around her plate with her fork.

"I am, I haven't been to a party in forever," I admit, still unsure if I am excited or not, now knowing the party is off campus. I lift my glass and take a sip of my freshly squeezed orange juice, perfectly prepared. I could live off orange juice if I were allowed, it's like my heroin.

"Oh, great," Blaire huffs as she straightens her back, going stiff. I follow her gaze, noticing she is staring at her brother with two other guys as they walk into the canteen. "What's up?" I ask, noticing how uncomfortable Blaire is, her knuckles turning white from squeezing her knife and fork so tight.

"Yeah, I'm fine. I just hate those two fuckers my brother is with. They are the biggest dickheads I have ever met." She looks back at me for a second before glaring at their backs. "Be warned, they are not the nicest boys and you do not want to get on the wrong side of either of them. Even Blake," she warns, her eyes tearing away from them, turning to me. Sadness fills her big brown eyes and I'm surprised she said that about her own brother, considering they seemed close at the game earlier. Maybe I was wrong?

"Who are they?" I question, intrigued. I raise my eyebrow,

staring at the three guys walking through the door. They make their way to a long table. It is situated directly in front of the largest window and looks over the rest of the canteen, as if they are the kings of the academy staring down at their subjects. I watch them take their seats, and I realize that they are probably the three best looking guys I have ever seen in my life.

"On the left is Charles Kensington, he's a duke and the Queen's nephew. His family also have side businesses where they make their billions, but I'm not sure what it is."

The first thing I notice is his shaggy, dirty blonde hair. He reminds me of Alex Pettyfer, resembling his double but more handsome. His hair is slightly darker, it looks untouched but in a purposeful way. His shoulders are broader and more masculine.

"In the middle is the biggest asshole of them all, Hugo Vandenberg. His father is an MP and is also running for prime minister in the next election. He thinks he owns everyone. He is a cruel, heartless prick," she whispers.

Honestly, I can see that.

As I stare at their table, he looks directly at us and I notice how dark his stare is. The way he looks screams authority, sitting in the middle of Charles and Blake. Hugo is huge, even from where I'm sitting you would think he was a body builder.

All three of them turn their heads, catching me in the act of perving on them. Blake grins as I quickly turn my gaze somewhere else, but from the corner of my eye, I can see him getting up from his chair, making his way over to our table.

Shit.

"Do you want to take a picture? It'll last longer, Africa," Blake retorts, pulling the vacant chair opposite us and taking a seat, his forearms resting on the table. His white shirt is untucked from his slacks, the sleeves rolled up to his elbows, exposing his tanned skin.

"Oh, shut up Blake, I was just telling Adelaide about your asshole friends," Blaire snaps as Blake stares her down, his veins pulsing on the side of his neck, clearly annoyed. I lean back in my seat, feeling uncomfortable with the situation, and keep my mouth shut. It's evident Blaire is wary of her brother and something doesn't feel right between them two. I want to figure out why.

"You're so delightful," Blake snarls, leaning back in the chair as he lets out a deep breath. The way he maneuvers is so lethargic, reminding me of a sloth, but I bet when the time is right, he could pounce. He rests his hands behind his neck, watching Blaire as she eats her dinner while ignoring his presence.

Blake finally slouches forward, flexing his hands and showing off the muscles in his forearms. "How are you getting to the party tonight?" he questions Blaire, sounding irritated.

"I have a ride, thank you," she replies bluntly, trying to finish off her dinner.

"Is Africa coming with you?" he probes, leaning in and waiting for an answer. He's flexing his hands but then he stops, tapping his fingertips on the wooden table. He can't sit still. His face tightens as he squints his eyes at Blaire, the irritation very clear.

"Yes of course she is. Stop being such a dick Blake. Her name is Adelaide, so use it." She sits back in her chair and crosses her arms, giving him the filthiest look I have ever seen.

"Well in that case, be warned Africa. Our parties can get a little … extreme. You are in for a treat," he insists as he stands up, his eyes scrutinizing me before he smirks and heads back to his table.

"Don't worry about it, the parties are awesome. He's just trying to intimidate you," Blaire says and thankfully we have finished our dinner and once our plates are cleared, Blaire grabs my hand, dragging me out of the canteen so we can get back to the dorm room and get ready for the party.

Oh joy.

We manage to get ready after a few hours, with Blaire insisting on doing my hair and makeup. I lean in close to the mirror to see her handiwork. My eyes widen. I'm surprised by how good I look. She created a smokey look on my eyes, adding some false eyelashes and red lipstick. My hair is pulled into a sleek ponytail, then curled softly at the ends. Blaire opted for a cobalt blue skintight dress that also just about covers her ass, and pairs it with black heels. Her hair is straightened, the sleekness showing off her amazing jaw line.

She looks hot.

We meet Maisie outside in the courtyard, where she is waiting for us in her brand-new BMW i8. She assures me this is one of the cheapest vehicles she owns, and she only uses this one, so she doesn't damage the others. I jump in the back of the car whilst Blaire takes the front seat, connecting her phone via Bluetooth to play some old songs for us to sing along to.

"Whose party are we going to?" I question.

"We are going to Royce Huntington's mansion; he throws parties all the time. It's literally the party house," she says with a shrug.

I'm not sure if I heard her correctly, because she can't be speaking of Royce Huntington the actor.

We arrive at a mansion in the middle of nowhere, and already we can hear the music pounding from outside. Cars are parked all around the driveway and a few people are standing in the doorway, smoking cigarettes. Maisie parks the car in an available space which happens to be the furthest away from the house, meaning we have to walk across the gravel in six-inch heels.

This is torture.

From the outside the house looks magnificent. The modern structure is built with white cedar wood and red brick decorations. Tall large windows, asymmetrically placed on either side so you can see the fluorescent lights from inside, where bodies are already dancing.

Blaire links our arms together as we step through the doors into what looks like a palace. The grand marble staircase, with intricate steel work for handrails, is the first feature I see when walking through the main entrance. His parents must be very lenient. My father would never allow me to throw a party at his house. Not that I'd even be able to, considering he doesn't want to be associated to me. I shake the thought out of my head before it ruins my night and put on my biggest fake smile possible.

"We need to get to the kitchen. I want a stiff drink," Blaire says as she pulls me into a modern kitchen. I have never seen so much alcohol before, it looks like they bought a whole store's worth.

"Oh, look it's the foreign bitch," I hear Ruby say as she comes into the kitchen.

"Ruby, it's always such a pleasure to see you," Blaire says as she pours us both a vodka and cola. Ruby just scoffs and walks through the glass double doors, heading out into the back garden, and Blaire hands me my drink.

"Well, cheers to your first party in Darlington!" Blaire sarcastically says, rolling her eyes at me as we clink our glasses together, both downing our drinks in one go. We pour ourselves another and head into the huge living room, where loud drum and bass plays. Bodies grinding on each other and couples make out in every available space you can find.

On the edges of the room are small alcoves with seating areas, and in one of them I see Blake, Hugo and Charles sitting and laughing amongst themselves. A white powder lays on the table directly in front of Blake, which I assume is cocaine. Blaire grabs my hand, annoyance carved onto her pristine face, and drags me along with her towards her brother. As we approach them, I notice Royce Huntington. It really is him, I thought it wouldn't be true. Royce is one of my favorite actors, he plays in many big-time Hollywood movies. I know that he followed in his parent's footsteps and started acting when he was eleven years old.

Yes, I know a lot about him. Serious fan girl here.

"What the fuck Blake, are you serious?" Blaire shouts at her brother whilst he sniffs a line and ignores her. Hugo and Charles sit there staring at her with amusement and before I know it, I feel an arm snake around my shoulder.

"Who is this fine piece of ass?" I hear before I lock eyes with Royce. He rakes his gaze over my face and all the way down my body.

"Hi," is all I can say to him before he removes his arm and sits down next to Charles, helping himself to some cocaine. His light brown hair is clearly not styled, the top curly and disheveled, falling into his eyes as he leans forward.

"Do you want a bump?" he asks me with a rolled-up bank note

in his hand, the sea green colour of his eyes hidden by black pupils blown wide from the drugs in his system.

"No thanks, I'm not into drugs."

"Blaire, how about you take your only friend and fuck off," Blake curses, his face scrunched up into a frown. The other guys burst into laughter, embarrassing Blaire even further.

"Don't talk to her like that, you piece of shit!" I snap at Blake, and his eyes widen in surprise as I grab Blaire's hand to drag her away. I get us a couple of tequila shots and we find ourselves on the dance floor, trying to forget what happened with Blake.

After a few hours of dancing nonstop and losing count of how many shots we have consumed, Maisie finds us and drives us back to the academy. We get changed into our pjs and eat a few snacks while gossiping about how tonight went.

"I still can't believe you stood up to my brother for me. You should have seen his face!" Blaire rolls onto her back, laughing so much that we both end up with happy tears.

"I just can't get over the fact that Royce Huntington goes to this school. And he put his arm around me!" I wink at Blaire as I tuck myself in my bed. It is two in the morning and today is the first day of classes. I know for a fact that I am going to be hungover.

"Right, it's time for bed. I'm going to regret this when I wake up in like five hours," she says. I turn the lights off and settle myself before closing my eyes. Already I can hear Blaire's faint snoring. In a weird way it is rather comforting to know that I have someone here with me, rather than being alone.

My stomach aches, the roiling feeling of alcohol and nerves combined together. I'm still unsure of how I feel towards the academy, what with the students not being all that welcoming, but I'm glad that I have Blaire and Maisie already. Hopefully with them by my side, I'll have a good time.

Chapter Four

*I*t's seven in the morning. The alarm has just gone off and my head is pounding. I hear the faint noise of the shower and notice that Blaire's bed is already made. I climb out of bed, yawning like life my life depends on it, and stretch my arms above my head. I seriously need some painkillers to get rid of this headache. I stand up and start making my bed as the door opens to the bathroom, the steam hitting me in the face.

"Hey, how are you feeling?" Blaire says cheerfully with a big smile on her face.

"I feel like I'm dying. You on the other hand, seem to be rather perky for this time in the morning." Blaire laughs and I make my way to the bathroom, grabbing my towel on the way.

I stand under the hot stream for god knows how long, letting the water crash on my face as memories flood my mind. I can't stop thinking about my mum and how much I miss home, or the fact that I haven't built a relationship with my father. My heart aches to the feeling of not understanding why he isn't supporting me in the way a father should. The somber takes over my mind, the sadness clouding over any ounce of happiness I felt a mere few hours ago.

All these questions and no answers, but this is a sad truth that I am used to.

After washing and conditioning my hair, I scrub away all the toxins from my skin and rinse off before finally getting out of the shower. After brushing my teeth and hair, I finally put my uniform on. When I head back into the bedroom, I find Blaire only wearing knickers and sitting at her dressing table, finishing off her make-up.

"Well, I was certainly not expecting that," I say, laughing whilst throwing her pajama top at her.

"Oh honey, it's only a pair boobs. You'll be seeing me naked like all the time now." She shrugs and throws the shirt back at me.

I roughly dry my hair and end up deciding to curl it. I also apply some light make up to freshen up my skin and make me look less zombie-like, so at least I look half decent for my first day. Finally, I give myself a once over in the mirror and decide this will have to do.

I grab my phone from my bedside table and notice I have a text from father.

Do not forget about our agreement, it reads.

"Hey, you okay?" Blaire asks, which means I must be wearing my pissed-off look.

"Yeah, sorry I'm fine... just nervous." I smile at Blaire, hoping she lets it go.

"Good, we need to go. We'll be late for homeroom," she says.

We both leave our dorm room and walk through the girl's dormitory, quickly realizing that all the girls are staring and giggling directly at us.

"What's up with them?" I whisper, feeling all eyes on me. I start to panic in my head, thinking I did something wrong or maybe I forgot my skirt. I look down and examine myself, but I look fine.

"Hey girlies." Maisie comes out of her room and joins us.

"Does anyone want to share what is going on?" Blaire turns around, shouting at all the girls as they all quickly shut up.

"Haven't you seen the posts on Instagram?" Maisie pulls out her phone and loads the post on her phone, handing it over to me. My jaw drops. A whole post dedicated to me and some guy I was dancing with at the party with the words 'Slut' written all over them. I don't understand who or why someone would do this.

"Why would someone take photos of me and call me a slut?"

My mind goes blank, the enrage filling my veins as I read the comments. My body trembles as the anger reverberates through me, and to make it worse, it's on the gossip page for Darlington so I don't even know who posted the photos.

"Whoever did this will pay," Blaire hisses as she passes the phone back to Maisie.

"At least the photos aren't that bad?" Maisie shrugs her shoulders and follows behind us.

I walk into the homeroom that I luckily share with Blaire, heading towards my assigned seat, and I feel everyone's prying eyes on me. "Slut," a girl coughs as I walk past her desk.

I take one glance at her and she gives me lazy wave.

"Everyone settle down and take your seats," a distressingly ancient looking women says as she walks through the door. She's wearing a horrible khaki colored skirt which reaches her knees, a matching colored blazer and a white shirt buttoned all the way to the top, tied together with an antique pearl broach.

"My name is Ms. Glover and I will be your homeroom teacher for the next four years" she says, starting what looks like a slide show on the interactive board. After a few minutes of listening to Ms. Glover babble on, the door shoves open, slamming against the brick wall and interrupting my daydream.

"Mr. Crawford, I am so glad you decided to join us." She rolls her eyes and gets back to her desk as Blake takes his seat, which happens to be assigned next to mine.

"Africa." Blake nods his head in my direction, not with respect but mockingly.

"I heard a little rumor that you got a bit slutty last night," he says without even looking at me.

I decide to ignore his comment and get back to filling out all the forms Ms. Glover handed to us. As soon as the bell rings, I pack my things, without a backward glance at Blake, and make my way to my next class, Business Ethics.

I decide to make a quick pit stop at my locker, and notice Royce leaning against it with folded arms. He's missing his blazer, the sleeves to his shirt folded up to his elbows.

I observe him as I get closer, his light brown hair still wet from the shower and curls falling over his eyebrows. The cheeky smirk on his face makes my heart thump harder and my palms sweat. I'm concerned there will be an ulterior motive to his visit.

"Can I help you?" I ask with hesitance, staring at him warily. I may be in awe of the guy, but I don't want him to know that. I need to play it cool.

"Adelaide, it was such a pleasure to meet you last night," he says, the corner of his lips curling up into a grin. His beautiful sea green eyes feel like they are penetrating my soul, and all of a sudden, I am lost for words. He steps close to me and I shudder, a tingle running down my spine, causing goosebumps to appear on my skin.

"Although, I did hear a little rumor," he whispers in my ear and I feel his breath tickling my neck.

I gulp, still, my heart thumping hard, but I melt at the scent of his cologne, lavender notes with a hint of spice and woodchips hanging in the air. It's intoxicating.

"I heard that you were a little naughty, and that you were working at my party last night," he continues.

I take a step back from him as he just stands there with a huge grin on his face. I stare at him, raising my eyebrow and frowning.

"Now I don't mind that you do it for extra money, but I would appreciate it if you let me know and maybe let me use your services," he says casually, and I can't seem to form words to come out of my mouth.

"W-what are you talking about?" I stutter, and Royce's brow furrows, confused.

I try to take another step back away from him, but he moves closer with every step until I can't move anymore, my back hitting the wall behind me.

Before I know it, he has pinned me against the locker with both arms above my head and he stares directly at my mouth, then back to my eyes. His lips part slightly before the edges curl into a smirk.

"You know what I am talking about. William, the guy who is in those pictures on Instagram, said you gave the best blowjob last night." he chuckles under his breath.

I am trapped against a locker, with Royce fucking Huntington in front of me, and I'm whimpering like a dog with its tail between its legs. I am unable to even produce a sentence to stand up for myself and this guy has me lost for words, which is a rarity.

"Look, I don't know what you're talking about. I didn't give anyone a blowjob," I retort eventually, trying to push him away from me.

Royce removes his arms from above my head and starts to walk backwards.

"Next time you want to whore yourself out to all the guys at my party, give me a little notice," he demands and winks before walking off in the opposite direction. I stare at him as he wraps his arm around another girl's neck and leaves the building.

After my first few lessons, I meet up with Blaire and Maisie in the dining hall at our usual table. All my classes this morning were full of girls whispering about me and calling me names, as well as guys asking me for my number or to have sex with them.

"I can't believe someone started this rumor about you, it's so childish," Blaire sneers.

To be honest, Blaire is more pissed than I am. I know people start rumors about the new kid and I expected this to happen. I'm hopeful it'll blow over soon.

"I will find out who started it, and I will kill them myself," Blaire declares, and I am starting to feel sorry for whoever did make all this shit up.

"It will blow over soon, if I don't retaliate then no one will care." I finish off my pasta salad and take a sip of water. When I look at the head table from the corner of my eye, I see all four of the douchebags joking and laughing around.

Royce looks over to our table and sends me a little finger wave, looking all smug. I look away instantly, not wanting to give him the satisfaction. I stand up from the table and say goodbye to the girls.

It's my free period and I have to go to the library to sign up for a tutor to assist with the academics.

I make my way through the dining hall and straight away I bump into someone, and once I realize who it is, I get shoved back and nearly stumble on my ass.

"Watch where you're going, whore!" Ruby bellows.

"I apologize, I didn't see you there." I take a step back, holding out my hands in surrender.

I straighten my blazer and get ready to leave, but Ruby just starts laughing at me.

"Don't touch me again, I don't want to catch AIDS from someone like you," she sneers loudly and the whole dining hall goes silent to witness the altercation. I push past her two cronies, through the double doors and back into the main corridor. I rush all the way to the library and before entering, I settle my hand on the brick wall, as my heart thumps in my chest, my anxiety taking over. I close my eyes and count to ten to calm down my breathing, but my body continues to tremble. I repeat the mantra until my breathing is under control and once, I have contained my emotions I open my eyes and take in a deep breath.

Soon after walking up to the main desk where the librarian sits, I find the book where I can sign up for tutoring and I put my name down. Then the librarian hands me a timetable and rule book. I check the time on my phone and seeing as I have another forty-five minutes to spare before my dance class, I decide to take a seat at one of the large round tables and get started on my homework.

After a few minutes with complete focus on my assignments, a book slams down on my desk, jolting me in my chair.

"Can I help you?" I recognize the boy standing in front of me to be Hugo, who Blaire told me about yesterday. He stands there staring at me with a dark, disdainful look.

"You need to be here next week, Monday, five in the evening on the dot for your tutoring session."

And then it hits me.

"Are you my tutor?" I ask, raising my eyebrow. He looks too

good looking to be smart. Not to bring the boy down or anything, but it seems to be rare to find a guy who is super-hot and has brains.

"Unfortunately, yes. So please don't waste my time." He scowls.

"Yes, sir," I jokingly salute him, but I have a feeling I am agitating him even more.

He walks away, shaking his head and growling quietly.

Following my brief encounter with Hugo, I decide to make my way to the dance studio, which I am really looking forward to. Dancing is my way of expressing my feelings and letting off a bit of steam, and after today I need to blow off a lot and just dance it all away. The dance studio is amazing, with dark hardwood floor and surrounding walls consisting of floor to ceiling mirrors.

"You must be Adelaide Adams, I am Miss Young," a petite, blonde woman says as she makes her way over to me. She looks like she could be a student here and is stunning.

"Yes, I am." I smile back at her, placing my gym bag on the floor.

"It is so lovely to have a new student," she continues. "I better warn you now that there will be a dance recital in three months' time, and you will be expected to partner up with one of the lovely gentlemen in the class." She claps her hands in front of her and all the students make their way to the middle of the floor.

"Class, we have a new dance student. Please let me introduce you to Adelaide, who has just transferred here." She wraps her arm around my shoulder as she presents me to the rest of the class and luckily, I don't recognize anyone here.

Taking a sharp breath, I give a small wave to the class sitting in front of me, all pairs of eyes on me with welcoming smiles on their faces.

"So, Adelaide, just to inform you I will need you to perform a routine to the class so that I can determine who to partner you up with. Is that okay?" she smiles sweetly, so I nod and accept. I don't mind performing in front of an audience, so I feel rather excited.

Everyone sits at the edges of the classroom as they get ready for my little performance. I put on one of my favorite songs.

'Ghost of You by My Chemical Romance'

I decide to mix and match my dance routine with modern dance and ballet. I move around the room, not feeling the prying eyes watching every move that I make. Every time I dance, I imagine my happy place, somewhere on a beach where all I can hear is the waves crashing along the shore. I can hear the seagulls gawking above my head and smell the crisp saltiness of the water. I let myself go and forget all my troubles when I dance. I forget about my mum passing and the fact that I started a new school in a different country.

The music runs through my veins with every twist, twirl, and spin I make on the dance floor. I can hear my racing heartbeat and feel the sweat dripping off my forehead as I work every muscle in my body.

The song comes near to the end and I am on the floor with my head resting on my knee, in the splits position. I hear the clapping noises of my fellow students and Miss Young shouting, "Well done!"

I look up to the small audience and try to catch my breath. A huge grin appears on my face and suddenly, I feel as though a weight has been lifted from my shoulders.

Chapter Five

Once the bell rings to signal the class is over, Miss Young requests that I stay behind. "I am really pleased with your performance; you have done so well. Which is why I think you will be an amazing partner for Miles Digby," she clasps her hand on my shoulder while gesturing her other hand to someone behind me to come forward. I turn around and see a tall guy walking over, a big grin from ear to ear on his face. His teeth sparkle, matching the angelic look of his white blonde hair and pale skin.

"Hi, I'm Miles. I hear you are my new partner," he sticks his hand towards me, and I take it.

"Adelaide, lovely to meet you."

My heart thumps wildly as I stare at him, taking in his symmetrical features. This guy could be a model, his cheek bones are to die for. Miles drops my hand, taking a step back, raking his hands through his damp hair as he grins down at me.

"Right, meet me here three times a week. I'll email you a schedule," he says, winking before he leaves.

Soon after, I leave the dance studio and head back to my room. Walking down the corridor near the gymnasium, on the left I notice an old, medieval style door slightly ajar. Unfortunately for me, I am the nosiest bitch ever and curiosity takes over me.

Straightening my back, I stare at the door. Biting my lip, I check both ends of the corridor to make sure no one is watching and I walk to the door. Pushing what feels like a ten tone of bricks, the hinges creak loudly as I shove further in. The natural light from the corridor illuminates the tunnel walls as I take a few more steps forward.

Taking out my phone, I switch my torch on so that I can see more ahead of me. As I head in deeper, a loud bang goes off behind me, making me jump. I turn around and notice the door has shut completely. I move as quick as possible back to the door to try and open it back up but it's no use. The door won't budge.

I look down at my phone, noticing that I have no signal to send out an SOS. "Fuck," I sigh.

I figure banging my fist on the door is no use seeing as no one will be around. Classes have finished and everyone is either outside in the courtyard or in their rooms, so no one would hear me. I brace myself deciding to see where this dark tunnel leads to.

Tunnels must lead somewhere, right?

I shine my phone torch ahead of me, the light revealing that I'm surrounded by old brick walls and an uneven brick path. My heart pounds against my chest, and I inhale a deep breath to calm my nerves and prevent an anxiety attack.

We all know in horror movies this is how people die.

Curiosity killed the cat.

My head keeps imagining sounds and I turn, expecting to see something but there's no one there. These tunnels must be haunted. This castle is so old, I wouldn't be surprised if people died in it. As my torch lights up the walls, I instantly jump, nearly falling back. My mind is playing tricks on me, imagining there is something in here with me. I shine the torch back in front of me, noticing a scary gargoyle staring right back at me, and I let out a big breath of relief before carrying on through the eerie tunnel.

I walk for what feels like miles and am unsure of how far away I am from the academy. Eventually I enter a larger space that has three other doors and my breath hitches in my throat.

Why would someone put three doors at the end of a tunnel?

I make my choice and head to the middle door. I turn the doorknob, but the door won't budge. I try and push it open with my shoulder, but it makes no movement.

When that doesn't work, I try the exact same thing on the door to my left.

Again, it doesn't budge.

I try my luck with the door on my right, and with one push, the door swings open easily. Someone must have come down here if the door in the academy was already open. So, they must have come through this way.

I carry on with the journey, and after a few minutes, another door is at the end of this tunnel and natural light is seeping through the cracks. I push open the door, which is not as heavy as the others and end up in what looks like a basement.

A basement filled with beer kegs.

Where the fuck am I?

Looking around the basement, I see an industrial style metal staircase which I climb slowly, trying not to make any noise. Pushing the metal door at the top open, I come out in a red colored hallway with dim yellow lighting. Sighing to myself and unsure of where to go, I take a right turn.

"Hey there, you lost?" a friendly female voice startles me from behind.

Taking a deep breath and preparing an excuse, I slowly turn around and put a fake smile on my face. "Hi, yes I am so sorry, I seem to have gotten lost trying to find the ladies room." Hopefully, she buys the little white lie that I just formed.

"Oh honey, that is fine. It took me a while to get used to round 'ere."

The lady, who hasn't formally introduced herself yet, puts her arm around my shoulders and guides me through to a large speakeasy. "You must be here for the job interview, I am Samantha," she grabs my hand to give it a firm handshake, and all I can do is nod along to what she says.

"Um yes, I am Adelaide," I introduce myself, thinking that it would be helpful to get a job around here, especially during my free time. Samantha shows me around the extravagant club with the walls painted in a deep red and crystal wall mounted lights. There are several round tables covered in red and black tablecloths with a small candle in the center for decoration scattered around the room, all facing a large stage with red velvet curtains. Directly in front of the stage is a lowered level floor with red upholstered seating booths, which I am guessing may be VIP seating.

"Okay, so as you can see this is the bar on the left where customers can sit and have a drink, but usually people sit at the tables and the waiters take drinks to them," Samantha explains, but I am mesmerized by the bar itself.

The shiny mahogany wood looks as though it is hand carved to create the intricate details of the old Tudor Rose. On the wall behind are glass shelves with every bottle of spirit you can find.

"Have you got any bar or club experience?" Samantha brings me out of my daze.

"Yes, I do. I used to work in a pub back home," I say with a smile.

"Great, well will you be able to do a trial shift this Saturday?"

I instantly agree with her. I mean it can't be that hard, going from working in a small pub in South Africa to what looks like a huge club here?

We shake hands and Samantha escorts me to the main entrance. Thank god I can order an Uber from here to take me back to the academy. I don't even know where or how far away I am.

From the outside it looks welcoming, cheerful, and beautiful. Plastered walls and marble stones make up most of the building's outer structure. It's as alluring inside as it is on the outside. I stand in the parking lot, patiently waiting for my Uber to arrive, my attention focused on a large sign with lights around the edges.

"Club Envy," I read aloud. This must be what the club is called.

I should have asked really, but I should technically know if I was supposed to go for an interview. I just don't understand how a tunnel from the academy leads straight to Club Envy and who would use it. Or even yet, what the connection is between them both.

After only waiting for five minutes, my Uber arrives and drives me back to the academy. Thankfully, by road it is only ten minutes away and I am surprised that I haven't noticed the building before.

When I arrive back at my dorm, I find myself alone as Blaire isn't back yet- probably still in class. I decide to take this time alone to study on my bed with some music playing in the background, while I nibble on a few snacks that we have in our small fridge.

After a few hours, I can't handle any more information in my brain. Pulling out my phone, I realize I missed a call from my father. Rather than calling him back, I send him a quick text asking what he wants, as he never usually calls.

Sighing to myself, I decide to go for a bubble bath to relax. My legs ache after that long walk through the tunnels. Slipping into the tub, my first thought is that nothing beats a hot bath. I lay there for a while, reading a book whilst my skin prunes in the water. I hear the door slam from the room, meaning Blaire must be back. I wash my body and get out of the bath, wrapping my body in a fluffy towel and leave the bathroom.

"What the fuck?" I jump back, startled to see Blake sitting on Blaire's bed.

"What are you doing in here, and how did you get in?" I check myself over, making sure that I'm still holding the towel to my body.

Blake lifts his head slightly from looking down at his phone and looks directly at me. His oceanic blue eyes rake over my body in repulsion as I stand in the bathroom doorway, my hair and skin still dripping wet.

Flustered and breathless, I tighten my hold on the towel, embarrassed Blake caught me off guard, looking like this. The droplets of water fall to the floor as the silence takes over the room. Eventually he looks back down at his phone.

"I have a key."

"Well, that doesn't mean you can just come in here whenever," I grit out. Storming over to the door, I open it and point out to the corridor. "Get out."

Blake sighs, standing up from Blaire's bed, slowly walking up to me, putting his phone in his pocket. His facial expression doesn't change. His nostrils flare as his protruding stare doesn't avert my gaze., the ferocity very clear.

"Please," I plead.

My gaze trails down to the ground, not brave enough to look him in the eye and Blake pins his right hand to wall next to my head, enclosing in on my proximity. He brings his mouth to my ear and barks out a wry laugh.

"Never, ever talk to me like you did at the party again."

Quickly, I bring my eyes up to meet his and all I can see is the resentment and fire in his eyes.

"Do you understand?" he grits out.

My body trembles, a shiver running down my spine and the only way for me to respond is by nodding my head in agreement.

"Good, otherwise I will make sure what you get next is worse," he threatens, storming away out the door and down the corridor.

I slam the door once he's gone and sink to the floor, my knees too weak to hold me up as my body trembles after the altercation. It must have been Blake that started the rumors in the first place, and all because I told him not to speak to Blaire in horrible way.

What a prick.

I get up and quickly dress into my pajamas, getting straight into bed. Looking at my phone, my father has texted me back requesting my attendance at a dinner on Friday night, which I agree to. My chest tightens at the fact of another social event, but I don't really feel like arguing with my father now either.

∼

Sitting in English class at nine in the morning after a sleepless night is torture. I'm unable to hear the words coming from my teacher, as all I can hear are the whispers from the students. After my altercation with Blake in my room, I can't get the image of his furious face out of my mind, nor the murderous glint in his eyes and how repulsed he was when he saw me in my towel.

That guy has some serious anger issues.

Once the bell rings, I gather my things in my satchel, waiting for the students to clear before I head to the dining hall.

"Miss Adams, do you have a minute?" Headmaster Valentine requests as he appears in the doorway. Instantly I pick up my bag and follow him to his office.

"Have I done something wrong?" I question as I take the seat across from him at his desk.

He crosses his arms then sits back in his leather upholstered chair, his hard stare boring into me.

I wait patiently for him to speak, rubbing my sweaty palms on my skirt. Why do I have a feeling this might be about the rumors? And that he might actually believe them?

"Well, I must admit. Since you have started at this academy, a certain rumor has been brought to my attention."

Quickly, I try to defend myself. "Sir, I can—"

Mr. Valentine holds up his right hand, interrupting my explanation. "Look, I understand you are new here and that is why I am treating this as a stupid rumor some other student created." He places both hands on the desk in front of him and stares at me with intensity. "I will let this slide, but if I hear of something like this again, I will be forced to take action."

"Yes sir, I understand," I say, standing up and leaving before he changes his mind.

As I walk past the reception desk, I notice Blake leaning against the wall, a smug expression on his face and staring directly at me. Without trying to make any contact with the prick, I straighten my back and look directly ahead of me so that my eyes don't meet his.

However, when I try to walk past him, he grabs my arm, his fingers digging into my flesh as he squeezes tighter. "See Africa, this is just a taster of what I can do to you. Do not disrespect me again," he hisses directly in my ear.

My head turns, finally facing the monster next to me, and my wide eyes meet his. The blue of his iris disappears as his pupils dilate, turning them darker.

"That was for kicking me out of my sister's room. You need to learn your place around here, Africa." He gives me a murderous smile, sending shivers down my spine as goosebumps break out all over my skin.

Unsure of how to respond to him, I stand there blankly, trying not to let the tears pricking my eyes fall. Blake finally let's go of my arm, undoubtedly leaving a bruise, and storms off in the opposite direction.

~

*A*fter a long dreadful week, with all the whispering and snickering everywhere I go, I am thankful it's finally Friday and I get to go to my father's house this evening but I'm still in a bundle of nerves knowing I have to sit around a table with people I haven't met yet. Considering this was only the first week in Darlington, it has surely been eventful. Nothing that these posh fucks say about me even breaks the seal of being hurt. I bet none of these twats know what losing a parent feels like. They were probably all raised by a nanny or something.

I manage to get through the morning classes without any comments or incidents. I am hoping that the rumor has fizzled out and no one will be bothered by my lack of retaliation. As I don't share a class with Blaire, we arrange to meet in the dining hall and have lunch. I take a seat at our normal table and wait for the girls. I notice the head table where the three royals sit – yes, I call them royals as they may as well be – has a group of people I haven't seen before siting in their places, and I'm pretty sure that will cause some problems.

Well speaking of the devil, the three royals that spawned from Satan have arrived and they all look displeased upon noticing their table is occupied. Unsurprisingly, the table is cleared within seconds and they didn't even need to say a word.

My nickname of the 'royals' fits. It's like they are the kings of the school and even the teachers are afraid of them. I wouldn't want to be on the wrong side of the Queen's nephew either and I have already had a run in with Blake.

Waiting patiently and avoiding any contact with the royals, I scroll through my phone, taking interest in my social media again. I don't particularly want to draw attention to myself, but I also feel like a loser sitting on my own, so I text Blaire telling her to hurry up.

Thankfully after I text her, I see Blaire rushing through the canteen to join me.

"I am so sorry I'm late, the class was running behind," she says, trying to catch her breath.

We order our food and suddenly a thought crosses my mind. I can't help myself from being nosy. I raise my eyebrows, looking at Blaire. "So, weird question," I ask. "You and Blake aren't twins, are you?" I bite my lip, hoping that I'm not being too intrusive.

"Oh no, we're not," she laughs, finding my question humorous. "We have the same dad but not the same mum. My dad cheated on my mum with Blake's, so both our mothers were pregnant at the same time."

Nodding my head, my eyes widen as my eyebrows raise. That does explain a lot, especially as they are in the same year at school. I just assumed one of them was adopted or he got held back a year, which wouldn't surprise me.

Our food arrives and is served to us by the waiter. I haven't eaten a thing today and my stomach is rumbling like crazy. While eating, I wonder if Blaire has any knowledge of her brother's confrontation with me and how she would feel about it. I guess they aren't that close. I mean they don't really communicate with each other during the day.

"Hey, what are your plans for this weekend while everyone goes home?" Blaire asks and my breathing quickens as I have no idea what to say. I can't just tell her that I'm going to my father's house or that I have a trial shift this Saturday at a Speakeasy.

"I am staying here all weekend. I might venture out into town, but I think I will just study," I shrug, hoping that I am convincing enough. Blaire stares at me as though she is trying to figure me out, so I give her a sly smile which works, and she gets started on her lunch.

"What about you? Doing anything nice?" I ask her, figuring that I may as well try and suss her out.

"Blake and I are off to our dad's house. Won't be anything special, but we are expected to attend some sort of gala."

Hmm, how the other half live I suppose. Always attending galas and posh parties. I can see why my mum wanted to leave this life behind. Seems as though so much is expected of you at such a young age.

Chapter Six

After what felt like a relatively normal day, classes are finally finished, and everyone is leaving to go home for the weekend. Luckily, Steve isn't picking me up until eight this evening, so I have some time to pack my bag and possibly do some studying. I look at the time, noticing it's only five, so I come to a decision to go down to the dance studio and get some practicing in for my routine.

Walking the halls of the castle is like walking through history, but with ghosts. I wouldn't be surprised if the castle were haunted. I feel as though the painting's eyes are moving and watching my every move like I'm in an episode of Scooby-Doo, or even better, Harry Potter. Now that would be cool. A shiver runs through me as I think about an actual ghost approaching me. I'm not sure I'd want that to happen.

It takes ten minutes to get to the dance studio from my room, and that is with speed walking. I notice on my way up that the door leading through to the tunnels is shut. Maybe they locked it when they found it open while I was inside?

Reaching the studio, I pull the door open and walk inside. The good thing about everyone going home is that I don't just have the castle to myself, but also the dance studio. Not even a teacher in sight. Well, apart from the skeleton staff, but they don't really do much. This week Miles and I didn't have dance practice, but I thought I'd come up with a few ideas to run by him next week. Peeling off my leggings and hoodie, I'm left wearing my leotard. Usually I don't wear it because I don't like people seeing me with nothing on, and it really doesn't leave much to the imagination, but it's perfect to dance in. It gives me much more flexibility. I put on 'Call out my name' by The Weeknd after I have stretched out my limbs. I start a random routine, dancing for another three more songs, until someone starts clapping their hands.

Immediately, I grind to a halt and gasp, because Royce Huntington is leaning in the doorway, and has gone undetected until now. That sly bastard.

"Wow, you are an impressive dancer, I must say," Royce says with a mischievous grin on his beautiful face.

"Can I help you?" I ask him, raising my eyebrows, a little annoyed.

Grabbing my gym towel, I wipe the sweat away from my face and chest just as Royce takes a few steps into the room. He looks around the studio, his face morphing into an appreciative smirk as he looks back down to me.

Sighing, I answer, "I am kind of busy."

"I thought everyone went home this weekend. I wasn't expecting to hear music from the hallway and find you dancing in here," he grins, raking his gaze over my body and making me feel exposed. I shudder.

There really isn't anything left to the imagination with the leotard hugging every curve of my body. My heart races with the proximity of Royce affecting me in a different way. It's exhausting.

"Well I am a foreign exchange student, remember. I don't have a home," I murmur, grabbing my stuff so that I can leave. Royce grabs my wrist to stop me from leaving the room, but I yank it out of his hand and scurry away as fast as I can.

"I must say, you have amazing body," he shouts from behind me and I don't look back.

I walk as fast as I can back to my dorm to try and get away from

Royce. Realizing that it's already half past six in the evening, I haven't packed, showered, or studied.

Passing the door to the tunnels on my way to my room, I see the door is ajar. "What the fuck," I whisper. Someone has clearly used it again. I wonder if someone uses the tunnels as a short cut to Club Envy. Then again, there were other locked doors, so maybe they used one of them. I still want to find out why the tunnels from Darlington lead to a club of all places. I doubt the club was there hundreds of years ago when the castle was built. Maybe it is a coincidence?

This is why I need that job as a bartender, so I can investigate. Why of all things does one of my traits need to be being nosy?

Back at the dorm I have a shower and pack my bags. Before I know it, Steve texts me to let me know he's here. I make my way to the courtyard to meet him, really hoping that I do not bump into Royce again. I don't want him to see me being picked up in a chauffeured Bentley and have him snooping around my life. Father would literally kill me. Steve opens the door behind the passenger seat for me and packs my bag in the boot.

"How was your first week Miss Adelaide?" he asks, glancing at me through his rear mirror.

"It was okay thank you, still trying to get used to everything," I respond bluntly, not really wanting to make conversation, even though he seems nice enough. Steve is a big guy. His persona is intimidating and unapproachable, which makes me wonder what his past profession would have been, to now be chauffeuring my father and occasionally me around. I must admit that he's a good-looking guy too. He has the whole rugged bad boy look. I wouldn't fancy getting on the wrong side of him.

Forty-five minutes later, we pull up to my father's mansion and Steve uses a fob to automatically open the gates, which must be new, as last time he had to intercom through. On the right as we enter the estate, I notice a little hut with a security guard sitting inside. As we drive past, he gives Steve a curt nod. I wonder why my father has all this security. I know he's a billionaire, but he isn't a celebrity of any sort.

Once I get into the house, Mrs. Blossom is standing at the grand staircase waiting for my arrival. "Dinner will be served at nine this evening Miss Adelaide. I hope you have settled in at Darlington Academy," she says with a soft smile before picking up my bag and making her way up the stairs to the west wing, where my room is located.

"Thank you, Mrs. Blossom," I shout back at her so that she can hear me from the top of the stairs. I come to a decision to find the kitchen and get myself a drink. I might even have a snoop around the house. The last time I was here I didn't have a chance to explore, so why not now?

I manage to find the grand kitchen, in the shape of a big U with an island in the middle. The breakfast bar is strategically placed to look toward the floor to ceiling windows, overlooking vast gardens and a lake. The counter tops are made out of a glittering marble and the cupboards are all painted in a pebble cream. An enormous silver range cooker catches my eye, where a chef is cooking tonight's dinner. The old Italian-speaking man looks directly at me and then tries to shoo me out of his kitchen. I hold out my hands in surrender to apologize.

"Hi, sorry I just wanted a drink," I say to him, hoping that he understands, as I don't speak a word of Italian. A lady standing at the island, cutting vegetables, gestures for me to sit down on one of the tall stools at the breakfast bar, and I oblige. I don't really want to say no to a lady with a very sharp knife in her hand.

"What drink can I get you Miss Adams?" she says once I've taken my seat. Why is everyone calling me Miss Adams for Christ's sake?

"Please call me Adelaide," I insist with an edge to my voice. Hopefully, she gets the idea that it pisses me off. "I'll have a glass of orange juice, if you have any, please." Nothing is better than a fresh glass of OJ. The lady - who's name I'm still not aware of - pours me a fresh glass of orange juice from the American style fridge and hands it over to me before getting back to cutting the vegetables. She looks young, possibly even my age, wearing the classic kitchen staff uniform in black, her blonde hair tucked up in a black cap.

"So, what's your name?" I directly ask her No point beating around the bush.

"It's Sally, Miss Adelaide," she instantly replies with a soft smile and I down my drink in a few gulps. "Well, nice to meet you Sally, I'm off to explore more of this palace my father calls home." I smile back at her, leaving my empty glass on the side. I leave the kitchen and end up in a narrow hallway, following the direction of where I can see the most natural light.

"Wow."

My jaw literally drops to the floor as I walk into the ballroom and catch my breath. The room is easily bigger than a normal house. The floor is so white, glistening from the natural sunlight coming through the French windows. Three large crystal chandeliers hang from the tall ceilings, gleaming with every stroke of light. At the other end of the ballroom, a dais is situated where I'm guessing the performances take place.

I stroll through the room, out of the French doors and onto an outside balcony that looks over the botanical gardens and fountains. Who knew my father lived this lavish lifestyle and couldn't be bothered to see his own daughter or support his family?

I do wonder if he has another wife or maybe other children. Maybe he treats them better. If I'm honest to myself, I am coming up with different conclusions and have never been told the full story.

I head back inside and go to my room as dinner will be served soon and I don't want to be late. The entrance I used to walk in must have been the staff entrance, as a fancier looking door leads straight behind the grand staircase. This must be where the guests come through.

～

*A*fter having an amazing bubble bath in my whirlpool bathtub, and blow-drying my hair, Mrs. Blossom has left me a black box with a note on the top on the bed. I open the note. "For Dinner, - Father," I read out loud. I open the box to find a red lace cocktail dress, which is way too posh for me.

"What a lovely dress, Miss Adelaide," Mrs. Blossom says from the doorway, as she enters my bedroom. "You will look stunning," she says excitedly. She wanders into my bedroom and picks up the clothes I wore earlier, putting them into a washing hamper and replaces my towels. Mrs. Blossom places the dirty washing hamper near my door and heads towards my wardrobe, picking out a pair of black heels.

"Oh my God," I shriek, seeing the pair that Mrs. Blossom pulls out. "Those are Louboutin's." I can't contain my excitement. I quickly put them on to see what they look like. I mean, I know they are just black heels, but they are beautiful, and I finally have a pair of my own.

"Yes dear, most of your clothing and shoes are expensive name brands. Your father always wants you presentable." She looks at me through the mirror as I twirl and pose with just my shoes and under-wear. You don't wear these shoes, they wear you.

Slipping on the red lace dress, I give myself a once over in the mirror, my face scrunching up in displeasure. "I really hate this dress," I huff. I look like an old lady trying too hard.

"Dear, I think you look lovely." Mrs. Blossom brushes my shoulders and gives me a reassuring squeeze. I wonder why my father wants me all dressed up for a pointless dinner. Unless he has invited guests, which he could have warned me about.

Mrs. Blossom leads me down the grand staircase and into the study where my father is already standing, looking out the window as he takes a call with a tumbler of whiskey in hand. Mrs. Blossom leaves, shutting the door behind her, so all I do is wait. Father notices my reflection in the window and shuts the call off straight away.

"Ah Darling, I hope you are pleased with the dress. You look like a lady for once," he says, patronizing me. He takes a seat on one of the leather upholstered chairs and crosses his left leg over the other, gesturing for me to sit down opposite him. I sit, taking in my surroundings. The whole study is surrounded by bookshelves. Maybe it's a decoration thing.

"Do you read?" I ask him, trying to make some sort of conversation in an attempt to get to know him. I have no idea what his interests or hobbies are. All I get from him is that he is strictly business.

That reminds me, I don't even know what business my father even does. Shall I ask him or just wait for him to tell me?

"I read all these books a while ago, but now they are simply for decoration," his voice comes out rough as he gulps down the rest of his whiskey. I respond with a curt nod and look straight back into my lap. My palms are sweating so much right now.

"We are just waiting for our guests to arrive and then dinner will be served." He stands up, sauntering over to the little bar in the corner of the room where all his drinks are displayed in crystal decanters. He pours himself another glass, also filling a second one. He offers me the drink and I instantly take it. I am going to need it to get through this evening.

"How was your first week at the academy?" he asks, sitting back down and observes me.

Do I tell him it's been a living hell or just let this one go?

"It was okay, I am still trying to settle in," I lie. I gulp down my whiskey and put the glass down on the little table with a coaster. I wipe my hands down on the dress to get rid of the excess sweat and my father stares at me, with calculating eyes.

"I heard a nasty little rumor got around, I hope it's not true," he hisses.

Shit, how did he find out about a stupid rumor at my school? Unless someone has been informing him.

"It was a stupid rumor some idiot started on the new girl. I am sure this happens all the time. I haven't even retaliated." I roll my eyes at him, instantly noticing the anger flash in his eyes. My throat suddenly feels dry and scratchy.

"This is exactly why I did not want you going to the academy and tarnishing my last name," he snaps, leaning forward in the chair, resting his elbows on his knees, waiting for me to look directly into his eyes.

"It won't happen again," I whisper, my body shaking. I give up, no point trying to defend myself to someone who doesn't know me.

"Dinner is served," a gentleman announces, breaking the

tension as he enters through a door opposite the one I entered through - This one must lead through to the dining room. I follow his lead, and I'm met by the unnerving eyes of all the guests already seated, following me all the way to my seat.

Silence fills the room until my father is the last to be seated. All the guests are male with no female in sight, which means I'm on my own, and my heartbeat has tripled in beats. The young man who called us in for dinner offers red wine to everyone sitting at the table and I instantly pick my glass up for him to fill it. I don't normally like red wine, but this occasion fucking calls for it.

"Gentleman, may I please introduce my daughter Adelaide. She has recently moved back to England from South Africa," my father introduces me, the guests whispering their greetings. I just smile and give a small wave to everyone before finishing off my wine, then gesturing to the waiter for more.

The whole room gets loud again as they converse about business and I couldn't be more disinterested. The gentleman haven't even introduced themselves, ignoring me for most of the evening. My only guess is they could be my father's business partners or employees, but the suits they are wearing seem too expensive and they all look immaculate. The man sitting across from me looks a lot like Blake Crawford, the same chestnut brown hair and ocean blue eyes.

"Excuse me Adelaide."

I turn to the man who spoke.

"I just thought I would introduce myself. I am Mr. Huntington," the gentleman next to me says.

I immediately recognize him. This is Royce's Father. They are literally a spitting image of each other. The light brown hair, big sea green coloured eyes and the same mischievous smile. How did I not put two and two together?

"Hi, it's such a pleasure to meet you. I am a massive fan of your son's work," I say to him, bouncing a little in my seat. Even though his son has been the ultimate dick to me this week, I still never thought I'd meet his parents. Well, his dad. He faintly smiles at me before being interrupted by another man sitting next to him. He gives me an apologetic look then turns his back to me.

"Adelaide, remember. Not a word of any of this to your school friends, understood?" my father whispers to me.

"Yes Father," I nod, which puts a satisfactory smile on his face.

After sitting at the table with all the random men for hours, I managed to indulge myself in a three-course meal, feeling completely bloated in my dress. I really hope my stomach doesn't show too much of a food baby. Now that would be a lasting impression.

Once the guests say their goodbyes and leave the house, I head up to my room to get in the shower again and rinse off all the sweat I accumulated throughout dinner. I just want to curl up and watch some Netflix in bed before I go to sleep.

Putting on my pajamas, I hear a knock coming from my bedroom door. I go to open it. Disappointment fills me as I see that it's not. My father stands in the doorway, his hand on the frame.

"I have decided to enroll you in one to one classes for elocution lessons, where you will also become a debutant," he says sternly. Wow, I did not expect that. I thought debutants were a thing of the past, given that Queen Elizabeth abolished the ceremony in 1958.

"I didn't realize they did that sort of thing anymore?" I say, which is clearly a big mistake.

"Of course, there is. This isn't a request Adelaide. You will obey," he grits his teeth before walking away, and as soon as I try to retreat back into my room he turns around. "Oh also, I won't be here tomorrow evening, I have a gala to attend."

Maybe it's the same Gala the Crawford's are off to? For a second, I wonder why I wasn't invited, but also thank god I wasn't

"I'll be going back to the academy tomorrow anyway, I have loads of studying to do," I tell him.

He doesn't acknowledge me. Rather, he saunters off down the hall into the east wing. I haven't been that way yet but apparently Mrs. Blossom says its off limits to anyone but my father and certain staff.

Thankfully, after a few minutes I've settled into my bed covers and Mrs. Blossom brings me my hot chocolate with marshmallows. Oh yes. Now my film marathon can begin.

Chapter Seven

I wake up to Mrs. Blossom pulling my curtains open, the sun beaming straight through and hurting my eyes. I didn't even manage to have a film marathon last night. After my hot chocolate, I instantly fell asleep and had the best night's sleep in a long time. This bed is amazing.

"Why? It's so early," I mumble, trying to hide my face under the duvet covers but Mrs. Blossom is having none of it. "Breakfast will be ready in half an hour Miss Adelaide. As it's such a lovely day, breakfast will be served outside," she teases. I throw the duvet off and get out of bed to climb in the shower for a wash.

After I'd showered, brushed my teeth and gotten dressed, Mrs. Blossom leads me through to the outside courtyard where my father is sitting, reading his newspaper. Pastries and fruit are laid out on the table. I can already smell the sweet nectar of coffee and that's the only motivation I need. I sit myself down facing the grounds and notice by the side of the house is a glass-covered structure.

"Hey, what's in that glass house?" I ask my father.

"That's the pool house," he murmurs from behind his newspaper. My curiosity piqued; I might have to check that out later before

I go back to the academy. I nibble on a few croissants and drink my coffee, enjoying the rays of sunshine on my face. After I'm done, I stand and stretch, receiving a "look" from my father. Before I go back to my room to pack my bag and ask Steve to take me back to the academy, I decide on a slight detour to check out the pool house.

It isn't as big as I thought it would be, but it has an average sized indoor swimming pool with a hot tub on the side. The glass doors fold back, leading to an outdoor kidney shaped pool with a waterfall feature, and a little bar on the right. Maybe father has pool parties here in the summer?

After checking out the grounds of the estate I venture back into my room and find my bag has already been packed by Mrs. Blossom, left on the bed ready for me. I get dressed back into my academy uniform before I ring down to Steve to have the car ready in five minutes. When I get downstairs, he is waiting for me outside next to the Bentley, talking to someone else. As soon as he sees me, he nods and opens the back door for me to slide in. Once I am settled in, Steve drives out of the driveway and onto the main road.

"Going back so soon Miss?" he asks.

"Yes, I have so much studying to do so I thought I'd go back," I say. Hopefully, he doesn't ask too many questions. Once again, I'm not really in the conversing mood. I decide to use this time to read a book for my English Lit class.

Arriving at the academy in the late afternoon, I drop my bag off at the dorm and decide to head to the dining hall to grab a bite to eat. I doubt I'll have any food later at the club, so I best eat something now. The dining hall is empty, as expected, which I am grateful for. I order myself a light meal of steak stir fry, which hopefully won't bloat me out too much. I still haven't decided what to wear but going by what Samantha was wearing, it seems as though the requirement was smart casual.

I have a few hours to kill before I need to leave, so I figure strolling down to the library won't hurt. I need to fit in as much studying as possible while here. My grades really need to improve or else my father will kill me.

My tutoring sessions begin on Monday with Hugo and I must

admit, it's not an occasion I'm looking forward to. He scares the living shit out of me and seems as though he would be cold and impatient. I'll be surprised if I last more than a week before he gives up on me.

The library is cold and eerie, located in the old construction of the castle which has been newly renovated, but kept the design of medieval times. The flame style wall mounted sconces would have been candles for light back then, and the chandeliers hang high along the wooden beams. The stained pictorial glass windows are so high you would need a ladder to reach them. The sun beams through in bright colours, shining a rainbow down on the cold concrete floor.

Searching for the correct books in Egyptian History leads me all the way to the back of the library. I have no idea how they sorted this out, but it seems they have books for bloody everything possible. A faint sound startles me from my search, and I halt my steps. Moaning sounds echo in the air around me and I am unsure if it's a moan of pleasure or if someone's hurt. I make my way around the maze of books shelves, following the sounds, the moaning getting louder and louder. That's when I find the culprits.

I gasp, automatically stopping in my tracks, and I accidently drop a book from my hands to the floor. It's Charles and some girl who I haven't seen before. It appears my presence hasn't interrupted them, and I immediately scurry off to the other side of the book-shelf. The image of Charles fucking a girl whose legs were wrapped around his waist, her skirt scrunched up on her hips and her knickers left on the ground has been imprinted onto my brain.

My heart is beating so fast in my throat it takes me a while to compose myself. I grab my book and hurry back to my table, trying to pretend I didn't just witness that. I scrub my hands over my face and steady my breathing to calm down, but before I realize, a presence is standing over me. All of a sudden my heartbeat is back to running a marathon. I open my eyes to find Charles looming over the table on the opposite side with a sadistic grin spread on his beautiful face.

The sunlight shines on his golden locks from behind, making

him look angelic, but I know he is far from it. They say that the devil comes to you in a form of unimaginable beauty, with his charming smile and alluring personality, and that is exactly how he draws in his prey. He wants you to submit to him and succumb to all of your desires.

"Did you enjoy the little show, Africa?" he purrs, his voice so seductive he practically talks sex. He stares at me from his golden-brown eyes and the grin just keeps on getting wider. His hair falls onto his face, just about covering his eyes as he leans his forearms on the spine of the chair opposite me.

I take a deep breath, "Um, I hardly saw anything,"

I have no clue what to say to him. My brain has gone dead. In a weird way, I am jealous of the girl and I have no clue why. I am as inexperienced as they come for an eighteen-year-old. Yes, I am still a virgin and the furthest I have gone with a guy is kissing and that was years ago.

"Oh really, well it didn't seem that way," he chuckles with a mischievous tone. "Now you know my little spot," he winks at me. I try and swallow my gasp, but I end up holding my breath for longer than normal.

What the fuck is wrong with me?

"Well, I won't tell anyone about your little secret spot." I roll my eyes at him, hoping it will send the message of- I don't care, go away.

He chuckles under his breath and stands up straight to shrug on his blazer. He buttons up the last two gold buttons and wipes it down, as if to take out any creases that are visible. Surprisingly, there isn't.

"I wouldn't recommend using it either," he says and now I'm confused, which he can read from my scrunched-up face "For your business," he continues on and that's when I realize what he means. How do people still believe this shitty fucking rumor?

"How about you fuck right off and let me get back to studying," I snap at him. He starts walking backwards, holding out his hands in surrender and an apologetic expression etched into his face, but I know full well that it is far from what he intends. God if he is anything like Blake, I will be reminded of this later.

~

Since arriving at my dorm room, I have showered and blow dried my hair but now I'm staring into my closet, trying to pick out an outfit. I stand inside the closet in my underwear, tapping a finger on my bottom lip and staring at all the clothes in front of me. Maybe one will just pop out at me and that's what I'll wear. I decide after ten minutes to put on some jeans, a black vest top and a black cardigan matching it with some black pumps. Hopefully, this will be suitable, if not Samantha could always tell me for future reference.

I order myself an Uber from the app and I have about twenty minutes until it arrives, so I put on some mascara to make my blue eyes pop and a nude pink colored lipstick. I don't want to overdo it. I pick up my small shoulder bag where I put my lipstick and purse and hang it over my shoulder. Giving myself a once over in the mirror, I am pretty pleased with the outcome. I quickly tie my hair up in a ponytail as I don't want my long hair getting in the way this evening.

The Uber arrives dead on time, and I check my surroundings to make sure no one else is around. Once the coast is clear I quickly jump in the back seat and greet the driver. The drive is not far, but I have some time to contain my nerves. I don't know why I'm so nervous. I have worked as a waitress and bar staff before, so it's nothing new, but I think it's because I know I'm also doing it to find out why the tunnels lead there.

I should probably just have been clever and actually asked someone before I put myself in what could be a potentially dangerous situation, but hey. You only live once. We arrive at the club and I'm grateful I that I'm still early by ten minutes. This will give me some time to finally settle my nerves, I hope.

The parking lot isn't busy with cars, so I am guessing it's still too early for everyone to come out. I walk on the gravel ground and head through the old wooden door and into the hallway. I catch a glimpse of Samantha sitting at the bar, writing on some notepad, and as if she can feel my presence, she turns her head around with a wide smile and waves me over.

"Hey chick, how are you today?" she asks with a gentle smile. I don't know the lady, but she seems so warm and welcoming I feel instantly safe around her which is good.

"I am very well, thank you for asking," I respond with a shaky breath and Samantha picks up on my nerves.

"Hey, don't be nervous. Tonight, is an easy night." She slides off the bar stool and guides me to a little closet where a locker is situated to place my bag. She then shows me behind the bar and all the drinks that they serve from the menu, which thankfully I have knowledge in. That seems to put me in her good books.

"So tonight, the shift will end at twelve if that is okay with you?" she asks, and I nod in response. After half an hour, the club has attracted some customers who all end up sitting at the bar and ordering drinks. Luckily, timing is on my side and it isn't so busy that I am unable to provide a bad service.

The building seems to heat up quickly and I take off my cardigan, so I'm left in just my vest top, showing some cleavage — which attracts a few comments from the older men, but due to my experience of this before it doesn't faze me. Samantha observes me from the sidelines and gives me a thumbs up occasionally before she joins me at the bar taking orders. The club seems to be piling up with more customers tonight and Samantha apologizes for it being so busy. But in my opinion, it makes the time go fast when you're busy and I'm having a lot of fun. This makes me feel normal again, like I don't attend some posh, expensive academy just around the corner.

Another lady called Lily starts her shift at ten in the evening, and she seems generous enough. We don't have time to converse as she's straight to work. Samantha pulls me to the side in a quiet room to have a little chat and now the nerves are creeping up my spine again. Fingers crossed.

"I am so impressed with you tonight," she gushes. "I will definitely be hiring you after this evening," she continues and all I do is smile at this lovely lady.

"So, here at Club Envy we do host private events, which you will be invited to work if we need staff," she starts, explaining what I should expect so I nod along, taking it all in. "We also have our own dancing girls that do performances on some nights." My eyes go wide as she instantly catches my attention. I smile at Samantha, intrigued.

"Dancing girls?" I ask, raising my eyebrow at her.

"Yeah, we have erotic dancers, burlesque and occasionally pole dancers," she explains to me. She pauses for a second before continuing. "But not stripping. It's more of a classy establishment," she assures.

I would love to see that. It's not a form of dancing I have performed myself, but I agree that dancing is an art form, even if it is erotic dancing or even pole dancing. That takes some strength. I mean the most erotic dancer that comes to my head is Dita von Tease, and her routine of dancing in a giant martini glass was epic.

"If you're free next Saturday for a shift, we have the dancers on then."

I can't wait for next Saturday already. We swap numbers and Samantha adds me to the work group chat and I already feel part of the team. This is probably the best thing that's happened to me since being in England and all it took was a little job at a club.

Clearly, I am easily pleased. My grin grows wider at the thought. The butterflies flutter in my stomach, excited for next Saturday already.

Once my shift has ended, I take an Uber back to the academy and before I know it, I am tucked up in bed by one in the morning, looking forward to a lay in. I put my earphones in and listen to some music to help me fall asleep, but the image of Charles fucking that girl against a bookshelf is still fresh in my mind. The heat rises in my stomach as my imagination runs wild, replacing that girl with me in his arms. My legs wrapped around his waist, my arms holding onto his broad shoulders and breathing in every single kiss he gives. My breath quickens, my heart pumping against my tight chest. Why am I imagining something that could never happen to me? I would never be able to have someone like him.

The Queen's naughty nephew. Seeing as I am all alone in the dorm, I figure I'll explore myself a little and imagine Charles' manly, manicured hands all over my body.

Wow, I have lost the plot.

Chapter Eight

Monday has rolled around quickly, and the academy is swarmed with students again. Blaire arrived early this morning, waking me up from yet another dirty dream of the cheeky, mischievous Duke.

"How was the Gala?" I ask Blaire as I sit up, covering my chest with my duvet.

"It was really boring if I am honest, but I did meet a guy and we swapped numbers" she gives me a cheeky wink whilst putting her uniform on. "But that is all I am saying for now. I don't want to jinx it."

After showering and getting dressed in my uniform, we make our way down to the dining hall, my belly rumbling in starvation. I ended up missing lunch and dinner yesterday, since I spent my whole afternoon in the dance studio coming up with different routines.

We take a seat at our normal table and Maisie is already there waiting for us, having kindly ordered our breakfast for us. I need coffee and a glass of orange juice. Glancing up, the Royals are already seated at their throne and I instantly recognize the blonde girl that was with Charles in the library, sitting next to Ruby. Heat

flushes my cheeks in discomfiture, and that's when I realize I'm staring, because Blake has a grin plastered on his face. He stands up and
struts toward our table.

"Oh god, what do you want Blake?" Blaire huffs, looking up
from her phone screen while I forget how to breathe again.
Goddamn it, why did he have to come over here after he caught me
staring?

"You really are such a lovely sister, aren't you?" he drawls,
pulling a chair out opposite me, the legs scraping against the tiled
floor as takes a seat, his dark gaze set upon me.

"What do you want?"

"I was just coming to ask Africa if she enjoyed the little show at
the weekend, that's all," he chuckles under his breath. "I heard you
got all pervy, watching Charles fucking Constance in the library," he
declares, louder than normal. The whole dining hall falls silent and
all the students watch us with anticipation.

"That is a load of bullshit. I hardly saw anything. But if he
didn't want to get caught, he should find a better…" I pause trying
to find the correct word, "spot."

Blake's expression falls from roguish to malice in a split second.

His mouth tightens in a thin line and his nostrils flare. "Are you
calling me a liar, Africa?" he sneers, and I shrug my shoulders as I
lean back in my chair, folding my arms across my chest and lifting
my chin up in defiance.

I'm done with this prick thinking he can intimidate me.

A few students gasp, waiting in anticipation for Blake's reaction
to my statement. Finally, I stand up for myself against this prick and
he doesn't like it. Well tough shit. You can't always expect everyone
to bow down to your feet.

Blake stands up so abruptly, the chair falls back hitting the
ground behind him and Blaire copies his movement. "Blake, fuck
off right now," she shouts at him in front of everyone, their faces
falling in disbelief. She's never stood up to him in front of an audience, and I can't help but feel pride.

Blake ignores Blaire, his nostrils flaring as he points an index
finger in my direction. He then leans forward on the table, one hand

clawing the surface. "You will regret this Africa. Don't think Blaire will always stand up for you," he speaks through clenched teeth. "You'll wish you never came here. I promise you," he clenches his jaw, the veins in his neck straining against the skin. He turns on his heel to walk away, smacking down a tray of food a poor guy was holding in his hands. The food flies everywhere, landing on the floor and on a few students. The other Royals follow Blake out of the dining hall and finally noise from conversation breaks the silence.

My body is trembling, shaking with anger over how this fucking prick treats people. It's always directed towards me, not anyone else and I don't know why I am suddenly a target. Just because I am new? How the fuck does that work?

"Ade," Blaire whispers - she had given me the nickname Ade, which is so much better than saying my whole name — why didn't I think of it before? - "Do not let that low life get to you. He won't do anything. I'll make sure of it."

~

Morning classes are dreadful. No one's spoken to me since this morning, aside from Ruby tormenting me in classes, calling me a slut and a working girl.

"I bet you wish it was you don't you, Charles fucking you against the bookshelf," she purrs with a mocking smirk. "But why pay for an AIDS ridden slut when he can get it for free," she cackles and the whole class burst into laughter.

My breath hitches in my throat, as the bile starts to rise but I endure all the comments and insults until the bell rings to signal that it's finally lunch time.

I pretty much sprint to the dance studio and strip out of my uniform, until I'm left in my leotard. Then I put on 'Messed up' by Fredrik Ferrier, and I just dance. I let out all my anger into every move I make. Pushing myself to the point where my body wants me to stop, but I carry on. I punish myself to the point of exhaustion and my feet ache from the constant contact with the hard floor. Sweat pours from my forehead, my breath trying to catch up with me. Suddenly I feel faint from the lack of food and all the exercise, and I end up falling to the floor. I roll until I'm lying on my back, waiting until my heartbeat calms down to a normal rate.

"Jesus woman, you're going to pass out one of these days if you carry on like this," a voice speaks out from the other end of the studio.

Glancing through a mirror, I recognize Miles and pull up my arm to give a small wave. I can't even form words right now, so that's all I've got.

"You okay? I heard what happened," he asks with sincerity in his voice.

I roll myself over so that I'm lying on my stomach on the cold hardwood floor, cooling down my red-hot skin. "I will be," I reply.

He nods in acknowledgement and doesn't say another word. It's like he knows I need this time out to just dance. Maybe he does sometimes too.

Miles saunters over to me, stretching out his arm, lending me a hand to stand up. In his right hand, he has a remote and instantly presses play. A rock song booms from the surround system, 'Bad Girlfriend' by Theory of a Deadman. Wow, I did not see this coming.

"Come on, let's get some of that anger out of you," he smiles at me and starts to twirl me out of his arms. I haven't really danced like this to rock music before, but he's making it fun. I haven't laughed this much in a while, and it feels refreshing. We playfully do the air guitar, pretending we're rock stars, head banging, and adding some weird tango to the mix. This is interesting and a change of dynamic. I feel like a little schoolgirl, acting foolish for the sense of fun. The tightness in my chest fades away, the light flutters easing. I can still feel the adrenaline, but I finally feel comfortable with someone other than Blaire and Maisie.

"See, I am putting a smile on your face," he calls out through the loud music. We enjoy the whole song and I think we have danced around every inch of the floor space. We even end up on the balance beams at the side and jump off them, pretending we're jumping into a crowd and everyone loves us.

He grabs me by the waist, leaning my head back to end the song and we're both hysterically laughing. "Wow that was amazing!" I shout, my ears ringing from the loud music.

Miles chuckles, grabbing us both a bottle of cold water and a towel to dry the sweat from our faces.

"Now that is letting yourself go. That is why I love dancing," Miles takes a big gulp of water from the bottle, while I stare at him in appreciation. The way his Adam's apple bobs from every gulp he takes, the sweat running down his pale skin. I shake off the weird feeling I'm having and gather my belongings in a bag to head towards the showers and freshen up before class.

"Thank you," I whisper to Miles, glancing over my shoulder before I leave.

He nods and turns around to pack his own bag.

～

Thankfully, I'm not late to my next class after lunch and Blaire is waiting for me at the entrance; everyone has already taken their seats.

"Where have you been?" she raises an eyebrow at me and touches my wet hair, which I put in a messy bun on top of my head.

"Dancing?" she confirms then wraps her arms around me in a brief hug before heading into the classroom.

Hmm, okay.

"Really, you're fresh from a client and come straight to class?" Ruby bellows, staring at me through the slits of her eyes. "Good thing you washed before you came back. You still smell of sex though."

"Shut the fuck up, Ruby," someone says as they enter the class and it's Miles. I didn't even know we shared a class together. He looks and winks in my direction before taking his seat on the other side of the room.

"You know Miles Digby?" Blaire asks from behind me.

"Yeah my dance partner, I was with him at lunch," I tell her, wondering why she sounds so surprised.

Ruby is staring at me like a lion stares at their prey before attacking. What the fuck have I done now? I don't give her the satisfaction of looking back at her, but just continue sitting there, carrying on with my assignments. This is probably the only class I am academically advanced in, science.

I mean, this is a weird university. You go to high school like normal people, but whereas most students go to college or university, this is an in between for the rich and elite. It's the only school of its kind and all the elite from around the world attend here. I didn't even check to see how much it costs to attend and I most definitely do not want to know.

This is also the only class I don't share with the three Royal douche bags. Thank god.

The whole classroom is quiet as the sub teacher has sprung a little pop quiz on everyone for them to enjoy. I scan my eyes across the room, my eyes locking with Miles. He curls his lip into a smile for me from across the room, which sends a shiver down my spine and butterflies form in my stomach.

He really is gorgeous; you'd think his face was sculpted by the Greek gods a thousand years ago. He made me feel so alive during lunch with our little dance around the room. Made me forget the other pricks at the school and realize I still have some good friends on my side.

Ruby catches onto our little staring session and throws a note at Miles' desk. He opens it, scans it quickly, and tears it apart, sticking his middle finger up at her in response.

I barely contain a giggle because Ruby does not look too pleased with that outcome.

The bell signals for the class to end and everyone hands in their tests to the sub. Ruby is the first one out of the classroom, mumbling shit to herself. Miles bumps his shoulder into mine and gives me another cheeky grin before leaving after her.

Damn, his dimples when he smiles.

"Ade, Miles is Ruby's stepbrother. She will kill you," Blaire sighs as we walk out together. "He's also a dick, playboy of Darlington and never has girlfriends," she explains.

One, I did not even know they are related, but they're step siblings, so why would Ruby be so pissed off about us? Two, I wasn't interested in him that way, or even for a quick fuck, but now that I think of it… I wouldn't mind being bedded by Miles Digby. His lean body pressed against mine and his devilish mouth…

I quickly shake the thought out of my head before my imagination runs wild again. "We're just dance partners for the recital and at lunch he cheered me up," I explain. "Nothing is happening," I say to Blaire. I kind of feel like I just lied to my best friend. And although nothing has happened between me and Miles, I want to see if something can.

All classes are done for the day, and I have about five minutes to get to the library for my tutoring session with Hugo. The library is at least a fifteen-minute walk from where my last class is, so running is my only option.

I don't want to get on the wrong side of Hugo, adding him to my list of tormentors. The hallways empty quickly as everyone goes to their dorm rooms before dinner, so running through the hallways is a little easier than having to push people out of my way.

I make it in time, bracing myself for an hour of torture, catching my breath and wiping the sweat from my forehead with the sleeve of my blazer. I round the corner and catch Hugo already seated at the table, all the books and papers meticulously organized around him. He looks sweet and innocent sitting there, writing something down in his book. My opinion changes when he looks in my direction.

Okay there it is, the cold-hearted murderous look on his face.

Taking in a deep breath, I take a seat directly in front of him. Hugo hands me a piece of paper, which is one of my pieces of homework already marked by the teacher. How the fuck did he get this? I look at the page and then at Hugo in confusion.

He stares at me blankly before speaking. "I took it," he shrugs as though it's a normal thing to do.

I roll my eyes and look back down at the paper in shock. I got a C on my math's paper, which is probably the best I have ever done.

I secretly whoop in my head and as if he can read my mind, he grabs it out from my grasp and sighs.

"Don't get too excited. It's not that great," he drawls. Hugo shrugs off his blazer, sliding it on the back of his chair.

Oh Jesus Christ. My mind goes blank and my mouth goes dry as I can faintly see tattoos peeking out from where he's taking off his tie, unbuttoning the few buttons at the top of his shirt. His neck is now on full display and it's covered in tattoos. You would never know with his blazer on, but now that I look at him closely, I can see the black ink hiding behind the white fabric of his shirt. I swallow the hard lump in my throat and try to distract myself with something else.

"With my tutoring, I want you to achieve an A on everything. Nothing less." His voice sounds raspy and I see his whole persona matches the way he looks – dark and mysterious.

His raven black hair shines in the sunlight beaming from the stained-glass windows, highlighting a slight dark blue tinge in his hair. I kind of wish my hair were that colour. It matches his dark ocean blue eyes and tanned skin.

Hugo is the only Royal who hasn't insulted me yet, but I feel it coming. I doubt he will continue to play nice, especially after my slight altercation with Blake in the dining hall this morning.

"We will work on this paper this evening, as there will be another math's test soon," he says bluntly, handing me a worksheet to work from.

I nod, scared to say anything in case I offend him. He starts to explain formulas to me, and we work on the worksheet together. He gives me another practice test to do now so that he can mark it before our session is over and I immediately start. I try and answer each question. I glance up and watch as Hugo completes his own homework. I try not to stare at him too much, but my eyes keep drifting back towards this god in front of me. A slight draft wafts through the library where students keep opening the door, and the smell of him teases my nostrils. The delicate scent of pinewood and orange fills the air around me.

I catch myself and shake my head, continuing with my test. I'm acting like a horny little teenage girl around these Royals. I've never really thought about boys before. I was always too busy with school, my social life and surfing in the ocean. It never crossed my mind to even look at a guy and think I want a relationship or even to jump his bones.

Moving to England has changed me in ways I never thought possible.

Hugo holds out his hand to take my test once I have finished, handing him my test. He has a little tattoo on his wrist of a sword with a snake wrapped round the blade. I sit back in my chair, waiting for him to mark my answers.

"Not bad, but you need to study more," he purrs without looking at me. The markings on the page are all in red when he slides it back to me. I stare at it in disbelief, he's given me a B.

Woohoo! I scream in my head.

Hugo stands up, packing all the books away in his backpack and holding onto his blazer. "Same time Wednesday," he says and then suddenly he's disappeared. Maybe he is the quiet one out of the three? I imagine having either Charles or Blake as my tutor.

No fucking thank you.

After my tutoring session with Hugo, I head off to my official dance practice with Miles for the recital. This time we're not alone and the whole class joins us to practice, which I am thankful for so that my head stays in professional mode rather than flirt with Miles mode. We sit on the floor in the corner of the room looking through his phone playlist to pick a song for the routine.

"So, I think the performance needs to be broken down into three different routines. That will get us a good grade and show-case our talent" Miles states, as he scrolls through his Spotify playlist.

"I agree, so I think three songs and three routines?" I suggest, the corners of my lips tugging into a smile. I know we can achieve this as we work so well as a team.

"That is a brilliant idea, we can start off with Ballet to set the mood, and then possibly ballroom to then tango. So, we are building the suspense?" he says as his eyes go wide to match his grin.

My belly fills with excitement, and my skin flares with goosebumps at the thought of our brilliant idea.

The first song we decide on is a piece by Pyotr Ilyich Tchaikovsky, 'Swan Lake', which will be ballet dancing. The second song to break the classical number is 'I Don't Care' by Apocolyptica, as Miles loves his rock music and thinks we can do a romantic number with this one. I agree. We start practicing some techniques with the first two songs so that we have a flow going before we decide on another. We practice for nearly two hours straight and into the evening before calling it quits.

"Hey, it's still dinner time, do you want to get dinner together?" he asks, his dimpled smile automatically making me agree. We walk to the dining hall together, discussing our routine, choice of music and what we could do to make it better.

"We can ask Miss Younge to go last, as our performance will probably go on the longest?" I suggest to Miles, which he nods and agrees to.

"I also think an outfit change in-between could be awesome?" Miles says, as his beautiful eyes connect with mine. My mind goes blank and I have to shake the admiration off before I digest what he said. An outfit change between routines could also add more dramatics. I smile at Miles and nod before tearing my eyes back down to the ground. My cheeks burn as I start to blush and feel giddy and before I know it, we are walking through the dining hall doors.

All the student's eyes land on us as we walk through the double doors and lucky me, the Royals are at their table. I forgot that I'm dressed in gym shorts and sports bra, instantly turning my cheeks red from the heat. God, I wished I'd gotten changed before anyone else could see me. I really don't like my body on display for everyone to view. I am so self-conscious it's unreal, always comparing my body and looks to other pretty girls. I obsess over the way I look but, in the end, I am still not happy with how I look.

We take a seat at another table in the hall, furthest away from the Royals, which I am guessing is his usual table. We order some chicken fajitas for dinner tonight to load up on carbs and protein.

"So…" I drag out the word. "I didn't realize Ruby Lockhart is your stepsister," I say, resting my chin on my hand and staring at him.

He clicks his tongue on the roof of his mouth before turning to look at me. "Yeah, her mum married my dad only last year," he whispers. He seems hesitant to talk about it.

"What about you, why are you here?" he questions me in turn, affection in his eyes and I can't help but fall for his sweet persona. So, I decide to open up and tell him what I haven't told anyone else here. Not even my best friend.

I take a deep breath, whispering to Miles so no one can overhear.

"My mum was murdered a month ago."

Miles leans in closer, his leg brushing against mine and I feel comforted. "She was shot in the chest, in front of me, by some random guy whilst we were shopping," I continue with a shaky breath. Sometimes I forget there are still emotions there as I tell the story. "She went into hospital, was in a coma for a few days before my step-dad called me and told me she didn't survive."

I stop talking about my past before I spill too much. I still don't want to confess who my father is, and I don't want to know what the consequences would be if my father found out I told someone our secret.

Finally, I am saved by the waiter bringing our dinner to the table. We tuck in and talk about each other's hobbies and interests which is a nice distraction from telling my story "So what did you do for fun in South Africa?" Miles asks before he takes a sip of his water.

"Umm, well I love surfing as I grew up near the beach and dancing. That's all I ever really did" I smile, my blush creeping up my cheeks again. My heart thumps against my chest as I expose myself further to Miles. "What about you?" I ask in return.

"Well, dancing was always my passion, but I grew up around horses, so I played Polo a lot when I was younger" he says with a grin on his face

Chapter Nine

$\mathcal{M}$iles and I finish our dinner and indulge ourselves in a dessert. Normally I do not eat a lot of sweet things due to dieting, but we share a caramel ice cream sundae. Considering the day, it is needed. We leave the dining hall and thankfully the Royals have already left without saying anything else.

We end up splitting ways on the first floor where the boy's dorms are situated, but unfortunately for me girls' dorms are on the top floor, so there are two more flights of stairs for me to enjoy.

I had promised Blaire at lunch that we would have a girls evening and watch loads of chick flicks tonight, which I am really looking forward to, so I hurry up the last flight of stairs. I stop in front of my door, facing a note stuck to it that is addressed to me. I grab it and quickly open the dorm room to find Maisie and Blaire sitting on the floor, painting each other's toenails.

"Hey sorry I'm late, I went to dinner with Miles after practice. I was starving."

They face each other with concern and it clicks in my head what they are thinking.

"We are just friends," I sigh, but I know for a fact they don't believe me. I put my satchel on the table near my bed, clutching the note in my hands.

"Hey, did you two see the note addressed to me stuck on the door?" I ask, but they shake their heads.

"Have you read it yet?" Maisie asks and I shake my head, slumping down on my bed.

The girls follow my lead, sitting next to me on the bed, intrigued to see what the note says. I rip it open and find that I don't recognize the handwriting and neither do the girls.

"We know your secret," I read aloud and my heart stops.

Do they know who I really am? Who my dad is?

The girls look at me with questioning faces, but do I lie, or do I tell them the truth?

"I have no idea what secret their talking about," I shrug, ripping the note up into a million pieces before throwing it into the trash can.

"It's probably someone playing a stupid prank on you," Blaire insists, and I hope she is right. It could just be someone trying to scare me off.

I get changed into comfier clothes before joining the girls for our movie marathon.

"Hey, what film do you girls wanna watch? We have Mean Girls or John Tucker must die?" Maisie questions whilst setting herself up on the floor.

"Defo Mean Girls because Ade reminds me of Kat!" Blaire squeals, and I roll my eyes at her but then giggle. It's nice to see her excited for something. I mean I could see the resemblance, only due to us both moving from Africa, but nothing else besides that.

"I think we should dress up as Playboy bunnies for Halloween this year," Blaire insists as we watch the scene where Kat dresses up as a zombie bride. To be honest, that would be me.

"Halloween is still a few weeks away," I say, secretly hoping we do not dress as Playboy bunnies. My dad would murder me if he saw me dressed like that.

"Well it's never too early to start planning costumes. Halloween is the biggest party of the year and it's literally only four weeks away." Maisie comments in between.

"We'll have to go shopping," Maisie squeals and I roll my eyes at them both. The thought of attending another Darlington party makes me feel uneasy. I might not even go to this stupid Halloween party.

We watch a few more films before Maisie retreats to her own dorm and Blaire and I settle in our own beds. I aim to have a good seven hours sleep tonight without any interruptions. Blaire puts earphones in to help her drift to sleep and the faint sound of her snoring helps me relax.

The following day I follow through with my normal routine, but today I woke up earlier than normal from a restless night's sleep. Already I can tell that everything will get on my nerves so I after I get dressed into my uniform I blow-dry and curl my dark locks into soft curls. May as well make myself look as presentable as I can. I put on some mascara and nude lipstick

Seeing as I am up this early, I text Blaire to let her know that I'll meet her in the dining hall for breakfast, but for now I make my way to the library to pull out some more books to read for my business economics class. I take a seat at my usual table, pulling out my laptop to jot down notes for my assignment later and I insert my earphones to drown out the silence that surrounds me.

Not realizing anyone else has arrived in the library, the sudden thump of a book being slammed on the table frightens me out of my concentration. I look up to see two Royals and an actor. Charles, Hugo, and Royce stand in front of me with their arms folded across their muscled chests. I take out my earphones, stopping the music from playing.

"Good morning to you too," I sarcastically say. Charles and Royce have huge grins on their faces, whereas Hugo looks bored as fuck. Royce takes a seat next me, hanging his left arm off the back of my chair.

"Wow, Africa you must take your job seriously, starting this early," Charles teases, but in my head, I know he means it.

"You are sitting at our table Africa," Hugo drawls and takes the seat directly in front of me. Charles follows suit, taking the seat next to him.

"Am I supposed to believe you study this early in the morning?" I sit back in my chair, arms folded with displeasure at being disturbed.

"Wow, Africa I must say you look a lot better with make-up on," Charles confesses, playing with my pens that are laid out on the table "You should really wear it more often. It takes you up to a number…" he pauses, thinking about what to say next. "Three, yeah I'd say three," he chuckles under his breath.

Hugo turns to face him, not looking too pleased. He clenches his jaw, defining the sharp edges.

"Don't listen to that fucking idiot," Royce says, his hand from the back of my chair coming up to brush the loose strands of hair off my face.

I flinch in my chair and he chuckles, noticing my nervousness and my pulse quickens as my heart races.

"Don't worry beautiful, I won't hurt you," he reassures me, but the fact that my favorite actor just touched me has my knickers literally soaked, just from that little display of affection. I secretly scream in my head.

As Royce brings his arm back around to place on the table, I see the exact same tattoo on his wrist as Hugo's. Maybe it's a best friends tattoo? I pretend to get back to my reading so that I can try to catch a glimpse of Charles' wrist, seeing if he has the same. As he's playing with my pens, he picks one up to throw at Royce and just my luck, his blazer rides up and I see the exact same tattoo. I wonder if Blake has the exact same one.

I check the time on my phone and notice its nearly breakfast time, so I pack my things away, disappearing from their weird morning antics. I have no idea why they sat with me, but like Hugo said, it's their table.

But they didn't ask me to leave either. Hmm…

"Hey Ade," I hear my nickname from behind me, which only Blaire uses. I turn around to see that Royce is jogging to catch up to me, but instead of stopping I carry on.

"What do you want Royce?" I groan. But seriously, what does he want?

"I think we got off on the wrong foot and I'd like to be your friend." his face lights up with his big smile, but all I can do is scoff.

"Are you serious or is this some sick joke?" I snap. Why should I believe him when his friends hate me?

I carry on walking in the direction of the dining hall with Royce in tow, but he doesn't say a thing. People's eyes are drawn to us as we walk down the hallway, confusion clearly displayed on their faces. I'm confused as hell too.

"Let me join you for breakfast." he flutters his long eyelashes at me, and I know I'd feel bad for saying no, so I nod and walk to our table. Thank god Blaire and Maisie are already seated, so I don't have to have an awkward conversation with Royce or sit in silence wondering what to talk about. Fuck that.

"Royce, I didn't realize you were joining us for breakfast." Blaire raises her eyebrows at me, and I shrug it off. Let her deal with his crap.

"I thought I'd get to know Ade better," he wiggles his eyebrows, giving me a devilish grin before sitting next to me.

"Oh wow, you even use my nickname for her. Cute," Blaire mumbles and I can tell she isn't too pleased with this arrangement.

"Hey Ade, how about we have breakfast another time?" Royce leans in, whispering in my ear, his hot breath caressing my skin and sending jolts of electricity through my veins.

Royce stands up from his seat, smoothing down his blazer before leaning down and giving me a kiss on the cheek. Instantly heat rushes to my cheeks, turning them red from embarrassment. I catch Blaire gasping from the other side of the table in disbelief and she's not the only one.

What the fuck just happened?

"Just me and you next time," Royce adds before he walks away from me, joining the Royals table.

"What the fuck just happened," Blaire mouths to me as Maisie giggles behind her hand. "Royce doesn't just kiss people on the cheek," she says, her eyes bulging out of her skull and I have no clue what to say to her, so I just eat my fruit salad in silence.

After breakfast, the girls and I amble to our first class, English literature, where unfortunately for me I share with all the Royal douche bags. Just to add the cherry on top, I sit next to his royal asshole, Blake Crawford.

Taking a seat at my desk, I organize what I need for this lesson along with my homework. I skim through the completed assignment to make sure I'm happy with the outcome, hoping I get graded at least a B. I let out a long sigh, rubbing my palms over my face. I am not eager for this class to start. I've never been the academic type, more of a doer which is why dancing and gymnastics has always been my top graded class.

My thoughts are interrupted by Blake pulling out his chair then slamming his bag on the desk as if it's an inconvenience. He takes out his workbooks and pens before throwing his bag on the floor beside him, then he takes a seat. I try to keep my eyes forward so that I'm staring at the interactive white board, but something about Blake is distracting my thoughts. I can feel the anger and hatred seeping through his skin. Every movement he makes is to distance himself further away from me. I haven't been this close to Blake since outside the headmaster's office where he cornered me, the memory sending shivers down my spine, triggering my skin to prickle.

Blake's right leg starts to bounce under the table, shaking the whole damn thing, his arms flexing as he plays with his pen, making little tapping noises on the wood.

My eyes start to twitch with annoyance and unintentionally I snap, "Can you stop moving so much?" I try and keep my voice down so the teacher doesn't hear us, but a few students have, and they turn their heads to stare.

Blake slightly turns his gaze in my direction, nostrils flaring, and clenching his jaw before he leans in a little closer to me. "Africa, I warned you, and now you have royally pissed me off," he spits through clenched teeth, spittle landing on my cheek from the close proximity.

"I will make sure you wish you never attended this university, maybe even have you begging that you were back in the bush with your tribe," he threatens, leaning back in his seat and turning to look away from me again. He focuses his attention on the teacher at the front and all I can think about is how good he smelled. The smell of cloves mixed in with oakwood and vanilla, the smell of a king, and he really is a king here.

But soon after my pulse quickens, and my breath hitches in my throat. I don't take too kindly to threats.

Before the class is finished, the teacher comes over to Blake, handing him his already completed homework assignment and I catch the big red A on the front.

Colour me impressed.

He grabs it from the teacher and that's when I notice the tattoo on his wrist, just like the others. So, he also has one. I almost ask why but stop myself, remembering who I was about to talk to. He stands up, pushing the chair back with his muscly calves, and picks up his bag before storming out the room.

The dude needs some help with his anger. I really feel sorry for Blaire having to put up with his sulky attitude all the time.

~

*A*fter the day is done, I decide I need to relieve some stress but this time I want to go swimming. I haven't tried out the Olympic-sized swimming people in this castle, but I am sure it's extravagant. Lucky for me, I get the pool to myself as no one else booked a session. Being by myself is just what I need right now.

I've been swimming since I was three years old with my mum, and I've enjoyed it ever since, especially as I built some core strength. It was vital for swimming in the ocean against rough tides while surfing. Which reminds me, I need to get down to Stonewall beach one of these days and go for a surf. That would make me feel complete.

I get changed into my academy issued swimsuit, which is black with the academy logo resting on my right breast, and wrap myself in a white fluffy robe before stepping out into the pool room. I look around at the vast space with seating stands on three sides of the room for when competitions take place and a score board right at the front near the jumping boards. Ahead of me lay the water which looks perfectly still.

Slipping the robe off, I throw it on the bench near the wall and make my way to the edge of the pool. I climb down the steps and my toes hit the water. Expecting freezing temperatures, my tense body relaxes the deeper I head into warmth and heat. This is a posh school so I guess they can afford the heating. I float for a while, stroking my arms to keep me afloat before I clutch onto the side and start my laps.

I place my feet against the wall, still clutching onto the side as I prepare myself to start. Pushing myself off the wall, I start to front crawl with my face in the water, only catching breaths after a few strokes.

Once I've completed ten laps, I give myself a rest stop where I began, staying afloat for a while before putting my head under the water for a few seconds. One of my favorite places in the world is below the water, listening to nothing but just silence. I let myself sink to the bottom and sit on the pool floor, feeling the water move around my skin and just trying to keep myself down, holding my breath for as long as I can.

Sitting there, I let my memories join me, releasing them out of the closed cage I keep locked. A picture of my mum pops up first, and my lips curl up into a smile remembering how beautiful she was. She was my best friend, and she didn't deserve to leave this horrid world so early. My feelings well up inside me, threatening to explode. She was supposed to be here for me, graduating with a degree, and one day be at my wedding to the man of my dreams, but some lifeless dickhead had to take that all away from me too early.

Now I'm stuck in my own little cage called Darlington Academy with stuck up cunts, a billionaire father who doesn't even have an ounce of love in his heart, and possibly no future for me here because I can't even pursue my own dreams. Dreams that were stolen from me the moment I boarded that plane to start a new life in a different country.

Naturally, I can hold my breath for at least three minutes before I need to come up for air, so after a few minutes of dwelling, I put my memories back in the little cage at the back of my mind and I start letting myself float naturally to the top of the water. My favorite part is when the water slides off my face and taking that first breath again. I open my eyes as I make my way up and a few shadows hide the light of my passage from above. I can't see who it is or how many people stand there but as my head slightly pops out of the water, I get to take a fresh breath. Just as my lungs expand with this new air, a strong hand grabs a fistful of my hair, pushing me back under the water.

Whoever it is, they hold me under for a few seconds before pulling me back out. I gasp, grabbing another quick breath before they push me back down. I struggle against the hold, my scalp stinging with how hard they're gripping my hair. I try to remove their strong hold with my own hands, but nothing seems to budge.

Who the fuck is doing this?

They pull me back out, still holding my hair and I struggle to take a breath. The water falls from my eyes and they start to focus. The shadows start to form into Blake, who is holding my hair as he kneels down on the side with a murderous grin on his face. Beside him is Hugo and Charles, their arms crossed in front of their chests. Charles has a Cheshire Cat smile plastered on his face as he enjoys the view of Blake trying to drown an innocent woman, but Hugo stares down with no expression on his face. He's blank like a void and has no visible emotions, but that doesn't surprise me as he seems like he has a black soul. My body tremors as I start to panic, and my chest tightens under the restriction of air.

"Enjoying a little swim, are we?" Blake chuckles under his breath but it's not sincere. I can tell he's finding pleasure in hurting me. I stare into his icy blue eyes, trying to find any humanity but there is not a glimmer of remorse behind them, just darkness. I manage to yelp as he pushes me back down into the water and my hands fly up, trying to scratch him off me, but he doesn't shift. He's too strong for me and my mind goes into overdrive, thinking of the worst that can happen. I'm going to die at the hands of Blake Crawford, and he doesn't care.

Why would he care who I am, because to him I'm just an exchange student from another country who has no family so no one would miss me, would they?

"I warned you not to mess with me and pay back's a bitch," he roars, pulling me back up again, hot tears rolling down my cheeks and I can't contain my emotions. I hyperventilate and the pain in my lungs are unbearable as I cry out to plead. The salty tears sting my face as they stream down before hitting the water and Blake chuckles even further.

"You now have an enemy which you wish you never crossed."

He pushes me down under again as I take my breath, my mouth still open as I descended, the water replacing the oxygen in my lungs. My head starts to feel hazy whilst my body stops struggling, giving up on me. My life flashes before my eyes and the faint picture of my mum returns with her hand holding out, ready for me to take it so that I can go with her. Something is dragging me back. My hands keep drawing back even further and she starts to disappear like a distant memory again.

"Adelaide!" I faintly hear my name being called. My mum is calling my name, reaching out for me.

"Adelaide!" I hear again but clearer this time, recognizing Miles' husky voice. It wasn't my mum. I can feel my chest heaving heavily, with every breath Miles pushes through my lips, trying to get rid of the water in my lungs. He continues three more times before I cough up the contents from my lungs and come back to full consciousness. "Adelaide!" he shouts, "oh thank god." he sighs in relief as I push myself to sit up, feeling the cold wet tiles under the palms of my hands.

My eyes scan the surroundings, realizing I'm next to the pool.

"What happened?" I try whispering to Miles, my throat raspy, feeling as though it's been cut with razor blades. I look at Miles for comfort as he stares at me with his soft blue eyes, edged with worry before answering.

"You were drowning, and when I found you, you were unconscious," he whispers before taking my hand and lifting me up to stand, putting his arm under me.

"Let's take you to the nurse's room to make sure you're okay."

Miles grabs my bags and throws a fluffy robe around me before escorting me to the nurse's office. His hands resting on my hips, comforting and guiding me the whole way there.

"Are you okay?" he asks before knocking on the door. "Yeah I'm fine," my voice comes out a bit raspy. I give him a soft smile, reassuring him that I am okay but really my heart is racing a thousand miles per hour and I still can't remember what happened. Trying to remember what happened, all I know is that I was swimming. The next thing I knew, Miles was giving me the kiss of life. Although, I can remember his soft lips against mine and the worry in his eyes.

Miles saved my life.

The nurse answers the knock on the door with a smile on her face, welcoming us both in and gesturing for us to take a seat.

"I'm Miss Watson dear, how about you tell me what happened?" she says in a soft tone as we take our seats.

"Well, I was swimming and I'm not sure," I try to answer as much as I can, but my memory fails and I shake my head in disbelief. Miles grabs my knee and gently squeezes to comfort me.

"I actually found her in the swimming pool, unconscious and I had to pull her out, so I gave her a five rescue breaths and CPR then she came around," Miles explains what happened and how he found me while I stare at him in disbelief.

How the fuck did I drown?

I mean, I am an incredibly good swimmer.

"Oh dear. Well let's check you over to make sure everything is okay," the nurse – who's name I've just learnt to be Miss Watson – says. She spins around, leaving towards the medical storage room to get her supplies.

"I'll leave you to it then," Miles says, lifting from his seat and getting ready to leave.

I grab his hand before he can, pleading with my eyes for him to stay. He smiles at me, understanding, before taking a seat again and lacing his fingers through mine, not letting go. I look down at our intertwined hands and smile inwardly.

Miss Watson re-enters the room, taking the seat opposite me, taking my blood pressure, and shining a light in my eyes.

"Well everything is looking fine, but due to the lack of oxygen to your brain, you may feel dizzy for a few hours. So I think it's best that you go back to your dorm and rest." Her soft wrinkled face is reassuring, reminding me of my grandma, Paul's mum from back home, who's soft grey hair was long but always pulled into a bun on the top of her head. Her soft wrinkles had shown her age and even though she was sixty years old, she had the energy of a twenty-year-old. In fact, she taught me to surf and showed me the wildlife around the Savannah.

God, I loved that woman.

Miles escorts me back to the dorm, shooting Blaire a text to let her know where I am. He settles my belongings next to the door and leads me through to the bathroom.

"I must go. I have to teach a dancing lesson to someone else, but I'll come back later to check up on you." He holds my hands in his, kissing me on the forehead before heading out of my room.

I hear the door close softly and that is my cue to peel off the robe and my swimsuit. I climb laboriously into the hot shower, letting it warm up my cold skin. I almost fall over from that dizziness the nurse was talking about while I tried to wash my hair with my favorite honeycomb and coconut shampoo, and scrub off all the chlorine still stuck to my skin. I finally tuck myself into bed, hugging my body tightly, but I'm too anxious to close my eyes in case something bad happens again. My body begins to shiver, not from the cold but in fear and sweat coats my skin as my adrenaline piques. My mind plays tricks on me as the smallest of sounds make me flinch, so I tug the duvet tighter and up to my chin for comfort.

I already know that I won't be able to get any sleep tonight, so I plug in my earphones and listen to calming music to help drown out the silence and distract me from my own dark thoughts.

Chapter Ten

I bolt upright in bed before my alarm goes off, sweat dripping from my forehead, unable to catch my breath. I peel the duvet off my sweat soaked skin, shakily climb out of bed, and head to the bathroom. Placing both of my hands on the sink for balance, I stare at my reflection in the mirror for a moment. Turning on the faucet, I cup cold water in my hands, rinsing my face.

Little snippets of my nightmare keep playing over in my mind. Blake, Charles, and Hugo drowning me. I'm underwater, looking into the eyes of a demon with black eyes. His cackling echoes in the water while he holds me under. Hugo and Charles stand behind him with sin in their eyes, enjoying the view of me struggling, while I scratch the skin from Blake's arm.

He doesn't budge.

I spray some more water on my face to shake off the nightmare. Why does this feel like a memory? Surely, they didn't drown me. I would have remembered something like that. I shake my head. My mind is playing tricks on me.

Checking the time, I still have an hour before my alarm goes off, so I climb back into bed and scroll through social media. Exhaustion fills every part of my soul and my eyelids flutter closed. This time when my alarm goes off, I get up. but thank god I fell back to sleep. I needed it.

"Good Morning hon, how are you feeling?" Blaire comes over, sitting on the edge of my bed still dressed in her satin night gown, looking as flawless as ever. She takes my left hand to hold and gives me a reassuring squeeze. "Are you up for classes today?" she asks.

I withdraw my hand from hers to help myself sit up.

"Yeah I'll be fine, the sleep did me good," I give her a reassuring smile and she sighs in response, lifting herself up from my bed, heading to the bathroom.

My phone pings from beneath me as I left it on my bed when I dozed off. There's a text from Miles asking me if I am okay. I smile, sending him a quick reply to let him know that I am fine and still attending classes today. He replies immediately saying he will meet me down in the dining hall for breakfast.

After Blaire and I have gotten ready for the day, which took me a little longer this morning as I caked my face in concealer to hide the big blue bags under my eyes and my blotchy skin, which was still pale after yesterday, we make our way down to the dining hall where we meet Maisie.

Disappointment rushes through my veins and my shoulders slump as I see Miles hasn't arrived. I'm sure he will be here soon, I tell myself. He's the only guy who has been so genuine since I've started here, and not propositioned me for sex like all the other dicks.

Plus, the guy saved my life, so I kinda owe him one now.

We take a seat at the usual table, both girls pestering me, checking to see if I'm okay. I try and reassure them as much as I can but it's nice to have someone worry over me.

"What are you ordering Ade?" Blaire asks as she eyes the menu.

"I'm not really that hungry," I murmur as I rest my chin on the palm of my hand, but Blaire's eyes dart from the menu straight over to me in a split second. My eyes go wide in response, and it's evident that I said the wrong thing.

"You have to eat something. If you don't choose something, I will be forced to do it for you," she challenges as her dark eyebrows raise.

I'm lucky to have them in my life. I smile and my heartstrings tug as I watch them fuss over me, constantly asking if I am okay. I order my breakfast, settling on yoghurt with fruit and granola, not overly hungry but in need of some sort of boost. And of course, coffee and an orange juice.

Sitting in silence, I pry into everyone's conversations near me, luckily none of which are about me, for once. Two large hands grab my shoulders from behind, startling me out of my daze and I find Miles cracking up. He takes a seat next to me, grabbing my hand and threading his long fingers in between mine.

"How you are holding up?" he whispers in my ear.

Blaire and Maisie stare at us from over the top of their phones. A frown graces Blaire's mouth and I know she isn't pleased. I think she can at least like him for saving my life.

"I am fine, thank you for asking." I give him an honest smile, because I feel a lot better now that he's sitting next to me. "I want to say thank you, but I don't know how to repay you." I stare down into my lap, not wanting to see his reaction but he grips my chin in his long elegant fingers, bringing my eyes to meet his.

"How about, I take you out this Friday?" he asks, plastering a cheeky smile on his face, his eyes staring directly into mine as he waits for my answer.

I put on my biggest grin and nod. "Yeah, I'd love that."

"Good, it's settled then." Glancing over his shoulder, "well I have to run, I ordered my breakfast to go as I am busy this morning, but I'll catch you later?" He stands to leave, winks at me and then heads off.

Wow, who knew drowning was a way to get someone's attention.

Blaire and Maisie have shock written all over their face, the bottoms of their jaws pretty much hitting the table and their eyes wide as saucers.

"Oh my god!" Blaire shrieks behind her hands, covering her mouth while I giggle like a little schoolgirl who's crush just asked her out – oh wait, that is me.

My first class of the day is Business Economics, which is actually what I should be studying for my degree. I don't share this class with the girls, but I do with Blake.

Today is the first time I step foot in this class, and other than Blake I have no idea who else will be here to taunt me, and the only reason why I know Blake is in here is because Blaire warned me when she saw my class schedule.

I am the first one to arrive and Mr. Aldridge is sitting at his desk, organizing papers.

"Ah, I am guessing you are Adelaide?" he asks, taking of his glasses and throwing them onto the desk. I give him a smile and an awkward wave, and he points to a seating plan on the board.

Oh, for Christ's sake, next to Blake again! Why do we have to sit in alphabetical order? I grunt with a sigh, dragging my feet to the desk where I don't want to sit. I'm starting to think the universe is against me.

Today is the first morning I haven't seen any of the Royals, so as soon as Blake enters the room, I feel nauseous with dread, almost frightened of him. My pulse quickens as he looks over at the seating plan, his disappointment radiating all the way from the other end of the room. The girls already in the room all play with their hair, pushing up their boobs to show extra cleavage for when Blake walks past, which he surprisingly ignores. Blake takes his seat next to me, being sure to move it away from me as far as possible without leaving the desk entirely. I don't say a word to him, taking his last warning into consideration.

Thinking this day can't get any worse, in steps Hugo and Charles. Luck is slightly more on my side. Because of the seating plan, they don't sit anywhere near me. I sigh in relief and lean back in my chair, playing with the pen in my hand. I could do with a stress ball.

Mr. Aldridge begins the class with an introduction to the first units and sets up a little assignment to complete within forty-five minutes. Blake still hasn't said a word to me, but why would he? I scan the room to find Charles slumped back in his chair, his arm resting on the back of his partner's, looking around the room before his eyes find mine. His lips curl up into a sinful smile and he gives me finger wave. I immediately snap back to my assignment, trying to ignore his taunt.

I manage to finish my assignment within thirty minutes and Blake isn't too far behind me. I notice Hugo finished at least ten minutes before me, which doesn't surprise me as that guy is smart. He's got the looks of a Greek god but the mind of an evil genius, and he uses them both as a weapon. I sit there daydreaming and biting on my pen, not realizing I'm still gazing at Hugo until he cocks his head my way, breaking my little daze. We all hand in our papers, and Mr. Aldridge sets an assignment which will take the whole year to complete, but then drops the bomb that we will be working in pairs with the person sitting next to us.

Fuck my life.

Blake and I don't say a word to each other about the upcoming assignment, but I am pretty confident we can come up with a plan of just splitting it in the middle, without any conversing. The class starts to filter out the door, but Hugo and Charles make their way to my desk, I assume to wait for Blake.

"Do you enjoy staring at people like a fucking weirdo?" Hugo says with a sneer on his face, and Charles' head rolls back as he roars with laughter.

"I didn't mean to, I was daydreaming," I roll my eyes at him.

Oh god why did I just tell him I was daydreaming. Now he's going to think I was dreaming about him!

"That's fucked up," he drawls, already bored of the conversation. They stand in front of our desk waiting for Blake, who is talking to Mr. Aldridge, possibly trying to get a new partner. That would be a dream come true.

"You all good mate?" Charles questions Blake as he storms back over to us. Clearly whatever he was talking to Mr. Aldridge about, or the request for a new partner was denied. Goddamn it.

"Yeah, he's a fucking cunt. Hate the dude," Blake spits as he picks up his bag from the floor, stuffing all his stationary and books into it, then they all make their way to leave. Blake spins on his heel, turning to face me again nearly halfway through exiting.

"Oh Africa, I forgot to ask you earlier…"

His eyes turn from their beautiful Indian ocean blue, to a black hole filled with nothingness. "Did you enjoy your swim last night?" he releases a slow chuckle and the other two follow suit. I drop my books, realizing my nightmare was in fact a memory.

Blake tried to drown me.

"Don't forget tutoring tonight Africa," Hugo adds nonchalantly before they leave me alone in the room. Tears sting the back of my eyes and my breathing hitches as my chest tightens. I try to withhold the hyperventilating cry that lies in my aching chest. Wiping away the tears that managed to escape, I pretty much run to the bathroom to check my makeup. I apply some more concealer to try and hide the red around my still stinging eyes, holding the cry that's begging to be released, but I won't let it. No, I'll release it through dance later. I won't let these fuckwits ruin my day.

The rest of the day goes by with a blink, considering I still have tutoring with Hugo this afternoon. I've even checked to see if anyone else can replace him, but there isn't any other tutors available. For now, I have to cope with Hugo and his frustrating personality.

Entering the library, I notice he's not at our usual table, which is unusual for him as he's always early. I get all my assignments set up on my laptop, stick in my earphones and play some loud rock music that matches my mood to block out everything and everyone around me. Getting on with my assignments, I haven't kept my eye on the time. My earphones are ripped from my ears, leaving a stinging sensation behind.

"It's time to work, not head bang," Hugo says, clearly agitated. I frown at him as he takes his usual seat, starting his normal routine of organizing all the papers, books and stationary on the table.

I think he has some form of OCD.

"To be honest, I don't really care what you think, I don't really want you as a tutor anyway," I snap, putting one earphone back in and continuing with the assignment.

"And why is that Africa?"

Is he for real? I know Hugo is smart, so why he's acting stupid is beyond me. "Umm maybe because your fucking dick of a friend tried to drown me, and you just stood there." I grit my teeth, clenching my jaw, trying not to flip the table over and punch Hugo, even though I'm pretty sure that would be unsuccessful.

"Oh, that. Yeah, Blake didn't try and drown you, do you think he's stupid and would actually kill you?" he asks, chuckling to himself and handing me an assignment to complete.

"I beg to differ." I put my other earphone back in and turn up the volume, knowing he can hear it. He studies me for a moment before getting back to his own assignment and I can feel the awkward tension in the air. I still want to kick the shit out of him, but he's huge so I'd never win. I think if I tried to punch him, he wouldn't flinch, and my hand would be worse off. I finally get into a rhythm with my assignment and once again Hugo has to be a dick, pulling my earphones out again.

"What the fuck do you want?" I am seething by now.

"You're listening to some pretty heavy shit," he says, and I look at him in confusion. I mean I knew my earphones were loud enough for him to hear, but I didn't think he would want to start a conversation.

"Yeah well, the occasion calls for it," I roll my eyes at him.

"Yeah. Slipknot will help you with all the anger you're holding in," he surprises me, recognizing the band I'm listening to. But not just that, he knows how angry I am. I suppose I am radiating a dark aura around me.

"No shit sherlock, obviously I am angry."

He shakes his head at me and grabs my assignment from underneath my hand, stuffing it in his bag along with the other things before he leaves.

What the fuck was that all about?

Almost as if he is angry with me, but what the fuck does that asshole need to be angry about? I have every right to be furious with the prick.

The end of the week soon comes round and I'm getting ready for my date with Miles. Well, I think it's a date.

Blaire still insists on giving me a talk as she doesn't think this is a good idea. "I really think going on this date is a bad idea. He is the biggest playboy I know and plus he is Ruby's stepbrother," Blaire warns as she packs her bags. She turns around to face me, placing a warm hand on my bare cold shoulder.

"I just don't want you to get hurt, that's all," she says.

"I know you are only looking out for me, but I haven't felt like this with someone, ever. And he treats me so well, so I would love to see where this may go," I explain, offering her a soft smile. I have heard whispers that Miles and Ruby are close, but I haven't seen them communicate in any way.

"Right, well, have an amazing evening. Don't forget to text me later. I'll see you on Monday," Blaire smiles as she lifts her bag and leaves the room. Thankfully she leaves just in time for me to get ready, so I get the room to myself in peace. I style my dark brown hair with soft curls and apply a full face of makeup along with red lipstick. I am going all out tonight to look my best and I'm glad that it's with Miles.

Every time I think of him my heart skips a little beat in excitement and the butterflies in my stomach flap their wings ferociously. We have such an amazing connection, not just as dance partners but also as a possible couple and he's gorgeous too. A lot more beautiful than what I usually go for, but that is probably because a gorgeous looking model has never looked my way before. I pull out an off-shoulder white skater dress, with a tight-fitting bodice and pair it with some red heels. Taking a picture of my outfit in the mirror, I send it to Blaire and Maisie in our group chat for their approval. They both reply instantly with the heart eyes emoji.

At exactly seven, Miles knocks on the door as promised and the butterflies feel more intense than before. I quickly check my make-up before answering the door, and as soon as I do, I am left breathless.

Miles looks handsome in tight fitting jeans with a white crisp shirt, sleeves rolled up to the elbow and smart brown loafers. He looks like the typical posh boy. He even styled his hair differently, spiking it up a little and making it look effortless.

"Ade, you look fucking amazing," he breathes, eyes wide and raking from my feet all the way to my face, with a devilish grin on his face.

"It's not too much, is it?" I ask, giving him a little twirl but the look on his face shows appreciation. It seems to say 'I want to rip your clothes off' which makes me even happier.

"Hell no!" he says, grabbing my hand and escorting me to his car, which is parked in the courtyard at the back of the academy. Students are allowed to have their vehicles on site, as long as they park it in a secure garage behind the academy, and pretty much everyone has their own car. Everyone apart from me of course.

"Where are we going tonight?" I question, but Miles just looks at me with a mischievous smile and doesn't say a word. We get to the garage and my mouth almost drops. I haven't seen so many expensive cars all in one place in my whole life. I bet this cost more than a fucking country. He directs me to an electric blue Maserati which is tucked away in the corner and it takes my breath away. I don't think I have ever seen a car so beautiful. I mean, I'm not one for cars, but even I know this is a limited edition.

Miles chuckles to himself as he can see the appreciation in my eyes.

As a perfect gentleman, Miles opens the passenger door for me, letting me slide in gracefully. The leather upholstered seat hugs me in, making me feel safe and comfortable. Once Miles has climbed in, he starts the engine with a button and the car roars to life. The sounds making me feel as though I'm at an F1 race rather than the academy, and then Miles gently pulls away from all the other cars, leaving the estate, making me in charge of the music, so of course I choose the most cheesy songs ever.

"Seriously, you decide to go for this?" He side-eyes me, the corner of his lips curling into a grin.

I laugh, my hand covering my mouth as 'All the small things' by

Blink 182 starts playing and to my surprise Miles starts singing, knowing the words off by heart. So, I join in.

We sing the song all the way through, with Miles tapping along to the beat on the steering wheel.

"Might I suggest that you stick to dancing and not singing," Miles jokes as he winks at me. I playfully slap his leg, then he grabs and holds my hand, leaving it on his thigh. My heart leaps as my eyes travel down to watch this sort of affection and a small smile tugs my lips. "I can say the same for you," I wink back, enjoying this type of banter between us.

I see a sign on the way to our destination that reads 'Stonewall Beach'. It takes us forty-five minutes to get there, which flew by. He pulls up in a parking lot, which is directly in front of the beach. He opens my passenger door, holding onto my hand and pulls me out to stand. I breathe in the salty ocean air and my heart warms, remembering how much I love that smell. I really need to get down here to surf.

The moment Miles clasps his hand in mine, my heartbeat quickens, and I suddenly feel breathless. We take a stroll, hand in hand to a little seafood restaurant that is directly sitting on the beach. A waiter takes us to a private table on a balcony where we hear the waves crashing against the rocks of the restaurant. We both take our seats, and already a bottle of red wine has been put on the table. "I took the liberty to pre-order the wine. I hope you like it," he says.

The waiter pulls the cork out, pouring us a little in a wine glass to taste and I moan in satisfaction, tasting the sweet grapes and a hint of oak from the barrel. "It is amazing."

We are lucky to enjoy the gorgeous sunset at dinner on the balcony, the indescribable orange and crimson with flecks of gold in the sky, just like an oil painting.

"This really reminds me of home, where the sunsets in the savannah are to die for," I whisper to Miles as I stare into the horizon in adoration.

"Well, you look stunning with the sunset reflecting in your blue eyes," Miles compliments, as he grabs my hand from across the table, his thumb brushing against my soft skin. I briefly close my eyes, savoring this moment and my pulse races along to the hammering of my heartbeat against my chest.

After our delicious dinner, my stomach full on seafood paella, we decide to take a stroll on the beach. The sun has fallen, and the moon is resurrected in its place, the silver colour reflecting off the blue ocean and brightening the scenery. My toes sink into the golden soft sand, tickling my skin with every step I take. My arm is in Miles' as we admire the setting, listening to the bustling of people around us and the soft waves hitting the shore.

"This is… amazing. I have needed this," I admit, hugging Miles's arm tighter and giving him a soft smile. Cocking his head to look at me, the slight breeze blowing through his silver blonde hair, he smiles. My heart aches with lust, my body itching to get closer to him.

Walking on the beach with a slight breeze, I have to hold my dress down to prevent it from blowing up and everyone seeing my underwear. In the corner of my eye, I notice a large bonfire on the other side of the beach, with a few girls dancing around it still in their bikinis.

"Wow, I miss having parties on the beach with my friends back home," I mumble, Miles pulling me down to sit with him on the sand facing the ocean.

"They have a lot of parties here in the summer. They're really fun," he says, putting his arm around my shoulder and bringing me in closer. I can smell his spicy cologne in the breeze as it wafts past me, surrounding the air I breathe.

It smells almost like Christmas.

"Hey, do you want to do something crazy?" Miles wiggles his eyebrows at me with a cheeky grin and I am liking where this is going. "Want to go for a swim? The water is still warm at this time of year."

"Oh, hell yeah!" I agree and we both start peeling off our clothes, until we're left in just our underwear. I'm wearing a matching set of white lace, but because it's dark no-one will really see, plus the girls are drunk at the bonfire so they won't care. We both end up racing to the water and Miles is the first one to dive headfirst.

"Come on!" he hollers, cupping his hands around his mouth. He floats effortlessly in the water, the moonlight catching on his pale skin. I run further in but don't take the leap as Miles did when diving in, and soon enough I reach him. He grabs my waist with his soft hands, pulling me towards him.

"You're right, it's actually pretty warm in here," I whisper as I stare into his cosmic eyes. I snake my arms around his neck and wrap my legs around his torso, feeling his hard, lean body against mine.

We swim around for a while, splashing water in each other's faces, joking around which makes my heart feel lighter than it's been in a long time, and being here with Miles feels right. He makes me feel comfortable, making the memory of me drowning disappear as if it never happened.

He grabs my legs, wrapping them back around his waist so that he can hold me, my hands brushing along his biceps as I snake my arms back round his neck. His eyes stare at me intensely again, but this time there seems to be a look of regret and pain.

"Are you okay?" I ask, my lips so close to his that if I let out another breath they would touch, and just the thought of us kissing sends heat from my core to the rest of my body. I'm shivering but not because I'm cold, more like desperate for him to kiss me, but I don't want to push him and be rejected.

He doesn't reply to my question but instead his lips crash against mine, his hand gripping the back of my neck, fingers tangling in my long hair and holding me in place while his other hand stays on my slender waist. He parts my lips with his tongue, invading my mouth and sending shivers through my spine, heat radiating from both our bodies. His tongue is so sensual, but almost apologetic. He kisses me as if this is the last time, as if he will never kiss me again.

Miles pulls away and rests his forehead against mine, both of us trying to catch our breath. "I am better now," he whispers, hauling me up from the water and bringing me to my feet. We walk out of the water, back to our discarded clothes on the sand. I stare back at the bonfire, watching the girls now all sitting down on their towels, drinking beers, and laughing.

All of a sudden, my gaze connects to three sets of eyes, sitting on sun loungers and hiding behind the fire, the orange hue brightening the dark features on their faces. I stand there in my white soaked underwear, staring straight into the depths of hell at three demons called Blake, Charles, and Hugo. Each with a beer in their hand and girls surrounding them along the ground.

I hear another man's voice call out from behind them, and I instantly recognize it to be Royce. He stumbles behind the sun loungers, wearing white trousers and a blue shirt with a white cardigan tied around his neck. Looking ever so posh, I must say. Before I know it, they are all staring directly in my direction and a creepy grin curls up onto Royce's face as he leans down to whisper in Blake's ear. I try to swallow the big lump in my throat, but it doesn't seem to budge.

I promptly pick up my dress and slide it over my wet underwear. At this moment I don't care; I just need to get away. Looking at the three of them has brought up the memory of me drowning and their dark, sadistic faces enjoying it. I try to catch my breath before Miles wraps his arm around my waist, leading me back to the car.

I can't believe they have just witnessed me in my underwear, but mostly I wonder if they saw me kiss Miles in the ocean. My body fills with dread, thinking about the ways they will taunt me once we're back at the academy.

We're both back in the car on the way back to the academy, my soaked underwear leaving wet marks on my dress. I rest my head back on the plush, luxurious car seat and listen to the playlist I put on, my eyes daring to close in exhaustion. We don't say a word to each other on the way back to the academy, but Miles rests his left hand on my knee, drawing small circles on my skin with his long, slender finger.

We walk hand in hand to my dorm, my other hand holding the jacket he rested over my shoulders to create a barrier from the cold breeze. A true gentleman. We stand outside my door for a few moments before Miles leans his hard body into mine. He cups my chin in between his fingers, and slowly brings my lips to meet his. This time he kisses me tenderly, not like the first time where it was rough and passionate. Miles doesn't slide his tongue in my mouth, instead just giving me a feather light kiss, leaving me wanting more.

"I had an amazing time tonight Ade," he purrs under his breath, his eyes still closed. I cup his angelic face in my hands, trying to bring him closer, but he gives me one last kiss before taking a step back. He leans his back against the opposite wall, putting his hands in the front pockets of his jeans, staring at me with hooded eyes, waiting for me to unlock the door to my dorm.

"I had an amazing night too, thank you Miles," I smile at him one last time before retreating into my room and closing the door on him.

I take a long shower, spraying my hot, flushed skin with cold water and smiling at myself for how giddy I feel. Miles is the first guy I have ever gotten so close to, enough to enjoy being in their company. It still baffles me as to why Blaire and Maisie warned me off him, because apparently, he's a 'playboy'.

Standing under the shower, I wash and scrub the salty ocean from my skin, leaving it red raw with my honeycomb bodywash. This really is my favorite scent; I'll have to ask Blaire where we can order some more.

I text the girls in our group chat informing them of this evening's activity, and they seemed pretty excited for me when they text back. Hopefully, they're coming round to the idea of Miles and I as a couple because I certainly am. Getting changed into my PJ's, I tuck myself into bed, fatigue completely taking over my body and I'm asleep instantly.

Chapter Eleven

I don't wake up the next day until noon, sleep has completely taken over me. My phone vibrates on my nightstand, a hint that I should join the living. I check my phone. I have texts from Miles, my group chat, and – someone who normally doesn't give a shit – my father. He usually only texts me when he wants something. Irritation fills me up, making my blood feel as though its boiling. I think I'll read that one last.

The text from Miles instantly puts a smile on my face.

I had an amazing time last night Ade, see you soon x

I send him a quick text back, telling him how much I enjoyed last night, and I can't help but help giggle to myself, rereading his last text. It takes me a few moments to collect myself before I read the text from my Father.

Your first elocution lesson is tomorrow at the house, be there at 9.

My response back is a simple OK, not expressing how I really feel about these shitty elocution lessons. I really don't know why the fuck he's trying to change me; I mean why bother flying me across the world to not even see me.

Prick.

Grabbing my pillow, I shove it into my face, screaming as loud as I can to drown out the noise. Getting up, I get change into some yoga pants and a sports bra so that I can hit the dance studio early to let out some frustration. I should have read my father's text first and then Miles'. Maybe my mood would be better. Knowing I have to be there at nine in the morning doesn't help either, considering I have a shift at the club tonight starting at ten which probably won't end till after midnight.

Poking my head inside, no one seems to be in the dance studio, which I am grateful for as I like practicing on my own. I lay my towel and bottle of water on the side and connect my phone to the Bluetooth speakers that surround the room. I put on 'Heart shaped Glasses' by Marilyn Manson and practice my routine for the recital.

I dance for another few songs before someone rudely interrupts my rhythm and shuts the music off. "What the fuck?" My head swings around and I see the intruder.

"Oh, someone's feisty today!" Royce steps into the room holding his hands up in surrender. "I heard music and thought it might be you," he grins.

Picking up my towel, I wipe the sweat from my blood-red tinted face and take a swig of my water. "What do you want Royce?" I cock my hip out, resting my hand in the dip on my tiny waist.

Patiently, I stand there waiting for Royce to respond, but instead he circles me like a shark in the ocean waiting to attack his prey. The grin on his face is as sadistic as ever and I know for a fact he's going to mention seeing me last night.

Fuck my life.

"Oh, you know, just thought I'd say hi. Can't I be friendly?" his beautiful face changes from a smile to a deep frown. He halts in front of me, staring me down and making it obvious that he's drawn to my cleavage.

"See something you like?"

"Oh yes very much. Especially since I saw you in that lovely white number last night," he says, tipping his head back and roaring with laughter. I have to bite the inside of my cheek to stop myself from commenting further. I turn away from Royce, taking another sip of my drink before stretching out my limbs in front of him.

You have to act like you don't care Ade, I think to myself. My chest tightens under the pressure of his eyes and I continue to take a big gulp of water to help ease the dryness of my throat.

"You looked good." He shrugs his shoulders, taking a step closer to me, his eyes roaming my body through the mirror in front of us. His face doesn't hide the lustful sexual thoughts, I mean, I should be happy right? Royce fucking Huntington is checking me out, and he said I looked good!

"Well, thank you, but if that's all?" I say.

He chuckles under his breath again before turning on his heel to leave. I notice he's wearing the same outfit from last night, so I'm guessing they must have stayed out all night and have only just come back.

"I'll catch you later Ade." He winks, then leaves the room and the breath I was holding releases into the room with a whoosh. I end up sitting on the floor, exhausted from my routine, but also the fact that my heart is racing ten times faster than it should be.

How is it all these boys make me feel more worn out, and set my heart rate higher than when I dance for hours? I guess it doesn't help that they are the most gorgeous men I have ever seen in my life. It should be a crime to be that beautiful.

I bet Royce isn't aware that I've met his father at that awful dinner party the other weekend. I wonder how he would react knowing I shared the same table and ate next to him. Just the thought tickles me.

After my little outburst in the dance studio, I go to the dining hall to get some breakfast in me. Dancing on an empty stomach is really not a good idea. On my way up there, I walk past the wooden door to the tunnel, noticing it's open again. It's been closed all week. It clicks in my head that the door is usually only open on the week-ends, so possibly the staff use it.

I am going to find out why it leads to Club Envy.

Shaking off my Nancy Drew thoughts, I continue on my merry way to the dining hall. I walk past the Royal's table with three of them and Ruby sitting there, which is also unusual considering it's the weekend and they normally go home. I suppose due to last night's antics, they probably wanted to stay and party. I take a seat, looking at the menu but my gaze bounces around the room, self-conscious to the fact that everyone's eyes are on me. My mind starts to cloud with darkness, as I feel the way people judge me from across the room and it doesn't help that I am vulnerable and alone with the Royals present. My mind repeats a mantra of counting down from ten. Beads of sweat form in my hairline as I stare down at the menu. Eating alone has always proven difficult, and now that my safe wall of Maisie and Blaire are not present to shield me from prying eyes, I feel the pressure more than ever. I take in deep breaths, calming the beats of my heart and my quickened pulse, but all that runs through my mind is that the prying eyes are laughing at me. Laughing at how I look or my eating habits. These eyes stare at me with disgust and I know what they all think.

Ade is fat, she shouldn't eat.

Ade needs to lose weight

She should learn to control herself around food.

But in reality, these people around me aren't even concerned about how I eat, or what I eat. When you suffer with an eating disorder and body dysmorphia, it's hard to get rid of these demons that haunt our minds on a daily basis.

Soon after my mental argument with myself, I order some boiled eggs and fruit to provide some protein and energy, which should hold me up until lunch. I only plan on studying this afternoon, so I am sure I won't work up such an appetite. Knowing that the demon eyes are all watching me, I pull out my phone and browse through my social media. The only two friends I have added on any platform are Blaire and Maisie, and I intend to keep it that way.

I check Facebook messages and see that my best friend from back home has posted some of my belongings which I was unable to bring on my travels. Knowing what is in the package puts an instant smile on my face and I can't contain my excitement any longer. I send her a quick message back thanking her and telling her I miss her.

Finally, my breakfast arrives at the table, but something more unwelcoming decides to ruin my morning— the four dickheads, who's heads are so stuck up their own asses I'm surprised they don't eat their own shit.

Blake takes a seat directly in front of me, while the other three fan out around me taking the other available seats. Blake is dressed in his hockey uniform, looking beautiful and rugged with his chestnut brown hair, tousled with how many times he rakes his hand through it. Hugo looks immaculate, his raven dark hair perfectly tailored to a high part fade showing the tattoo just above his ear. He's wearing a black tight-fitting t-shirt and black joggers and I think he's been working out, but my god does he look devilishly handsome. I could eat him for breakfast. I want to look at him in appreciation but hold myself back, not wanting to attract their wrath.

Charles's shaggy hair falls into his eyes as he looks down on his phone, wearing grey shorts and a matching grey t-shirt that shows off his lean muscles. He's really got the preppy but surfer dude look going on, and I love it.

Ruby is sitting next to me with her arms crossed over her chest, leaning back on the back two feet of the stool and I am so tempted to push her over. I'm not that evil though, so my next though is I hope she doesn't fall back and hurt herself.

Damn, I'm too caring.

"To what do I owe the pleasure?" I deadpan, folding my arms across my chest, which is clearly distracting the boys - I'm still in my sports bra, which shows a lot of cleavage. I should have gotten changed before coming down. Two sets of eyes stare at me with fire burning within, the dark holes drawing me in, hoping I can add some light. They look troubled and angry and I can't figure why.

Charles and Ruby are now distracted by their phones, not even bothering to look in my direction, as if looking at me is a crime and they would be punished, or I'm not even worth their time. You know what? I bloody wish I wasn't.

Hugo's jaw clenches, the muscle ticking and bringing out his sweet dimples as he crosses his arms in front of his huge chest, his biceps straining against the tight sleeves of his shirt. I can pretty much see his veins popping out with how muscular he is. I wonder if he takes steroids to be able to get that big, but I don't think he would be too pleased if I ask him that question.

"Well, we thought we would be good friends and ask how your evening went, that's all," a venomous sneer shows up on Blake's face, complimenting the venom in his voice when he speaks to me. He looks down at his phone before turning it to me. I cough, almost choking on my drink. He's got a picture of me straddling Miles in the ocean and kissing but looking as if it were more.

I raise my eyebrow, confused. "Why the fuck have you got a picture of me kissing Miles?" I ask, not giving him the satisfaction of retaliating just yet. His hateful sneer is still plastered on his face and he puts his phone back in his pocket. The other dickheads just laugh, apart from Hugo who's silent but deadly, nonetheless.

"Well, going by that picture it looks like you did more than just kiss," he continues but I don't want to bite just yet. "You're such a disgusting slut, parading around having sex with all the boys, you're fucking repulsive Africa," he cringes, leaning forward as he says what's clearly on his mind, not having a care in the world.

"You're kidding me, right? First you try and drown me, now you have a picture of me kissing Miles. You're the pathetic one Blake," I grind out through my clenched teeth. God, I wish I could punch the fucking cunt in the face right now.

I'm so distracted by my standoff with Blake, my body goes into shock and a scream escapes my lungs as someone grabs a fistful of my hair, slamming my face into the table. I feel the blood spluttering out of my busted nose as she pulls my head back, forcing me to stare at Blake. The blood continues to pour until it hits my lips, and I taste the coppery tang.

Blake forcefully stands, slamming his fists onto the table and bringing his face so close to mine that I can smell the malice radiating off of him. "Listen here, you tribal fucking cunt. I warned you about the hierarchy here and you just didn't pay attention. You get what you deserve." He puts a finger under my chin, lifting my eyes in defiance to look at him, Ruby still gripping my hair making my scalp sting in pain, but I won't let them know that. He grips my chin even harder, the pain running through my jaw and I know for a fact it will leave a bruise.

"I am sick of you thinking you're better than us, so you will fall in line like everyone else does at this academy. Because bitch. This is our school."

Blake storms off with Charles and Ruby in tow, but Hugo waits a moment longer, handing me some napkins to clean the blood off my face. I stare at him with fury in my eyes, refusing to take them, so instead he throws them in my direction and leaves to follow his Satan of a leader. I pick up the napkin from the table, trying to clean as much of the blood off as I can.

No one was in the dining hall to witness what just happened and the waiters were nowhere to be seen. I suppose they all have a blind eye to what the Royals do.

Without eating my breakfast, I pick up my gym bag and run back to the dorms. I jump in the shower, spraying my skin with scolding hot water, letting it fall onto my aching scalp through to wash away all the blood. I watch as it goes down the drain. The tears fall and mix with the water. Unable to control my breathing, it hitches in my throat as my knees give way beneath me. I fall to the floor, crying and taking heavy breaths. The hot water washes away the blood and tears, washing away the semblance of a life I had here. Crouching in the corner, my head falls to my knees as I suddenly feel deflated.

I sit there for god knows how long, but eventually I stop crying and pick myself off the tiled floor, turning off the shower and checking the damage to my face in the mirror. I have a bruised nose which I am sure will be more prominent tomorrow. Fear takes over my body thinking what father will say when he sees my face. I'm sure concealer can hide most of it, but I'm fairly sure my nose is broken.

Tears prickle at the back of my eyes again as I stare at my reflection in the mirror. Anger takes over my whole body and I slam my fist into the mirror where my reflection is, glass flying out around me, leaving specks of blood on the mirror.

Now it's as broken as I feel.

*T*arrive at work an hour early, as I was not able to concentrate back at the academy. I walk through the doors and then through the foyer, feeling lethargic as I try to hide my face and hands from anyone seeing them. As I hang up my leather jacket on a hook, Samantha rounds the corner and her eyes go wide as she notices the damaged skin and bruises.

"What the fuck happened chick?" she says, and within a few strides she's standing before me, grabbing my chin in a gentle touch. Samantha tilts my hand from side to side as she inspects the damage. My heart is racing against my chest as I fear that this could get me fired.

"Umm, my face was smashed against the table by some girl, and then I got angry and punched my mirror," I admit, taking a gulp as I look towards the floor in shame. My eyes begin to water as I feel embarrassed to be seen like this. I tried my best to hide the bruises on my face with make-up, but nothing gets past Samantha.

"Oh hon, how could this happen to you? Let's get you cleaned up. I have cleaned a lot of cut hands so I know what I am doing," she offers with a soft smile, one that she never usually exposes and I sigh in relief as the tension in my stomach settles. My heart rate slows down, and I manage to exhale a deep breath as Samantha guides me to her office. She is amazing, helping me disguise the bruises on my face and cleaning my cut knuckles so it's hardly noticeable for when I work. When she said that she does this all the time, I am guessing she either means cleaning other people cut knuckles or her own.

I get straight to work with the other girl called Lily, who seems to be on the timid side. I figured she didn't talk to me much last time because she was either really busy, or she doesn't like me. I help her in the basement, where the tunnel leads to, and I want to ask her about it, but I get a feeling she doesn't like questions much.

"So, how long have you worked here for?" I decide to ask her, thinking that it can't hurt to try and get to know my co-worker.

Lily doesn't look my way when she answers. "Um, about a year I think," she says, and I am grateful that I managed to make some progress in conversation.

"Oh cool, do you enjoy it?" I continue, hopefully not pushing her buttons.

"Yeah it's alright, but you get some right bastards in 'ere," she shrugs, passing me a heavy box and directing me to put it by the old, crooked wooden door.

This could be my chance to find out about the tunnel.

"Hey, I don't suppose you know where this door leads to?" I bravely ask and Lily cocks her head up from looking through a box.

She chuckles under her breath before responding. "You ask a lot of questions."

"Sorry, simply curious. Looks old and I love history. Thought there might be some historical facts." I give her a crooked smile, hopefully she buys my little white lie. It is partly true; I am intrigued about the history.

"Well, I think it's some old tunnels that were built hundreds of years ago, but I never bothered to ask. Honestly, it doesn't fascinate me." She passes me another heavy box to stack up.

I think that's enough pressing for one day. I don't want her to hate me. We finish up in the basement just in time to start work behind the bar before any customers saunter in. I clean a couple of the wine glasses with a hand towel and organise the bottles of liquor on the shelves. I suppose I might have slight OCD. Wish it were the case in my own room. With my back against the bar, I hear a slight wolf whistle behind me, the hairs on the back of my neck instantly standing up.

"Hey Africa, what you are doing here?"

I turn around with pursed lips, avoiding eye contact with the asshole.

"I work here now," I mumble to Royce, wiping the counter tops.

"Oh, does that mean free drinks on you?" he chuckles sarcastically with a smile on his face. He pulls out the bar stool and takes a seat, folding his arms on the countertop and still grinning at me.

"Can I get you a drink?" I ask as politely as I can. He is a customer after all, so I need to be nice. Even though he wasn't there this morning when I had my face smashed to the table by Ruby in front of the other Royal pricks, he's still friends with them and I do not trust anyone who is remotely friendly with them.

"I'll have a whiskey, neat but with three cubes of ice."

He ruffles up his perfectly styled caramel toned hair, looking kinda sad sitting here on his own and lacking his normal cheeky personality. I fix his drink up, handing it over to him before I serve the other customers rolling in. It's weird seeing Royce sitting at a bar when I've had posters of him in my childhood bedroom, always admiring his movies. He hasn't starred in a film since he started high school, expressing to the public in an interview that he wanted a normal school experience. Can't blame the guy. His family is always traveling the world shooting films, clearly never spending time with Royce as he's always here. I guess that's how he gets away with his house being party central. But I am still wondering what his dad was doing here, of all places at my father's house eating a three-course meal next to me.

"Are you just going to stand there staring at me Ade?" Royce whispers, breaking the trance I was in, not even aware I was staring at him.

"Sorry, I was actually staring behind you, wondering what the performance will be," I say, hopefully that was a good save.

Royce takes another sip of his whiskey, the ice clinks gently in the glass as he rolls it absently between his hands.

"Oh, you wait and see. It's magical." His haughty expression glares my way, and he shakes his now empty glass in my direction, signaling for a top up. I roll my eyes at his arrogance, thinking he can order me around because I'm the one working behind the bar.

I refill the glass with whiskey and three cubes of ice, exactly how he requested it earlier, and hand his drink over. He grabs the glass, brushing his elegant long fingers over mine, sending a jolt of electricity through to my limbs and making me feel numb. I quickly retrieve my hand, clearing my throat.

He takes a sip of his drink, eyeing me over the rim of the glass, clearly aware of my reaction to that silly little accident of us touching skin to skin. I'm seriously fan girling in my head right now, I never want to wash this hand again.

Well I will but still, it's just an expression.

As I load the empty glasses into the dishwasher under the bar, where its well-hidden, I can feel Royce's glare penetrate my back. I turn around and find him staring at me with narrow eyes, his chin resting in the palm of his hand. Plucking up my courage, I finally ask him what's been bothering me since he arrived.

"What's wrong, you seem … off?"

Resting one of my hands on my hip as the other rests on the surface, tapping my fingers against the countertop. Royce stares at me absently, opening his mouth to say something but nothing comes out. He scrubs his hand over his face, taking in a deep breath before bringing his sea green eyes to meet mine.

"I am sorry," he declares, and I'm taken aback. I raise my eyebrows at him as he takes a sip of whiskey, blowing out another big breath before continuing.

"For what the guys did to you. Just know that I am not part of that," he says, raking his eyes away from mine, landing over on the stage. My body steels itself as I'm taken aback by surprise and my stomach flutters from this revelation. My thoughts freeze and his cheeks flush red as he swivels on the bar stool, his attention now on the dais where the lights have been dimmed, only a spotlight now covering the stage. I guess the show is just about to start.

The lights in the room go completely dark, leaving only the candlelight to illuminate the room, the incandescent flames dancing and creating shadows on the audience's faces as their eyes gaze over to the stage. As everyone's attention is at the front of the room, I stand behind the bar watching Royce, not even realizing the spotlight on the stage has come on. His eager expression lights up when the music starts playing, welcoming the first performer.

The song 'Pour it Up' by Rihanna starts playing and the beautiful brunette woman is already on the stage, seated on a chair backwards, wearing a trench coat and not leaving any skin visible. While the music continues, the woman starts her routine by removing the trench coat, revealing the most stunning outfit I have ever seen.

She's wearing a black rhinestone corset which accentuates her big bust and small waist, matching black frilly knickers which cover her whole ass and six-inch black heels.

I'm gawking at this beautiful woman on the stage, my gaze following every graceful move she makes, how she dances on the whole stage using the chair as her prop, looking sexual without removing any part of her clothing.

This is mesmerizing.

I keep watching the performances throughout the night whilst fixing up the drinks for the waiters to serve to the customers, still astounded by how sensual the routines are. I know this is supposed to be an erotic dance show or 'Burlesque', but unlike a stripper these girls don't remove any part of their clothing, apart from their bra but even then, they are at least wearing nipple tassels. They make it seem so beautiful.

I want to learn Burlesque.

Royce spins around on the bar stool, requesting another whiskey. The performances are done for the evening, so a lot of the customers are starting to leave, but Royce stays behind. "Do you want me to take you back to the academy?" he asks.

Do I go with him or should I get an uber? I mean, I know he apologized for his friends but what if there is an ulterior motive? "Um, if you don't mind waiting ten minutes then yeah." I smile at him; fairly certain he's being genuine.

Packing up my things, I slip on my leather jacket, meeting Royce back at the bar. He gulps down the rest of his whiskey then pulls out a wad of money from of his wallet, placing it on the bar for Samantha to take. I am fairly certain he's overpaid for his drinks. We walk outside to the parking lot in complete silence, stopping at an all-black Aston Martin One-77 and I am in awe. This car is worth over a million fucking pounds and they only ever made seventy-seven of them, hence the name.

I don't know a lot about cars, but I have heard about this one.

"Are you fantasizing about my car, Ade?" Royce teases as he opens the passenger door for me. I slide into the luxurious interior, breathing in the scent of fresh leather. Royce climbs into the driver's seat and turns on the engine. The car roars to life and a slight squeal slips out from my lips. Royce chuckles under his breath, clearly aware of my reaction.

"This is just … fucking amazing," I admit, brushing my fingers along the hand sewed seams of the seat. He turns on the music from his plush steering wheel, slowly reversing out of the parking lot, driving onto the main road. I feel as though I am floating on air with how smooth the car drives, I can't feel any bumps from the road and every turn Royce takes is with ease.

"How did you find the Burlesque dancers?" Royce asks, breaking the silence between the two of us. He hasn't looked in my direction since we got in the car, which surprises me as he normally doesn't care if I find him ogling. "It was hypnotizing, I've never seen anything like it," I confess. "I didn't even realize they did these performances when I took on the job," I continue, turning my head slightly to look at Royce, but his eyes stay firmly on the road ahead of him.

He frowns, the curve of his lips turned down. "Why did you take the job there?" Finally, he turns his head, bringing his dark sea green eyes to look at me.

I shrug my shoulders, biting my lip before I answer him. "I wanted something to do, rather than sit in the academy all the time, plus I used to have a part time job at home so it's nothing new."

I glance away from him, looking out of my window even though it's dark outside and I can't see a thing.

We arrive at the Academy in record time with how fast Royce drives. He probably didn't want to be in the car with me any longer than he needed to. We go our separate ways, saying goodnight at the stairs leading up to my dorm. I trudge all the way up to the third floor and head to my dorm room, finding another note stuck to the door. I rip it off the door, opening the envelope to yet another little letter.

"We know your secret."

Who the fuck is sending me these notes?

Chapter Twelve

$\mathcal{I}$ arrive at my father's house by half past eight in the morning, feeling exhausted by the lack of sleep last night, the note playing on my mind. I still can't work out who would send that note or even what secret they may be aware of. Maybe they found out about my father, the truth that I'm in fact not an exchange student or poor as they think? Other than that, I have no secrets.

I sit in the kitchen, enjoying a cup of coffee as Mrs. Blossom enters into the room holding a big brown box.

"Miss Adelaide, this has just arrived for you," she says, placing the box directly on the counter in front of me. Unable to contain my eagerness, I jump off my stool and pick up a pair of scissors from a drawer, cutting the tape that's holding the box closed. Squealing in excitement, I rip open the rest of the parcel tape, opening the box and seeing my whole life packed away neatly. My heart races as I pick out the first photo album, which holds all my memories of my mum and family back home.

I put that to the side on the counter, not wanting to look inside just yet. I'll wait until I'm on my own before I reminisce. I rummage through the rest of the contents of the box, packed with scrap books, jewelry, and trinkets from my friends. The tears in my eyes start to well up, the sadness taking over me with the knowledge that my old life is packed into such a small box. I wipe away the tears that fall and pack the contents back in the box, taking it up to my room for me to organise later at the academy.

I'd rather have these kept close to me than being kept here.

The clock ticks at nine and the doorbell rings, signaling the elocution teacher is here. I stand at the bottom of the stairs as Mrs. Blossom answers the door to Ms. Veronica. A blonde, pale middle-aged woman dressed in a matching light pink skirt and blazer walks into the house with a huge grin on her face and the biggest sunglasses I have ever seen.

"You must be Adelaide?" she says, taking off her bug sunglasses. Her bright grey eyes go wide, scanning my body from head to toe.

"You really are a beauty, aren't you dear?" she says in a patronizing tone.

Biting the inner side of my cheek, I try to repress the sarcasm from pouring out. I take a deep breath before I finally greet this overbearing woman in front of me.

"Hi, yes I'm Adelaide and thanks," I say with a brief smile before it falters. Mrs. Blossom leads us into the drawing room, where a pot of tea and two teacups with saucers are already placed on the table with a couple of finger biscuits.

Seriously, these posh twats.

"I can see why your father wanted you to have elocution lessons. We need to get rid of that horrid accent of yours," she drawls, taking a seat on the grey sofa and pouring us both a cup of tea.

Rolling my eyes and trying not to snap at this woman, I take a seat in the grey armchair facing her, crossing my left leg over the other. She tuts, waving her finger at me. "Oh dear. First lesson, you need to sit like a lady." She shows me how her legs are closed at the knee, leaning to one side and her spine dead straight.

She kind of looks like she has a stick stuck up her ass.

I imitate and sit like a 'proper lady', feeling thoroughly uncomfortable. Ms. Veronica picks up her tea, taking a sip but her pinky finger sticks out, so I mimic her actions. The corners of her lips curl up slightly, pleased.

We carry on sipping our tea with no conversation until she demands for me to walk from one side of the room to the other.

I thought this was elocution lessons, not learning how to walk.

"I need to see how you walk Adelaide, so I can assess your mannerisms." She stands up from the sofa, observing my walk. I do this a couple of times from one end to the other, watching the concentration on Ms. Veronica's face as she taps her index finger on her chin.

"You walk like a lazy, homeless person," she articulates, sauntering over to me on the other side of the room. She pushes my back and stomach in and adjusts my shoulders. "Right, chin up and stare at the blue vase on the other side of the room, then walk over to it."

Why anyone would ever walk like a cardboard cutout baffles me. This is uncomfortable.

"You should feel as though you are floating on the air. Walk as if you're a proud woman," she sings. Closing my eyes, I try and block her out, counting to ten and controlling my breathing so I don't bite. I open my eyes, walking over to the blue vase and following her instructions. She claps to herself, squealing with delight. "Well done dear!"

We take a seat back on the sofas, where I sit with my legs closed, back straight like she taught me. She pours us both another cup of tea before continuing with 'Speech Therapy' as she likes to call it.

"We need to try and practice your speech therapy. We need to get rid of that dreaded accent of yours. It shan't do in this society, and you come across too harsh." She huffs before taking a sip of tea. I fidget with my fingers as I pick the skin around my nails, offended by her honesty but I nod along.

"Ladies need to be graceful, as if you were whispering but firm at the same time" she hums and I tilt my head to the side, lifting my eyebrow as she contradicts herself.

How the fuck can I be whispering, but be firm at the same time? I feel like she can't make up her stupid mind.

"Adelaide?" I hear my name being shouted out from the foyer. My father calls out again before opening the door and entering the drawing room. He stands in the doorway with his hands in his trouser pockets, all suited up as if he were in a business meeting. His hair is neatly cut and styled, not a strand out of place. He screams business and dominance.

"Ah, Ms. Veronica, I hope my daughter isn't any trouble. I know she needs a lot of fixing."

My eyes open wide as I glare at my father in disbelief.

Inhaling a deep breath, I reply, "I didn't realize I needed fixing, father."

They both look over in my direction My father's dark eyes meet mine, the anger noticeably clear at my interjection. He purses his lips before his face softens and he chuckles.

"Yes dear, of course you do. Whatever your mother did to you in that country is just not suitable. I want a lady for a daughter, not an orphan who looks and acts as though she got lost in the wilderness for years," he mocks, causing Ms. Veronica to laugh, cackling with her hand on her chest.

Bile rises from my stomach into my throat and I try swallowing it down. I conceal my anger by picking up my cup of tea, sipping the hot drink and counting to ten in my head.

"I shall leave you ladies to it, then." Father exits the room, leaving Ms. Veronica panting with a flushed face. Oh god, she fancies my father. Now I want to be sick.

"You heard the man, let's get straight back to work," she announces and that's what we do for the whole day, not even with a ten-minute break. She teaches me how to eat properly, what cutlery to use for what dish, which wine or champagne glass should be used at a dinner table and so on.

I am officially spent. How do ladies live like this? Constantly worrying about how they look, how they walk or eat and drink. It's fucking stupid.

The grandfather clock in the far-right corner chimes, signaling the time has just hit seven in the evening. "Oh, will you look at the time!" Ms. Veronica announces, straightening her back as the clock chimes. "I think it's best to end the lesson and carry on another time. We have accomplished a lot today. I will organise with your father the next session, as we have a long way to go yet."

"Okay, Ms. Veronica. Thank you for today," I offer a fake smile, trying my best not to scream at her. After the devil woman leaves, I stomp back to the kitchen, not taking her advice to always walk 'properly' whilst grab myself a glass of orange juice. I gulp it down and pour myself another.

God, I wish this were straight tequila or something.

I huff and puff around the kitchen, not noticing Sally in the corner by the pantry, laughing behind her hand.

"I am so sorry, I didn't know anyone was in here," I tell her, my cheeks flushing red because she just saw my little episode.

"It's okay, I understand why you're upset. She sounded dreadful," she says, making her way over to the fridge and pulling out a few groceries. She places the contents onto the countertop and plucks out a big pot from under the counter.

"Do you want something to eat? I am making stew," she wiggles her eyebrows at me. I take a seat at the breakfast table, my chin resting in the palm of my hand as Sally chops up the vegetables.

"I'm just so pissed off that everyone thinks I need to be *fixed*," I emphasize with two fingers. Tears prickle at the back of my eyes and my face feels hot as the anger fizzles up in my veins again. I scrub my hands over my face, trying not to let the tears fall, but they come anyway. I have never cried this much in my life. It's as if no one takes into consideration that my mum died a few weeks ago. The fact that my father mentioned me being an orphan too… well, I may as well be. No one at the academy even knows I have a family, so to them I am an orphan. What's even worse is I haven't told my best friends about my father because every time I come close, fear takes over me and I hesitate.

"Adelaide, you do not need to be fixed. Your father is an exceedingly difficult man. He's got his skeletons and it won't be long until you find them," Sally murmurs and I lift my head to look at her, but she isn't looking in my direction.

Skeletons? What does she mean by that?

I wipe away my tears with the sleeve of my top, feeling pathetic all over again. Sally puts a bowl of beef stew in front of me with some dumplings. I didn't realize how hungry I was until I smelled the wonderful aroma of food.

~

I stayed at the house a little while longer enjoying the company of Sally and eating a good hearty meal for once. The stew she made was delightful, I even had another helping which is very unlike me, but she made me feel comfortable so I didn't even think about my weight or the fact that I can't really eat a hearty meal in front of someone.

She let me blabber on about my mum, and all my friends from back home, which was lovely. Even though I didn't ask her a lot of questions about herself, she told me a little about her life. She's a few years older than me and started working for my father over a year ago. She dreams of becoming a Michelin star chef one day, and honestly with the food she cooks I don't think she is that far off. Apparently, the Italian chef who cooks all my father's meal was a big-time chef, but he decided that he didn't want the stress anymore and only wanted to work for rich people in their home kitchens. He fully supports Sally in her dreams, though. He sounds like an ideal idol to have. Where's mine?

Steve drives me back to the academy before ten so that I have some time to study. Once I get back to the dorm room, I find Blaire sitting on her bed and as soon as I close the door behind me, she runs up to me, hugging me so tightly around my arms. A fat tear runs down her cheek.

"I am so sorry for what my god-awful brother did to you, I also heard about the drowning," she sobs, turning her gaze to the floor.

I wasn't prepared for this, but I guess I should confide in her more.

I let out a big sigh. "I should be the one who's sorry for not telling you Blaire. I was scared. He is your brother after all," I deflate, and Blaire takes my hand, dragging me to sit down next to her on the bed.

"I was embarrassed, I mean I don't know what I did wrong," I shrug my shoulders, still unable to look directly at her.

She lifts my chin up with her fingers, moving my head from side to side to inspect the damage, but lucky for me the concealer has removed the evidence. I am surprised my father didn't notice when he saw me earlier.

"You have nothing to be embarrassed about Ade. Blake is such a prick and I really do not understand what's come over him," she says with concern in her voice, clasping her hand on my shoulder as her big brown eyes stare directly into mine. She truly looks apologetic, and I know she is on my side. "Plus, you did some good work at hiding it with make-up," she innocently chuckles, and I join her, feeling as though a weight has been lifted off my shoulders. I still have so much to tell her but expressing little bits of myself at a time works for me.

I run myself a bubble bath so that I can read a book and relax. After the weekend I've had, it's needed. Blaire has gone to the dining hall to pick up some food bits for us to nibble on later while we put on a film and have a girly night. I wash my face, rubbing away at the make-up, revealing the purple bruises under my nose and eyes. My nose is a little swollen but luckily, it's not broken. The bags under my eyes are so apparent from where I didn't properly sleep the night before, so I'm really looking forward to climbing into my memory foam mattress bed to sleep it all off.

Once getting changed into a satin night dress, I tie my hair into a messy bun on top of my head, before bracing for the fact that Blaire will now see my face with no make-up. Now she will really see the damage.

Opening the door to the bedroom, Blaire's hands automatically hide the gasp on her face. "Oh Ade," she says, her brows furrowed, eyes narrowed as she stares at my broken purple face. "Put it this way, at least you look tough," she shrugs her shoulders and I know she's joking.

I toss a pillow at her to shut her up, both of us laughing it off.

We put on one of Blaire's favorite classic films, 'My Fair Lady', which is about a cockney lady played by Audrey Hepburn, who sells this gentleman flowers and learns that he can teach people how to speak 'proper' and pass them off to be either a duke or duchess at a ball. Eliza Doolittle actually goes to this gentleman for help as she wants to become a proper lady and I can't help but giggle to myself at the thought. This man - Professor Henry Higgins – believes accent and tone of another person's voice are important in high society and that you can tell if you are basically rich or poor by it, to put things bluntly.

At least Eliza Doolittle had the choice and actually asked for help whereas I am being forced to do it. Also, the fact that this is the same attitude in the real world and not just a stupid film is ridiculous. In fact, the film is brilliant. I'm enjoying every second of it, and Audrey really plays her character well. Once the film has ended, we switch off the TV, tucking ourselves into bed ready to sleep.

"Ade, I just want to say I am so sorry again," Blaire whispers from her bed, and I can hear her rustling between the bedsheets.

"You shouldn't have to apologize for his behavior, Blaire. It's not your fault," I reason, my voice cracking as I speak. I swallow the thick mucus building up in my throat, and I hear Blaire sigh to herself before she speaks again.

"I know I shouldn't, but I honestly have no idea what has gotten into him lately. He has changed and I feel embarrassed. I get why you were scared but you can tell me anything Ade, I will always have your back," Blaire apologizes to me once more, feeling guilty for all of her brother's behavior. It's not her fault that he's the Antichrist, destined to make my life hell. Maybe that is why he was put on this Earth? To make me fall to my knees, begging for mercy. Testing my patience and making me beg for forgiveness for any sin I've ever committed.

Maybe this is what I deserve…

*A*s I wake up, Blaire is already in the shower. Without thinking about it, I rub my eyes, wincing at the slightest touch to the bruises. It will be a painful experience just putting on some make-up.

"Good morning sleeping beauty," Blaire hums, exiting the bathroom only wearing her white fluffy robe and a towel wrapped around her hair. She looks flawless even wearing a bloody robe and a towel turban on her head, whereas I'd look like a drowned rat.

"Morning," I yawn, grimacing at the pain.

I sit on the edge of my bed trying not to finish rubbing the sleep from my eyes, knowing how painful it will be.

"Oh hon, is it that painful?" she asks with concern.

"Yeah, but I'll be fine," I assure her. I quickly jump in the shower, being careful when washing my face. I dab the wet cloth over my bruises, attempting to clean around my nose. I swear at myself a couple of times in the mirror every time I press too hard, rage fueling in my gut, ready to scream.

Count to ten Ade and breathe.

Attempting to put some make-up on, I grimace, trying to hide the purple and blue bruises, but they seem to be more prominent today. The bristles of the makeup brush sting my skin with every stroke as I blend the concealer. I apply some mascara to my long eyelashes, and a bit of blusher to hide the rest. I suppose I'm wearing a mask today like I do every day, looking fine on the outside but underneath I'm battered and bruised.

Styling my hair, I curl the ends and clip the top half, creating a half up half down do. I finish my look off with some nude lipstick and stare at myself in the mirror, happy with the outcome. The bruises are hidden, and my nose is slightly contoured to look less swollen.

Blaire whistles from behind me in the doorway. "Damn girl, you look hawt," she says in an American accent and I pout, shaking off the feeling of discomfort. I probably won't be able to move my face much throughout the day, which is hard considering I frown a lot.

"This will look cute," Blaire exclaims, taking out a blue ribbon from her drawer in the nightstand. Facing me, she ties a cute little bow in the clipped half of my hair. I look in the mirror, suddenly surprised by what she means. I am really starting to look like a girly girl. Maisie is already at our table in the dining hall when we arrive, and the food has already been ordered. This girl is a literal saint. She knows exactly what we want in the morning and orders our breakfast, not forgetting the coffee and of course my orange juice. I have no idea how I lived life before these two.

Well, my life here anyway.

We eat our breakfast in peace without any comments from the Royals and it's a blessing. Hopefully, they feel guilty after what they did to me on Saturday, which is why they can't even make eye contact. Weirdly enough, Royce hasn't even acknowledged me this morning, which is out of character. Maybe I don't like this little blessing in disguise. I have a horrible feeling about today which makes me anxious. Blaire notices too, assuring me nothing will happen on her watch and that she will be by my side the whole day. Lucky for me today we have classes together.

The whole day passes quietly, without a single remark from any student in the academy. No one even makes a sex joke, or a comment about me being tribal or riddled with diseases. Hopefully, everyone has gotten over the fact that I'm the new girl and that I haven't retaliated. I make my way over to my locker with Blaire and Maisie in tow, gossiping about their weekend when I discover a note sticking out from my locker.

My face turns pale and my chest tightens, alarm bells ringing in my head. I quicken my pace so that I can get it over and done with, ripping it open. It's the same handwriting but not the normal note stating they 'know my secret'. No, this one is different. The girls stand behind me with concern on their faces, so I turn around and read the note aloud.

Meet us in the dining hall at six this evening.

We're about to uncover your little secret from the grave.

Blaire rips the note from my grasp, studying it before she rips it into shreds, throwing it over her shoulder.

The colour from my face has vanished, leaving me looking

ghostly, my makeup not even hiding the anxiety. My heart rate goes a thousand miles per hour, my blood pumping rage around my body making me feel distressed and numb.

Blaire shouts, "Who is this?!", and the other students pause as Blaire loses her shit. Her rage just about matches mine, but instead of freezing up and becoming a mannequin, she goes batshit crazy. I don't blame her.

I even see fury and rage within Maisie's hazel eyes, a new emotion to me from her, considering she is always so cheerful, but now I see determination. Determination to help me find out who this sick fuck is.

"I guess we have a date at six," I shrug, not so fearful knowing I have my two best friends backing me up. I know they will make whoever sent these notes pay.

Chapter Thirteen

After the day has finished; we go up to our dorm room with Maisie joining us.

"You are not going down on your own. We will go together as a united front," Maisie suggests, whilst she perches herself on the edge of the bed.

"You girls don't have to. I can do this by myself," I add, grateful that they would stand by my side, but this is my own battle.

"Ade, we are your friends and we will back you up, no arguments. We are going down with you," Blaire declares in a firm tone but softness in her eyes.

After a few moments I agree that we'll go down together as a united front, no matter what happens. Annoyance still floods within me, fury pumping through my blood, turning my cheeks a hot chili pepper red. Am I mentally prepared for what might happen? Or what secret they might uncover? This is probably my only chance to come clean and tell the girls the truth about me, better they hear it from me than some sick fuck exposing me in the dining hall at dinner time.

sighing, I drop down to sit on my bed. "Hey, I have got something to tell you girls, so you best sit down," I break, my nerves taking over and my rage is deflated by the butterflies in my belly.

Blaire sits on her bed with her legs crossed and Maisie lounges comfortably, as if she's ready for a story telling. I tell them every-thing- from when my mother died, to my father's rules and regula-tions. Why I attend this school, even down to the stupid elocution lessons and the fact I need 'fixing'.

Their eyes go wide at my revelations. Not a word has been spoken since I confessed and now I feel as though I have lost my friends forever. I end up sobbing in my hands, not able to face the girls after basically lying to them for weeks. My bed dips as someone sits down next to me, and I look up to see it's Blaire with teary eyes.

She grabs me and pulls me into a hug, squeezing the hell out of me. Maisie does the same, joining in the group hug with teary eyes, and we end up giggling at the fact we're all crying.

"I understand why you didn't tell us. Your father is a nasty piece of work and I have only met him maybe twice," Blaire says with a slight smile. I was unaware that she had met him, but I kinda guessed considering they may have attended the same gala.

The alarm on my phone goes off, warning us it's ten to six, so we stand up from my bed, giving each other another hug before making our way down to the dining hall. We stay clothed in our academy uniforms, not bothering to change, and luckily my makeup has stayed intact. "Right, let's go see which sick fuck wants to expose you," Blaire jeers as if she's declaring war, which is exactly what we are doing.

We make our way down the three-story high stairs, striding down the halls until we come up to the grand doors that lead into the dining hall. Two students stand outside guarding the doors, clearly expecting my arrival. I push the nervous feeling in my belly down, breathing in and out, calming myself down.

Ade, you've been through so much worse.

The two guys give us a haughty smirk before opening the wooden double doors, where we're met with the eyes of the Royals. All of them, including Royce. The heat from my skin radiates in the air and I can feel Blaire's deathly stare on her brother, who is in the middle of everyone, looking superior. His pompous expression is plastered on his face as his hands are tucked behind his back. Hugo is expressionless as usual, but the look in his eyes says it all. The disgust is apparent in the way his emerald green eyes rake over my body. My breath quickens, my chest feeling tight as my hands clench into fists at my sides.

Charles' mischievous grin takes over his whole face, his brown eyes glistening with excitement. Royce on the other hand stands on the far end, not being able to face me. Instead his gaze is fixed on the ground, resting his chin in the palm of his hand. He's the one I am disappointed about the most, the guy who apologized to me just two days ago for what his friends have done. But here he stands with the fucking demons of Darlington Academy, not even daring to look me in the eye.

The fucking pussy.

Blake lets out an exaggerated breath, cocking his head to one side as he stares me down. "I am so glad that you received our notes Africa." His hands stay wrapped behind his back as he prowls forward, circling his friends, but his gaze doesn't break away from mine. I look at Blaire, feeling the anger roll off her. The hurt in her eyes says it all.

She didn't think it would be her brother doing this, but here we are.

I turn my gaze to Maisie, who's teeth are bared like a predator ready to attack their prey, her arms crossed over her chest as she leans on one leg, the other slightly bent.

"We thought we might take you down memory lane, you know, for fun." Blake carries on, now standing before me. He's holding a remote. My chest heaves and my nostrils flare as he presses a button, bringing down a white screen covering the windows, removing any natural light from entering the room. I look around the room to see that we have been joined by the whole academy, but I can't see Miles anywhere in the crowed. Ruby is sitting on the Royals table, her face plastered with an evil grin, chewing on some gum as she enjoys the show.

Blaire takes a step forward. "Blake, what the fuck are you

doing?" she confronts her brother, but Blake doesn't budge. He nods his chin towards some other students, and they grab Blaire and Maisie by the arms, pushing them to the floor on their knees. Blaire screams the whole room down, trying to break free but it's no use.

"Right, well let's get to it," Blake slaps his hands together, rubbing them hungrily in front of his chest. "We had a lot of digging up to do, but surprisingly it wasn't so hard. All we had to do was give them some money and … voila," he chuckles, taking a brown manilla file from Ruby. As he opens it my attention falls onto the white screen, where a picture of my mum has been blown up, showing her lifeless body with the shot wound.

It's the day she was shot.

I am unable to breathe, but I can't contain it any longer. "What the fuck?!" I scream, trying to run towards Blake, prepared to punch him. Someone grabs my arms, kicking behind my knees and pushing me to the floor. I refuse to look ahead of me, but this guy grabs my hair and forces me to look up at the screen.

"Zara Adams, murdered with a gunshot to the chest. She was rushed to the hospital but remained unconscious for a few days until she died," he reads from the file.

My breath is hot, coming out in puffs from my lips. Anxiety has taken over my body, and all of a sudden, I can't breathe, choking on the tears daring to spill out. My body gives up against the strong hands gripping me, and I hear Blaire shouting at her brother from behind me while Maisie does the same.

Blake crouches down, cupping my chin so that I'm forced to look at his dark, amused eyes. "Why did you kill your mother, Africa? Was it your plan to come here?" His breath lands on my skin as he speaks.

I'm unable to reply, tears spilling down my bruised cheeks, exposing the blue and purple skin as the makeup washes away. My tears crash onto the hard wood floor beneath me and Blake looks victorious.

His conquest to destroy me has succeeded. I feel dead inside.

"You're are a murderer Africa," he whispers and the whole academy laughs, shouting out 'murderer'. The voices all blend into one, becoming faint whispers as everyone starts to filter out of the room. Inhaling a deep breath, I swallow the bile in my throat.

"I didn't kill my mother, you sick fucking cunt."

I grind my teeth to the point my jaw starts to hurt. Blake shrugs his shoulders at me and turns around, facing his friends. Royce is still unable to look me in the eye, his hands now in his trouser pockets.

What a fucking prick.

Hugo and Charles stand with Blake having a conversation, and Blaire has been let go by the guy who was holding her. She storms towards Blake and slaps him in the face, the sting leaving a hand mark on his perfectly chiseled cheeks. She and Maisie then scurry towards me as I'm still kneeling on the floor, my arms wrapped around my waist, my body trembling with anger and anxiety. I'm unable to move and it takes both of them to pick me up from the floor. They put their arms around my shoulders, letting me lean on them as we make our way back to the dorm.

I still haven't said a word to them, and they're trying to get me to talk but I can't bring myself to do it. My throat is in agony from the screaming, every swallow I take feels like someone has stuffed stinging nettles down there. My eyes are blood shot with the tears still pouring out. We get back to the dorm, where I promptly lock myself in the bathroom, crouching down on the cold tiles of the shower. I don't remove my uniform, instead I turn on the shower, letting the scalding hot water fall onto my skin, burning with every drop. My uniform is now heavy as it soaks up all the water, my skin red and raw from the heat of the liquid still pouring down. I seem to be making this a habit.

A knock at the bathroom door startles me out of my daze. I turn off the shower and peel off my academy uniform, leaving it on the tiled floor. I wrap my white fluffy robe around my body and tie my hair up in a messy bun on the top of my head.

"Ade, are you okay?" Blaire whispers on the other side of the door. I can hear the disappointment in her voice after what her brother did to me. I know how bad she feels, not knowing her brother would set me up like this. She's been an amazing friend since I started at the academy, even standing by my side against her own brother.

Opening the door, I face Blaire whose eyes are rimmed red from all the crying she has done. She leaps and wraps her arms around my neck, nuzzling her face into the dip between my neck, sobbing. I hug her back tightly to reassure her that everything will be okay.

"Hey, don't worry about me Blaire. I'll be fine."

Understatement of the year.

$\sim$

A few weeks have passed since the incident in the dining hall. I have hardly spoken to anyone other than Blaire, Maisie, and Miles. I've kept to myself, concentrating on my assignments, my dance routine with Miles, and working at the club. I have refrained from visiting my father's house and haven't had another elocution lesson in a while.

Thank god.

I think if I saw Ms. Veronica anytime soon, I'd punch her in the throat.

The Royals have also been leaving me alone, apart from Ruby and her stupid friends. I still have my tutoring sessions with Hugo in the library, but lucky for me he takes his tutoring sessions very seriously so not even bullying is allowed. I still haven't spoken to Royce, after seeing the pain in his eyes when he was standing before me with the Royals, not able to look me in the eyes. Even after he apologized, it hurt me the most. It felt as though he stabbed me with a sword straight through the heart and twisted it. I would have been a lot better if he just didn't apologize to me in the first place, but that was probably the plan.

Destroy Ade – complete.

I'm sitting in English lit, right next to the demon himself, Blake. I can't even pay attention to what the sub teacher is saying at the front of the class, my chin resting in the palm of my hand. My long dark hair - which I haven't even styled in weeks - falls around my face, hiding my features as if it were a mask from Blake who doodles on his notebook. I had handed in my assignment on 'Romeo and Juliet' early thanks to Hugo, so I'm expecting my grades to be higher than normal. Fingers crossed.

The sub teacher, who's name I didn't even register, comes over to our desk and hands both mine and Blake's assignments, both marked. Oh, so he also handed in his assignment early. Staring at the red markings on my assignment, my eyes go wide at the big B on the first page. I faintly smile to myself, proud that I have improved since last time. I don't dare to look at what Blake received. To be honest I don't care anymore. I don't see this as a competition anyway, as long as I'm happy with my grades, that's all that matters.

As I go to put my assignment in my folder, Blake tears it out of my hand, scanning my grade, clearly pissed off.

"Do you mind?" I snap, tearing it back from him and stuffing it into my folder away from him. I'm surprised by myself, snapping at Blake, considering these are the first three words I've said to him in weeks. I wouldn't be shocked if he took offense to it and got me back later, but I don't think he can do anything worse to me than what he did.

Accusing me of being a murderer and killing my own mum.

"How the fuck did you do better than me?" he retorts, shaking his head as he stands up from the chair. Now I am happy. I know I said it's not competition but the fact that I did better than Blake is comical and rewarding. Instead of responding to him I turn on my heel, not concentrating and bumping into a rock-hard chest. My hands linger on the muscular chest, feeling how ripped Royce is even under his button up shirt. I look up and our eyes meet for the first time since the club. The pain is still evident in his eyes and his jaw ticks, not removing his eyes from mine.

Immediately, I take a step back, looking down at the floor before I barge past him, our shoulders brushing as I leave. I don't look back. The guy actually had the audacity to approach my desk, and after all this time, he looked at me. I want to ask him if he's okay, give him a big hug and tell him it's going to be okay, but for what? Why am I feeling like this? Those guys ruined my life and I'm not sure how much more I can take.

I practically speed walk to the dining hall to meet Blaire and Maisie at our usual table. Blaire hasn't spoken to her brother since the altercation either and Maisie has ignored all of the Royals, who she used to be friends with. They seemed to have broken all three of us, but technically, they didn't do anything to Blaire and Maisie.

Blaire stares at me with concern. "How was your day hon?" she asks, looking up at me from the top of her phone screen. She's just as worried as I am, not knowing what else the Royals will do. Could be anytime soon that they pounce, and we want to be prepared.

"Well, I got a better grade in English Lit than Blake, and to be honest, he didn't take that too kindly," I chortle in joy.

"Hopefully, that doesn't fuel his fury."

I order myself a chicken salad, as I can't stomach a lot of food without feeling queasy. The girls think my eating disorder has gotten worse over the past few weeks, my body turning into skin and bone. Even Miles has noticed, saying my energy levels have gone down and it's evident in our routine.

But at least I'm eating, right? It could be worse.

"We seriously need a girl's weekend away to rejuvenate, and I am really feeling a makeover," Blaire suggests, wiggling her eyebrows.

Actually, that sounds great. I need something that will make me feel like me again and a makeover could do exactly that. I haven't even cut my hair in months, my long locks just below my ass now, which is getting harder to style. The colour is so dull and boring, I need something that will brighten up my face. Smiling in Blaire's direction, I say, "I think that is a brilliant idea."

"How about instead of going to the Halloween party, we have a girly weekend then?" Maisie suggests, and that is the best idea I've heard in a long time. I couldn't think of anything worse than attending a stupid Halloween party with drugs, alcohol, orgies and of course, the royal assholes. I'd much rather get pampered and have a makeover with my best friends. Blaire and Maisie have both been so supportive since finding out about my father, not telling a soul about my secret. In fact, they find it entertaining that I have to take part in elocution lessons to become a 'proper lady' and the fact that I want to practically murder Ms. Veronica.

Unlucky for me, this weekend I have another one of my elocution lessons at my father's house, which I am not in the mood for. The only reason why I'm excited to visit is so that I can pick up my box of photo albums that I left behind last time I was there. I also have a break from working at the club this weekend. Apparently, they're hosting an especially important private meeting and only a few of the staff are allowed.

After I demolish my chicken salad, the girls and I split ways in the main hall as I make my way to the dance studio to meet Miles for practice. When I'm on my own, the other students still tend to whisper and shout out 'Murderer' in passing. I've even had the pleasure of my mum's picture plastered on my locker with the word 'Murderer' written in red paint. I seem to have grown accustomed to their accusations and just let it slide, hoping they give it up when they realize it's no longer affecting me.

I put on a brave face, walking the halls of the haunted castle, but as soon as I enter the dance studio, the mask slips and I break down. I can't perform my usual routine of sitting in the shower and letting scolding water burn my skin, which makes me feel another sort of pain. I suppose it's a form of self-harm.

"Hey, there you are. I was wondering when you were going to turn up," Miles says as I throw my gym bag over the bench, removing my hoodie and sweats. Every time I do this, Miles eyes never stray from my body, passion burning in the mauve colour of his eyes, taking in the black leotard I'm wearing today. He gives me a cheeky smile when I turn to face him, making me forget about today already.

We have sort-of been dating but haven't gotten serious yet. He sometimes sneaks into my dorm room and we end up having a make-out session on my bed. He wasn't at the academy when the whole shit show went down with his beloved stepsister and the dickheads. He's been my rock in all of this, and if it weren't for him or my two best friends, I would have ended my life right there and then.

His lips turn up into a grin. "I got you a little surprise," he says, his arms crossed behind his back to hide whatever it is. I try and move around him to grab whatever he's hiding, but I'm unsuccessful. Throwing his arms up in the air, holding what looks like tickets, I try to jump to reach them but it's no use. Miles is a tall guy, just over six feet and I'm five feet nothing.

"Give me a kiss first," he winks, bringing his lips closer to mine. I can smell the mix of sweat and cologne mixed in together from his practice earlier. I lean in closer to give Miles a kiss as he brings down his arms towards me, wrapping them around my tiny frame. I have to go on my tiptoes just to reach his lips, which makes him chuckle.

As soon as our lips meet, I'm in a trance, forgetting where I am or even why I am giving him the kiss in the first place. He feels like my safe zone. Whenever I am around him, he makes me feel like no one can hurt me. Eventually, Miles pulls away from my lips, and I let out a small involuntary whimper, missing the feel of his lips against mine already.

"I got us two tickets to go see a band called Nightfall at Stonewall Auditorium in a few weeks' time," he says, showing me the two tickets. I was never into rock music before, but since I have met Miles, he's introduced me to some pretty awesome bands, and I have a newfound love for rock music.

My face lights up, giving him another peck on his soft lips. "I would love to go."

I look at the dates on the tickets and it's the weekend straight after Halloween, which means I can get dressed up, showing off my new makeover and I can't wait.

Chapter Fourteen

Sipping my orange juice, I swing myself around on the stool. I'm seated at the breakfast bar in my father's kitchen, gossiping with Sally as she fixes us both a fruit bowl. I've informed her all about my little run in with the Royals, how I've told Blaire and Maisie about my father, which Sally warns me to make sure my Father doesn't find out.

Thankfully, he's not home this weekend and is away on a business trip, so I don't have to see him or hear about how disappointed he is in me. Sally joins me at the breakfast bar, sitting in the stool next to me, which is completely not allowed but it's just us two and Mrs. Blossom in the house so we think we can get away with it. My father warned the staff not to get close to me, stating that because they are staff, we shouldn't form any friendships. It's frowned upon.

Well, fuck him. I'll befriend who the hell I want.

Ms. Veronica and I have a lesson in an hour, and today she is bringing a whole new wardrobe for me as I should also dress as a lady.

"I swear to god, if she tries to put me in one of those matching skirt suits, I'll scream," I huff, furrowing my brows as Sally keeps laughing at me.

"Oh darling, you will look spiffing in one of those matching suits," Sally jokes, putting on a posh accent and I can't but help laugh along with her. Sally likes to joke about how prim and proper I'm becoming – well, being forced to become – and how I wouldn't survive a normal life around here anymore.

Sally is as London as they come. She even has a bit of a cockney accent which is refreshing to hear, considering I'm around people who hardly move their upper lip when they speak. Sally seems to think that my slight South African accent sounds American or even better, Australian, and always forgets where I'm from.

We like to speak to each other in different accents sometimes, taking the piss out of each other for some banter. I mean, in this house it's needed. It's always so serious and Mrs. Blossom is always warning me to make sure I don't miss behave when my father is around otherwise there could be consequences. I'm unsure as to what kind of consequences she's talking about, but I take her warnings very seriously.

I clear the bowl of fruit that Sally prepared for me. It seems like the only time I really eat is around her. She doesn't give me a lot of choice, always making me my favourite foods and sticking them in front of me. She really is an amazing cook and makes spag bowl that tastes like heaven.

"Miss Adelaide," Mrs. Blossom calls through to the kitchen. I look at Sally, pouting my lips, knowing exactly what she's here to tell me. Sally hides her laugh behind her hands, trying not to get in trouble.

"Ms. Veronica has arrived."

Oh boy, here we go.

"Wish me luck," I whisper to Sally as I leave the room, already dreading spending time with this woman. She reminds me of Effie Trinket from the Hunger Games films, so overbearing. I can't wait to see her shocked face when she sees I'm wearing ripped jeans and a t-shirt. Entering the drawing room, I find that it's been turned into a wardrobe. There are racks everywhere with all types of clothing on the rails, in every colour imaginable. Ms. Veronica is perched on the grey sofa where she sat last time, pouring a cup of tea. Her eyes go wide, scanning my outfit in disdain.

"Oh Adelaide, such a pleasure to see you again."

I perch my ass on the grey armchair facing Ms. Veronica, picking up my cup and saucer to take a sip of my tea. I sit in the position with my legs closed at the knee, slightly leaned on the side and back straight. When I pick up my teacup, I even let out my pinkie finger. Her brow goes up, and a smile creeps up on her face.

"I see you have been practicing," she says, and I nod in response with a plastic grin on my face, not wanting to make conversation.

I take in her outfit, the baby blue matching skirt and blazer which was exactly the same as the pink one. A white frilly blouse that reminds me of a pirate's costume and a little pearl broach on the lapel of her blazer. I bet she has that suit in all colours.

Who's she trying to be? The fucking Queen?

I notice she's put on some classical music in the background today, breaking any of the silence that occurs between us, which is often. We get started straight away, concentrating on my walking again. This time she puts a fucking book on my head because she says it will help me practice my posture.

I didn't even think this shit was real. I oblige, doing as she says so that we can get this over and done with. I don't want to prolong this any longer than I need to. I walk with the stupid book on my head with elegance, not dropping it once and I feel triumphed.

Take that, bitch. I can follow orders.

We practice the walking and sitting a little longer before we continue on to speech therapy. Apparently, I need to try and smile every time I speak, like a robot. This can't be hard. Then she actually gets me to recite 'The Rain In Spain' rhyme a hundred times over until she's happy with it. Ms. Veronica made it noticeably clear that her and my father want my accent to be completely gone in time for the Debutant Ball next year. How exciting. I roll my eyes.

Ms. Veronica picks out a few outfits for me to try on, because I need to find something to wear for an afternoon tea party that's in a few weeks, before Christmas. My eyes go wide when she explains this to me, unawares, that I would have been expected to attend tea parties and pretend to be a robot in front of other people.

What the fuck has my life come to, seriously?

I try on a few pencil dresses and a matching skirt and blazer suit. Even cute little tea dresses with kitten heels. She also expresses that when a lady wears a dress, she needs to wear nude coloured stockings at all times.

This woman is as sexist as they come. I'm biting the inner side of my cheek, stopping myself from snapping at her. The anger fuels in the pit of my stomach as she gets me to walk, sit, drink tea, and even pick up a cucumber finger sandwich in this tight yellow pencil dress.

Hours later, after Ms. Veronica had to leave to attend another appointment, I get some time to myself. I run a bubble bath in the whirlpool bath, my aching muscles could do with the jets penetrating my skin. I'm also going to read a good book with a glass of gin and tonic.

Now this is luxury. Laying back in the bath, my hair tied up whilst by head rests on a bath pillow, I read the first book of the 'Beholden To Balance' series by Cilla Raven, loosing myself in the fantasy world I wish were mine, rather than this shitty life I have now.

I take little sips of my gin and tonic, constantly adding hot water to my bath to keep it hot. My skin turns into a prune but I don't care. I'm definitely going to have a Netflix night tonight in my queen-sized bed. My phone pings on the side of the bath, and I pick it up, reading a text from Miles saying that he misses me. My heart flutters every time I see his name, wishing he were here with me, having a romantic evening.

He could be the one I lose my virginity to, but how do you know when you're ready? We haven't done anything sexual, but we have gotten pretty close.

I've expressed my feelings to him about how I want to wait for the right time, making sure I lose it to someone I love and trust, which he understood and agreed with. I know for a fact that Miles has slept with a few girls. Around the academy, he's renowned for being a bit of a playboy, and the girls still swoon all over him. I don't blame them, what with his angelic, gorgeous looks. Every time he smiles, I'm hypnotized.

I think I'm going to be doing a lot more for myself tonight than just watch Netflix.

~

*T*he following day, I'm sitting in the conservatory for breakfast by myself and enjoying the view of the open landscape, the rose gardens on my right and the sound of the water trickling in the water fountain. Breathing in the fresh countryside air, I enjoy the peace and quiet, as I stuff myself with a full English breakfast. Yes, Sally made it for me, saying that I need to put some meat on my bones. I agree with her, I look like a walking corpse at the moment. My eyes are black from the lack of iron in my blood and my skin has gone so pale you'd never think I come from South Africa.

Seriously, I need to really sit and revaluate my life, and pull my finger out. I know what the Royals did to me was horrific and not a lot of people would let that go, but losing my mum was the worst thing that has ever happened to me.

All I'm left with is the photo album of all our memories and that's my whole life. When I feel lonely and depressed, all I want to do is sit on my bed looking at the pictures, remembering all the good times we had, and keeping her memory alive by doing what we both enjoyed.

I need to get back into surfing.

I wrap myself in my big fluffy cardigan, hiding my skin from the crisp October air while I drink the best nectar that humans have created- coffee. Every sip I take warms up my insides, counteracting the cold outside.

I really just want to get back to the Academy today and practice my dance routine with Miles. He didn't go home this weekend, deciding he would rather stay behind because he didn't want to put up with Ruby all weekend.

I don't blame him. The stories he tells me about her are insane. She sounds like a spoiled brat, who clearly has daddy wrapped around her finger. No surprise there. Eventually, I go back to my room, and my bag is already packed by Mrs. Blossom even though I tell her I don't mind doing it. She even put the box of my stuff next to my bag, so I don't forget it this time. Mrs. Blossom comes across like an old grumpy woman sometimes, but I know she cares for me and wants what is best. She's kind of like my grandmother when I'm here.

Steve picks me up in the Bentley at the front of the house, packing my bag and box in the boot whilst I slip into the back seat. Throughout the journey Steve doesn't speak to me, which is abnormal as he normally asks me how the academy has been.

Looking at him through the rear-view mirror, I can see the vein in his neck pulsing, his face in a prominent frown. He's clearly irritated by something. Sticking my earphones in, I listen to some of the bands that Miles thought that I would like. A lot of them are too heavy for me but there are a few that I like. Especially the band 'Nightfall' that we're supposed to be seeing in a few weeks. I honestly can't wait for another date with Miles, outside of the academy. We've both been so busy with work and assignments, we haven't had the chance to go on another proper date outside of the castle walls.

More importantly, I'm feeling thrilled to spend a weekend with my girls. That's when the new Adelaide Vaughn, or should I say Adelaide 'Adams', will emerge from the pits of hell. I keep trying to think of how to change it up a bit. Maybe I should cut my long locks and dye my hair bleach blonde? Maybe then no one will recognize me, and they'll leave me alone. Now that would be a dream.

Unpacking my little box of treasures, I leave the photo album of my mum on my nightstand and pack away the scrap books into the drawer beneath my bed. I can't wait to show the girls later. I get changed into my yoga pants and a pink sports bra, leaving my torso on show.

I look at myself in the mirror, and I'm disappointed with myself for letting it get this bad. The faint lines that were the start of my lean muscles have disappeared, and my ribcage is prominent from the lack of food and too much exercise. I would be incredibly surprised if Miles found me even remotely sexually attractive when I look this sluggish. I need to get my shit together and starting from today, I'm putting my foot down.

In my own world, strolling towards the dance studio with my earphones plugged in, a pair of strong hands grab me from behind, pulling me to the side and a small whimper escapes past my lips.

"What the fuck do you…" I start rumbling, turning round to see that it's Royce.

He removes his hands from my shoulders, putting them into his trousers. He looks like a really posh twat that has gone sailing. Cream trousers, with a pale blue Ralph Lauren polo shirt, a cream coloured cardigan tied around his shoulders and bloody brown loafers.

His bottle green eyes darken as they rake over my body, clearly mortified by how I look. Good, I'm not here to impress this lying prick anyway.

Taking a step back, I cross my arms over my chest – which has gone down a size – lifting my chin up, hiding the fact that Royce's presence affects me. I want this man to grovel and beg for forgiveness for what he did to me. I won't forgive him or any of the other Royal cunts that walk this school.

Ever.

Rolling my eyes, I exhale. "What the fuck do you want, posh boy?"

Royce notices how agitated I am, and he rubs the back of his neck, his eyes falling to the floor before bringing them up to meet mine. He still has the sadness lying beneath the sea green colour, but this time they are darker, like the ocean has been polluted and turned black from all the lies and deceit. He leans forward, enclosing on my proximity.

"I haven't had a chance to see you Ade, I just wanted to make sure you're okay."

My eyes narrow at his declaration. "Oh, so suddenly you care about my feelings?" I scoff.

His hand comes up, grabbing my arm painfully, his eyes refusing to stray away from mine. "I had no choice… We had no choice, Ade."

I pull myself out of his grip, completely outraged by his statement.

How dare he say that they, or him, had no fucking choice?

"No choice? Everyone has a choice. Now leave me the fuck alone."

Turning on my heel, I walk away in the direction to the dance studio, my body shaking, unable to take these confrontations. I'm so angry that if I were a cartoon, steam would be coming out of my ears as my head blows up. These boys are going to be the death of me.

I enter the dance studio, looking around to see that Miles still hasn't turned up. Hm, that's unusual as he's normally here before me. I put down my belongings on the bench and start stretching all my limbs before I practice my routine.

I put on a playlist from Spotify and start off with 'First position'. My heels touch, my toes are pointed forward and my arms rounded in front of me. I always mix ballet with modern dance, the elegance meeting with modernity has always been my style. It makes me feel free, like I can do what I want.

'Haunted' by Beyoncé starts playing whilst I lift myself onto the tip of my toes, performing pirouette en pointe. My toes ache from the weight of my body as I choose not to wear my ballet shoes, and I welcome the pain, torturing myself as I lift my body weight and leap across the room, twirling without my heels touching the floor. My breath quickens as I move around the hard wood floor, putting my body through the paces, sweat pouring out of my pores.

Some people fight with their bare hands to get their fill, but me? I bruise and batter my body by dancing, pushing myself to the point of feeling faint. The rush it gives me is addictive, like heroin for some people, but to me this is better. When I get onto the stage in a few weeks' time, my pain will all be worth it.

Once I've had my fill and collapsed on the floor, I check my phone and find that there's no missed message from Miles. It's been two hours since I arrived, so I would have heard from Miles by now, but he hasn't even acknowledged my text. I doubt that he would purposely stand me up, so possibly it's a family emergency or something.

I secretly hope that's the case in a weird way, so I know it's not me.

Chapter Fifteen

*N*eeding to replenish my energy, I'm sitting on my bed, legs crossed, eating a tuna sandwich. My gaze is fixed on watching the wind bristle between the oak and holly trees. The low winter sunlight beams through the double-glazed window, blanketing the whole room in yellowy, gold tones. As it's such a lovely day, I debate whether or not to head to Stonewall Beach and go for a surf. The winter chill has never stopped me before.

Removing my yoga pants and sports bra, I pull out my wet suit from my wardrobe and slide into the tight fabric. I googled and found out that I could hire a surfboard just down the beach, which is perfect because I wasn't able to bring my surfboard with me from across the globe. I throw on a clean pair of yoga pants and a hoodie over my wetsuit along with some trainers, before tying my hair up in a messy bun on the top of my head.

I order myself an Uber which meets me out front in the courtyard, taking me all the way into Stonewall. The driver drops me off directly in the parking lot where Miles parked for our first date, the memory making me smile of that time in the ocean. I stand by the wooden beams along the side, scanning my eyes over to where the beach hut is to hire the surf boards. It looks like I'm not the only one who decided to surf, the waves are really on our side today. I stroll towards the beach hut, noticing how busy the beach front actually is. Even though its winter, people are still walking around buying ice cream and savouring the pleasant day. The smiles on their faces say it all. I've always said living by a beach is the way forward. Breathing in that ocean air everyday just makes you feel so... alive.

Clearing my throat, I try to get the attention of the gentleman who's back is turned.

"Hey, can I hire a surfboard please?'"

The burly man turns around, exposing his sun-kissed blonde hair, the wavy locks resting on his shoulders whilst the top is tied up in a top knot. He looks like a Viking beast. His skin is so tanned, you can tell he practically lives outside in the sun. I give him a slight smile, a blush tinting my cheeks, and he arches his blonde eyebrow in disbelief.

"Are you sure?" His blue sapphire eyes narrow as he stares at me.

"Do you even know how to surf?'"

He leans in, placing both forearms on the counter and clasping his hands together, his head cocking to the side. Is this guy for real? Now, because I'm a girl, I can't surf.

"I'll have you know, even though it isn't your business, I can surf just fine."

I cock my hip out, crossing my arms across my chest and standing my ground. The Thor look-alike stares at me blankly before standing himself upright. He shakes his head and turns towards the surf boards all placed on shelves, picking one out for me. He chooses the brightest pink one there is, in fact it's the brightest one I have ever seen.

"Wow, so because I'm a girl you think I should have bright pink?" I scoff, my eyebrows raised. I grab the board from him anyway, pushing it into the sand to stand upright. A grin replaces the frown he had on his beautiful chiselled face whilst I start taking off my yoga pants, trainers, and hoodie. I'll show this fucker. Grinning at him, I place my discarded clothes and bag on the counter.

"I'll let you look after my belongings," I tease, grabbing the pink monstrosity and making my way to the blue and white waves. Yeah, I'll show that fucker. Sexist prick.

Laying down flat on the board, I paddle out far enough to where the other surfers are sitting, waiting for the waves to hit. The ocean here is completely different to South African waters, I mean, before, I always had to be wary of great white sharks, but thankfully I was always okay. At least the ocean here is a lot safer, although the waves aren't as big, but that doesn't matter. The first wave approaches and I get ready to stand on the board, which is attached to my foot by a leg rope. The water is freezing cold, nipping at the visible skin on my hands and feet, but the good thing about my wetsuit is that it retains heat, so I'm warm enough without freezing to death.

As I stand on my board, I spot the Viking standing outside of the beach hut, leaning his shoulder against the wood, his arms crossed over his chest as his feet are crossed at the ankles. His gaze follows me as I take the waves, along with the other surfers. I'm the only one in this goddamn ocean with a colourful board, the dick. I think he did it so that I would be easy to spot. The other surfers watch me as well, clearly surprised by a girl surfing in their waters.

I take out my last wave before I go back to the beach to get a drink of water, my muscles aching like crazy. It doesn't help that I pushed myself dancing this morning and now I'm surfing. My muscles are screaming at me to stop and just relax but I can't. I don't know how to. Walking on the wet sand and holding the bright pink board under my arm, I approach the sexist pig from earlier, who's also looking after my stuff. I lean the board against the beach hut, taking my hair out from the bun and letting it fall gracefully around my face. Then I unzip my wetsuit just enough that my cleavage is on show.

The egotistical Viking -whose name I don't yet know - doesn't move from his spot. His lips curl into an arrogant, condescending smile as he takes in my now on show cleavage. He picks up the pink board, tucking it under his arm as he takes it back into the hut, placing it back on the shelf. For once a smirk creeps up on my face, an overwhelming feeling of arrogance which I haven't felt in a while. I take a sip of my water, the satisfaction of cold water relinquishing my thirst.

Picking up my clothes and bag from the counter, I walk back over onto the beach, perching myself on the golden sand, preparing for the early sunset. I place my belongings next to me and lean myself back, resting on my forearms. I better let myself dry for a while before I get an Uber to pick me up. I don't think they would be pleased if I climbed into their car and soaked the seats.

As I'm watching the lavish golden sun descend and the shadows of the surfers in the water, a figure approaches me. His wet blonde hair is now curled, emphasizing his sharp features as he holds a black board under his arm. Hands rake through his hair, causing the water to drip onto his high cheekbones, the wetsuit straining against his muscles. A sinful grin takes over his face as he notices me resting on the golden grains of sand. My breath hitches, remembering when he had a girl wrapped around his waist, the moans still playing in my mind.

"Well, who do we have here?" Charles teases.

Oh great, I can't go anywhere without bumping into one of the fucking pricks.

And now I know this particular fucker also likes to surf.

I don't acknowledge or respond to Charles, removing my eyes from his muscular form to keep staring at the ocean and the other surfers. Hopefully, he will leave me alone.

"Nice surf," he winks and saunters off without another word.

Thank god.

Just when I think I'm getting time to myself; the sexist Viking guy sits next to me on the sand. I turn my gaze over to him, my hair blowing in my face with the slight breeze.

"I must say, I'm lost for words… I'm impressed," he admits.

Smiling, I tuck my hair behind my ear then turn my gaze back towards the ocean. "Well by the looks of the other guys here, you don't have a lot of woman surfers?"

"You're right we don't, like at all. So, I truly was impressed when I saw you out there," he confesses, and my ego keeps building. We both sit there in silence, admiring the view of the early winter sunset. The guy stands, holding out his hand towards me. "By the way, I'm Zach. How about we move over to the bonfire over there and get you warmed up?"

Taking up the offer, I give him my hand, feeling his rough hands in mine as he hauls me up. I wipe the sand off from my ass and pick up my stuff before we walk over to the bonfire. "I'm Adelaide, but I suppose you can call me Ade," I wink.

We walk over to the bonfire where someone's car is parked on the edge, blaring pop music and with cooler boxes placed in the boot. It also seems to be where Charles is, with girls surrounding him, all giggling to whatever he just said. Zach leads me to the beach chairs where I take a seat, savouring the warm feeling that is emitting from the fire, the heat prickling my cold and exposed skin. I don't plan on putting my clothes back on until my wetsuit is reasonably dry.

Zach offers to get me a drink from the cooler box, which he assures me is his friend's and that they won't mind, so I accept. I look around the bonfire, a little anxious as Charles eyes never stray from mine. He looks in his element, the demon that he is by the fire. I can see the flames dancing in his dark eyes as he flirts with another girl. She will probably also end up around his waist at some point this evening.

Oh god, why am I thinking about that?

If this is Zach's friend's little party, does that mean he's friends with Charles?

Hopefully, Zach doesn't have the same trait of being a cunt like Charles.

Zach approaches, handing over a can of cold beer. "I am guessing you know Charles Kensington'" he asks, taking a seat in the unoccupied chair next to me. I open the can straight away and take a massive gulp. Having to put up with Charles' presence means that I need to drink.

"Yeah, we attend Darlington Academy together," I roll my eyes without meaning to and take another big gulp of beer.

Zach raises his eyebrow, shaking his head in displeasure. "Oh, you're one of them, are you?" He's taking smaller sips of his beer, clearly savouring it.

"What do you mean by 'one of them'?" I emphasize, but I know exactly what he means. He's asking me if I'm a stuck-up brat asshole like the others. "I might attend that academy, but that doesn't mean I'm anything like those assholes," I tell him, and Zach roars with laughter in response. Hearing him laugh is like a breath of fresh air, it sounds real and rough. It matches his hard Viking persona.

"I'm guessing you are friends with his royal douchness?" I ask, positioning my body so that I'm looking at him clearly, waiting for him to answer. He doesn't stop laughing at my serious facial expression and takes a sip of beer before answering me.

"Fuck no, he's a dick. He just surfs here a lot and we have the same circle of friends," he clarifies.

Thank god.

I let out a big breath, my anxiety starting to fade away as I start to feel comfortable with Zach. We end up chatting for most of the night, getting to know each other, and I must admit, it's lovely getting to know someone who is normal like me. We have similar interests and the most obvious one is surfing.

"So, tell me about the beach hut? How did that come about?" I ask Zach, intrigued.

"Well, I love surfing and this is a great location for tourists and locals to come down and surf but a few years ago they stopped the surfing lessons, so I thought why not" he starts, then takes a sip of his beer and I watch the orange flame from the bonfire dance around his chiselled features. "I guess I also saw it as creating a hobby for the kids and adults around here, you know?" he adds.

"That is amazing. I think it's great that you could do it" I smile as my cheeks flush from admiration for this guy.

"I have noticed that Charles keeps staring at you. Literally the whole night, he hasn't stopped," Zach laughs, but I doubt that's true. "Want to piss him off?" Zach questions, a mischievous grin dancing on his face and I have no idea what he means. Me being here probably makes Charles angry enough. When I catch him looking over at us, I can see the hatred and disgust in his eyes, his face turned into a frown, a girl hanging herself on his arm.

"What did you have in mind?" I quickly turn my gaze to Zach and that's when his big, rough hands grab my face, pulling my lips to his. His tongue slips past my lips, kissing me passionately and raw. His hand slides across to the back of my neck, holding me in place as my body goes numb.

I'm really enjoying this kiss, like, way too much.

Zach lets go, chuckling against my lips, making me ache for more. My skin tingles with the rush that goes through me, and the pit of my stomach fills with heat. I haven't felt like this before with a guy, not even Miles. The way Zach kisses is captivating, enthralling and in control, almost as if he's claiming me in front of the others.

Oh my god.

We both smile at each other, before looking around to see Charles has stormed off, clearly furious at us. We both high-five each other. I want to do more than high five this man. We both stand up from the beach chairs and Zach walks me over to the parking lot where I'm meeting my Uber. He did offer to drive me back to the academy, but he doesn't believe in drunk driving and I'm grateful he won't put me in that position. Although, I realize when Royce drove me to the academy, he had had a lot to drink.

Now I feel guilty.

"Thanks for a surprisingly fun evening. I didn't think I'd be out this late," I joke and Zach nods, agreeing. I don't think he expected it either, especially after his arrogant and sexist persona to begin with. I think I'll let that pass.

"Can I have your number?" Zach blurts out as I open the passenger door of the Uber and I turn around to face him, my cheeks feeling flushed as the guilt passes through me.

"I already told you that I am currently seeing someone right now." I raise my eyebrow in question, leaning my hand on the car door as Zach shifts from one foot to the other.

The corner of Zach's lips curls up into a coy smile before he speaks. "I know, this is purely platonic. It's just for when you want to come down and surf that's all". Giving in, we swap numbers before

I get into the Uber that takes me back to the academy, and I can't help but think that I would love to see Zach again. Even if it's platonic.

I will most definitely be coming back to surf with Zach

~

*S*itting in my Business Ethics class, I keep thinking about the weekend and Zach. How he's imprinted on my mind and that kiss… I can't stop thinking about it. Whenever I do, the heat in my core rises and a pool of desire fills my knickers. He's left such a mark on me and I can't wait to have an excuse to see him again. I haven't heard from Miles at all since he stood me up yesterday, not even a text to let me know he's okay.

I complete my assignment in class and sit patiently, playing with my pen as Blake is still working on his. I try and face the front of the room, but I end up doodling loads of little hearts on my notepad in front of me, careful not to write Zach's name.

I am seriously schoolgirl crushing right now.

Today was the first time in a while that I decided to put on some make-up. My bruises have gone, and my nose isn't swollen anymore from the battering I suffered. Even though the outside of me has healed, the inside is still screaming in pain. I still have a long way to go with putting weight on my body, trying not to look like a skeleton but I am excited for our girls weekend of pampering soon.

Blake finishes his assignment and leans back in his chair, bringing his arms up so they are resting behind his head. His blazer is neatly hung up on the back of his chair. I can smell his scent of vanilla and oakwood with a hint of cloves, and if he weren't such a dick, it would be addicting. I take a sly glance to the side, watching as he flexes his arms above his head, stretching the muscular biceps. The button up shirt strains against his sporty, lean frame. I scan my eyes lower, peaking at the slight skin visible between his slacks and where the shirt has risen. My breath quickens at the sight of this demonic man. How can he look so perfect yet be so devilish and cruel? I think about what it would feel like if my hands were to brush along his tanned, toned body; feeling every bump on his torso knowing full well it will burn.

I shake the thought from my mind, giving myself a mental slap and reminding myself that he's a dick. I shouldn't think about or have any sexual tendencies towards this asshole.

Maybe I can tame him?

No, no. Focus Ade.

When the bell rings to signal class is over, I make my way over to the library where I'm meeting Hugo for my tutoring sessions. Why the hell can't some other tutor become available so that I can get away from these guys? I slide into a seat at our usual table, pulling out my laptop containing all the assignments that I need help with, and plug in my earphones until he gets here. He gets really moody when I listen to my music. Always says what I'm listening to is so heavy and angry. Well, it's better than listening to his fucking voice.

I listen to some music which I haven't listened to in a while and start on my assignments, tapping my foot to the beat. Without realizing, I end up singing the words to one of the songs, a little louder than I should. Hugo takes a seat across from me before ripping out my earphones.

"Do you have to rip them out every single time?" I wince, my ears stinging from where he pulled them so hard. He is so strict, and I wouldn't be surprised If he wanted to become a teacher or even better, a prison guard. He would do well with that.

"You know how I feel about you listening to music while you are supposed to be studying. Plus, I don't want you to fucking sing," he hisses.

I mock him by copying his words, which lands me a death glare. I take the warning from him and pack my earphones away, but I still hum my tunes. Hugo sighs.

"Well done by the way, on your Business Ethics paper."

My eyes go wide at the fact he just said something nice, and actually praised me on my work. There is a god. He shows me the paper which I completed earlier – I'm still baffled by how he gets them so quick – and in red is a big letter A. I can't contain my squeal, so I let it out. Hugo winces as he hands me my paper, which I might just frame. Hopefully, father will be proud of me.

I mentally give myself a fist bump, knowing Hugo would never do that.

We carry on with whatever Hugo gets me to do and I'm still humming, happy with my grade. Hugo keeps looking up at me from his paper, his jaw ticking with annoyance and I couldn't care less. If I could, I would stand on the library tables and dance, that's how ecstatic I am.

Eventually he leans back in his chair, dropping the pen to fold his arms across his taut chest, emerald green eyes narrowed as he bites his lip. A frown takes over his face. "How are you so happy after everything we've done to you?"

Great, what a way to ruin my mood.

I inhale a sharp breath, unprepared for a question like this.

"You know what Hugo? I'm not happy. I'm fucking broken and ruined because of you and your dickhead friends. This is the only thing that has made me even smile in weeks, and there you go ruining that for me too," I say through clenched teeth, my hands tightening into fists on the table. I can feel my long nails piercing the skin of my palm, the blood dripping from my skin onto my notepad, leaving specks of blood.

What a metaphor.

The one thing I'm happy about, and these cunts have to ruin it by taking blood from me, making it visible for everyone to see.

"Are you happy now?"

I unclench my fist, grabbing a tissue from my inner blazer pocket, wiping the blood from my palms but the blood has already soaked through the pages in my notebook. Hugo leans in over the table, bringing his beautifully perky lips near to my ear, his hot breath caressing my skin as adrenaline runs through my veins. The heat between my thighs turns my legs numb. Goosebumps appear all over my body, making me shiver and the smell of Hugo so close to me is fucking intoxicating.

"I like seeing you in pain. It turns me on," he whispers, tilting his face so it's now facing me. His eyes are half lidded, letting me in on one of his secrets. I try and swallow the knot in my throat, but it doesn't budge. Hugo chuckles under his breath as he leans back in his chair, continuing on with his assignment.

Why am I so turned on right now?

Attempting to get back to my assignment, I try to ignore the feeling that's left in my stomach, how Hugo affects me so much. The image of his big calloused hands ripping off my uniform, caressing my tiny frame as he takes me right here on this table floods my tainted mind.

Oh, how just a look from his emerald eyes drive me into a frenzy.

Hugo infects every brain cell in my mind, and just the thought of those perfectly rounded lips on mine could send me into an orgasm itself. I shake the thought from my corrupted mind before Hugo notices I'm having a sex daydream about him. Why do I have to have these thoughts over these cruel, heartless boys? They haven't even showed any type of affection towards me, so why is my mind and body betraying me?

Chapter Sixteen

I haven't seen Miles for almost two weeks, so when he sends me a text to apologize, I'm stunned. His excuse is that he had a tough few days and had to stay home for a while. I'm unsure how to respond to him, so a simple 'okay' will have to do. I have tried to text him, asking him if he's okay, but now I think that giving him space might just be what he needs. I don't want to come across like a needy girlfriend, even though I'm not his official girlfriend. I kept thinking to myself - is he ignoring me because I haven't had sex with him yet? But I instantly get rid of that thought, as I don't think he would be like that.

Well, I'm hoping that he isn't inclined that way.

As Blaire hops the shower, I relax on my bed, scrolling through social media when another text pings through. I open the notification, hoping it's Miles, but to my disappointment, it's my father.

I want you at the house next Sunday for dinner, 6pm – I'm not asking.

Oh great, another dinner party which I will need to attend, probably with all those men again, making me feel uncomfortable whilst I eat my three-course meal. I roll my eyes at the thought.

Undoubtedly, he's also expecting me to be all prim and proper, just as Ms. Veronica taught me to be.

"Oh, I'm so excited for our pamper day!" Blaire gushes as she exits the bathroom, wearing a cute, frilly baby blue tea dress. I smile up at her from where I'm resting against my headboard, waiting for both her and Maisie to get ready. I was so excited when I woke up this morning that I got showered and dressed before they woke up. I even managed to fit in some study time. A knock sounds from the door and Blaire opens it up finding Maisie dressed in a similar dress to Blaire, but hers is white. Her auburn hair falls elegantly around her small face. These two have really gone all out in their outfits today, and then there's me, wearing jeans and a nice cream jumper. It's winter, why would I wear a goddamn dress?

"Let's go bitches!" Maisie says, so I get up from my bed and tuck my phone into my little black shoulder bag. Then we're on our way.

Maisie drives us to the next town over from Stonewall, called Bayside Hill, which has a massive shopping mall and several designer shops. It takes over an hour to get to Bayside Hill, but as soon as we near it, I can tell we're away from the beach town of Stonewall and more into the countryside, where green forest surrounds the winding main road. Just ahead are the towering buildings and as we turn off right by some traffic lights, the view is replaced into a big glass palace they call Bayside Hill shopping district. My eyes go wide at the scene in front of me and I sit forward in my seat, my neck craning to see it all.

"It's amazing, isn't it?" Blaire says as we pull into the parking lot, my mind still in awe over how magnificent this structure is. This is something I'd expect to see in London - even though I have never been to London - not the countryside, but it looks like a city in and of itself. Climbing out of the car, we walk past an extravagant water fountain. A naked roman lady stands tall at six feet, holding an old roman water container above her head. I read the plaque as I walk past, 'Lady Maria of Bayside'. Hm, interesting.

We walk on the beautiful Carrara marble tiled path with matching marble columns on each side supporting the roof, as we enter through automatic glass doors. The whole inner mall structure is built on glass and marble, looking like a palace inside and out.

Our first call of duty is the hair salon and I'm really nervous, deciding I want to cut my long locks from my ass to at least sit just below my shoulders.

Maybe I might add some highlights? Who knows?

We find the hair salon that Blaire booked us in, called Eden, and it's surrounded by plants with a water feature that actually looks like the garden of Eden.

All it's missing is Blake as its serpent.

All three of us girls have our hair appointment at the exact same time, Blaire made sure of it, so we're allocated to our seats for stylists to work their magic. I explain to the lady how I want my hair cut, and maybe a change of colour too. We get served a glass of champagne and some truffles whilst the stylist gets to work and I'm still in admiration. This is like living in an alternative universe, and I'm not used to being so pampered.

I have never coloured my hair so this will be a first for me, and butterflies form in my stomach when I see that both Blaire and Maisie are getting their hair refreshed with colour. I have just learned that Maisie's beautiful auburn hair is not natural, and that she's naturally a mousy brown colour. Well, learn something new every day.

''Right, so the hair dye needs to be left on your hair for around forty minutes, and then after wards we will rinse it off then cut and style it" The stylist explains as she wraps a plastic cap over my head to contain the heat. I nod my head in agreement and she smiles at me before leaving me to it.

I sit in my luxurious leather throne, drinking my champagne and reading a juicy celeb magazine while I wait. When the timer goes off the stylist leads me through to the basins where she rinses the colour off and gives me the most amazing Indian head massage. Oh, my goodness, I need to come back here just for the massage.

Once I've sat down back at my chair, the stylist gets to work on cutting my long mane, and I'm not even nervous anymore. It's time for me to get a new look and build my confidence back up again. As soon as she cuts my hair and blow dries it into bouncy curls, she turns my chair to face the mirror so that I can see the finished product. Both Blaire and Maisie come over, standing behind my chair, their hair already done with just a trim and gloss. They both look fabulous. Looking at me in the mirror, they cover their mouths with their hands, squealing.

My hair has been dyed, the ends lightened with a technique the stylist calls Balayage – a French term for either sweep or paint – and it looks amazing. The roots are still the same colour but with gloss to add shine, and the ends are not too light but a lovely caramel tone, working well with my tanned skin.

"Oh. My. God. You look amazing," Blaire gushes, still shrieking and clapping her hands in front of her chest. My hair is now cut so that the length rests just below my shoulders, and layers have been added for volume. I am stunned with the magic this stylist has performed. I can see now that my old, dull brown hair was drowning my face, making my skin tone look boring. But now I can even agree I look hot, and I can't wait for everyone to see the finished product.

Since leaving the salon, we have gotten our nails done, been to an eyebrow bar and I even got eyelash extensions, making my blue eyes pop. It also means I don't need to wear mascara all the time and it's amazing. We rest our feet for a bit, stopping off at a cute little blue café that sits in the middle of the mall. I order myself a large coffee –I haven't even had one today – and a blueberry muffin.

We sit at a round table in the corner of the café, sipping on our coffees as we talk about how the morning has gone so far.

"I am so glad not to be home this weekend. I cannot face being around Blake right now or even my father. They have both been acting so strangely since my father took on an extra business deal" Blaire says, her face looking deflated as she mentions her brother. "But I am glad to be here with you girls. We needed a day like this." She continues, but within a second her expression changes and she now has a smile on her face.

"If you need to talk about it Blaire, we are here for you too." I console, offering her a soft smile as she nods in my direction, but from the silence I can tell she isn't ready to reveal anything as of yet but luckily, I am patient. Maisie raises her dark auburn eyebrow in my direction.

"So, when are you next seeing Miles, or even better … Zach?" she asks, taking a sip of her coffee. The girls are still not sold on the idea of me and Miles, but as soon as they heard about Zach, they were all for it.

"Well, Miles has hardly texted me, but I've heard from Zach. We've exchanged a few texts; he's wondering when I'm going down the beach to surf." I shrug, trying to ignore the cheeky smirks appearing on both their faces. Blaire straightens her back, a huge grin forming before me as she comes up with an idea.

"We should all go down and try to surf."

I know exactly why she wants to join me down the beach - so she can ogle all the other male specimens. I don't blame her. There were some extremely hot and attractive men, and even Charles looked to die for in his wet suit. It's not every day you see the Queen's nephew looking rugged. Blaire waves her arms around, gesturing for us to move.

"Come on ladies, we have some shopping to do."

The rest of the afternoon we literally shop until we drop. I haven't been in so many stores in my entire life. I used to find one shop I liked and that's the only place I would go to. The girls made me buy a few new dresses, skirts, and cute little tops, plus way too many shoes. I even get changed out of my jeans and jumper into a little yellow wrap around dress to match the girls as I felt out of place in my too casual clothing, and I feel amazing.

Who knew that getting pampered like this and a whole new wardrobe would be so comforting?

∽

*W*hen we arrive back at the Academy, we drop off our shopping bags back at the dorms and head straight to the dining hall for dinner. This day has left me starving and I could eat for ten people. All of the sudden I feel nervous knowing that most people will see my new look. Not every student has gone home this weekend as it's supposed to be the big Halloween party.

We are skipping the party and have three ladies coming to the academy later this evening to give us all a full body massage. That's exactly what my muscles need. I can't think of anything worse than attending that stupid Halloween party, knowing for a fact I'd be setting myself up for another taunt or humiliation from the Royals.

Entering the dining hall through the double wooden doors, everyone's eyes have fallen onto us. A slight smirk appears on my face, blood rushing to colour my cheeks bright red as people notice my new look. I mean, what I did was drastic. At least I think it is. The Royals are all seated at the high table by the floor to ceiling windows, eating their dinner, and still dressed in their academy uniforms. I guess the party doesn't start till later this evening if everyone is still here, not even dressed yet.

For some reason Blake looks furious as he watches me, Blaire and Maisie walking over to our table. The muscle in his jaw ticks as he clenches his teeth, his hand wrapped around his sharp knife tightly, turning his knuckles white. I know he would use it on me if he could. Charles has a smirk on his face, shaking his head before looking down at his dinner and taking another bite of his steak. I wonder if he's laughing at me.

Royce is leaning back in his seat, his eyes studying me as I walk past their table, brows furrowed, and I can see his mouth twitching. He looks as if he wants to say something, but he's holding it back. I look at Hugo last, knowing he's emotionless but he makes me nervous the most. His face is pure poker face as usual, but his eyes are blazing with vehemence and I can see he wants to see me in pain, just as he admitted to me the other week. He wants to see me beaten and bleeding on my knees for him, praying for mercy. He wants to be the god that will grant me my freedom.

I would happily fall to my knees for Hugo, just for one night of passion in his arms. He looks at me as if I should be punished, and the Royals are providing me with the hell that I'm caged in, punished for my sins. They are the demons instructed to crack the whip.

Flipping my hair over my shoulder, I stride with confidence to my seat and just as I'm about to sit down, Miles appears. His eyes go wide, scanning my body, his smile gleaming with passion as he studies my new look. I give him a confident smile.

"Damn, where the fuck did Ade go?" he says.

I sit down and Miles takes the seat next to me, giving me a kiss on the cheek.

"You look … amazing."

We order our dinner, and as I'm feeling confident, I splurge on a big meal, not worrying about anyone else judging me. I don't want any of the other students to think that the Royals broke me. I'd rather them believe that I might have fallen, but I have picked myself back up again.

"Are you not going to the Halloween party tonight?" Miles questions, and it hits me that I completely forgot to tell him that we have decided not to attend. I hope he wasn't thinking about us two going together.

"I'm so sorry I completely forgot to tell you, but we're not going tonight," I whisper. I don't want the rest of the students knowing that we decided against it. The party seems to be the biggest party of the year, thrown by the Royals of course, and it's absurd if no one attends. Well, fuck them.

Miles nods and kisses me on the cheek before leaving me again, exiting out of the dining hall.

Once we have eaten our dinner, the girls and I get ready to leave the dining hall and head back to the dorms to prepare for our massages. As I stand from my chair, someone taps me on the shoulder, and I turn around to face the lovely Ruby Lockhart with her two cronies, Constance Evergreen and Priscilla Voss. All three of them are standing in my pathway with their hands tucked behind their backs, making it impossible for me to get through.

"Oh, look everyone. Africa decided to get a little make-over to try and fit in," Ruby cackles, and the whole room turns around to stare at us, giggling behind their hands. Ruby tuts, a scowl replacing the grin. "You think because you got your hair dyed and some eyelashes, that all of a sudden everyone is going to love you? Ha."

I stand in front of her, arms crossed over my chest, raising my chin so she thinks she's not affecting me but secretly I'm shitting myself.

"You look even more like an AIDS ridden whore now than you did before, and it doesn't take away from the fact that you're still a murderer."

It's how she drags out the word 'murderer' in her hyena tone voice that makes me see red. Blaire and Maisie are behind me,

"Leave her alone Ruby!" Blaire warns, her eyes wide as she confronts Ruby, but she isn't listening to her warning.

No, they're all grinning at me and I can't pluck up the courage to even lift my fists or to bite back with words. Nothing wants to come out. My body has gone stiff like a mannequin and it's so frustrating, knowing I can't stand up for myself.

"Trick or treat…. Bitch," Ruby growls, and that's when Blaire and Maisie are pulled away, students surrounding me and the three bitches in a circle. Before I know it, I'm having rotten Halloween pumpkin insides thrown at me. Covering me from head to toe. I try and block out the shit by crouching away, my arms covering my face but it's no use. I am drenched and I fucking stink. The whole room bursts into laughter, enjoying the fact that I'm covered in rotten pulp and I'm standing here taking it.

I am a coward.

When the escapade ends, I try and pull off as much pulp from my body, hair, and face but the rotting smell still lingers. My new dress is soaked and ruined.

I want to scream and hit everyone in this room with a baseball bat, breaking their bones and making them bleed, just as they do to me on the inside. I run back to my dorm, immediately discarding the dress in the bin when I get into the bathroom. I jump in the shower, scrubbing off the rotten smell and it takes nearly three washes to stop it from lingering on my skin and hair.

What the fuck have I done to the fucking cunts here, apart from attend? Seriously, these posh twats need to get a grip. Is this what rich people do for fun? Do they pick on the poor, helpless people because they know they can't do anything back? These people are

supposed to be our future politicians, businessmen and woman...
and even better, they are in the royal fucking family.

These are the people who run the world and let the poor people
suffer, and it doesn't surprise me. I'm glad I got to live a normal life
in a beautiful country rather than with a parent who doesn't love me
and just views the world as money bags.

Fuck them all.

I try to forget about how humiliated I should have been, but
honestly it was the nicest thing they've done to me so far.

I'd rather the Royals disgrace me by throwing rotten food all
over me than call me a murderer, forcing me to look at my mum's
post-mortem photos and drowning me. It sounds messed up, but I'm
not easily humiliated. I'd take it a hundred times over again.

Chapter Seventeen

An entire week has passed with the whole academy calling me names and throwing food at me. Apparently Ruby has ordered everyone to throw rotten food at me every chance they get, and they truly do get me at every opportunity. The worst one was when someone threw rotten tomatoes at me, making it look like I was covered in blood, and called me a murderer. It's sad that I have to admit that I'm used to the taunting and bullying from other students. Blaire and Maisie feel really guilty as the other students leave them alone and always make sure they're either not there, or they are being pulled away.

I was stupid in thinking a make-over would make me feel more alive, but in reality, it painted an even bigger on my target on my back.

This afternoon, I'm spending my Saturday in the club. I offered to assist Samantha with clearing the storage room and helping with deliveries, due to the fact I'm taking tonight off to go and see 'Nightfall' with Miles.

Sitting on the bar stool, I complete the inventory while watching the dancers practice their performance on the stage for tonight. I can't keep my eyes off of them, they look so free. All the girls wear wigs and masks to hide their identity when they perform so that customers don't stalk or bother them for sex when they finish. Apparently, it's happened a few times.

I want to be that free.

I inhale a sharp breath. "Samantha, how do I become one of the performers?" I finally ask, feeling like a weight has been lifted off my chest. I so desperately want to try and do this, and its technically good practice for my dancing.

Samantha side glances at me from behind the bar with a smirk on her face. She can see how I stare at these girls with desperation in my eyes.

"Well, can you dance, chick?"

My face lights up, ready to answer her question. "Yeah… I am studying dance for my degree," I ramble on, shocked I never made her aware. I guess it's never come up. She doesn't really like the Darlington Academy students, she thinks they're all posh twats with sticks up their asses, and she's not wrong. Luckily, she likes me.

"Oh, well, I'll book you a slot for an audition and then we will take it from there, yeah?" she asks.

I squeal in excitement.

My father would kill me if he found out I want to dance in Burlesque in front of an audience, but like I said, the girls hide their identity so how would he know?

Quickly sending a text to Miles, I tell him where to pick me up from so that we can go to the concert later. I haven't told anyone that I work here, apart from Blaire and Maisie, so I'm unsure of how he will react.

Getting back to the inventory, I pick up my drink and take a sip. I'm drinking a rum and cola to get me into the mood for later tonight. I'm really looking forward to seeing and spending time with Miles as I haven't really seen him unless it's during dance practice.

He says he feels guilty about Ruby and her escapades and wants to make it up to me later. I'm grateful we get a night out to let our hair down.

The dance recital is in a matter of weeks and we have been nonstop perfecting our routine. I'm feeling more motivated now than ever and can't wait for the whole academy to see me in my element, so I can show them exactly what I can do. I have been putting blood, sweat, and tears into this, to ensure that the routine is as perfect as it can be. I won't let anyone take that from me.

Once the inventory and deliveries have been sorted, I go into the ladies' room to get changed before Miles arrives. I decided to wear some leather trousers and a cute red crop top paired with heeled boots and a leather jacket. I even go all out and put on a full face of make-up with red lipstick. Now I'm ready to go and have some fun with my date.

We might even take it to the next level in our relationship.

As I'm roughing up my hair and admiring myself one last time in the mirror, my phone pings with a text from Miles to say he's waiting for me outside. "Right, I need to go Samantha. I'll see you next weekend?" I shout out just before leaving the club.

I walk on the gravel path to the parking lot and see Miles' Aston Martin parked up, and the butterflies in my stomach begin to flutter. The nerves are creeping up my spine the closer I get to the car, knowing I'll be seeing Miles on our second official date. I love the way he makes me feel when I'm round him. He makes me feel so safe and secure, even though his stepsister is a bitch, but Miles is different. I can feel it.

I know he wouldn't hurt a fly, let alone hurt me.

"Wow, you look... stunning," Miles says as I hop into the car, my leather-clad ass scooting along his leather interior, which doesn't bode well as I'm already sticking to the seat.

Already Miles has the music turned up high to get us in the mood for the concert and he even brought me a beer to drink on the way up. I look over to see his eyes haven't strayed away from my outfit and I mentally give myself a high five.

"Is something wrong?" I ask, just in case he doesn't actually like my outfit. But, to be honest, it's so he can boost my ego.

"Hell no. I have just never seen you look so... different and sexy," he growls, grabbing my face in the palms of his hands, bringing me closer to him as he parts my swollen red lips with his tongue. The way he kisses still mesmerizes me, it's as if he's always saying goodbye. I can't quite put my finger on it.

He pulls away, giving me a cheeky grin before getting back to actually driving the car so that we can make it to the concert. I take a deep breath, clearing my throat as I flick open the beer can and take a huge gulp.

I am going to need it.

It takes around forty-five minutes to get to the venue, and the cars are already queuing to get in the car park. Miles booked VIP, so we get to go in straight away. It's a bigger than a normal parking space, but I wouldn't expect anything less with the car he has. With his VIP passes, we skip all the queues, so we're straight into the actual arena. Miles got us standing tickets, as he says the experience will be a lot better in the mosh pit rather than sitting down and not having any room to move, and I agree. I'd much rather dance around with loads of other sweaty bodies than sit next to someone grumpy.

We queue up to get some drinks, which are an extortionate in price but lucky for me Miles insists on paying for everything, even though I always like to offer to pay for half. While getting our drinks, we leave our coats with the attendant who stores them in a locker for us, so we don't have to carry them around as it's going to be extremely hot. Usually I couldn't think of anything worse than dancing with loads of sweating, gross bodies, but tonight, I'm up for new experiences.

We arrived a little later so the support bands are playing on the high-rise stage. Miles grabs my hand as he escorts me to find a great space near to the stage. He pushes his way through a load of already drunk groups of teenagers dancing, and they all look a little worse for wear already. People are stumbling into each other, sweat dripping off their faces as some sway from side to side, unable to stand straight. I have no idea how they're going to cope for another half an hour before 'Nightfall' comes on and plays.

When the band takes to the stage to play the whole arena goes crazy, and as I'm a little tipsy, I do to. We end up dancing around stupidly together, enjoying the music, jumping up and down with the rest of the crowd and it's exhilarating. For a posh boy, I'm surprised Miles would even attend a gig like this because it means he has to stand around with commoners. But he's proven to me that he isn't like that, so I guess not all rich people are the same.

We dance for a couple of songs before Miles offers to get us another round of drinks. I offer to stay behind so that we don't lose our spot. I carry on dancing, enjoying the music, not paying attention to who I'm even dancing with. I'm swaying my hips, not realizing just how tipsy I am, and when I stumble back, I hit a hard frame along with the drink that's in their hands. I turn around and my eyes widen, staring directly into the green emerald abyss of Hugo's eyes. I squint just to make sure it's not the alcohol making me see things, and then I stretch out my hand to touch the muscular form before me.

Yup, he's real.

I gasp, my hand cupping my mouth. "Oh god, I am so sorry," I slur my words, clearly too drunk to deal with this situation but Hugo does nothing. His drink spilled down his tight black t-shirt, all the way down to his black ripped jeans, and he throws his empty cup into the crowd. "Do you want me to buy you a replacement drink?"

He doesn't even respond to my question. Instead, he looks around the crowd before his eyes are drawn back to me. He turns around and without me noticing, grabs my hand and yanks me behind him, dragging me along.

Oh god, he's going to lose his shit. Where the fuck is Miles?

Hugo drags me all the way to an outside smoking area that is filled with sweaty, drunk people, swaying to the music blaring through the speakers. To my surprise, Hugo lights up a cigarette and offers me one.

"No, thanks. I don't smoke." I wave my hand in front of me, turning away the death stick.

"You shouldn't be here on your own," he drawls, taking a drag from of his cigarette as his eyes take in my outfit. I suppose he hasn't really seen me in anything other than my academy uniform and jeans, or that cute yellow dress which was ruined by pumpkin pulp.

I think he likes it…

I stand in front of Hugo, taking in his relaxed aura, which is rare. This is the first time I have ever seen him in anything but his posh boy outfit Instead, he looks normal and goddamn gorgeous. The tight t -shirt shows off his taut muscles and the ink covered skin of his arms and neck. He truly looks magnificent, even with a cigarette in his mouth.

Almost… intoxicating.

"Hang on, do you like rock music? Because I'm sure you always complain about how loud mine is…" I tease, cocking my hip out and folding my arms loosely around my chest. I haven't got my leather jacket to wear so I'm exposed in just my red crop top, but I can appreciate the feeling of the cool air on my sweat soaked skin.

Hugo looks back down at me and considering how tall he is and how small I am, he has to dip his head to look at me. He blows out a puff of smoke before answering.

"There's a lot you don't know about me, Africa," he purrs.

I should be scared right now, standing next to Hugo, but for some reason I'm not. He has done some dreadful things to me but there is something drawing me into his sadistic, demonic ways and all I can think about is his beautiful body covering mine.

I bet he's kinky as fuck.

"To answer your question, I'm not alone. I am actually here with Miles, he just went and got us another round of drinks," I tell him, raising my chin as I gaze around at the other couples who are pretty much fucking each other on the benches. Sensing my discomfort, Hugo smirks at me, baring his teeth, looking cruel as ever and I can't help but laugh.

Hugo's eyebrows furrow in confusion.

"What are you laughing about?"

He takes another drag of his cigarette, finishing it off before stubbing it out in the ashtray. I stare back at him, realizing how dilated his pupils are, so he's either absolutely fucking drunk or on some sort of drugs, but he is hiding it very well.

"You. You're just so…" I start, tapping my finger onto my lower lip before I find the correct word to use, "Uptight and mean." Now I feel like an idiot. Why the fuck did I just call Hugo mean? I need to sober up a little more. Shit! That reminds me, I wonder where Miles is. He's probably looking around for me.

Hugo's head rolls back, roaring with laughter, clearly amused by my comment. I can't tell if it's an evil laugh, where a villain cackles before killing his victim, or if he's actually amused. His smirk switches to a frown in an instant.

"Wow Africa, you don't know what mean is until you've crossed me," Hugo says, baring his teeth as he takes a step closer. I try and take a step back, but the back of my foot has hit the brick wall and I'm trapped. My breath quickens and Hugo notices the rise and fall of my chest. He stands closer to me, his left hand rising as he places his palm on the brick wall above my head so I can smell the spicy aroma of his cologne.

"You might think Blake is the cruel one, but cross me, and you will find out just how much of a heartless bastard I really am," he whispers in my ear, the venom from his lips caressing my senses, leaving me feeling tingly and slightly turned on.

His fingertips caress my left arm, leaving a hot trail behind. He takes a step back, and I can see the change in his eyes. They have turned into a black pool of nothingness. Nothing but a black hole, but they're still sucking me in. Since I laid my eyes on him, from the very start, I've had nothing but sinful thoughts of this demon. I want more, but I know it's impossible.

A guy like Hugo doesn't go near girls like me. We're not cut from the same cloth and it's evident. My eyes go to the floor as I shuffle my feet.

"I need to get back inside," I whisper, still affected by Hugo. I need to get back to Miles – my safe haven, a guy who actually likes me, and the one who I might finally let in.

Hugo turns towards the door, beckoning with his head for me to follow. So I follow. We end up back in the drunk, rowdy crowd, Hugo's big frame pushing through the sea of people and they split. Just one look at him and people want to scatter. I know I would if I didn't know him. He's scary as fuck.

Luckily, he takes us back to the exact same spot and scares off the people that were in our place, but Miles isn't here. I'm wondering if he went looking for me or if the queues are so awful that he still hasn't come back.

Hugo whispers in some guys ear, who I am guessing is his friend who came with him to the gig.

"He hasn't come back yet," Hugo says in my ear so that I can hear him, and I am taking another guess that his friend knows who Miles is. I stand in front of him, deciding that I am still going to enjoy my evening and dance the night away. Even though Hugo is a prick, I doubt he would leave me alone here, unattended. After a while I start getting worried because Miles still hasn't returned, and it's nearly been an hour. My nerves start kicking in and I start feeling sick.

Turning around, I notice an emo looking girl with bright purple hair hanging off of Hugo's arm. Maybe they came as a group and he's fucking her? I decide not to tell him where I'm going. He looks occupied and I don't want to be a cock block for anyone. I walk in the opposite direction to where we went out to the smoking area, bodies pushing me around and making me feel even more nauseous than I did. Hands grab me from every direction and I'm too drunk to really tell anyone to fuck off.

Stumbling back through the entrance to where the drinks queue is, I see Miles in the far corner, still waiting. I let out a big sigh, happy that he hasn't got lost or murdered. I stumble my way over, and he immediately sees me and gestures for me to join him in the queue.

"Hey, what are you doing here?" he asks, lifting an eyebrow and giving me a soft smile. I look at him in confusion, wondering how he didn't realize how long it's taking for him to get a stupid drink.

"You've been gone for a while and I got worried," I tell him, snaking my arms around his arm to steady myself. Miles looks at his watch and curses under his breath. "Oh, I suppose an hour is a long time to wait for drinks. Sorry, babe."

Aww he called me babe, that's new.

As I'm in the queue waiting with Miles, I scan my eyes around the room and notice Hugo standing by the entrance doors, staring at me, his lips set in a thin line. He shakes his head before re-entering the arena.

What the fuck have I done now?

Once we get back to the Academy, Miles has to carry me to my dorm room as I am too drunk and stumbling everywhere.

"Wow, you definitely are worse for wear," Miles chuckles as we get to my room, and I fumble in my clutch bag, trying to fish for my keys. "Here, let me help," he offers, taking my bag from me and in an instant, he finds my keys. Luckily, he isn't as drunk as I am, otherwise we would be stuffed.

When he manages to open the door, he leads me through and guides me to my bed, which I instantly flop back onto as my eyes start to close from exhaustion.

"Are you going to be okay? Because I need to go. I am getting picked up to go to my father's house," Miles says, his large hand rubbing my leather clad thigh.

"Yes, you go. I will be fine, I just need sleep," I mumble, waving him off with my hand.

Miles gives me a peck on the lips before he stands to leave, and within a few seconds I hear the soft click of the door once he is gone. My head feels dizzy, and even with my eyes closed the rooms feels as though it is spinning. Luckily, sleep takes over me rather quickly.

~

*W*aking up to a massive hangover after an eventful night, I'm lying on my bed, waiting for Steve to come around and pick me up from the academy. I awoke with my mascara and eyeliner smeared under my eyes, my lipstick still glued to my lips and still fully clothed in my leather trousers and red crop top. I have no idea how I managed to fall asleep in the tight leathers, but it somehow worked, and I slept like a baby.

I scrubbed my skin in the shower, removing any of the remains of last night still stinking of alcohol. I blow dried my new hairstyle, curling the ends and put on a full face of make-up, trying to look alive and presentable before going to my father's house. We have another stupid dinner party tonight and I'm really not looking forward to it.

My phone pings with a text. I open it to see that Steve is outside waiting for me, so I pick up my shoulder bag and head straight out to the courtyard. Forty-five minutes later, we roll up onto the drive of my father's house and as always, the front door is already open with Mrs. Blossom waiting for my arrival. I climb out of the black Bentley and make my way into the house while Steve drives off to park the car.

"Good Afternoon Adelaide, I like your new style," she says, and I am pleased she noticed. It was a huge thing for me to change my hairstyle and I'm wearing more make-up than usual. I smile at her sweetly. "Thank you, Mrs. Blossom."

She escorts me to the kitchen, because she knows I need a coffee and an orange juice. It's my ritual whenever I come here, and I spend a lot of my time in the kitchen. As I expected, a fresh coffee and glass of juice with a blueberry muffin is waiting for me by the breakfast bar. Sally is already in the kitchen with the head chef preparing our dinner. I greet the staff quickly, especially Sally, knowing she can't talk while she's hard at work. The food smells amazing already and I can't wait to see what they have come up with for tonight's dinner.

Mrs. Blossom beckons me with her head to leave the kitchen. "Miss, let's get you into your room and I'll bring up your drinks and muffin." I notice she's acting very formal towards me and she knows how uncomfortable I am with formalities, so something strange is happening right now. I just can't quite put my finger on it.

When I get up to my room, I open the door to a rack of clothing, all dresses in colour co-ordination on a rail with matching shoes and purses. It seems as though tonight's dinner is important; I just don't know why father has never mentioned anything.

I exhale sharply, my brows furrowed. "Is something wrong Mrs. Blossom?"

She looks puzzled and conflicted as she stares at me. "No Miss, but I must warn you, your father is..." she starts, but we're interrupted by a harsh knock on the door.

Mrs. Blossom's face goes pale before answering the door, and my father is standing on the other side, his hands tucked into the pockets of his slacks. The redness of his eye's glows under the dim light, and his frown prominent with the wrinkles in his skin. His lips are pressed firmly together before he goes to speak.

"Mrs. Blossom, some privacy please," he says, anger radiating through his tone. My heartbeat races, sending blood to my face and making me feel overly hot and anxious. I try a smile. "Father, how are you?'"

My father stalks closer to me, his hands pulling out of his pockets as he gives me the glare of death. Confusion plays in my mind whilst my face stays placid. I don't want to show any fear because I know he will enjoy that.

"Father? What's going on..." I try and ask but before I know it, his back hand connects with my face, the force so powerful it sends me to the floor, a scream escaping my lips.

Tears flood my face, burning my red-hot cheek as they stream down. I try not to make another sound. Bringing my hand up to rub the side of my face, my fingertips wipe away the tears. But, as I check my hand, I find blood. My nose is bleeding from the force of the blow, clearly still sensitive from only healing a few weeks ago. I taste the coppery essence of my blood as it pours down my lips, staining my white blouse, but I don't try to clean it up. No, I stare into the dangerous eyes of my father, the abuser.

He looms over me, baring his teeth before he speaks. "What the fuck have you done to yourself? he starts, stalking closer towards me. "I never gave you permission to change your looks, and now you look like a whore!" he shouts.

I'm still laying on the floor, leaning on my forearm as my hair falls around my face, my eyes glassy as they stare at the monster before me. I have no words. My chest tightens from holding the cry that threatens to burst out, but I can't give him the satisfaction.

I know my father was an abusive man before, my mother

warned me once about him. She told me how dangerous he was, but I never listened. I just wanted to know my father.

"Get yourself cleaned up and ready. You need to look presentable as we have guests arriving shortly" he says with a calm demeanor, walking out of my room without another glance.

Shortly after he leaves, Mrs. Blossom comes running in, assisting me off of the floor, and takes me to the bathroom to get cleaned up.

She takes out a first aid kit from above the bathroom cabinet while I take a seat on the closed toilet seat, my body trembling with adrenaline and fear. I can't hold onto the cry anymore. I let it all out, spreading the blood and tears around my face and staining my blouse even further. Mrs. Blossom gives me a hot towel to put over my nose and runs me a bubble bath so that I can get in and relax but my body doesn't want to move.

"It's okay dear, please don't cry," she says, wiping away the blood and tears from my face and helping me get undressed before guiding me into the bath. The cry from my chest doesn't stop for a while and I break down, resting my face on my bent knees, wondering why the fuck I deserve all this pain and deceit from everyone around me.

I don't know what to do anymore

Chapter Eighteen

I'm sitting on the edge of my bed in a silk robe, staring at the rack of gorgeous dresses that I'm supposed to choose from to wear for tonight's dinner party. My body is still traumatized from earlier and it doesn't want to move. I lean over my bed, grabbing my phone from the nightstand and connect it to the speakers so that I can play some music.

I put on 'The Dope Show' by Marilyn Manson, matching my mood. I feel anesthetized, as if someone shut off my emotions by pressing a button. I really have to put on a show tonight, wear a mask of elegance, glamour, and the least of my favorites — a fake smile. Standing up, I walk over to my dressing table and stare at the bruise my father put on the left side of my face. I touch the purply, black blotched skin, immune to the pain now. I stare into my own eyes in the mirror and I can see the sadness there.

Be brave Ade.

Painting on my make-up, once again covering bruises on my face, my nose swollen again from the blast and my eyes puffy from all the crying. I cake on foundation and concealer, putting on some rouge and a little eyeliner to hide the puffy look. I add some red lipstick, the colour of blood, because it suits me. I'm so used to seeing blood on my face, I like how the colour compliments my skin. There's nothing better than wearing blood red. Mrs. Blossom fixes my hair into a chignon, hiding all the highlighted ends, my hair looking plain again.

I practice my smile in the mirror, getting used to the stinging feeling of moving my cheeks. I wince a few times before it becomes bearable and I look as though nothing has happened.

I look like a robot.

"Miss, we should get you changed. Guests are already here in the ballroom," Mrs. Blossom says, coming behind me and placing her lovingly soft hands on my shoulders. I can see how bad she feels that she couldn't help me. Now I know why everyone was acting so formal towards me. What I don't understand is who told my father dearest, because no matter what I do, it gets to him.

Is he spying on me…?

I stand up from my dressing stool, shedding the silk robe to the floor. I'm already dressed in a nude coloured corset, pushing up my breasts and holding in my waist. I'm even wearing nude coloured stockings which are connected by suspenders, and I must say, I look hot. I have never, ever thought in my life that I would have to dress like this all the time under my dresses, but according to Ms. Veronica, it helps with posture and makes you feel more 'lady like'. Peering through the dresses on the rail, the colour of the rainbow before me, I decide to choose a dress that matches my soul.

The black one.

Backless with a halter neck, beaded bodice, and puffy skirt. The underlayer is blood red, matching my lipstick and adding the glamorous factor. I look like a gothic ballerina. Mrs. Blossom pulls out a pair of Louboutin's and they are picture perfect. I smile at her, which she returns, knowing exactly what I'm up to. I am making a statement. The shoes match my whole outfit, the red and black ombre matching my dress and make-up down to a T.

I'm escorted down the grand stairs by Mrs. Blossom and toward the double wooden doors that lead into the ballroom. A waiter stands at the doors, next to a table filled with crystal glasses of champagne, and he hands me a glass. He goes to open the door, but

I shake my head, not feeling ready just yet. I down the glass of champagne, giving myself some dutch courage. The waiter eyes me in surprise, but a smirk covering his face.

Grabbing another champagne glass, I nod my head to the guy, which he obeys and opens the double doors.

Oh boy. The ballroom is heaving with bodies in expensive, elegant dresses and sharp suits. To think, my father told me it was only a dinner party. Yeah, right.

Taking a deep breath, I glide into the ballroom, remembering how perfect the room was when I first saw it. The crystal chandeliers brighten up the white space, and I look towards the dais, noticing a violinist and a pianist playing classical music, adding to the ambiance. People are dancing hand in hand. It looks glamorous. My father has pulled out all the stops for this soiree. Gulping down the champagne already in my hands, I place the empty glass back on the passing tray as I grab another one. I should really slow my drinking but when you're as pissed off as I am, you can't help but drink your sorrows.

"Adelaide!"

My name gets called out by the host himself, beckoning me to join him as he talks to a group of men. I obey and saunter over, trying really hard not to roll my eyes but it doesn't work. Plastering a smile on my face, I put on my obedient mask, acting as the perfect daughter, like a robot, as expected. My father places his hand on my shoulder, causing me to flinch, squeezing his fingers really hard into my flesh as a warning to behave.

My gaze falls to the gleaming marble floors as my father introduces me to the circle of men, hoping they haven't noticed me flinch from when my father touched me. But if these men are anything like my father, they would enjoy it too.

"Adelaide, this is Zach," my father says through gritted teeth, and I lift my gaze from the floor to the gentleman standing in front of me. I start at his shiny black dress shoes, working my way up, taking in his broad frame, and how tight the suit is around his body until I finally meet his sapphire blue gaze.

Zach from the beach.

My breath hitches, and my eyes go wide in surprise. The words do not form, and I panic as my chest tightens. Does my father know I have met this man, or even worse, does he know about our hot kiss the other night to piss Charles off? Swallowing the knot in my throat, I hold out my hand, intending to shake his hand and introduce myself.

Zach knows who I am, he recognized me straight away. He smirks, his beautiful eyes gleaming from the crystal chandelier lights above us.

"It's a pleasure to meet you Adelaide."

He grabs my hand in a firm handshake, and I exhale sharply. The group carries on their conversation as I stand there with my father, my gaze still on Zach, the Thor look alike. His hair is tied in a bun at the back of his head, making him look so handsome my knickers could melt. As I'm looking into his beautiful blue eyes, he tries to gesture for me to go somewhere away from these boring fucks and I so goddamn want to.

I smile at the group, "Will you excuse me father, I need some fresh air," I excuse myself and my father nods. Walking through the French doors, the crisp winter air cools off my heated skin. I walk over to the ledge, placing my palms on the ice-cold stone, focusing on my breathing as I wait for Zach.

"Well, you could say that I'm awfully surprised," a hard voice sounds from behind me, sending shivers down my spine. The memory of Zach when he grabbed my face and kissed me plays through my mind. Like a god taking ownership of his possession and it was hot. The Viking king laying his claim. Well, I wish he were.

Spinning on my heel, I come face to face with Zach, who's standing behind me with his arms crossed behind his back. He looks as handsome as I remember, but this time a posh boy, in an expensive suit like the rest of them. And he had the audacity to ask me if I was 'one of them' when he questioned me about Charles? I raise my dark eyebrow at him in defiance, smirking at the handsomeness before me.

"Oh really, shouldn't I be the one who's surprised? Considering you said you hate stuck up snobs?"

I can't help but melt around him, the way he made me feel before creating a pool of desire within my core. Zach's head rolls back in laughter, the sultry growl coming from his chest turning me on even more. My breath quickens, still unsure of what to make of this encounter and my skin goes all prickly from the crisp air.

"Okay, you got me. I hate posh snobs, but unfortunately my parents are one of them and I had to be here tonight," he says, stalking towards me and joining me against the stone wall, the only sound is the water trickling in the fountain before us.

Zach sighs, his shoulders going slump. "Don't worry. I know why you couldn't tell me your real name. Your father is a very … unique man, and I know he ordered you not to tell anyone," he admits, not looking at me but at the fountain, the water glowing from the coloured lights in the statue, creating a beautiful display.

So, he knows all about me, then. But did he know about me when we met?

"And no, I didn't know who you were when I met you, I only just put two and two together." He turns around to face me, grinning with that sinister smile of his.

I scoff, rolling my eyes. "You read my mind."

The dick.

We stand there in pure silence, listening to the sound of crickets and the water fountain. Zach's shoulder brushes against mine, making my whole-body tremble with just the slightest touch. The thought of his big Viking hands touching my soft tanned skin crosses my mind. The way his searing hot kiss took control over my whole mind and body, the neediness in my kiss, longing for more than just his mouth.

Shaking off the thought, I bring myself back to the moment and Zach's side eyeing me with a wry grin, clearly aware of the effect he has on me. I take in a deep breath and turn on my heels, ready to head back inside, otherwise father will be looking for me. As I go to leave, Zach grabs my wrist, his fingers digging into my tender skin. I look down at his hand clenched on my wrist, and his suit has ridden up to reveal a tattoo.

The exact same tattoo as the Royals.

My eyes go wide, as I tear my wrist away from Zach, turning to face him as he inserts his hands into his slacks pockets, his gaze now shifted to the floor. How have I not noticed the tattoo before?

"Why have you got the same tattoo as Charles and his friends?" I whisper, my body shaking. Is he in on all this? Does he know how much they torment me?

Maybe this is a game to him, to woo me and then break my heart. Zach's gaze lifts from the floor, staring directly in my eyes. The lights from the ballroom dance in the sapphire of his eyes but the longer he stares at me, the blacker they become.

He's just another demon in disguise.

Zach clenches his jaw, shifting his weight from one foot to the other, clearly uncomfortable with the situation. I stand before him, my chin up in defiance, and I can't help but clench my fists to the point my nails cut the palms of my hands. I can feel the blood spread between the wrinkles. Zach sighs, his right-hand scrubbing over his stubbly jaw.

"There's a lot you don't know Ade...I," he starts to say, stalking closer to me, but I take a step back, not wanting to get close to him right now. As soon as I do, I lose all my senses.

"What is the tattoo about Zach? Why have you all got one?" I question, my voice coming out in shaky breaths.

"It's a stupid tradition that's been around for hundreds of years, created by Lord Darlington himself," he says, and my nose crinkles at the stupid sounding ritual. Of course, there's something traditional about it.

"They call us the Darlington Knights," he adds, and I can't but help let out an exaggerated laugh. He must be joking.

"Seriously? The Darlington Knights? What are you, some kind of secret society or something?" I joke, still unable to contain my laughter at this stupidity. "That's usually something they do in films," I add, and I can see by Zach's face that I'm getting under his skin. Good, I hope I piss him off.

"I know you think it's stupid Ade, but we cannot talk about it here. I will explain everything, when I am able to," Zach says, gritting his teeth, aggravation clear on his face so I decide not to push further. His face shifts from annoyance to almost one of fright.

I turn around to see where his gaze has wandered off to and find that he's staring at both of our fathers, who are standing by the French doors. Both with vicious smiles on their hard, rough faces. They almost look inhumane.

~

*M*y father parades me around the room, greeting everyone that attended this evening. I can't remember when the exhaustion hit me first. Once I have done my rounds and drunk tons of champagne, I say goodnight to my father and make my way to my room, only waiting until I get into the hallway to take off my shoes and walk barefoot to my room. They may be the most beautiful shoes I have ever seen, but my god are they uncomfortable. I unzip my dress in the bathroom, letting it pool around my legs. Washing my face, I'm careful not to scrub too hard at my tender skin. The bruises start to make their appearance, reminding me of the altercation with my father earlier.

At least the alcohol numbed the pain for the whole evening.

Staring at myself in the mirror, I'm surrounded by vanity lights and I am surprised no one noticed my swollen nose. I'm starting to feel sorry for my face, the amount of battering it has received, it hasn't even had time to heal. I wouldn't be surprised if I permanently looked like this from now. A slight knocking sound comes from my bedroom door, and I'm really hoping it's my hot chocolate. It must be one of the servants, because Mrs. Blossom never knocks.

"Come in!" I shout from my bathroom, hoping they will just leave the hot chocolate on my bed side table and leave. What I wasn't expecting was to see Zach leaning in the bathroom doorway, holding my hot chocolate.

"What are you doing in here?" I ask, through the mirror I'm shocked to see the handsome Viking leaning against the door frame, his hair now taken out of his man bun. It's unruly, falling gracefully around his face. He's holding my mug in one hand and the other is in his slacks pocket, a few buttons undone showing his toned chest. The black tie is now untied and hangs around his neck. And here I am, standing in front of this godly man, only wearing my corset, suspenders, and stockings.

I don't know how to feel about this situation, but my heart is racing, the rise and fall of my chest prominent. Zach ambles towards me, his eyes taking in my lack of clothing. He places the mug on the counter beside the wash basin, my back pressed against his hard body. Both hands now free, he places them around my shoulders, and I flinch. The slightest touch from his fingers brings my nerve endings alive, his fingertips trailing down my arm, leaving a burning sensation behind.

It takes me a while to register that he's touching me sensually and that he's not here to hurt me. I wouldn't be surprised if he wanted to punish me for aggravating him earlier, but in a weird way, I would love it. My eyes close of their own accord, my head falling back onto his shoulder as he brings his lips to my ear. His nose nuzzles my neck, scraping my hair to one side.

"Who did this to you?" he murmurs, the rough growl in his voice turning me on even further. My mouth parts, taking in a deep breath as I open my eyes. I stare back at Zach through the mirror, and his fingers now grip my chin as he inspects the bruising.

My body immediately wants to shut down, forgetting how horrendous I look right now. I'm watching both of our reflections in the mirror as Zach waits for my answer, but I shake my head, not wanting to express that my monster of a father did this to me. My cheeks flush red with embarrassment, and I tug myself away from Zach, already missing how he feels against me. But I don't need this right now.

I'm supposed to be with Miles, and I for one am not a cheater.

"You have to leave. I really need to get to bed," I tell him, hiding myself in my closet to get undressed and prevent any further conversation. But also, to stop the inevitable from happening. The sexual attraction is clearly there, and I know if he stayed longer, I would get lost in those sapphire eyes and forget the consequences.

He reeks of temptation and I want to commit the sin.

Wrapping up in my silk night gown, I hear the slight click of the door closing behind Zach as he leaves. I quickly rush to the bathroom and pick up my hot chocolate from the side, taking a sip of the sweet nectar that will help me sleep tonight. Although I doubt I'll be sleeping much. Zach has just imprinted himself onto my mind.

I tuck myself into bed, even though my intention was not to stay here. It's too late to ask Steve to take me back to the academy now. He will have to take me early in the morning. I text Blaire to let her know I won't be back tonight, and not to worry about me. Even though I'm tired, I can't sleep so I turn on the television, watching a film on Netflix and hoping that sleep will take over me soon. As I get comfortable under the duvet, my phone pings with a text and I pick it up immediately, thinking that Blaire has responded to my text, but its Zach.

I just wanted to let you know how beautiful you looked tonight. Zach x

A smile crosses my face, and I text him a thank you before setting my phone back on the nightstand. I put on a romantic cheesy film, feeling giddy after my encounter with Zach, and nothing beats a good rom-com. Before I know it, my eyes have closed, sleep taking over, but my dreams are haunted. Haunted by the Royals, my father and Zach. The tattoo takes over my sinister dreams, and the feeling that they are out to get me preoccupies my mind.

Chapter Nineteen

After a few slow, painful weeks have passed, and I have been preoccupied with exams, dancing and working at the club. I haven't been back to my father's house since the dinner party and ever since that day, I have been anxious to hear from him.

Miles has noticed that whenever he goes to touch me, I flinch, frightened that I might be hurt again. My mind has been plagued by Zach's confession over the 'Darlington Knights', but I haven't tried to press any further, worried I might push him away. I am sure Zach will tell me in his own time.

I'm sitting at my usual table in the library, waiting on Hugo for our tutoring session this afternoon, but my mind keeps wondering off to my safe place. I picture that I'm back home in South Africa, on the beach surfing with my mum, staring at the brassy African sunset while enjoying life in general. Doodling on my notepad, I haven't realized that Hugo has sat down in front me, organising his stationery and books as per usual.

Fingers snap in front of my face and I jolt from my seat, snapping out of my daze.

"Hello, Earth to Africa."

"Sorry."

Hugo frowns, cocking his head to one side in confusion. I look at him through my absent eyes, my chin resting in the palm of my hand, waiting for him to scold me about something today like he usually does. "You always look so fucking depressed," he says, stating the fucking obvious.

I look back at him through narrowed eyes, the corner of my lip twitching at his comment but I don't respond. I sit there in silence.

Hugo shakes his head before handing me a completed assignment from Business Ethics. Wow, I got another A. Father will be pleased. "Wow, something is definitely wrong, because you're not even squealing about your good grade," Hugo mutters, but once again I do not give him the satisfaction. I almost forget that he's one of the boys who drowned me, he was there when my face was smashed into a table. But then he was kind of pleasant to be around at the concert, looking after me for a while. In my head, there is a hidden agenda somewhere and I need to find out what it is.

Do I ask him about the tattoo and tell him I know what it means?

"Who do we have here then?" a voice shouts from behind me, and hands are placed on my shoulders tightly, making me cringe. I wince without meaning to, even though I'm not in pain, I'm just waiting for it. No, expecting pain to be inflicted. Hugo notices the terror in my eyes and stares at me, then back at his friend Charles.

Charles finally takes his hands off of my shoulders and slides into the seat next me. It's then that I realize he's not on his own as Royce takes the seat next to Hugo. I keep my head down as they begin a conversation, blocking out their voices, not wanting to hear about them fucking other girls or whatever else they get up to. I feel Royce's stare burning into me, so when I look up, I confirm my suspicions. His sea green eyes haven't left me and suddenly I feel even more uncomfortable. Charles' knee slightly grazes my bare leg and I quickly try to move it. I even shift my chair slightly, hopefully going unnoticed, but Royce has been watching every movement since he's arrived.

Why the fuck are they here right now?

"Have you done something to her?" Royce says, now looking at Charles, his top lip curling into a snarl as he lifts his chin.

Charles looks offended, and he leans in closer to Royce with narrowed eyes, an expression that screams insulted.

"What the fuck are you on about Royce?" Charles says through gritted teeth. Hugo looks at me and then back to his friends, shrugging his shoulders, clearly bored with what's going on.

Even I'm confused, although I don't look up from the assignment Hugo gave me. But I can't concentrate, not with them both here as well.

Royce's light brown eyebrows furrow in confusion.

"The girl flinches whenever you move, you literally speak, and she cringes."

Looking up at him, I see a worried expression. I have no idea why he's so worried about me when all he's done is fuck me over. All four of them have ruined my chance of happiness at the academy and honestly, I can't see them doing anything worse than what they have. They don't feel any kind of remorse or empathy to people, let alone to me.

Charles clicks his tongue, and sighs.

"I haven't touched the fucking girl, I wouldn't go near her gross fucking body," he says, turning to face me with disgust in his expression. "No offense Africa. I just don't want to catch aids."

I sigh, packing my laptop and assignments in my satchel and throwing my completed worksheet in Hugo's direction before leaving.

I storm out of the library and down the hall. Once I'm out of sight from prying eyes, I lean against a brick wall, my body trembling as the tears fall down my red cheeks. Why the fuck am I so sensitive right now? Usually, I wouldn't care, but life has been so hard lately and all I want to do is scream and cry at everything.

Wiping the tears from my cheeks with my blazer sleeve, I try to pull myself together again before heading to dance practice with Miles. Our dance recital is in two weeks, just before the Christmas break.

I walk into the studio, and Miles is already sitting on the wooden bench waiting for me. He lifts his gaze from his phone screen to look at me and he can tell that I have been crying. He stands up, putting his phone in his sweats pocket, and snakes his arms around me in a hug. I let out a big sigh and relax into him. I feel so much safer and relieved to be in Miles' arms, knowing no one can hurt me here and that he would protect me.

Miles has been so patient with me recently, knowing that I want to take my time before having sex. We're taking the relationship slow and he has respected my boundaries. There's been a few times where we came close, in my dorm room after a great make-out session, but thankfully nothing has gone past kissing.

I can't help but feel bad for the guy, seeing a girl who is frigid as fuck.

He kisses my forehead then looks down at me. "Are you okay?"

I offer him a sweet smile and a nod, assuring him everything is ok. For now.

Soon after, I undress from my academy uniform so that I'm left with just wearing my black leotard and put on some ballet shoes this time, otherwise I will be breaking my toes and we really can't afford for something to go wrong. Our grades depend on it. We start our routine by ballet dancing to 'Swan Lake', I'm standing in fourth position with Miles behind me, holding onto my hand that's in front of my chest. As the music continues, he spins me round until I'm in a 'releve' position and then a 'pirouette'. When the music transitions to classic rock we change our routine and add modern dance. We practice the same routine another three times before taking a seat and drinking some water to quench our thirst.

"We're definitely ready," Miles says, smiling softly at me. I'm wiping my face and chest with a towel to try to get rid of the sweat, but my mind isn't with it.

The comment Charles said is playing in my mind like a broken record and I'm starting to believe him. I must be disgusting. Why would anyone come near me? I'm surprised Miles is still here. I suppose as my dance partner, he can't really break up with me until the recital is over.

I offer Miles a weak smile, picking up my gym bag and walking to the door.

"Yeah, we're definitely ready."

It's seven in the evening already and everyone has gone down to the dining hall for dinner, but hunger doesn't even cross my mind. I've fallen into my old habits and I haven't eaten a decent meal in a while. I'm losing the muscle around my bones again and my ribs are showing through my skin.

I'm punishing myself for not being perfect or wanted, and I relish in the pain. I really am a sadistic fuck, I suppose.

Blaire enters our dorm room later with a little take out box in her hand. She walks over and sits herself down next to me on the floor. "Here I got you some food, you need to eat something," she says, handing me the takeout.

I take it from her and open it to see that she brought back some chicken and mushroom cream pasta. How could I refuse eating with Blaire staring at me with those puppy eyes?

I eat my dinner, well, half of it anyway, but my stomach is not used to all this food. Blaire has passed out in bed while I've just completed all my assignments. It's past midnight, and sleep doesn't take over anytime soon, so I get changed into a pair of yoga pants and hoodie, deciding to go for a walk around the campus. The eerie, haunted hallways of Darlington Castle are terrifying at night, the sound of the wind whistles through the crooks of the stone walls, making my body jump and shiver. The bright light of the moon illuminates the paths and reflects off of the shiny metal in the knight's armor.

As I walk around the halls, my feet end up taking me near the dance studio, where I find an orange glow. My heart is beating fast, warning me not to go any further but my nosy mind is telling me to go for it. I obviously follow the voice in my head and walk towards the light. It's coming from the tunnel, the door wide open and all the candles are lit on either side of the stone walls. Someone is down here. What do I do? Obviously go through the tunnel and follow the candles. I am curious as to who or why they would be using the tunnel and what I could possibly find out about the other doors.

The route I took last time is the exact same route this time, but I am still not able to get through the other two doors. They're clearly not in there. I bet they're at the club, and if I follow the path further, I will find out why this leads to the club. I manage to sneak through the metal door into the basement of the club. I had already ensured that no boxes or kegs were placed in front of the door. This is exactly why I offered to help arrange the basement or stock room, whatever they actually call this room.

I climb up the metal stairs as discreet as I can, careful not to make a sound in case Samantha comes around the corner. Lucky for me no one is around the back. I can hear the thump of the music blaring through the wooden doors that leads to the club. I am seriously praying to god right now that no one is standing on the other side of the door as I open it a fraction, just enough for me to peak through and see that no one is standing here.

Thank god.

Opening the door wider, I find the club crowded with men in expensive, sharp black suits. My eyes go wide, looking around the room. All the Royals are sitting around a table with a half-naked lady serving them their drinks. The waitresses wear nothing but red lace thongs, a matching lace bra and six-inch heels, but just as the performers, they're all wearing masks to hide their identity.

I peek in further to see a woman stripping off her clothing, dancing around a pole on the stage. It's unlike the performances we usually put on. This is a gentlemen's club and the bile rises in my throat from disgust. My heart pumps blood around my veins at full speed as I stare at the naked girls dancing on the men's laps around the room.

I wonder why Samantha hasn't mentioned this side of the business, or why she never asked me to work a shift here. I have a feeling it would involve no clothing and allowing men to grope my ass as I walk past, so no, thank you.

My eyes scan the room and I find Zach talking to a bunch of guys I've never seen before. He's laughing along with his friend, a whiskey in his right hand while his other hand rubs his thumb across his lower lip. God, that is a sexy look.

I turn my gaze back to the Royals' table but they're not there, and I can't see them anywhere else in the room.

Where have they gone?

"You shouldn't be here Africa," someone whispers behind me. I jump, quickly turning around as my heart beats out of my chest. I take a big gulp and find Hugo and the rest of the Royals standing directly behind me. They must have caught me staring from the corner and snuck around through the other door to get behind me.

Oh shit, I'm in so much trouble.

I see the four faces of Charles, Hugo, Royce and Blake glaring down at me with looks of menace. The hairs on the back of my neck stand up as I feel the presence of another body behind me, but I don't need to turn to see who it is.

"Ade, what are you doing here?" Zach hisses, clearly not a fan of me right now either. Or maybe it's the fact that I have just found out about their little meeting spot. This must be where the 'Darlington Knights' come out to play.

Hugo grabs my wrist, pulling me at such force and dragging me down to the basement. I don't say a word to them, knowing how much more trouble I'm in.

I think this is the first time any of the Royals haven't really said much either, all five pairs of eyes are on me as I stand against the wooden door that leads to the tunnels. My eyes don't leave Hugo as he stands directly in front of me, both hands in his pockets as he scans my body. His jaw is clenched, veins pulsing by his temple. He's clearly holding onto some anger but all I can think about is how fucking magnificent he looks in a suit. What's wrong with me?

All of them look irresistible in their black suits, even Blake. The way he leans against a wooden barrel, staring at the ground because I know he can't face me. The only time Blake looks at me is when he's being hostile and threatening. Zach smiles, stepping closer so that he's standing next to Hugo.

"I'm glad to see your face has healed, Ade," he says, breaking the silence.

"What do you mean her face has healed?" Hugo asks, cocking his head to Zach, clearly confused as to what's going on. Hugo's lips twitch, a frown which is permanently on his face, as he waits for Zach to answer.

I shake my head at Zach, begging for him not to out my secret. He scrubs his large hand over his lips before speaking. "She um, hit her face when surfing," he lies, and my eyes bulge out of their sockets, heat radiating from my skin with fear.

It will do. I'm just glad he didn't say anything about my father.

Blake finally looks up at me, a scowl etched onto his face. "Good. She fucking deserves it," he spits, ocean blue eyes turning dark, as if a demon has possessed his body. But I know for a fact it's just him and not a demon. He means every word he says, and I wouldn't be surprised if he would hit a girl. Fucking scumbag.

"Thanks Blake, you're so fucking charming," I hiss, rolling my eyes. I'm used to his little outbursts, but that is the cherry on top. His lips turn into a cruel smirk, showing me just how inhumane he really is.

"What are you doing down here Africa? Because you're in so much shit right now," Hugo adds to my disappointment, but it's expected. His hand rubs along the stubble on his chin, the atrocious glint in his eyes doesn't falter. I know he's holding it all in.

I wonder what would happen if he snapped.

Cocking my hip out, I cross my arms in front of my chest, trying not to show any fear because the four Royals can smell fear from a mile off. The scent of terror piques their interest and they torment you, make you fall and then they pounce to break you.

But not tonight, I'm putting my foot down.

Zach steps forward, giving Hugo a disappointed look. "What he means is, if anyone else found you, you would be in a lot more trouble."

I know he's a good guy, but who's to say he wouldn't hurt me like the rest of these cunts. I lean my back against the cold wooden door, noticing Royce and Charles haven't said a word to me yet. Charles is leaning against the metal staircase with no care in the world. A haughty expression doesn't leave his perfect, pale face throughout the whole of this confrontation. Royce on the other hand still looks sad and empty, and I haven't spoken to him properly since the Royals think they outed me as a murderer. He's a fucking prick and I hope he burns in hell.

"What? Is this your little secret society meeting of the Darlington Knights?" I tease, laughing at how serious these dicks are right now, but my humor doesn't last long. I'm pushed against the wooden door by my throat. Hugo's strong fingers grip my neck so tight I can't breathe, and I know that his fingers will leave a mark but I'm not afraid right now. I'm finding his carnal behavior erotic and my body comes alive like a spark has just been lit.

Hugo's eyes are dilated, baring his teeth as he's finally letting out the anger, the vein in his neck pulsing and I have the urge to kiss it. I want to tame the beast in front of me, express just how much his anger turns me on but with the rest of the dicks in here it's probably not a good idea. He lets go of my neck and finally I am able to breathe, and I let out a raspy cough, stroking my neck, already missing how Hugo feels against me.

God, what the fuck is wrong with me?

"I'm sorry, did I hit a nerve?" I retort, my voice croaky and harsh but fuck them.

What's interesting is how the dynamics have changed this evening, usually it's Blake who does the confrontation and threats at the academy, but tonight it's Hugo. He did say he was the most dangerous one, and I'm starting to think he's the real leader of this group, but at the academy he keeps it in check. Blake is just his puppet and Hugo pulls the strings on all of them. How interesting.

"What did you guys expect? I work here you idiots; did you really not think I'd find out?" I snap, and confusion is evident on all their faces apart from Royce, which means he didn't tell them. That's another interesting factor.

"You work here? Since when?" Charles now speaks from his little corner. He lets out a gruff laugh, shaking his head.

"A while. I'm surprised Royce hasn't told you since he knew already," I tell them. Now I'm the one with the arrogant expression as the group look between themselves and then to Royce.

Payback is a bitch, isn't it? Royce shifts from one foot to the other, scrubbing a hand across his face as he lets out a deep breath.

"I'll walk Africa back to the dorms, you guys can bring the cars around," Hugo orders. Look at that. They all file out of the room to follow his orders.

"Well, I didn't realize it was really you who is in charge," I say as condescendingly as I can. So, he's the reason for the other altercations. For me drowning, being smashed against a table, and worst of all, showing me a picture of my mums' dead body in front of the whole academy. He is the true devil in disguise, ordering his little demons around, but he's also the one who looked after me and has been the least confrontational. My perception of people is clearly really off.

Hugo chuckles, "I am always in control, and you wouldn't want to be controlled by me Africa. You wouldn't last a day," he whispers, the rough sound of his voice traveling along my skin, causing goosebumps to appear.

Heat pools between my thighs whenever he opens his mouth and those emerald green eyes are hypnotizing. I should hate him, I need to loathe him, but my body wants something else and I know for a fact that's impossible.

Hugo would never go near a little foreign, skinny, disgusting bitch like me.

We walk through the tunnels, Hugo following from behind to make sure I make it back to the academy. The hallways are silent, with just the noise of the wind and the moon glistening bright, illuminating my way back to my dorm room. I put my key into the door, and as I twist it Hugo spins me around so that my back is against the wall. What is it with this guy and constantly pushing me against a wall? I mean, I'm not opposed to the gesture, but still?

He lifts his left arm, placing the palm on the side of my head, caging me in. His body towers over mine, and he has to lean down to whisper to me. "If you breathe a word of tonight to anyone…" he starts, just as I was expecting. "You will wish you never left your bed tonight." His raspy voice kisses my exposed neck and my toes curl in my trainers, waiting for his threat. "And don't think tonight's little stunt won't go unpunished," he hisses, taking a step back from me, placing his hands in his slack pockets.

The moonlight highlights the blue tinge in his hair, two paralyzing eyes staring at me with ominous horror. The light emphasizes the structure of his cheekbones, creating a shadow which resembles demon-like features. He notices the rise and fall of my chest as I'm breathing so heavily, biting my lower lip involuntary, and I nod my head to obey his demand.

Probably not a good idea to go against his wishes, otherwise I will feel his wrath.

Chapter Twenty

$\mathcal{I}$ try to keep my head down for the next few days, not wanting to catch the attention of the Royals, but I have a feeling my 'punishment' is due any time soon. My anxiety is at the highest it's ever been, and I'm constantly looking over my shoulder.

Zach has texted me a few times to make sure I'm okay, warning me to stay out of the Royals' way but I haven't responded. I don't want to talk to that prick right now. He will have to do a lot more than just text to get my forgiveness. I want him to grovel, on his knees.

Doodling in my notepad again, my mind wonders somewhere else as I'm sitting in Business ethics class with Blake shaking the table by constantly bouncing his fucking leg. It's as if he's on drugs or some shit and he's having withdrawal symptoms.

"We're going to have to meet in the library at some point and work on our project," Blake mutters under his breath.

I immediately stop doodling, looking at Blake with narrowed eyes. I look around to make sure it's in fact me he's talking to and not one of his friends who happen to be behind me. I furrow my eyebrows, pointing at myself to make sure I'm not making a mistake.

"Yes, you. Who else would I be fucking talking to?" he says, back to bouncing that fucking leg of his again.

Shaking my head, I roll my eyes at him, getting back to my doodling. I am still stunned Blake spoke to me, let alone asked to meet in the library to work on our project. This could be a trick so I should be careful.

Once class is finished, I pack my bag and make my way out of the room to meet Blaire and Maisie in the dining hall. After lunch, the stags are playing a field hockey game and the whole academy is allowed the afternoon off to watch the game. I'm not too thrilled about watching Blake play sports in the cold, but it's an excuse to get out and enjoy the winter sunshine.

"Hey, we ordered for you," Maisie says, looking at me from the top of her phone screen offering me one of her sweet smiles. Blaire is typing really fast on her phone, and I'm guessing it could be the guy she was seeing. She hasn't really told me much more about him because she didn't want to jinx what could happen.

Blaire sighs, "Sorry, it's my father being a dick as per usual. Wants me and Blake to go home this weekend," she says, putting the phone down on the table. She puts both her hands on her cheeks as she frowns, but she actually looks so cute.

"Why, what's the matter?" I ask.

"We have another stupid gala to attend this weekend."

These posh people and their galas, it's like they have one every weekend and they usually say it's for 'charity' but really, it's not. It's a place to show off your money and parade expensive outfits. The waiter arrives at the table, placing our dinner in front of us and my eyes widen to find a cheeseburger and fries in front of me. I haven't eaten anything this unhealthy in such a long time, and I'm really stunned as to why Maisie would order me this.

"I know you don't normally eat unhealthy, but you need to get some sort of fat on your bones. Plus, you might enjoy it." Maisie shrugs as Blaire giggles at the shocked expression on my face.

She's right, I haven't eaten something this good and juicy and deadly in such a long time, and I do need to put on weight again.

This whole up and down thing with my weight is becoming a real issue with my dancing and if I want to get a chance at performing at the club, I need to bulk up a little.

I take a bite out of the burger, and I'm in food heaven. My eyes go wide, as I glance up at the girls. The juice runs down my lips, but I don't care if I look ungraceful right now. Why the fuck have I stopped myself from enjoying such a delicacy? All three of us polish off our burgers and fries, clearly needing comfort food and we slouch back in our chairs, stuffed from the big meal. Okay, maybe I should have a cheat day once a week at least.

"That was amazing. Good call Maisie."

We let our stomachs settle for a while before picking up our bags and heading to the hockey field, where the whole school will be congregating. We walk at a snail's pace, letting the rush of people past us as we don't really care if we get a good spot or not. We just want to sit on the benches and relax. I catch Miles leaning against the brick wall outside in the courtyard, staring down at his phone.

"Hey, you okay?" I ask, catching him off guard. He quickly puts his phone back into his slack's pocket, and That was a quick reaction, wasn't it? Maybe I'm just being paranoid for no reason at all.

He smiles, his eyes squinting against the rays of sunshine in his beautiful eyes. "I was waiting for you; thought I'd come sit with you three."

The four of us walk over to the benches around the hockey field, both teams already on the field. I really wish this were more of an exciting game like Rugby, not a boring old sport with sticks. I suppose posh people don't want to injure themselves.

I stare down at the field, watching Ruby hang off of Blakes neck as she laughs. He doesn't look so amused by her presence, his gaze anywhere other than her. His eyes find mine in the crowd, a smirk playing on his lips, then he dips down to Ruby and kisses her in front of the whole academy. Claiming her in front of everyone, warning others not to go near her. For some reason, a pang of jealousy plays in my mind, making me uncomfortable.

They deserve each other.

"Look at the two love birds, I wouldn't be surprised if they announce their engagement soon," Miles says, and I spin my head to stare at him, giving myself whiplash as Blaire winces from her seat. Something is going on that I don't know about.

"It's not confirmed yet, it might not even happen," Blaire mumbles, shifting in her seat, clearly finding this situation awkward. "It's just a business deal, two families merging for more money, it's not serious," Blaire adds to my discomfort.

My heart pulls at the thought of marrying someone for a business deal and not for love. I feel sorry for Blake because you can clearly see he doesn't love her. As for her, she is drooling after him. But she doesn't love him either, it's just lust. Although I can't imagine Blake having a nice side to him so what is she falling for?

We sit and watch the game for seventy long minutes, the cold air creeping through my blazer. I should have worn a coat. Miles notices my body shivering and places his coat around my shoulders, finally giving me warmth. "Thank you," I whisper, kissing him on the cheek. Afterwards, he walks me back to the dorm as Blaire and Maisie are going off to the library to study for their art exam tomorrow. Miles takes my hand in his, and a smile forms on my lips.

Oh god, in a weird way Blake is like a brother in law if we're both dating the siblings.

I shake the thought out my mind, enjoying our little stroll. When we get back to the room, I quickly change out from my uniform and into something more comfortable.

''Shall we watch a film? Be nice to snuggle up together and relax.'' Miles suggests.

''Yeah that would be great. I actually wanted to watch step-up if you want to?'' I raise my eyebrow, and smile because it somehow feels so relatable.

''Oh yeah, that sounds awesome.'' Miles agrees from where he is already laying back on my bed, his head resting against my headboard. I load the film up ready on Netflix, and lay myself next to him on the bed, resting my head on his chest, listening to the beating of his heart. He plays with my hair the whole time we watch the film and I lean into him further, curling my arm around his waist, and a warm sensation fills my whole body, and I

As soon as the film ends, Miles flips me over on my back, his lean form hovering over me as he stares into my eyes with a cheeky smirk on his face. He leans down, kissing my lips, parting mine with his tongue. My eyes close, enjoying the feel of his lips on mine. My body shivers with heat and excitement as he deepens the kiss, sucking on my tongue. I let out a soft moan, feeling ready to finally give into the urges, especially with Miles.

I think I'm in love with him.

I break the kiss, feeling out of breath. "Hang on, let me go freshen up and then I'll be right out." Miles lays back down on his back, smirking as I scurry off to the bathroom to make sure I'm shaved, and everything is up to standard.

My heart races with nerves. I'm having to consciously breathe in and out to calm myself down, but I'm just so excited to take the next step. I rough up my hair, brush my teeth and spray on some perfume, giving myself a once over in the mirror to make sure I'm happy. There's nothing much more that I could do, and I haven't really got any nice lingerie here at the academy, so this will have to do.

As I come out of the bathroom, I see that Miles has picked up the photo album with all my mum's pictures in it.

"Hey, what's this?" Miles asks.

"It's all the photos I have left of my mum." I come and sit back down on the bed with him. Usually, I would be nervous for someone to take a look into my old life and memories. In a weird sort of way, it's like I'm introducing him to my mum.

He looks at the first picture and smiles. "You really look like your mum — absolutely beautiful." he smiles softly, as a tear threatens to escape my eye.

"Hey lovebirds," Blaire bursts in the door, throwing her satchel on her bed.

Great, my time with Miles is ruined. Tonight is clearly not the night to pop the cherry.

He smiles, putting the photo album down where he found it and kissing my lips once more. "Looks like we will have to wait a little longer," he says against my mouth.

He stands up from the bed and picks up his bag from the floor, saying our goodbyes before he leaves.

"Damn, you are one big cock block," I tell Blaire, quirking my eyebrow at her as she laughs.

"I am so sorry."

I end up having a cold shower that night.

~

Sitting in the library, I'm waiting for Blake to turn up so that we can work on our project together and at this rate I'm starting to doubt if he's going to turn up. I plug in my earphones, ignoring the world around me as I start on my half of the project when a hand yanks the plugs from my ears. Hugo.

"Seriously, you need to stop doing that," I hiss. The fucking dick is going to get punched if he does that one more time. I look up, staring at Hugo as he takes a seat in front of me. I wasn't aware that he would be joining us.

Hugo rolls his eyes, shrugging. "It's still tutoring night. Plus, Blake will be a little late. he's fucking Ruby in the supply closet."

I scrunch up my nose at the level of detail given, rolling my eyes at how forward Hugo is.

He smirks at my discomfort. "Don't get jealous Africa. I'm sure anyone is willing to take your virginity," he says.

My eye twitches as I bite the inside of my cheek, trying not to explode. "How did you know?" I demand.

Hugo leans back in his chair, the emerald beauties of his eyes staring down at me as an arrogant smirk takes over his face.

The dick.

He sits forward, resting his forearms on the table, the arrogant smirk not leaving his face. It's weird seeing his personality change from being a completely reclusive asshole to a handsome tease. My eyes narrowed, I look at Hugo, wondering what's going to come out of his mouth this time and I know, somehow, it's going to be an insult.

He lifts his right hand, rubbing the stubble on his chin, his Rolex glistening in the light as he studies me further before speaking. "I can tell, whenever I'm near you, like right now for example..." he starts, rubbing his thumb along his perfectly plump lower lip.

Subconsciously, I bite my lip, my eyes drifting to the movement. I'm suddenly breathless, the palms of my hands moisten, and as I shift in my seat, rubbing my hands along my skirt. My eyes do not leave Hugo's conceited face.

"The way you just bit your lip, your breathing has increased rapidly, and the fact that you're squeezing your thighs together to ease the ache between them," he continues, his eyelids hooded as he leans back in his chair, not breaking eye contact.

Damn that smug look on his face.

The corners of his mouth turn into a smirk, the emerald gems in his eyes sparkle from the light that shines through the stained glass and I'm breathless. I'm not even sure how to respond to that, but in a way he's not wrong.

"Well, so what if I'm a virgin?" I retort, crossing my arms over my chest, raising my eyebrow at him as Hugo chuckles under his breath.

"I can smell the desperation on you. But don't worry Africa, I don't fuck virgins, especially if they're you..."

"Sorry I'm late, dude," Blake says, breaking the tension between Hugo and me. I couldn't be more thankful for Blake's presence. I shift in my seat, still affected by Hugo's words but I couldn't care less if he didn't want to fuck me. I'm not interested.

At least I don't think I am.

"Africa, you look like shit." Blake snorts with a mocking smile.

Rolling my eyes at him, I get back to my assignment, the words from Hugo playing in my mind over and over again. We all sit at the table in silence, working on our projects. The only words spoken are when it's something to do with our work, and surprisingly Blake and I are working well together.

After a while, Charles and Royce come over to our table, interrupting our quiet working environment. Royce takes the seat directly next to me and Charles takes the other. I'm sandwiched between two dickheads, one that loathes me and the other who I used to be obsessed over, but now I couldn't care less about.

Charles grins at the whole table, enjoying the sight. "Look at this lovely little study group," he teases, and

Blake gives him a death glare, warning him to shut up.

See what I mean by dynamics? Now Blake is in charge. It makes no sense.

The boys talk between themselves, ignoring the fact that I'm sitting there, listening to every word. I discreetly plug one earphone in, hiding the wire between my hair so they don't notice. Hopefully if I don't put the music loud, they won't hear it.

I put on 'Greatness' by Don Broco and Hugo shakes his head at me. He knows, but at least he leaves me alone.

"Hey Africa, you coming to the party this weekend?" Charles asks, titling his head in my direction. I shrug my shoulders, oblivious to what party they're talking about.

"No, probably not."

Charles' smug grin doesn't falter, his brown eyes looking more hazel today. "We promise to leave you alone, I mean it's nearly Christmas after all."

I don't believe him for one second. I wouldn't trust a word any of these guys say to me. Ever.

"Aww man, would have been so much fun. It's this Saturday at Club Envy," he wiggles his eyebrows and I crinkle my nose.

Fuck, I'm working behind the bar that night. I ignore Charles, putting my head down, listening to music and continuing with my project. I haven't felt this uncomfortable in such a long time, my body is shaking from being wedged between all four Royals and my anxiety is screaming at me.

"Suit yourself," Charles sighs.

Once the two hours is up and the bell rings to signal the end of the day, I go to stand up and leave, but Hugo tuts, waving his finger at me. "We aren't finished, we haven't actually done what I wanted you to do, so sit your ass back down." I groan in response.

Damn it, I really thought I'd be getting out of it this time, but since Hugo has been tutoring me, my grades have become so much better. I sit back down, taking out my other assignments that need to be completed and the other guys snigger at the annoyance on my face.

They stay the whole time.

Chapter Twenty-One

Saturday rolls around rather quickly, and I'm at the club already setting up for the party tonight. Apparently, it's Charles' 'unofficial' birthday party with only a few people attending, some from the academy. I'm dreading the fact that I'm working tonight. The rumors and torment about me being a murderer have died down a little, I mean I still get the odd remark and my locker painted red to represent blood, but I don't let it get to me as much as I have done. Not retaliating has had its benefits.

Apparently, this evening is a black and white theme party, so Samantha has asked the bar staff to adhere to the rules. I put on my leather skintight trousers, a white Bordeaux crop top and my heeled boots. I may as well look like I'm attending a party. Lily and I hang up the lavish black and white decorations around the club, covering every corner possible and placing a bottle of Dom Perignon on every table. This party must have cost a bomb.

As I go back behind the bar to get some champagne glasses, I hear a loud whistle coming from the entrance. I look over to the red velvet curtains where the Royals walk through, all dressed in their fine, expensive suits, not adhering to the rules of black and white outfits. Charles is wearing a grey suit with a white shirt, buttons undone halfway, showing off his pale chest. His dirty blonde shaggy hair still falls over his eyes, giving the 'I don't give a fuck' attitude.

Charles' lips curl into a grin when he notices me. "Oh Africa, I knew you couldn't resist the urge to join us," he chuckles, his perfectly cheeky smile showing off his pearly whites. "You're a little early though.".

I sigh, putting on a fake smile but it falters. "I'm working," I say. I do not want to deal with their arrogance tonight. Standing behind the bar, I tap my fingers on the wooden counter, my other hand placed on my cocked hip, waiting patiently for their drinks order. "Do you want to me get you anything?"

Charles stands in front of me, placing both his forearms on the bar, clasping his hands together as the other three surround him. I glance at Royce, who stands next to Charles, a little more under-dressed than the rest, wearing a pair of dark blue suit trousers and a white button up, folded at the arms. His light brown hair is tousled, as if he didn't even bother to style it, but somehow it looks great. He stands with both hands in his trouser pockets, ignoring me, unlike the rest of the gang.

"Shots. We need shots," Charles hollers, clasping his hands around his mouth.

He's way too excited for this early in the evening.

I look at the other two, raising my eyebrow and they nod. Okay, shots it is. I get out four shot glasses and the tequila, pouring them each one, adding a slice of lime and handing over the salt. They cheers and say happy birthday to Charles, clinking the little glasses before gulping the shot in one go.

My eyes automatically drift to where Hugo is standing, perfectly dressed in his navy-blue suit that hugs him in all the right places. The way the suit strains against his biceps as he lifts his arm to take the shot is tantalizing. I'm surprised it doesn't burst open. His ebony hair is perfectly styled, and come to think of it, I have never seen a hair out of place on his head. He looks as immaculate as ever.

Blake looks devilish in his charcoal grey suit, matched with a black button up, making the oceanic blue of his eyes pop. He would be better suited if he had red eyes with two horns coming out of his skull, but he is as handsome as they come. They all are. It's hard to believe that the most fine-looking specimens are all in one academy. I suppose it helps to be rich. They can afford to look this extravagant.

"More shots Africa, and I want you to have one to," Charles smirks, shaking his empty shot glass at me.

I smile at him, shaking my head. "No, I'm okay thanks."

He flutters his long eyelashes at me, his grin growing wider. "Oh, come on. It's my birthday."

I snort a 'fine' in response and get out an extra shot glass before filling them all with tequila. The boys all chuckle as I hand them their glasses and I take mine, raising it in the air and to cheers Charles, again. I swallow the tequila, pulling the most scrunched up face as the liquid burns down my throat.

Charles yells 'woo', clearly excited.

I can tell this evening is going to be hectic.

The bass from the music starts to thump, guests arriving and all wearing their white and black outfits, looking flawless. A few people I've never seen or met before arrive, clearly not from the academy, but of course the three bitches turn up. Ruby, Constance, and Priscilla are wearing matching skintight white dresses. The hems just about cover their asses, their cleavages on display, and for some weird reason they have silver glitter painted on their faces.

God help me.

Ruby walks past the bar, giving me a pouty smile as she flips her hair over her shoulder. All three girls walk over to the VIP area joining the Royals, taking a seat on their laps.

And they call me a slut? I'm not about this slut shaming thing and I think each to their own but calling a virgin a slut and then displaying your own sluttish ways is just being a hypocrite.

All the drinks have been covered by Charles, so the guests are definitely taking advantage. Shot after shot leave the bar, everyone getting so drunk a few of them can't even stand. I scan the room, my gaze landing on the VIP area where Constance is giving Charles a lap dance.

She's rubbing her pelvis against his dick, swaying her hair all over the place and I think she's trying to be sexy, but it really isn't working. I'm staring at Constance with such distain in my expression, I don't even notice Royce has joined me at the bar.

"She's really not working it. She doesn't even know how to dance, unlike someone I know," he says, breaking my stare.

I mumble, trying to find a response but nothing comes. I purse my lips and pour myself a glass of rum and coke, taking a sip of the sweet nectar. I'm more stunned because this is the first sentence Royce has said to me in weeks. All of a sudden, it's back to where it all started, when he apologized, but then betrayed me even further.

"What do you want?" I snap at him, my eyes wide as I look into his sea green eyes. I tie my hair up in a ponytail while he stands in front of me, my neck over-heating from the heat in the club. Beads of sweat are forming in my hairline.

Royce places a hand on his heart, fluttering his eyelashes at me. I cock my head at him, forming a fake smile. I won't let him get to me this time.

He sighs, pulling a bar stool out then taking a seat. I automatically pour his whiskey with three cubes of ice and slide it in his direction.

"I see you remember my drink," he smirks, taking a sip of the golden-brown liquid, which matches the colour of his eyes as they stare at me over the rim of the glass.

The music gets louder, drum and bass thumping in the speakers and it's not even midnight. It's going to be a long night. When the music gets softer, I notice a huge five-foot cake being rolled out onto the stage, and Charles running up the stairs to go inspect it. As he steps close, a half-naked red headed woman jumps out, only wearing a white silk thong. My eyes go wide at the nudity. I wasn't aware there was a giant cake stashed somewhere, or the fact it had a naked lady hiding inside. A wooden chair gets pulled onto the stage next to the cake, the red headed bombshell forces him to take a seat, and she starts dancing on his lap, rubbing her tits in his face.

I don't think I have ever seen Charles so happy in his life. A beautiful naked lady and Constance have both rubbed their pussies against his muscular body tonight. Blake and Hugo stand in front of the stage, cheering him on and laughing like I've never seen before.

I wish they were always this happy.

I raise an eyebrow at Royce, who isn't paying attention to what's going on. Instead he's downing his drink, looking depressed.

"Why aren't you up there enjoying the naked lady?" I ask.

He places the empty tumbler on a coaster, twirling the glass around as he stares at it absently. "Not into that."

I grab the whiskey from the shelf, filling up his glass to the rim. Clearly, he needs it. I grab another glass and pour myself a tipple, downing the brown liquid.

Royce smiles at me as I pull another vulgar face, not used to drinking spirits straight. Then he stands up, lifting his glass to me to say thanks and walks over to their VIP table, Priscilla pouncing on him straight away, licking the shell of his ear as he sits down.

What the fuck is going on right now?

A few hours pass, and the party is still in full swing, and people are drunk as skunks. The bottles of champagne are being downed by the bottle rather than using the glasses provided, waitresses replacing them each time. I dread to think how much this has cost him.

Walking around, I look for empty glasses to take back and get cleaned. Sweaty bodies dance around every open space available, the guests popping pills and snorting cocaine off of the tables, some of the girls doing body shots. Soon after, the Royals and the other guests pop open the champagne bottles, covering the top with their thumbs, shaking the fizzy liquid before spraying Charles.

It's showering Dom Perignon, and all the guests, including me, are soaked through. Charles is the worst, standing on the table as someone sprays the golden liquid into his mouth, his tongue sticking out to catch every last drop, the liquid covering his face and wetting his unruly hair. The guests all wearing white are now showing visible underwear, but Ruby and her two minions are not wearing a bra, so pointed nipples are on show for everyone to see.

What a surprise there.

I'm glad I put on a stick-on bra under my crop top, otherwise mine would be on show for everyone to see as well. Rushing to the ladies' room, I check my make-up and wash the stickiness off my hands. I look at myself in the mirror, reapplying my red lipstick, Luckily, nothing else has been ruined. I wash my hands and fore-arms, trying to get the champagne off my skin. I smell like an adult's sweet shop.

As I stroll back to get behind the bar, I notice Samantha's office door slightly ajar. I open the door, expecting Samantha to be inside but instead I find Hugo sitting in the red leather armchair, licking his lips as his hand rubs the stubble on his chin. The other hand is twisted in dark purple hair, a girl on her knees is sucking his dick. I gasp, my hands shooting to cover my mouth and my eyes go wide. Hugo notices, but grins and doesn't stop.

I quickly retreat, closing the door behind me and scurry off to the bar. I grab a shot of vodka as it's the closest bottle to me and down the clear liquid. It burns down my throat, all the way to my belly, making me feel warm, even though I'm as hot as hell right now. I'm fanning my face with my hand, unable to get any cooler, and seeing Hugo with that girl has got me bubbling with jealousy. The way she made him look euphoric, a look I never thought I'd witness.

Lucky girl.

Shaking the thought and the image out of my head, I serve the other customers at the bar, keeping myself busy. I notice throughout the evening that the purple haired girl is nowhere to be seen, but Hugo has joined the others back at their table drinking the cham-pagne by the bottle. I must admit, this has been an awesome party, and I can't wait to see how much it all cost.

The time hits three in the morning and the guests have left, leaving only the Royals, me and the cleaning staff left. The club is a fucking mess and I wouldn't be surprised if it needs a deep clean.

The Royals are still sitting in the upholstered VIP booth, smoking cigars, and finishing off their drinks. Cocaine is neatly cut into lines on the table, as they each have their turn getting their high.

"Africa, how about you bring that leather ass of yours over here and join us?" Charles purrs as I walk past, holding a tray with empty glasses. I look at the four boys, all with their button ups undone halfway, their suit jackets nowhere to be seen and apart from Hugo, their hair is so disheveled it kind of suits them. Hugo's hair hasn't moved an inch.

I may need to ask him what he uses so that I can use it for when I dance.

"Sorry, but I have work to do and then I'll head back to the academy," I retort.

Charles' brows furrow as a smirk takes over his cheeky face, his pupils so dilated you can hardly see the natural colour of his eyes. "Africa, I'm paying for tonight which means I'm paying for your time so you will come here, take a seat and have a drink," he patronizes, patting the empty space next to him.

Placing the tray down on another table, I wave goodbye to the last of the staff leaving for the evening. All four pairs of eyes stare at me, waiting for me to sit. I obey, perching down next to Charles, crossing my legs, and pouring myself a glass of champagne.

Charles' arm snakes around the back of the seat behind me and he chuckles, lifting his glass to cheers with me. We clink glasses and I down my drink in one gulp, craving the buzz after tonight's eventful shift. The music is still left on for background noise, and Royce pours me another glass of nectar, which I savor this time round.

Blake licks the top of his forefinger, dipping it into the white powder on the table and sucking it off clean. I'm watching him as he does this and Charles notices. "Do you want to try some?" he whispers in my ear, sending shivers all the way down my spine.

I turn to face him, frowning. "No, I don't do drugs."

He chuckles under his breath, and I can feel the low grumble from his chest along my side as he leans in. "Honestly, it's not that bad. it won't do you any harm if you only do it for fun. It'll make you feel good," he carries on. "I dare you," he hisses now, and I can feel the venom from his voice. He licks his finger the way Blake did, dipping it into the snow-like powder, bringing it up to his lush pink lips and sucking it off as if it's sherbet.

I lick my lips, swallowing the gulp in my throat, my breath

quickening. The boys are all staring at me, all the black holes of their eyes hiding their true identity. The red lights shine on each of their faces, looking like sin and there's me, the innocent angel.

Charles does the same again, dipping his finger and thumb into the powder. He turns so he's directly facing me, the sinful grin on his face as his powder free fingers cup my chin, bringing the forefinger to my lips. I bite my lip, staring directly into the abyss of his eyes. I open my mouth, placing my red painted lips around the slender finger. I swirl my tongue around, tasting the bitter drug mixed with the taste of Charles. As soon as he withdraws the finger, he pushes his thumb into my mouth, the other fingers stroking my soft face.

My eyes don't leave his, the rise and fall of his chest prominent through his white, wet shirt. I look around to the other guys, who are staring at me sucking Charles' thumb. Royce and Blake have haughty expressions, but Hugo is clenching his jaw, the veins in his neck pulsing as he watches me suck on his best friend's thumb.

Somehow this feel sensual. I'm being watched as my lips are around Charles, and as soon as he removes the thumb, his other hand comes up to the other side of my face. He cups me in place before he places his fine lips on mine, inserting his tongue in my mouth and tasting the bittersweet drug on my tongue.

He leans back, chuckling under his breath. All of a sudden, my anxiety spikes up. I bring my hands up to his hard chest, pushing him away from me. I quickly stand, looking at the rest of the table and scurry away without another word.

What.

The.

Fuck.

~

I wake up on Sunday in the afternoon, as I only got back to the academy at half past four this morning. I wake up with hot sweats, still hyperventilating after last night's events. I can't decide what's worse. the fact that I tried drugs for the first time or the fact that Charles kissed me, and it was the biggest turn on.

I basically cheated on Miles, and my stomach roils as the prang of guilt ripples through me.

Scurrying out of bed, I rush to the bathroom, taking a cold shower before getting dressed in my yoga pants and sports bra. I need to relieve some stress and right now, dancing is the answer.

I stride into the dance studio, and thankfully it isn't occupied like it usually is at this time. I throw my bag on the floor, putting on the most relatable song I could think about.

'Popular Monster' by Falling in Reverse plays and I dance to my heart's content.

Dripping in sweat, my limbs ache, growing numb. I fall to the floor, my body trembling as the tears stream down my face, my chest heaving. I don't even know why the fuck I'm crying. I wasn't high on the fucking drugs last night, but I am high on the fucking misery caused by the royal dicks.

Standing back up, I push my body to the point of exhaustion, carrying on dancing around the room but the tears don't stop. As I carry on, another one of their song plays, 'The Drug in me is you', and I bruise the tips of my toes as I carry my weight round the room, spinning and twirling. My body welcomes the ache I force upon it as I drag my limbs around, finding new ways to create pain to distract me, but a shadow brings me out of my depressive state.

A slender, muscular form stands, leaning his shoulder against the door frame. The golden-brown eyes watching me as I move, but I carry on until the song finishes.

I pretend that I haven't noticed Royce. He always knows where to find me, and whatever mood I'm in, you'll find me in the dance studio. As soon as the song comes to an end, I grab my hand towel and wipe the sweat from my face, chest, and arms. My whole outfit is soaked from top to bottom. I sigh, "What do you want Royce?"

Uncapping my bottle of water, I stare at Royce through the mirror, gulping half of my water in one go.

He takes a few steps forward, cocking his head to the side as he studies my skinny form. "I just came to check if you're okay after last night. You left in such a rush," he says, putting both hands in his brown chino trouser pockets, shuffling his feet. I turn around, now facing the posh actor in front of me.

Why the fuck is he here, asking if I'm okay?

I bet it's another game to him.

"Yeah, why?" I reply.

A frown takes over his face, the worried expression fading away from his perfectly symmetrical features. "Well it doesn't seem that way, I can see that you have been crying," he grits, his nostrils flaring in annoyance. Taking his hand out of his pocket, he scrubs the palm over his tired face, sighing. "Look, I know I'm the last person you ever want to talk to, but I'm not part of whatever the guys are doing... trust me," he pleads. Concern has edged onto his perfect face.

Shaking my head, I let out a sarcastic laugh, not believing a word he says to me.

"Okay Royce, whatever you say."

I pick up my bag, throwing my towel around my neck to soak all the sweat. I barge past him, leaving him alone in the dance studio. I can't be fucked with people who try to ruin my life or break my trust anymore. He sounded so sincere, but this is where I went wrong in the first place, and it broke me on the inside.

Chapter Twenty-Two

The whole week has passed in a blur, and soon enough, Miles and I are standing behind the curtain on the stage, getting ready for our dance recital to the whole academy and any parents who have attended. I know for a fact my father hasn't turned up. I did invite him, but he says dancing is a waste of time.

The recital is being held in Stonewall auditorium and anyone was able to purchase tickets to watch the Darlington Academy recital. My nerves are kicking in, I haven't danced in front of crowd in such a long time, and the fact I'll be on display in front of all my bullies makes me more nervous.

"Hey, you're going to do great. Our routine is amazing and so are you," Miles consoles, rubbing my shoulders as I shiver. It doesn't help that my outfit is minimal. I'm wearing a traditional ballet outfit but in black, with smokey eyes and red lipstick. My hair is gelled back into a perfect bun on top of my head. We're on last as we have the longest routine, mixing three songs and three routines into one, so it's a lot of pressure.

I do my breathing exercises, breathing in and out, but I peek out to the audience through the blue velvet curtains and it's heaving with bodies. The Royals are all seated in the front row. I'm not bothered if Royce watches me as he's watched me before, but the others haven't.

I'm hoping they don't throw this in my face, otherwise my dreams will be shattered too, and I don't take criticism well. Luckily, after tonight, I don't need to see their faces for a few weeks while on Christmas break. I'm looking forward to relaxing.

I watch the last act of the evening and then it's our turn. Every routine has been amazing, but I can confidently say they won't beat ours. As soon as they're finished, they bow to the audience and Miles takes my hand, squeezing it tightly to assure me everything will be alright. I had to take anxiety tablets before this evening, and I don't feel like they have kicked in at all as my breath is all over the place.

The host of the evening announces Miles' and my name to the audience, so I take a deep breath, following behind Miles. The curtains are closed as we get into position, and once we're ready, the curtains open, revealing a pitch-black audience. The only light available is the orchestra at the bottom of the stage. The first song, 'Swan Lake' starts playing and the spotlight gleams on us, displaying us to the audience.

Silence fills the room as the violin starts playing, and we ballet dance for the first verse before the music transitions to 'I don't care' where we modernize the ballet, adding jumps and more twirls. It's very romantic and perfect, smiling at each other the whole way through the song and routine. My nerves have eased slightly due to not seeing the audience, but I can feel their presence and their eyes boring into our souls as we dance.

The lights start to change as the song continues, revealing the audience and the orchestra. As Miles leans me back, my head upside down, I'm facing the four Royals, whose perfect faces hold no expression. They look bored.

Fuck.

When the lights turn off, the curtains close for a second whilst the orchestra still plays the violins and as quickly as possible, I put on a tight black dress that hugs my torso but flares out at the bottom for movement and a pair of four inch heels before our last piece of music plays. As soon as 'The Kill' by 30 seconds to Mars comes on, the curtains open and the lights shine back on me and Miles. The audience cheers at the new outfits before settling down. Our hands are clasped together as my other hand rests on the top of his shoulder. My gaze constantly fixates to the right of me as we take on our own form of the Tango. Miles spins me around the stage, twirling me round so that my dress lifts in the air, my bodysuit covered ass on display.

We cover the whole stage, and my gaze catches onto the Royals again. Royce has a massive grin on his face, but the other three still look bored as fuck, leaning low in their seats.

Great, they are so going to degrade me over this. We finish our routine, my heart pumping out of my chest and we bow to the crowd, the applause blanketing the whole auditorium and I honestly feel amazing. I smile and wave to the audience before taking another bow and then running off the stage with Miles.

"Oh my god, that was amazing!" he lifts me up in the air, twirling me round as we both laugh from the adrenaline. My body is shaking from pure ecstasy and I feel on top of the world. I forgot how much I love performing on stage for people and how much it made me feel. You know what? Fuck what the Royals say, and their pet bitches. We were amazing and I know for a fact we will get amazing grades for this.

We make our way to the changing rooms where I can finally get out of these uncomfortable outfits. A few of us are going out tonight to celebrate our amazing night, and I cannot wait to have a drink.

I pull out the tight bun on my head, brushing out the hard gel in my hair until I'm pretty much left with a bird's nest. My make-up is still on point though, so all I have to do is get changed into my clothes. I slide on a red mini skirt, and pair it with a black turtleneck and knee-high boots. I slip on my leather jacket, grab my bags and leave to meet Miles and the others at the front of the auditorium.

We end up going around on a pub crawl down the main strip, pushing down shots at every bar and pub until I start to feel tipsy from all the alcohol consumed. We're at the last bar of the evening. Miles has had to leave, as him and Ruby going on holiday to ski. I wish I had plans like that over Christmas, but I doubt father would want to do anything fun.

I'm sitting in one of the booths along with my classmates, sipping on a rum and cola, when I see Zach walk in towards the bar. My eyes follow his movements, studying the dark blue jeans and navy-blue jumper making him look less surfer dude, but less posh twat too. He's somewhere in between. He's with a few people I haven't seen around before, and one of the girls latches herself onto his arm, sending a pang of jealousy through my gut. Her dark purple hair is down to her butt, her pale skin looking as if she's never seen the sun, paired with heavy black make-up.

Hang on, that's the purple haired girl that sucked Hugo's dick. Wow, is that his type?

Zach's eyes wonder around the room and stop when he sees me sipping on my straw in the booth, the corners of his mouth curling up into a smile as he gives me a little wave. I wave back, quickly averting my gaze back to my group and away from him. I can hear his roaring laugh from the other side of the room, the beautiful sound making me quiver in my seat. A band starts playing on the other side of the room, and that is a cue for everyone to stand around them and dance. The girls all stand up, squealing and grabbing my hand to join them.

When the band starts, they sing songs that I haven't heard before, but it's still fun to dance to. I'm swaying my hips, enjoying myself with the girls, dancing for a few songs. I head back to take a sip of my drink to hydrate and find Zach leaning his back against the bar, grinning at me. He winks as soon as I look at him, a red flush taking over my face. I give him a sweet smile, and gesture with my head to come over and join us. He gestures with his hands he will be ten minutes, so I shrug my shoulders in response, getting back to dancing.

The band starts playing familiar songs and it isn't until 'Mr. Brightside' starts playing that everyone freaks out. Everyone standing jumps around to the song, singing their hearts out. As I'm jumping like a crazy woman, I feel two hands grope my hips, and I know it's Zach because whenever he's near me, the hairs on the back of my neck stand up, acknowledging his presence. I haven't spoken to Zach since the night they found me at the club when I shouldn't have been. I've been ignoring his texts, feeling bad about talking to him when I should be with Miles.

I'm still swaying my hips, but this time it's against Zach's pelvic region. The strongly tanned, rough hands still on my hips, the long fingers brushing against my knicker line. I can feel the bulge in his jeans, the fabric in the way of our skin touching. I should feel nervous next to him, but this guy has seen me in my underwear already and with a bloody, bruised face, so I feel completely myself around him.

"You carry on rubbing that sweet ass of yours like that against me, I'll have to bend you over my car," he whispers in my ear, one hand stroking my long hair away and exposing my skin between my ear and neck.

I feel the tip of his nose nuzzling that sweet tender spot and it's doing bits to my insides. I want to turn around and kiss this Viking god in front of everyone, claiming him to be mine, but that's wishful thinking.

Unable to respond to Zach, I carry on dancing, rubbing my ass against him. I know it's provoking him. I can feel the growl of frustration from his hard chest against my back, and it makes me smile. I feel sexy right now, which I haven't in a while. Miles makes me feel safe, content and wanted... but Zach makes me feel sexy and possessed.

When the pub signals its last call, the room starts to empty, and we all shuffle outside into the crisp, cold air, waiting for an Uber to arrive and take us back to the academy. Zach follows, grabbing my hand and dragging me somewhere else. "Come on, I'll take you back. I haven't drunk any alcohol tonight," he grins.

"Does your father know that you're out galivanting in town tonight?" I tease as we get to his black Ferrari, parked along the sea wall.

"He does, but I bet your daddy doesn't," he smirks, lifting a teasing eyebrow. Okay, he got me there. I think my father would kill me if he found me out galivanting in Stonewall, especially in a pub.

Sliding into his car is a task, considering how low it is and how high my high heeled boots are. I plop my ass down in the luxury seats, and Zach starts the engine with a button and roars off.

"I must admit, I really enjoyed your recital tonight," he says, eyes still on the road but the cheeky smirk hasn't left his flawless face.

I tilt my head to him, gasping. I didn't know he went to that. I don't think I even told him about it. I quirk up my eyebrow, scrunching my nose as I look at him in confusion.

"I didn't see you."

He chuckles, turning his gaze to me for a sweet second, the headlights reflecting on the side of his face and showing off the perfectly sculpted cheekbones. "Oh, I was there, that last outfit... it got me going," he winks, and I cover my mouth, smirking and laughing. I forgot how much fun I have with Zach, but once again something is telling me it's all wrong. This is too good to be true. The happiness drains from my face, turning into a frown and Zach can see the change in my mood.

"I will tell you everything when the time is right, Ade," he consoles, placing his warm hand on my thigh. Looking down at his calloused hands in admiration, I take in his worker hands from where he deals with the surf boards. Not hands that show he's a posh twat who doesn't lift a finger - now if only that hand would slide up a little further...

I clench my thighs to get rid of the pooling ache between them as his hand stays put.

My breath is ragged as I try to breathe. He knows exactly what he does to me.

~

The tea party is an absolute fucking bore. I'm sitting around an oval table, sipping on my beverage from a little teacup that holds one gulp. I'm taking the tiniest sips to make it last. Ms. Veronica is sitting on the left of me, cackling to whatever the woman has just said to her. I pick up another little slice of a sandwich, the only filling is a fucking cucumber, and I finish it in one bite.

This is boring as fuck.

Classical music plays in the background. The hall is extravagant, ivory walls with historical paintings surround the room. Crystal chandeliers hang low from the ceiling, brightening the vast space. The tea party is held at an old stately home outside of Stonewall. It has its own tennis court, stables with horses and three swimming pools, but no one lives here. It's a waste of space in my opinion.

Shifting uncomfortably in my seat, I try pulling the hem of my skirt down as it keeps riding up. I'm wearing a matching skirt and blazer suit in the colour of sage green, with a white blouse underneath and nude four-inch heels? My hair is curled - a half up, half down look - the top teased and backcombed into a slight beehive, pinned with pearl clips, the mix of dark brown and caramel strands resting on my padded shoulders. Fucking padding.

My make-up is minimalistic with a boring nude lipstick. I look pale, like a vampire drinking fucking tea, when I want to be drinking the blood of the dickheads that put me here.

"Oh dear, you look so delightful," a woman says to me, her lips not moving when she speaks, but I smile sweetly at her and mutter a thanks. Around the room are a few young ladies around my age, all going through what I am. The torture to be perfect.

This is the first event leading up to the debutant ball next Christmas, where we will be introduced to some suitors who will escort us from being girls to being 'Ladies'.

I couldn't think of anything fucking worse.

My gaze scans around the room, watching the robots that surround the beautifully organized tables. The soft, ivory tablecloths, porcelain crockery with gold trimmings, and the cutlery that apparently is real silver, polished so there isn't even a speck of dust to be found. The grand flower arrangements of peonies and roses are the centerpieces of each table, placed in a blue and white china vase, so tall you can't see who's sitting opposite you.

I stuff my face with tiny Victoria sponge cakes and biscuits as the chitter chatter fills the room. I haven't spoken to any of the

other girls here, not really interested in their lives. Ms. Veronica
has been babbling on with the lady next to her for the past hour.
Literally, I thank the lord in my head when it's announced that
the tea party is drawing to a close. I am the first one to stand up
from my seat, eyes on me as I walk out of the grand room. I
mentally stick my finger up at the ladies behind me as they watch
me leave.

When I arrive home, the Bentley pulls onto the gravel road
toward my father's house and a black Ferrari comes into view.

Zach is here.

As Steve pulls to a stop I don't wait for him to open my door,
and I get out of the car as quickly as I can. I just want to get this
outfit off of me and burn it. The second I stand my skirt rides up,
making me feel uncomfortable. I try and pull it down by the hem,
struggling to balance my heels in the gravel, and a familiar laugh
sounds out from behind me. I turn around to find Zach leaning his
shoulder against the wooden door frame of the door, ankles crossed,
and he's dressed in a fine navy-blue suit. Damn it, my ovaries can't
take this.

I frown. "What's so funny?" I bark, trying to stand straight and
walk over to him but this skirt is very restricting, my normal strides
are reduced to little ones, making it take longer to get anywhere.
Zach's hand flies up to his mouth, hiding the wide grin behind it,
still chuckling as I maneuver towards him. I'm biting the inside of
my cheek, trying not to snap at Steve and Zach. Poor Steve is also
holding in a laugh, his face turning red from trying not to burst.

"Okay, come on, let it all out," I gesture with my hand over my
body, giving them both permission and to my regret they both burst
out laughing. Clearly, this posh lady outfit doesn't suit me. I look like
an old lady dressed like this. I purse my lips, my eyes wide and
staring at both of them. I finally make it to the bottom of the steps,
realizing I have nothing to balance myself against so that I'm able to
get up the five marble steps.

Zach noticing my struggle, comes to join me down below. He
tangles our arms together so that he can escort me to the top.
Annoyingly, it's only five steps, but this skirt is so tight I can't lift my

leg up at a ninety-degree angle. Maybe only thirty degrees, and these steps are wider and taller than normal.

"I must say, Ade…," Zach starts but the laughter takes over again, unable to form the words from his mouth. I wonder why he's here at my father's house, dressed in a sexy suit.

I sigh, rolling my eyes. "What are you doing here?"

Zach escorts me to the kitchen, where I kick of my shoes and head towards the fridge to pour myself an orange juice. I need an OJ and a coffee. As I'm taking sips of the sweet juice, I turn the kettle on, turning my gaze to Zach's as I point to the kettle.

"Coffee please, doll," he winks.

I empty my glass in a few seconds, waiting for the sugar to hit my veins like a drug addict. "So, are you going to answer my question? What are you doing here?" I fold my arms across my chest, the arms of the blazer also restricting that movement.

Fucking thing, who wears this shit on purpose?

Raising my eyebrow to Zach, he doesn't seem too concerned and takes a seat on one of the high stools by the breakfast bar. He looks so handsome in a kitchen. I bet he can cook. The image of him in an apron, chopping vegetables … I trail off in my mind, forgetting I was still staring at him. Turning around, I get two large cups out of the cabinet and start to make the drinks. Just as I'm about to ask how he takes it; he beats me to it.

"White, no sugar. I'm sweet enough."

Barking out a laugh, I finish making the drinks and head over to pass it to him

"These are exceptionally large cups," he says, taking the handle and lifting the mug up to inspect.

"Yeah I needed a big mug, because afternoon tea party drinks are so small you end up thirstier than before," I reply. I put my mug down, leaning my torso against the counter as I look over to Zach.

"I had to come drop some documents off for your father. He's away on business with my father and I forgot to bring them earlier," he finally admits.

I wonder how many days my father is away for. "When are they back?" I mumble, taking a sip of my beautiful roasted bean coffee.

Zach puts his down on the counter, his hand flying up to his face, then he does the one move that makes my knickers melt away. His thumb brushes the corner of his lip, those sultry eyes boring into me before he licks those luscious lips. Shifting on my feet, I balance myself on my other foot, trying to get rid of the butterflies in my belly that want to travel down to my sweet core.

Down girl.

Zach bites his lower lip slowly as he tilts his head to the side. "You know, I normally hate posh girls that dress like that, but my god, you are turning me on," he purrs, the sapphire of his eyes half-lidded as he rests his chin in the palm of his hand.

I straighten my back, turning around to put our empty mugs in the dishwasher.

"I do love a domestic woman too," he teases, and I can't help but laugh.

"So, you loved your maid?" I joke, and he barks out a laugh, his head falling back. The sound is like a perfect melody and it sends a pang to my gut. I love it when Zach laughs. It's so infectious. He stands from the stool, straightening the suit jacket before repositioning the silver Rolex on his wrist.

"I have to go princess, but I'm sure you will see me during the break."

He starts to exit the kitchen while I stay where I am, but he stops and turns on his heel. "Oh, and to answer your question, you have freedom of three days before father dearest returns," he winks whilst walking backwards. Soon after, I hear the soft click of the door and the roar of the Ferrari as he leaves.

This is going to be a great Christmas. Not.

Chapter Twenty-Three

O nce the Christmas break is over, it's actually a relief to be back at the academy. I hardly saw my father the whole holiday and we only sat down for one meal together, which was our turkey stuffed Christmas dinner. Other than that, he wasn't around. I received lavish gifts from him, including jewelry, all real diamonds, the best clothes from around the world and surprisingly he turned one of the spare rooms into a full dance studio, which was the real winner. I was stunned when he showed it to me. He thinks dancing is a waste of time, but he likes the fact I'm keeping fit.

Unfortunately, I didn't even have the pleasure of Zach around since our last encounter, which made me feel… alone. The one friend, or whatever he is, the only one who is allowed round, didn't. Miles and the girls texted me a Happy Christmas, which was about the only thing that put a smile on my face.

Since being back at the Academy I've kept myself busy with my assignments and projects, as there's only a few months left of the college year and everything is due soon.

"Here are our gifts," Blaire says, placing boxes on my bed from her and Maisie. We didn't get to do our own little Christmas before the break, so we're doing it now on a Wednesday afternoon in January. Why not?

I hand them their gifts, which I managed to buy from my monthly allowance from father and my job. I open the first box to find a necklace with three hoops, encrusted in diamonds but on the back, it has our names engraved.

The strings on my heart tug, as this is possibly the best present I have ever received. I mean, back home in South Africa I got cute gifts, but my friends weren't rich, so we didn't really buy gifts for each other, whereas now, we trade fucking diamonds for gifts apparently.

What a change of lifestyle.

Blaire and Maisie open their boxes and the way their faces light up does something to me, and I giggle. I literally love these two with all my heart and having them as best friends is amazing. I would die if I didn't have them here with me at the academy. It looks like we had the same idea for presents but in my case, I got us all matching best friend bracelets. The platinum plated bracelets each have a charm of our initials and also a gem which are our birthstones, followed by a diamond.

Blaire squeals, "Oh my goodness," she drags out, putting on the bracelet. We all hug, tears filling our eyes as we say our thanks. I check the time and notice it's already after three in the afternoon and I'm late for meeting Hugo in the library.

Shit, he will kill me. Literally stab me.

Grabbing my bag, I scurry towards the door, turning my head to say goodbye to the girls. "I gotta go. Tutoring session with the devil himself," I laugh. I have two minutes to make it…

"You're five minutes late Africa," he hisses when I arrive, not bothering to draw his eyes to me as I slide into my chair. It's five minutes, for god's sake.

"I do apologize Hugo. I didn't realize the time," I snap, pulling out my laptop from my satchel. I cannot be bothered to write every-thing down to just re type it up, so why not do it all in one go, instead of doing things twice?

Obtaining good grades until the end of the year is an absolute must, my father warned me at Christmas and if I don't, I don't want to know the consequences. If he just hit me because I changed my hair colour, I dread to think what he will do if I slack off at the academy. Smiling, I turn on my laptop and turn to look at Hugo.

"Did you have a nice Christmas break?" I ask, trying to start a conversation, but I feel as though I'm poking the beast. We haven't ever had a normal conversation and as one of my new year's resolutions, I want to make the effort in getting to know the Royals and be nice. I have kind of forgiven them for what they have done. I mean, in a way, but it's not forgotten. Start this year off with no grudges – how hard can it be?

Hugo lifts his head, his upper lip curled as if my question has aggravated him.

"Are you being fucking serious?" he grits.

Okay, so I poked the bear and he didn't like it.

I hold out my hands in surrender, my lips in a thin line. "Goodness, I am so sorry for asking," I stammer. He doesn't say anything else, but he just puts his head down and continues writing notes. Maybe he wasn't the best one to start my resolution with. I've put last year's antics to the back of my mind, locking it in the cage where my bad memories are and hiding the key, so I don't unlock it willingly. I should throw away the key really.

Once my laptop is up and running, I start typing, my leg bouncing up and down without realizing and I notice that Hugo keeps looking at me with an aggravating stare. I try to stop bouncing my leg, but for some reason I'm nervous and the fact that Hugo is so close to me is unnerving.

The way you just bit your lip…

The sentence keeps playing in my mind like a broken record. Does he think about this all the time? Is he observing me now?

So many questions.

I want to be intrusive and ask him about the purple haired girl from the party, and ask if she's his girlfriend, but I feel as though that would put the icing on the cake of him hating me. So, I hold back my questions, locking them in the cage.

My cage is going to burst soon and then I'm going to break down... I can feel it.

When the hour is up, Hugo stands up abruptly, his belongings already packed. He must be in a hurry. He walks past me, leaving me on my own but as soon as I think I'm free, I wince in pain, my hair being pulled back with force.

"Just because it was Christmas and it's a new year doesn't mean I like you now. I still fucking hate you and you are due your punishment for crashing the club. So be warned Africa…" he says, hissing like a snake. He's threatening, no, promising me punishment and when Hugo says something, he means it.

My eyes are shut from the pain Hugo is inducing, the long fingers tangled in my brown hair. He lets me go abruptly, storming off out the library, and it takes a moment for me to catch my breath.

Am I scared? No. I am fucking terrified. But at the same time, my body calls to him and just the touch of his fingers on my scalp send my nerves into a frenzy. He reminds me of the song from Avenged Sevenfold – Scream.

He makes me want to scream in a good way and in a bad way.

~

Samantha texts me to let me know that I can audition to dance whenever I want, and I couldn't be more excited. The back of my mind is telling me how risky it is, but then the little devil on my shoulder tells me, 'you're wearing a wig and a mask Ade, no one will know…' I instantly agree with the little devil.

Since the Christmas break, I have put the weight back on my body, making me look like a human being rather than a walking corpse. My ass and boobs are so big I can't stop touching them. I'm just surprised they're still there.

I haven't spent any time with Miles, in fact he hasn't really been around the academy, so we still haven't traded our presents yet. Well, I got him a present, so I'm assuming he got me one too. Wishful thinking?

Lounging on the golden sand of Stonewall beach in my wetsuit,

I admire the view of the orange-hued sunset. The ocean is crystal clear, you can see the seabed in the shallows, the little fishes and the seaweed floating. It's breathtaking. Only a few people have turned up at the beach today to surf, the winter cold putting them off, but it doesn't me.

I like feeling the slight crisp cold nipping my skin.

The bonfire has just been lit, the aroma of burnt wood in the air, the orange and golden flames dancing on the faces that surround it. My hands dig into the golden sand, letting it fall between my fingers, the tiny granules tickling my soft skin.

"Africaaa!" someone hollers, breaking the trance I was in, enjoying the silence and alone time. A body plonks itself next to mine in the sand, settling their board down beside them.

I tilt my head, side eyeing Charles as he admires the view ahead of us. The sun is just setting, and you can only see half of the sun. The other half reflects off of the water, the slight ripples changing its shape.

"What do you want?" I utter, my knees bent to my chest. I cross my arms around them, creating a barrier. I haven't spoken to Charles since his birthday party, after he fed me some drugs and then kissed me. I still don't know how to feel about that situation.

Anyone would say he was a bad influence, to which I agree but it was my choice. If I said no, he wouldn't have forced it upon me. I know he said he dared me but I'm sure he isn't that cruel. I was in a rebellious mood, so I thought, why the fuck not.

"Well, I was surfing just like you, and thought I'd come say hi," he shrugs. "I haven't seen you since my epic party, and our little, um… incident," he snorts.

My eyes narrow and my upper lip curls. I don't know exactly how to take that. Does he just not want to admit it happened, or is it regret in his voice? Because he hides it well.

Clearing my throat, I fix my gaze on the ocean. "Yeah, it doesn't matter. It was a mistake anyway," I state, thinking that I might as well say it before he does.

Charles turns his head to look at me, the water dripping from his perfect shaggy hair, his face scrunched in a frown. The orange of the sun gleams from his perfect brown eyes, making them look more caramel. "Yeah… Yeah, you're right," he stutters, and I don't know if it's me, but he sounded slightly disappointed. He clears his throat, dipping his chin so he's looking at the sand between his feet.

I swallow the lump in my throat, unsure of what to say, but I'm unsure as to why he's even here. He hates me, and he made that perfectly clear before. My chest tightens, remembering the words that left his crimson lips, I wouldn't go near her gross fucking body. Biting the inside of my cheek, my fingers trail the granules, feeling the cold shards slip through my fingers. I better leave, before I disgust him further.

Standing to leave, I rub the sand off my ass with the palms of my hands and then pick up my board, Charles watching my every move. I don't even a mutter goodbye, I just walk off. I take my board back to the beach hut, and another guy working today, instead of Zach, takes it from my hands, placing it on the shelves behind him. I open the locker where all my belongings are, picking out my towel and bag before heading back to the academy. I slip on my yoga pants, a hoodie, and my trainers in the car park. I still haven't contacted an Uber to pick me up, but I didn't want to leave just yet. Charles just drove me away.

Looking around the area, I scan to see what else is around and I spot a cute little ice cream parlor. I could do with an ice cream sundae. I haven't had one of them in a while either, so I may as well spoil myself. Walking into the 1950's style parlor, I find an empty booth along the glass wall looking out to the ocean and take a seat. The waitress is so attentive, already taking my drinks order. I order myself a coffee and decide to go for a banana split. My belly is rumbling already.

It doesn't take long for my drink and dessert to arrive, so I dig in straight away. As I eat the ice cream, I scroll through my social media, looking at all the pictures my old friends have put on, showing off their summer holidays. Damn, I wish I were back home enjoying the sunshine, the heat on my skin. I definitely relish the sunshine. I'm starting to lose my natural tan.

A ping rings on my phone, a notification showing that I have been tagged in something on Instagram, on the Darlington Academy gossip page. It's a picture of me, mouth wide open as I enjoy my banana split. Already the comments are flooding in, calling me a fat bitch, a pig, and many more.

What fucking prick decided to ruin my start of the year?

I look around outside, to see if I recognize any familiar faces, but I don't. The only person who comes to mind is Charles as he was the only person I have really seen. If it's him, I swear I'm going to kill him.

The comments do not die down, they keep coming in so fast I can't believe it. A few comments saying that I should kill myself, slit my wrists… and the worst one says that I should have drowned. They are talking about the incident where Blake pushed me under water.

The colour from my face vanishes, my body temperature rising so high, beads of sweat form on my forehead, drip onto the table in front of me. My chest tightens as the comments keep rolling in, but I can't stop looking at them, my eyes are glued to the screen of my phone. Tears roll down my face, turning my cheeks pink, and I try to wipe them away, but they keep on coming.

I decide not to head back to the academy, feeling too anxious. So, I leave the ice cream parlor after I've paid my bill and find the closest pub so that I can drink my sorrows away. I end up going back to that pub where we watched the band, having only just learned that it's called the Queens Head. Fitting.

Taking a seat at the bar on a stool, my eyes go wide in surprise. The purple haired girl is working behind the bar. Jesus, I am going to have to drink a lot tonight.

She's wearing a black t-shirt, showcasing her colorful tattooed arms, and this time I notice a piercing above her lip and her nose. She looks pretty cool, I must admit.

"Shot of Tequila please, and also a whiskey straight with ice," I tell her, and she retreats to the side, getting out the glasses and pouring my drinks.

"'Ere we go," she says with a weird accent I can't quite place. I down the tequila and signal for her to bring me another, which she obeys.

"You're that girl that works at Club Envy aren't ya?" she says, leaning her hip against the bar, crossing her arms around her chest, showing off her amazing cleavage.

No wonder the boys have gone for her.

Nodding my head in response, I down the brown liquid, welcoming the burning sensation as it trails down my throat and into my belly. Pure bliss. She smiles at me softly, already getting the bottle of whiskey to top me up. Okay, maybe I misjudged her.

I drink and down a few shots for the next few hours, not moving from my spot but the pub is starting to get really busy. Bodies constantly coming in and out, I think a band even starts playing at some point. I'm too drunk to care, and I don't pay attention to the guy who is standing next to me. "Hey sexy, what's a pretty girl like you doing on your own?" he says, creeping into my little bubble by the bar.

My elbow resting on the bar, my head resting in my hand I turn to face him, and he's not a bad looking guy. Probably too old for my liking but it's nice to be called sexy, especially in a pub when wearing a hoodie and yoga pants. I smile sweetly at him, seeing two of him, or maybe there's a twin I don't know? I laugh to myself, and the guy laughs along with me.

"Do you want another drink?" he asks, and I nod a yes in response, I definitely need another drink. My feelings aren't numb yet and I need them numb. Downing a few more tequila shots and relishing in how it feels, I get even more wasted. I pluck up the courage to dance with this guy, who I have no clue what his name is, but I'm having so much fun.

The guy orders me another drink, whilst I run to the ladies' room, and I tell you, weeing with a wetsuit on is… fucking painful. I didn't think about this…

Arriving back to my seat, a whisky waits for me with the hand-some man - I'm seeing three of him now, and I know for sure I am fucking drunk. Thank fuck for that. After a while, my vision starts blurring, the room spins, and I start feeling really dizzy. The guy's arm snakes around my waist, pulling me towards the exit, and I faintly hear him speak to me as we leave. "Come on, baby. Let's get you out of here, so I can fuck that pretty little mouth of yours."

I'm unable to respond to the guy, my voice coming out slurred. He doesn't listen to me anyway. My body isn't able to struggle against his hold, and it dawns on me that this guy fucking spiked my drink. I should have been careful what I wished for because I'm finally numb. Against my will.

I keep falling in and out of consciousness. One minute, I can make out that I'm being pulled into a car... but the next time I open my eyes, the guy is being punched in the face while another body holds me close to them. Incapable of making out the faces, I suddenly feel safe, somehow knowing I'm being saved from being raped by a fucking dick.

I stop fighting the drug and let unconsciousness take over.

The following day, I wake up all alone in my dorm room, my clothes and wet suit taken off, replaced with my pajamas. Blaire isn't in the room either as she wasn't here this weekend, so who could have saved me last night?

Chapter Twenty-Four

For a few weeks, after the picture was released of me eating a fucking banana split, students have been calling me fat, a pig and every other fat shaming name you can come up with. I've been trying to ignore them, but with already having an eating disorder, I haven't eaten properly, refusing to eat in the dining hall. Blaire has to bring me food to eat in our dorm room. Even still, I only eat salads and I've completely cut out carbs. My muscle is melting away, my skin is losing the elasticity, and I'm turning pale. I look like a walking corpse again; the sockets of my eyes are turning black from the lack of iron.

I look like pure fucking shit.

Still unsure of who sent out that picture and started all this bull-shit, I still believe it's Charles, although my mind is still trying to figure out who saved me from the pub, and the fact that they brought me back to my room and changed my clothes.

I'm losing sleep over it all.

Nightmares take over my dreams at night, the image of the guy who's name I don't know still haunts me, and I see myself tied to his bed as he rapes me. I'm too scared to close my eyes in case he comes back, but I'm unable to escape the horror.

I really want to know who my knight in shining armor was, so that I could say thanks, but no one has come forward, and to be honest I haven't really asked anyone as I'm too afraid to know the answer. It could have been another prank for all I know.

Shifting in my seat in Business Economics, my head is in a daze as I sit next to Blake. He's bouncing his leg up and down, shaking the table, clearly agitated about something. Today we're supposed to hand in half of our project, which we actually worked on together, with no snarky comments or threats. Hugo hasn't really spoken to me either since he threatened me in the library, and I am patiently waiting for my 'punishment', whatever it is. I couldn't give a flying fuck what they throw at me now. They can kick me down and make me bleed, and I wouldn't even care.

I already feel as though the life has been beaten out of me.

Mr. Aldridge saunters over to our desk with a file in his hand and says, "Well done you two, keep up the hard work and this will be the best project in the class."

Wasn't today supposed to be the day we handed it in?

I scrunch up my face in confusion as Mr. Aldridge hands the file to Blake. "I handed it in yesterday, wanting to get it over and done with," he says.

I nod in response, unable to say anything. Well, too frightened to say something, incase it's wrong.

When the bell rings to signal class is over, I couldn't be happier. I quickly pick up my satchel and leave the room. I'm trying to scurry away through the halls, but the students won't let me pass. I sidestep from the left to right, but it's no use. A circle forms around me, the faces of the students grinning from ear to ear as they stare me down. My body starts shaking, my anxiety spiking up and the alarm bells start ringing in my head. What the fuck is happening right now?

"What's it like being a murderer? Did you come here to escape prison or something?" Ruby says from behind me, and I spin on my heel so that I can face her, and the other two bitches, Constance, and Priscilla.

Great.

Unable to say anything, my body too weak to even run, my feet are glued to the brick pathway of the haunting castle. I swallow the lump in my throat, my eyes narrowed as I face off with Ruby, the sinister grin taking over her beautiful face. But her ugliness shows through her personality. The Victoria's Secret model look alike clicks her fingers to signal something and that's when I feel the first punch to the back of my head.

White stars start forming in my vision, and I try to shake off the feeling but it's too late. Punches and kicks surround my body. I crouch down to the floor, protecting my face and belly, but they manage to get there too. I feel the blood pouring from my nose, ears and mouth. My ribs crack under someone's foot, a scream escaping past my lips and the tears start to roll down my cheeks.

What feels like hours of being beaten is actually a few seconds before it's done. My battered and bruised body lays on the ground as the blood pours. I wrap my arms around my stomach, stifling a cough, but as soon as it comes out, my ribs burn.

Ade, you need to stand.

Trying to listen to the little voice in my head, I sit up slowly, the pain taking over my body. I wince, my body trembling and unable to cope with the agony. I look down to find my uniform is torn, covered in blood and dirt from where some students kicked me.

Fucking pricks.

I balance my weight on my right hand, my arm shaking and ready to give out, but I need to try and stand. I curl my knees ready to stand but my body trembles, and I fall back to the ground. I am just too weak.

"Ade!" someone shouts from the other end of the corridor, the sound muffled as my ears are drenched in blood. I can't recognize who it belongs to.

"Ade, what the fuck happened?"

Royce leans over me, inspecting my body, concern on his face. He goes to lift me gently from under my knees and behind my neck. Lifting me with ease, Royce carries me to his car. "I'm taking you to the hospital, you are seriously injured," he murmurs.

My head is leaning against his hard chest, I can feel the beating of his heart and it's racing. My eyes close of their own accord, I think I may have a concussion as my head was punched and kicked a few times. Royce inserts me into the passenger seat, putting on my safety belt before he climbs in and races off to the hospital. The drive there is filled with music and I listen to it, trying to stop myself from falling asleep while Royce keeps asking me if I'm okay. At one point he grabs my hand and squeezes it for reassurance.

I still fucking hate him, but if he's here offering help, I won't refuse.

The nurse checks me over, the X-ray showing my broken ribs just inches from penetrating my lungs. I could have fucking died. My wounds are cleaned and bound, the blood having finally stopped pouring from my ears and nose. The nurse gives me some really strong pain killers and fluid as I'm apparently malnourished. She's keeping me here for a few days to recuperate.

Opening my eyes, I look around, noticing I'm in a private hospital bedroom. The walls are painted a baby blue with paintings of the ocean and mountains. I look to the right of me where the window is situated and notice the beautiful view of vast farmland, hills with cattle in the background. My stomach flip flops as I find the plush beige armchair is occupied by Royce. His uniform is covered in blood and he's slouched back, his head leaning on the palm of his hand as he stares down at his phone.

I wince as I try to move my body to sit up. Royce hears me and automatically stands, putting his phone in his pocket. "How are you feeling?" he whispers, those beautiful sea green eyes staring down at me with concern, but also unease. He knows my feelings towards him, and it makes him uneasy.

"I'll be fine. I'm in fucking pain though," my voice coming out raspy, making me cough. The rumble unbearable, pain sears through my veins. Even with the strong pain killers, I can still feel the throbbing. Damn, they got me good.

"What happened?" Royce questions, taking my hand in his, rubbing his thumb along the top. "Ruby and her cronies got some students to beat me down," I shrug wincing at the tiny movement. Sitting up, I grab my glass of water from the nightstand. My mouth feels like ash. I take a sip of the cold water, the liquid bringing my mouth back to life. I don't realize how thirsty I am until I've downed the whole glass. I shake the glass in Royce's direction for a top up.

"I'm so sorry you had to do all this. You probably have something better to do," I tell him, watching him fill my glass up.

"It's no bother Ade, you needed help desperately, and I wasn't going to leave you on the floor now, was I?" he comforted.

"Do you need me to get anything else?" he asks, quirking his eyebrow.

"Ade! Oh my god, you're okay!" Blaire comes running into the room, her hand covers her mouth in shock at all my wounds and then she scans the blood on Royce's uniform. "Who the fuck did this to you?" she demands, the anger evident in her chocolate brown eyes.

"Ruby and her skanky friends. I found her laying on the ground outside her Business class," Royce says before I get the chance to respond.

Blaire's face flushes, losing the colour. A tear escapes her eye and she wipes it away quickly. "I'm so sorry I wasn't there. Where the fuck was Blake when this happened?" she says, but I don't understand why she's apologizing or even wondering why the fuck Blake wasn't there.

This was probably his master plan, or Hugo's.

"He didn't know about it. He'd already left when this took place," Royce says, the green eyes not leaving me once when he speaks to Blaire. It's as if he's too scared to look away in case something else happens. Why is he being so fucking nice?

The nurse comes into the room, stating visitors have to leave. After Royce and Blaire say their goodbyes I fall into a deep sleep, letting the pain killers run through my veins, numbing the pain. I haven't slept so well in such a long time. No nightmares haunt my dreams.

❦

hen I'm finally released from hospital, I'm put on pills to help with my anxiety and depression. I was recommended a therapist who will see me weekly, but I'm a bit apprehensive. Maisie and Blaire pick me up from the hospital, taking me back to the academy.

"We are staying at the academy this weekend. We are not leaving your side!" Blaire declares, her tone of voice rather stern.

"Yeah, we will make sure you are properly looked after," Maisie smiles, offering her hand to help me get out of the car. I grab it and slowly climb out, using her for balance.

Once we get to the dorm room, Maisie guides me to my bed and I perch myself down slowly on the edge, taking my time to breathe. Every inhale and exhale sends a pang of pain through my chest.

"We are so sorry, Ade. I cannot explain to you how much we regret not being there with you when this happened," Blaire's voice breaks as her gaze falls to the floor. She shakes her head and I watch as she wipes a tear away from her eye, my chest tightening.

"It is not either of your faults. We aren't always together, and Ruby is just a dick. Honestly, I am fine, or I will be because I have you two," my voice cracks as my eyes moisten with tears, and I can't help but feel guilty that I cause so much trouble in their lives. I wipe away the tears that escape down my cheeks and clear my throat. "I honestly am so grateful for the both of you. I hope you know that," I smile, bringing my eyes up to meet theirs and they nod back in acknowledgment.

They take care of me the whole weekend, constantly at my beck and call and bringing me food. I don't leave my bed at all and it's pure bliss.

Headmaster Valentine said he couldn't get CCTV to find the culprits and as there were no witnesses, he can't suspend Ruby and the two sheep. I wasn't going to bother reporting them, but Blaire and Maisie insisted. The strange thing is that Miles hasn't been around. He didn't visit me in hospital and only text me a few times to check how I'm feeling, but other than that he hasn't been around.

I'm starting to question our relationship.

Is he avoiding me? Have I done something wrong, or even worse, do I embarrass him?

Am I being paranoid?

A knock sounds from the door, startling all three of us, as we're not expecting anyone to be around. Blaire opens the door to Royce... who is holding a bouquet of flowers?

My favorite flowers.

Sitting up from my bed, I lean my head against my headboard as Royce strides into the room wearing black slacks, a crisp white shirt with a few buttons undone and a black suit jacket. He's dressed exactly in the same suit when I found them at Club Envy. He rubs the back of his neck, clearly nervous to be here right now.

"I thought I'd come see how you are, and I brought you these," he says, gesturing to the flowers in his hand.

He's made more of an effort than Miles has.

Blaire takes the beautiful bouquet of calla lilies, roses and peonies from Royce and places it on my chest of drawers. The pretty pink and whites matches the décor of the room... Did he know what our room looked like? Is he the one who saved me from the pub?

Questions I need answers to, but I don't push.

I smile softly. "Thanks, you didn't have to, you know," I tell him, looking at how immaculate he looks in his suit.

His mouth goes into a flat line as he scans our room, shifting from one foot to the other. "I know, but I wanted to. Again, I'm so sorry Ade." He lets out a deep breath, shaking his head. He looks disappointed in himself. Unsure of what to say, I sit up further, my slipping duvet exposing my upper half. I'm wearing a white vest top without a bra. My nipples can be seen through the thin white fabric, which Royce notices and smirks. The glint reappears in his extravagant eyes.

I pull the duvet back up, hiding my perky breasts from his gaze, feeling too exposed right now.

"I better go, I have an event I need to attend to, but I'll check in on you again soon," he smiles, giving me a two-finger wave before he leaves.

Exhaling sharply and finally relaxing when he leaves, my heart races from the encounter. I look over to the flowers, still surprised he brought them for me. It's kind of sweet.

"What was that about?" Maisie looks confused, her eyebrows furrowed as she stares at me.

"I have no idea, I think there is a hidden agenda," I shrug, working on standing up. I'm still wobbly, but I manage to make my way to the bathroom on my own, for a shower.

The girls don't think I should be back in class tomorrow, insisting I still need rest and I need to heal further, but I need to get back and catch up considering I've missed a whole week. Hugo emailed me stating he was not happy about me not turning up and said that I was being a wimp and I needed to grow some balls, apparently. He sent all my tutoring work through email, which I managed to send back to him completed.

Fuck him and his inconsiderate ways. The cunt.

Chapter Twenty-Five

Going against the girls, I return back to classes the following day. The whispers follow me throughout the day, students calling me every disgusting name you can think of. Commenting how I self-harmed myself, which explains all the scars. Some even whisper saying I should have died and not come back.

I plug in my earphones to block out everyone around me, and the only time I take them out is when I need to go into class. I'm walking down the hallway, hugging onto my books when a hand reaches out and touches my shoulder from behind. I jolt, frightened someone is here to hurt me again. My heart races at a thousand miles per hour, threatening a heart attack. I turn and find Miles out of breath, placing his hand on his heart.

"I am so sorry, I kept shouting after you and you weren't responding."

I look him in the eye, trying to slow down my ragged breaths. With the music paused I remove the plugs and swing them in my hand. "Are you okay?" I ask, stunned that I'm seeing his angelic face for the first time in weeks. I try not to show any emotion towards him right now, but inside I'm holding down anger at how insensitive he's been.

He should be the one who came to my room, giving me my favorite flowers or visiting me in hospital when I could have died. He should've been the one to hold my hand, consoling me and making sure everything is okay, but instead he's been a ghost.

All the times in the past when I needed him, he hasn't been there. The only time is when I found him myself in the dance studio and we danced, but other than that, he always has an excuse. I don't want to assume or let loose on him until I know his reasons, because I could be an overreacting hormonal mess.

Usually we would spend time together when we dance but I haven't been able to, I'm too weak so the doctors signed me off for a few weeks, which had me excused from the class.

Is that it maybe? Is he angry because I haven't seen him in dance class? Too many thoughts take over my mind, and I'm staring at my supposed boyfriend, his blonde hair shining under the sun beaming through the church-style windows. He has the looks of an angel, the only thing he's missing is a pair of glorious white wings.

"I thought we could spend some time together, watch some films or something in your dorm? I've got snacks," his smiles gleams, holding out a bag and showing me all the chocolate and crisps. I suppose he's making an effort, so I nod. He takes a hold of my hand and we make our way to my dorm room. I text Blaire to let her know that I've got Miles over for a while, so she agrees to stay in Maisie's room for a bit.

We watch a few films. I even indulge myself in a few snacks, but I don't overdo it. We cuddle on my bed, but Miles seems distant and I'm unsure why. He doesn't really touch me like he used to or kiss me as often. I feel like a chore to him. Lifting my head off of his chest, I look him in the eye.

"Hey, are you okay? You don't seem yourself?" I ask, but he doesn't meet my gaze, looking away instead and clenching his jaw.

"Yeah sure, of course I am doll." He kisses my forehead, assuring me. Before I know it, I have fallen asleep and when I wake up in the middle of the night, Miles has gone, and Blaire is in her bed. I look at the time and it's three in the morning.

Unable to get anymore sleep, I get changed into my academy

uniform and make my way to the library. At least I can catch up on a few assignments in peace. I plug in my earphones, even though no one is around at this time of night I still feel safe with the sound of someone singing in my ear. It makes me feel less alone and keeps me sane.

When I get to the library the lights are already on, I take out one of my earphones and the sound of someone typing fast on a keyboard echoes throughout the eerie walls.

I thought I'd be alone.

Strutting in further to where the tables are, I notice Hugo is sitting at our usual table, so I ignore him and sit at another table. What the fuck is he doing in here at four in the morning, typing so fucking fast? I wonder if he had any sleep. He hears my footsteps on the concrete and looks up to where I'm standing, unloading my laptop and files from my satchel. He doesn't greet me and gets back to whatever he's doing. Thank god, I don't need Hugo Ego today.

My earphones are plugged back in, listening to some rock band I found the other day. I make sure it's not too loud so Hugo can't hear and scold me like he normally does. There's something in the air and I can't put my finger on it. There seems to be an unnerving feeling, and goosebumps appear on my skin, covering my body.

My breath hitches and when I take a deep breath in, I can smell the scent of Hugo's spicy aroma. The feeling around my body feels like a ghost has just passed through me, leaving a chill behind as it leaves. I do wonder if spirits haunt this castle. I have never seen one so I'm unsure if I believe, but nothing would surprise me anymore.

Hugo is walking the aisles of the library, concentration etched onto his sharp face as he hunts for a book. I want to offer my help, but I'm terrified to even talk to him. I get back to my work and when I look back up, he's nowhere to be seen, but his stuff is still on the table. I sigh, disappointed at feeling lonely again.

When I get used to not seeing him, my earphones are ripped out once again and I know exactly who it is, because he's the only fucker to ever do it.

"Hugo, what do you want?" I snap.

His brawny frame looms over me from behind, his large tattooed hand resting on the back of my chair as he leans in, his perfectly plump crimson lips near my ear.

"This is the book I'm looking for," he whispers.

Leaning in further, he grabs the book for Business Econ. But instead of taking it and leaving, he lingers. I can feel his hot breath in the crook of my neck, sending shivers down my spine. I try to swallow the big knot in my throat, but it doesn't go away.

"I can't wait until your punishment is due Africa. Just a warning… it's nearly here," the venom in his voice threatens. I want to plead and beg on my knees for no more. I can't take it. I won't be able to handle it. I am too broken. But at the same time, I really want to know what the punishment is and how he will deliver it.

He chuckles under his breath, taking the book and walking back to his table, refusing to make eye contact again.

When the clock hits six in the morning, the other Royals walk in, joining Hugo at the table. I don't think they've noticed me yet. Well, I'm hoping they haven't. I can hear their chitter chatter, so I turn my music up, blocking out their voices. I think I'm more taken aback that Royce hasn't acknowledged me yet. He normally does, and he said he was going to check in on me, but he hasn't yet.

Maybe I've pissed him off?

Forgetting where I am and who surrounds me, my music is so loud I wouldn't be surprised if they can hear. I end up bouncing my leg to the music, enjoying the sounds, itching to get back into the dance studio. I really want to get back to the club and audition for a spot on their Saturday performances as soon as I am able.

As I'm enjoying myself, I almost forget to take my tablets, so I lean down to grab my satchel and remove one of the pills and my bottle of water. When I sit back up, Royce is heading over to my table, a cute little smirk on his face.

"Hey, how are you feeling?"

He pulls out a chair, sitting in it the wrong way around, his arms folded as he leans against the spine of the chair. How does he look so good in the morning?

"I'm better thanks, and thanks again for the flowers," I whisper, not wanting the others to listen in on our conversation.

Royce scrunches up his face, the smirk hasn't disappeared. "You don't need to whisper, they know I got you flowers and stuff, I don't care what they think," he adds.

Biting my lip, I look down, embarrassed that they know. I would much rather no one knew.

"Aw, are you embarrassed?" Royce chuckles, the green of his eyes looking darker today. He rakes his perfectly manicured hands through his brown hair, making it more messy but sexy.

"I have to go. Thanks again," I murmur, packing away my stuff into my satchel, leaving Royce at the table. I'm not really in the mood to have a conversation.

~

*F*inally, after a few weeks have passed, I have my first visit to the doctor. They have given me the go ahead to dance again. I'm back to a healthy weight, muscle back on my bones, and I'm all healed.

The first thing I'm going to do this weekend is audition. Hopefully, this will help me get my confidence back. I text Samantha, asking if I can go in tomorrow before my shift to audition, to which she automatically replies and says yes.

I squeal, excited for something to be going right for once.

I'm staying at my father's house tonight, meeting with Ms. Veronica for another stupid lesson. Steve collects me from the hospital once my appointment has finished, and to my surprise he's already outside. He opens the back-passenger door for me, and I climb in. When I get to my father's house, I see that Zach's car is parked outside, but so is Ms. Veronica's. Great, just what I need.

Impatiently, I don't wait for Steve to open the door for me. I hate it when he does it anyway. It makes me feel incapable.

I make my way into the house, heading straight to the kitchen, needing an orange juice or maybe something stronger to be able to get through this. As soon as I enter, I see Zach and Ms. Veronica chatting by the breakfast bar. Her laugh blankets the room, and her hands are squeezing his muscles through the sexy suit he's wearing.

"Oh Zach, where did these come from?" she giggles, I don't think they realize I'm here.

I clear my throat to make my presence known, and Ms. Veronica lets go of his bicep, turning around to face me. "Oh, hello dear, I am early. Have you met the lovely Zach? He's a friend of your father's and used to be one of the male escorts for the debutant balls," she says, too excited. Her eyes are wide, and she has the biggest grin on her face that I have ever seen.

"We've met," I retort, grabbing the orange juice and filling up my glass.

"Can we have a moment Veronica, please darling?" Zach flutters his eyelashes and gives her a wink. I think she orgasmed just by that. Hm, so she has a thing for Zach and my father? Gross.

My eyes narrow at Zach. "Darling?" I tilt my head. "You big flirt," I smile.

"I heard what happened. Are you okay?" he says, the smirk disappearing, replaced by worry. He looks so handsome in his navy suit, his long blonde hair untied, his bangs nearly covering his eyes. He strides towards me, I put down the glass of orange juice on the breakfast bar to which Zach appears behind me, placing his warm hands on my arms. Just that small touch ignites something inside of me, the goosebumps covering my skin and I shiver.

"I love how you react to me," he purrs, and I can feel the vibration of his chest on my back when he speaks. I lick my lips and take in a deep breath, trying to calm my nerves.

I spin round to try and escape, but it appears as though Zach took it as an invitation, and both of his palms go to the counter, caging me in. I lean my ass back on the counter, my eyes traveling down to his beautiful plump lips, and I end up licking mine again. I want to taste them again, so badly. Not to make someone else jealous, but because I enjoyed it so much. I look up to his half-lidded eyes, the bedroom look really working it for me. On the outside I look calm, but I feel as though a hurricane is exploding in my stomach, the ache between my legs begging for his hands to touch me there.

I tilt my head, the curls sliding off my shoulder, exposing my neck to him.

Smirking, I take a deep breath. "I'm fine thanks. How did you find out?" I ask, evading the last thing he said, and I'm intrigued to how he knows.

He shrugs his shoulders.

"Royce mentioned it to me at one of our meetings."

His eyes go dark, as if a demon has possessed him. I push him away from me, uncaging myself. "I've got a guest, so if you'll excuse me," I tell him, walking off to meet Ms. Veronica in the drawing room. For the rest of the day, Zach occupies my mind, the sexual tension between us exhilarating.

Chapter Twenty-Six

*a*t the club, the dancers are practicing on the stage for their performances tonight. I'm drying the glasses and stare at them in awe. I wish I were that confident, able to get up on stage like that and dance so... erotically. It must be exhilarating. I didn't come prepared with a routine, so I decide that I'm going to wing it. Sometimes I work best under pressure, plus I wasn't able to due to my health, so I had no choice.

"I am so excited to see what you have in store for us," Samantha smiles. I have only her and Lily as my audience later thankfully, as I thought I'd have to do it in front of everyone. I pour myself a small whiskey, discovering I actually like it after I tried it once. I was intrigued as to why Royce enjoyed it so much, now I can't stop drinking the stuff.

"Ade, you good for five minutes time?" Samantha says, looking at her watch on her wrist.

I nod in response, the butterflies in my stomach starting to flutter. I feel slightly nauseous, but I'm sure I'll be fine. Quickly get changed into some booty shorts and a sports bra, I leave my hair untied. Making my way onto the stage, I stretch my limbs as Samantha and Lily take their seats in the VIP booth. It has the best view. I put on my chosen song 'To Be Loved' by Papa Roach. It makes me feel really wild and free, it's the perfect song to freestyle to. Using a chair as a prop like the dancer for Charles' birthday did, I improvise, taking in what she did that night.

Watching these girls, I notice they flip their hair a lot, so I do just that, swaying my hips, sticking my butt out and opening my legs. It's pretty much all my routine entails. I work around the stage, touching my body as I go. I feel like one of the girls from that film Coyote Ugly, dancing on the bar. I actually feel so free, and it really is adrenaline-charged. This feels addictive, terrifying but exciting. All my nerves are stimulated, I feel sexy but classy at the same time. I don't think I've ever swayed my hair so much.

When my routine has finished, my skin now sweating from the excitement, the girls stand up, clapping their hands.

"Damn girl, you really can move!" Samantha says, walking over to me. I sit on the side of the stage, dangling my feet on the edge, trying to get my breath back. It will take me a while to get my strength and stamina back, but it's a start.

Lily smiles, as she stands next to Samantha. "You are so good! I'm extremely impressed and I must admit, I was a bit skeptical at first, but you proved me wrong," Lily says, which is the most she has ever said to me in fact.

Jumping off the stage, I go back to the bar to get myself a bottle of water to quench my thirst. When I've finally got my breath back and the adrenaline has worn off, I go back to the ladies' room and get changed back into my work clothes, ready for an exciting night ahead of me.

The club isn't overly busy tonight, Samantha and Lily have left, leaving me in charge and to lock up, which is a great privilege in itself. When the club doesn't attract anymore newcomers by midnight I lock up, order an Uber, and get back to the academy.

Exhaustion has taken over me, I'm unable to even keep my eyes open in the Uber. When I get back to the academy, I have a shower and crash in my bed, falling into a deep sleep.

I wake up before my alarm the following morning, and I'm starving. Checking the time, it's only half seven in the morning, but the dining hall will be serving breakfast at this time. Hopefully, no one else is an early bird and gets breakfast this early. I get showered and changed within a matter of minutes.

I remember to take my pills for my anxiety and then make my way over to the dining hall. To my pleasure it's empty, no one is around and the food smell delicious, making my stomach grumble even more. I order myself some bacon and eggs with a coffee and an orange juice, for once excited about food. After last night I feel a lot more like myself, but I seem to have this mantra playing - as soon as I feel better, something bad happens. And so, I live every day negatively, expecting something to happen. I walk the halls constantly looking over my shoulder for trouble.

At least if it does happen again, I won't be so disappointed.

I scoff down my breakfast, almost licking my plate clean. I order myself another coffee to go, contemplating what to do today. It's nearly spring, so it's a little warmer outside. Do I go surfing, dancing or just study? So many options for the day. Collecting my coffee, I walk out of the dining hall, my feet taking me outside to the court-yard. I sit on a bench overlooking the vast countryside that surrounds us, the green hills in the horizon.

The garden flowers are blossoming, the bees starting to collect nectar to make their honey, and it's so peaceful. I take a deep breath in, relishing the clean country air. I sit there for a good hour, until my coffee is finished and then I make my way back to my room.

I text Zach, asking him if he fancies going surfing today, feeling a companion might do me good. And it's an excuse to see him. He texts me back straight away, saying he will pick me up as he was on his way there anyway. The butterflies start fluttering in my stomach again, so I hurry myself and slide on my wetsuit and put some leggings and a hoodie on over the top. I tie my scruffy hair into a messy bun on top of my head, not really caring what I look like. There's no point in putting make-up on if it's all just going to run anyway. Within five minutes, Zach texts to say he's in the courtyard waiting for me. My little legs hurry, excited to see him and of course to go surfing.

My face lights up as soon as I see the car. "Hey, thanks for picking me up," I say, climbing into the luxurious Ferrari. I think I've seen his car more than him.

The smirk on his face lights up the sapphire gems of his eyes, and his long hair is tied up in a bun on his head to, ready to surf. He looks so devilish with his hair tied up; I wonder what it would feel like with my hands tangled in it while...

No Ade, no. You have a boyfriend.

We get to the beach in record time, the sun beaming across the ocean, filled with surfers. Once again, I'm the only girl surfer amongst all the guys. I don't mind though; I usually prefer guys over girls anyway. The guy from before is in the beach hut, our boards are already waxed and waiting for us both.

"I called ahead," Zach winks. I smile in return, taking my clothes off to then put in a locker. We hurry ourselves, getting too excited for the waves and run towards the huge waves taking over.

We surf for hours. I haven't laughed this much in a while, but once I realize this, I stop myself. I'm terrified to be happy again. Who knows what's round the corner, Someone could take a picture of me again and start calling me names, and I know for sure I'll just want to die.

"Come on, we need food and something to drink," Zach says, giving me his hand to lift me up from the golden sand. I rub the sand away from my ass and my sweaty palms, grabbing my board to take back to the beach hut. When we put our boards away, Zach takes off the top half of his wetsuit, exposing that muscular torso of his. The broad shoulders, the abs, that V line....

My mouth waters like a dog in heat at the sight, and he takes his hair out of the bun, running over to the outdoor showers to rinse himself off. The way the water runs over his chest and abs should be illegal. Those big hands scrub at his face, the blonde strands sticking to the side of his face. I stare in astonishment at this Viking god before me, rubbing those big hands over his body. It's not until he comes out, wiping the water off, that he shakes his head, letting his hair sway to remove the water. I think I'm in heaven.

"You ready?" he asks, pulling me out of my own little porno in my head. I nod, unable to form words to this figure in front of me.

Good god, what's wrong with me? I mentally slap myself for having these thoughts over another man when I'm in a relationship.

Zach ends up taking to me a local fish and chip shop. We order some chips to share and a cod each with some fizzy drinks as we sit in a little booth staring out at the ocean. It's very relaxed in this little restaurant, letting us in with our wetsuits and Zach's is still halfway undone, tied around his waist. As he leans his head down, a few strands cover his blue eyes, water still slightly dripping off, falling onto his perfectly sculpted nose and lips.

I wonder if he knows what I'm thinking about...

"I've never been in one of these before..." I tell him, pouting my lips.

Zach looks at me in surprise, his beautiful eyes going wide at my revelation. "No way, this is Britain's finest cuisine. Have you ever had a chip buttie?" he asks, raising one of his blonde eyebrows at me.

I shake my head, my face scrunched up, wondering what the fuck a 'chip buttie' is.

Zach gasps, "That's it, you need a lesson, and I will show you." He asks the waitress to bring two rolls with butter once our food arrives, and it smells delicious.

The waitress brings over two buns, already buttered and Zach does the unspeakable... he puts the salt and vinegar-soaked chips into the bun, closes it and hands it to me.

My eyes go wide, unsure of how to feel about this weird concoction. When I take a bite out of this 'chip buttie', it is the best thing I have ever tasted. I moan in response, enjoying the taste of two carbs put together to create such a dish. Wow.

"My god, that is amazing!" I squeal.

Zach chuckles and makes himself one. We demolish the butties in seconds, and I have no words.

We eat the rest of our food, the fish battered to perfection and the chips are delicious. We end up playing a game as to who can catch the most chips in our mouths, and Zach seems to be beating me, but his aim at throwing chips at my face isn't that great. We have the most relaxed but amazing evening.

I'm flooded with disappointment when it's time to head back to the academy.

~

*B*laire strolls into the room after her shower. "Hey, how was your weekend?"

I sit up, resting my head on my headboard, looking at Blaire. She's had her black hair cut again so that it's resting on her shoulders. Blaire is naturally pretty; she has those amazing eyebrows that girls dream of. "It was good thanks; the doctor has given me the go ahead to dance again." Blaire squeals, jumping up and down before she jumps on me in my bed. I laugh at how excited she is because I know she just wants the best for me. She and Maisie are like the sisters I never had.

Blaire gets off of me, pulling me along with her.

I have a shower, wash my hair, then brush my teeth. I don't bother drying my hair, rather just put it in a ponytail on my head. I put on a tiny bit of concealer, hiding the black circles around my eyes, and add a little mascara.

Honestly, I couldn't care less about what I look like anymore.

When we get to the dining hall, Maisie is already waiting for us, a coffee sat waiting for me. I take my seat, ordering myself a fruit bowl for breakfast, not wanting to eat in front of the full room. Even though I have managed to get better with eating, I still have a bad relationship with food and what comes with it. Yesterday with Zach made me forget about my fears and I enjoyed it. I don't feel as though Zach judges me and it's refreshing. Recently though, I have had doubts replaying in my mind about Miles, considering I haven't seen him since our movie night.

I sigh when I notice the Royals entering the dining hall, laughing, and joking around with each other. Why should they be so happy when I'm so miserable? Life really is unfair.

Taking a bite out of my apple, an arm snakes round my shoulders. "Hey beautiful," Miles says, jolting me from my seat. I think he forgets when someone touches me, I have serious anxiety. He kisses me on the cheek then takes the seat next to me, his arm resting on the spine of my chair. "Are you going to the party this weekend?" he asks.

I shake my head, unaware of what party he's talking about. Plus, I do not want to go to a party where all the assholes are. "No, I haven't heard about it and I probably won't go," I state. I sound abrupt, but with the state of my mental health, the party sounds like a bad idea. The girls look at me with assurance in their eyes. They are way behind me and know for a fact I wouldn't go unless I wanted to.

"Well at least think about it. Nothing will happen to you if you're with me, doll. I need to go," he says as he stands to leave. Without a goodbye from him or even a kiss on the cheek like normal, he storms off. I think I pissed him off, but oh well.

In Business Economics, Blake and I are starting on the second half of our project. Once again, he's actually being civil, talking to me like a normal person rather than spitting or sneering. "Hopefully, if we meet in the library again and work on it together, we can finish this soon," he says, writing down a few notes to take away with him for later.

"Yeah, sure," I reply. I like this side to Blake when he's calm and not so stressed out. When he actually works in a team.

"Can you do this evening after classes end?" he asks, the blues of his eyes sparkling. This is the first time I have seen their true colour. They aren't so dark, as if a demon has possessed his soul, like before. I wouldn't be surprised if one did. It would be an easy job, seeing as he's halfway there anyway.

"Y-yeah of course, but I have a t-tutoring session with Hugo as well. I don't want to make him mad." I can't help but stutter, I have never had a normal conversation with this douche before.

"Fuck him, you're doing fine in your subjects now, so you don't need him," he kisses his teeth, frowning.

How does he know how well I'm getting on in my subjects... when we only share two classes?

The rest of the day drags by slowly. For some reason, I'm a little excited to meet Hugo and Blake in the library once classes have finished for the day. As much as they annoy me, they can sometimes be funny to be around. You forget that these people are supposed to be the future leaders of the world. Lord Darlington created this elite academy for the blue bloods of our society. An academy that has every subject you can think of, and that any normal student would beg to be a part of. The opportunities here are supposed to be endless and a kick start for your future.

Normal students who pay thousands of pounds to go to university would die for this kind of opportunity. I think about all the jobs I could get by having a degree in pretty much every subject there is. It's a shame they don't do what they do in America, a scholarship, giving a few less fortunate students the chance to attend to make a better life for themselves.

When it's time to meet Hugo and Blake in the library, I stroll in with my earphones plugged into my ears, blocking out any rude comments that come my way.

The tension between Blake and Hugo is so thick you could cut it with a knife. They're both scowling at each other, Hugo's teeth are bared, and Blake's clenching his strong jaw. Looks as though a fight could abrupt anytime soon. I really do not want to be part of it, but seeing these two huge guys fight each other might be interesting...

I wonder who would win? Hugo is built like he's been on steroids or something and Blake is slightly smaller, but he probably has good agility, a skill gained by playing field hockey.

Soon as I've taken my seat, Blake is the first one to break, tearing his eyes away from the true leader of their group. Taking out my laptop and worksheets, I organize my tutoring stuff first and then the project materials. I feel as though I could be here till really late tonight. "Here's your maths stuff," Hugo grumbles, and I take it from him, seeing an A on the front. I mentally high five myself. I really am getting better in all subjects now. That's probably how Blake knows. He's joined my tutoring sessions so that he can get his work done. That makes more sense.

"Africa, are you perhaps making an appearance at our little party this weekend?" Hugo asks, lifting his gaze from his laptop to me.

I look up, meeting his hard stare and shaking my head. "No, I will not be making an appearance," I utter.

Why the fuck is everyone asking me about going to this party?

"Oh, I think you should…I insist," Hugo grins, the mischievousness of his tone showing through. I can see it being a bad idea, especially as Hugo has said before that my little 'punishment' is due, but I do not want to find out what it is - yet.

"I said no. I am not going," I state, putting my foot down.

I'm clenching my pen so tight my knuckles turn white. Hugo and Blake notice and they both smirk at each other. Carrying on with my work, ignoring the pair of idiots next to me, I plug my earphones back in, not giving a shit if Hugo doesn't like it.

We're all in the library till gone nine in the evening, Blake and I working hard on our project whilst Hugo does whatever he does. Charles and Royce come in, bringing takeout food for the table but I decline their offer.

"Ade, you should really eat, you had a fruit bowl for breakfast and then you didn't eat at lunch…" Royce says.

I scrunch up my nose, my face turning into a frown as I look at him. "Sorry, stalker alert…" I say.

Charles roars in laughter, clasping Royce's shoulder. "Dude, that is pretty stalkerish," he continues to laugh.

"I'm observant, especially since the incident," Royce sneers, giving a deathly look to the table. If looks could kill, this one would.

"No, I'm fine, seriously," I assure him.

In truth, my stomach is aching, the scent of their burgers and chips is driving me nuts but I won't put myself in that position again, especially since I don't know who sent out that photo of me. I'm still adamant that it was Charles.

Chapter Twenty-Seven

"*A*re you sure you don't want to come to the party? You'll have me, Maisie, Miles and even Royce looking out for you," Blaire pleads. We're sitting in our room as Blaire tries on some dresses for tonight's huge-ass party in Stonewall.

"I'll think about it."

Laying on my bed, scrolling through social media, as soon Blaire goes back into the bathroom to start her beauty regime, I look under my nightstand for the photo album of my mum. I wanted some time alone with her, reminiscing old times before I decided on tonight. When I bend down to grab it, I can't find it. I get off my bed, leaning down on the floor to check under the bed, under my nightstand.

Everywhere.

I cannot find it.

My heart is now beating in my throat, my chest tightening in fear. "Hey Blaire, have you seen my photo album? I can't find it..." I shout, but she responds with a no.

"Oh my god, where is it?" I look around the room, pulling everything out of every nook and cranny that I can find, but it's nowhere to be seen. The last person to be in the room other than Blaire and Maisie was Miles, but I doubt he would take it.

Doubt forms in my mind, clouding my judgement. Did Miles take it? Or am I imagining it? I try calling him, but there's no answer, so I continue to try over and over but all I get is a text sent through that he's busy, and that he will see me at the party.

I told him I wasn't going, so why the fuck is he saying he will see me there?

"Have you found it yet?" Blaire enters the bedroom, wearing just her towel, her face covered in a green face mask.

I shake my head in response, tears threatening to escape but I won't let them. "I'll go to the party," I tell her, and she squeals, clapping her tiny hands in excitement before retreating back into the bathroom.

I suppose I better start getting ready.

Once I'm showered, shaved and every other beauty treatment you can think of, I blow dry my hair into bouncy curls, clipping the top half so it's out of my face. I apply concealer, mascara, and finish it off with some red lipstick. This is the first time I've worn make-up in a while, and it feels good. I'm looking through the closet for something to wear tonight, and I end up pulling out two dresses to try on. I can't decide if I should wear the black halter neck swing dress, or the tight strapless red dress.

Holding each dress up to my body, I ask Blaire which she prefers. "Hmm, not sure whether to go black or red."

She taps her chin with her index finger, "I like the black one, it suits you." She grins.

Once I've slipped on the black dress, I criticize myself in the mirror as always, looking for an excuse not to wear it, but I actually appreciate how much effort I made. I actually look good again for once. Slipping on some plain black heels and grabbing a red clutch bag, I give myself another once over just in case, and a mental pep talk.

Ade, you can do this, just go to the party, and ask Miles. That's all...

Taking a deep breath, I count to ten, calming my nerves before we get ready to leave.

Maisie doesn't bother knocking on the door and enters freely, holding onto a bottle of tequila. "Hey bitches!" she squeals.

Maisie looks amazing as ever, her normal auburn corkscrew curls have been tamed into soft curls which fall around her petite face. Her cherry red lipstick is the focal point on her face, matching her red, long-sleeved skater dress, buttoned up all the way to the white collar. She reminds me of Cheryl from Riverdale, the way she's dressed. All she's missing is the knee-high socks.

Blaire pulls out three shot glasses from her cupboard, which I'm guessing she's always had. Maisie pours us the tequila shots "This will help calm our nerves and we need a little boost before we head out." Maisie cheers and we clink glasses and gulp our shots in one go, all three of us are so used to drinking tequila that we don't even pull the face anymore.

We order an Uber that then drives us to the destination, which happens to be an abandoned warehouse in the marina.

"Is this the right place?" I question Blaire, and she hums a yes in response, but I don't have a good feeling about this.

As we walk towards the derelict building, I follow behind Blaire and Maisie, feeling underdressed for some reason. Blaire looks so angelic in her white-off shoulder dress, the chiffon fabric blowing around her knees from the wind. Her heels are a lot higher than mine; the platform alone is three inches high. I call them stripper shoes.

I catch up to them, linking all our arms together as we walk to the side of the building. I stare at the graffiti covered brick walls, garbage cans everywhere piled high with trash, the ground covered in potholes, flooded with dirty water. This is how people get kidnapped in films, or even killed.

My heart stutters as I follow the girls. Clearly, they know the way.

We come up behind the warehouse, up to a metal door which has been left ajar, and Blaire is the first one to enter. I'm the last one. Only one light illuminates the halls, the green hue which flickers every second, moths surrounding the broken glass that should cover it. This feels all too sinister for me, and I want to turn around and get back to the academy into my own bed. That would be perfect right now.

As we inch closer to another metal door, I start hearing the thump of music playing. I finally let out a breath which I have been holding in, relieved to hear an actual party taking place. We enter through the narrow door into a vast space, the floor covered in bodies, dancing to 'Smells Like Teen Spirit' by Nirvana, all jumping up and down to the beat.

I scan the abandoned warehouse, no windows are present, but the set-up is professional, strobe lights fixed to the metal railing above us in the roof. The minute they go off, its pitch black in here. Smoke machines surround the DJ booth, which is propped up by metal containers, and large speakers placed in every corner of the room for the full effect.

"We need to find the bar," Blaire shouts over the music, and I nod as we take each other's hands, ensuring we don't lose one another in this place. I don't recognize any faces yet. I thought this was an academy party, but it seems everyone is welcome. We push ourselves through the sweaty bodies, trying to get to the other side of the warehouse, finally finding the make-shift bar made out of wooden crates and barrels. Very rustic.

"Oh, look who it is. My sister and her two slaggy friends," Blake says, coming up from behind the bar, holding onto a beer with a menacing grin. I roll my eyes, folding my arms across my chest. I turn around to stare at the dance floor instead of his mischievous face. I have not got the patience for tonight. The only reason I attended was to speak to Miles and then head back to the academy.

Pulling out my phone, I text Miles, telling him I'm here and asking where he is.

"Here's your drink," Blaire says as she passes me a rum and cola.

I take a sip, my face scrunching in disgust. "God this is really strong. You trying to give me alcohol poisoning?" I grimace.

Blaire and Maisie laugh as Blake leans against the metal staircase behind him, not looking like he fits in. He's wearing navy blue chino shorts, a white Ralph Lauren polo shirt and a navy cardigan tied around his neck. Posh twat.

"And here I thought you weren't attending?" he purrs, wiggling his eyebrows at me. I ignore the bastard, taking another sip of my rum with a dash of cola, which will hopefully make me forget about this dick.

"Have you seen Miles, Blake?" I ask, pursing my lips at him, but he shrugs his shoulders at me and walks off into the ocean of people.

Okay then.

Blaire grabs my hand, pulling me into the crowd to dance, and we jump around, swaying our hips to 'My Bloody Valentine' by Machine Gun Kelly which happens to be her favorite song. Maisie has sauntered off somewhere with a guy, unsure if she knows him or not, but she is confident and meets guys all the time.

Once we've had our fill of dancing, we need another drink to quench our thirst. I see Royce hanging out by the bar, grabbing himself a drink.

"Hey," I say, coming up next to him.

As soon as Royce sees me, his eyes go wide in shock, his lips in a perfect 'O'.

"What are you doing here? I thought you weren't coming Ade?" he gushes. I stare at him in confusion, thinking he would be excited to see me but instead he's wearing the expression of surprise, but not in a good way. "You shouldn't be here Ade," he continues, grabbing my upper arm, squeezing tightly. I pull my arm away, biting the inside of my cheek before I lose my shit.

I raise my eyebrows at him. "What do you mean, Royce?" I spit. My hand lands on my cocked hip. "Why do you look so surprised that I came to a party everyone asked me to attend?" I say.

Royce scrubs one hand across his face before looking at me again. The sea green of his eyes avoiding mine, he presses his lips together in a flat line, sighing.

"Ade, I know where Miles is. Blake said he's outside. Come on," Blaire shouts over the loud, banging music. She grabs my hand to escort me outside, but Royce grabs the other, and I feel as though I'm in a game of tug and war.

"Ade, do not go outside… please," Royce pleads.

Do I listen to Royce? Or do I not? Eventually, I decide to follow Blaire outside into a large courtyard, surrounded by large brick walls. A huge makeshift bonfire sits in the middle, surrounded by different bodies, and faces of people I finally recognize to be from the academy. On the far side of the bonfire, I catch a glimpse of the Royals, seated in a makeshift seating area. The chairs and tables are made by wooden crates, but I don't see Miles anywhere.

"Nice of you to attend, Africa," Blake says, standing up from where he was sitting. The whole courtyard goes silent, turning around to look at me. Hugo and Charles stand up from their seats, walking behind Blake as he walks closer to me.

"Blake, what's going on?" Blaire asks, concern in her voice.

I knew coming here was a bad idea, so why didn't I just listen to my fucking gut?

Grimacing, I swallow the lump in my throat, lifting my chin up in defiance. Fuck them. I am not retaliating for whatever they have planned. My ears pick up on giggling from the three bitches who were sitting with the Royals, and I shake my head, looking down at the ground before I bring my gaze up to them. Blake's standing in front of me, Charles is on his left and Hugo on the right.

Clearly this is an academy event, otherwise Hugo would be the one in charge.

"Africaaa" Hugo drags out, purring my name as he steps forward, Blake taking the hint and stepping back. Oh, shit. I've definitely underestimated the whole who's in charge thing now. Blaire looks at me in confusion, clearly unaware of the real hierarchy between these cunts.

"Blake?" Blaire pleads. I turn my head around, noticing Royce is behind me, shaking his head before looking down at the ground. I look around at the familiar faces but then Zach comes through, parting the audience. He's out of breath, standing next to Royce as he stares at us in surprise.

Oh, so he's in on it too. Maybe all this time he was pretending to be my friend, the fucking prick. I knew I shouldn't trust him, especially if he knows my actual secret.

Has he told them?

Hugo tuts, shaking his head. "I did warn you that you were due a punishment, and now look. You turned up on time…" Hugo drawls, his hard face staring at me with venom in those dark eyes. He's clenching his jaw, the muscles in his neck pulsing. I notice the tight black shirt and black ripped jeans he's wearing, looking devilishly handsome as always.

Charles is wearing jeans and a white shirt, the sleeves rolled back to his elbows. Both him and Blake have sinister grins on their faces, and Blake stands with his arms behind his back, clearly hiding something.

Hugo looks over his shoulder to Blake, signaling for him to hand something over.

"I thought we could go down…. Memory lane? How does that sound?"

I shake my head, my breath picking up speed as I now have an idea what Hugo holds in those large, tattooed hands. "How…did you…?" I mumble, unable to get my words out.

Hugo grins, chuckling under his breath as he brings my photo album in front of him, opening the pages. I find Miles coming out from behind the Royals, wearing a nonchalant expression as he walks towards them. "Miles? What's going on…?" I ask, staring at my supposed boyfriend joining the Royal dicks.

"You should really dump him Africa. I mean, he is a complete dick," Hugo says, giving a derisive laugh as he takes a step back. Blake steps forward, taking the photo album from Hugo.

"He is the one you have to thank for tonight, Miles here is the one who pretended to like you, even date you just so he can get your dirty little secrets and tell us. The last task he was set, was to just dump you in front of everyone and express his hatred for you, but then… he brought us this lovely photo album and came up with a whole new plan," Blake says, his lips curling even wider into a mischievous grin.

Shifting on my feet, uncomfortable with this situation, tears start forming as my body begins to shake. "Miles, why are you doing this?" I stutter, staring at the man who I thought was angel, my comfort zone, the guy who helped me during my lowest points. But then it began to make sense. Recently, he's been so distant, not caring when I was in hospital, beaten black and blue by his sister.

He shrugs, smirking. "It was the only way to become one of them…"

I scoff. "What, a stupid Darlington Knight?" My eyes narrow at him. The crowd gasps at the fact that I just mentioned them, by name. Miles nods his head at me before taking a step back, joining Constance, who snakes her arms around his shoulders, licking the outer shell of his ear.

That's fucking gross.

"Blake I swear to god, I will never speak to you again if you do this…" Blaire shouts, running towards Blake but there's always someone around to grab her out of the way, and this time it's Zach. My chest tightens, my throat closing up, and I'm unable to breath. Blake takes out a photo, showing me the one of me and my mum hugging each other on the beach, but then he throws it into the fire. A scream escapes my lips, shouting for them to stop, but Blake carries on.

"Why?!" I cry out, trying to run to Blake to stop him, but my heel catches in a crack in the tar, sending me to the floor. My knees hit the rough ground, grazing my skin. The palms of my hands cut from the sharp stones as I try to break my fall. The tears are streaming down my cheeks, hitting the ground as I plead. The sound around me muffles, my senses all lost as I watch Blake burn photo after photo, the only thing I have left from my mum. The only thing to remember her by.

"Stop, please stop… What have I done to deserve this?!" I scream, my throat closing up as I beg on my bleeding knees. The Royals all laugh, the flames dancing around their dark faces, once again appearing as if they have just emerged from hell. The true demons that they are, are visible now, showing their true identity, away from the masks that they wear.

"Africa, we warned you. And this is the price," Blake hisses through his teeth, throwing the whole album into the fire. I crawl forward towards the burning wood, watching my life burn away. The pages disintegrate as I watch through the flames. The album turns into ash.

It's as if I'm watching her being cremated once again. I bang my clenched fists against the tar, cutting my skin further, not caring that I have an audience to see me break down.

And here I thought they couldn't do worse when they accused me of murdering my mother. But here they stand, the three fucking cunts actively murdering my mum's memory. Making me break down and crumble in front of everyone.

They have won.

I'm officially beaten, bruised, and now broken.

I'm cowering on the ground until the audience submerge back into the warehouse, leaving me alone. As soon as Blaire has been released by Zach, she runs over, grabbing me into her arms. My chest hyperventilates, my heart is beating so fast I can't even get a breath of fresh air into my lungs.

Zach joins Blaire, trying to speak to me but I can't hear anything. My focus is on the fire, watching the ash float around in the air. I get up on my own, the blood dripping down my knees from the deep cuts. I can't feel the pain. My feet take off, running through the warehouse and out again to where the Uber dropped us off. I quickly order an Uber which arrives in a matter of minutes and takes me back to the academy.

I storm through into my dorm, wiping the tears away from my cheeks. My body is shaking from the trauma caused, but I know how to stop the pain. I go to my side table, pulling out all my pills. My anti-depressants, pain killers and whatever else I can find. Stumbling into the bathroom, I fill a glass of water and down all the pills. This should stop the pain, and hopefully I can join my mum wherever she is. I stare at myself in the mirror, my face cherry red, my cheeks stained by my mascara and my red lipstick smudged all over.

I look like pure shit.

It's not long until I feel my body shut down, the numb feeling creeping through my veins. I fall to the ground, my knees hitting the ground again, but this time I don't feel a thing. As my eyes threaten to close, I hear shouting from the bedroom. Blaire comes storming into the bathroom and I hear another familiar voice, Royce.

"Call an ambulance! She's taken an overdose!" Blaire shouts.

That's the last thing I hear before my body shuts down on me.

"de."

"Ade?"

My eyes begin to open to the voice calling my name. My vision is all blurry as I awake, but it begins to focus, and I see Blaire standing over me. I try to speak but my throat and mouth is so dry, like the Sahara dessert. I need water.

I've only just woken up, but I feel exhausted, my body aching, screaming at me to move. I scan my eyes around, noticing that I'm back in a blue room, with the paintings of the ocean and farmland. I'm in the hospital. I try and use both my arms to push me up to sit, but my arms give way, clearly too weak.

Blaire notices and assists in lifting me up, adjusting my bed so that the head is upright. "What happened?" I ask, my voice coming out raspy.

"Ade, you had an overdose on all your pills. Royce and I got to you just in time."

Tears form in her eyes as Blaire explains.

"How long was I out for?" I ask her, grabbing my glass of water on the little table beside me. I take a sip as she contemplates telling me, awkwardly playing with her fingers.

She sighs. "Two weeks."

I nod, accepting the fact of what happened. Blaire tries to keep the details minimal, but the memories have flooded back already, my emotions experiencing it all again.

The nurse comes to check all my vitals.

"You are incredibly lucky, Miss Adams. If your friends didn't find you in time, you may have died. You took an excessive number of tablets and your body began to shut down," the nurse explains, her wide eyes staring directly into mine. "What you did was profoundly serious. I hope you understand that."

All I do is nod, agreeing with her.

No shit, I didn't do it for fun.

"A gentleman called Steve will be collecting you Miss Adams, as your father requested. It was agreed that the rest of your recovery will be at home where a nurse will be on hand twenty four seven just in case," the nurse adds and I hum in response, agreeing with her. I'm pleased that I will be able to go home rather than stay in a hospital. My nerves jitter again, frightened of what my father will say when I get home. Blaire helps me out of bed and to get changed into normal clothes, an IV still attached to my arm. I find myself in a mirror, and my skin is an ashy colour, my lips so chapped from being out cold for two weeks. My eyes are red raw still, as if I have only just stopped crying. I look like a ghoul, dead but still walking the earth.

That's how I feel too. My soul has left the vessel.

Before I know it, Steve has arrived, waiting for me outside as Blaire pushes me in a wheelchair to the car. She gives me a big hug, still crying since I opened my eyes, and then she helps me slide into the car. Steve packs my bags into the boot then climbs back in the car himself. We don't acknowledge each other the whole route, I stay quiet and just watch the outside world, the beautiful green farmlands, and woodlands. My eyes threaten to close again but I'm enjoying the view too much, so I force myself to stay awake.

As soon as I get home, I'm asking father to transfer me to a normal university, not this stupid academy for the elite shit. I'm done with it and this life. We pull into the driveway, no other cars present, which means father isn't home yet. Mrs. Blossom is standing at the bottom of the marble stairs, waiting for the car to come to a halt.

"Oh, my dear Adelaide, let's get you to your bed and I'll bring you some hot chocolate," she says as soon as her eyes land on my fragile form. She pulls me out of the car, letting me lean on her as we go through the house. Climbing the stairs, we head into my bedroom. She helps me get into the bath, washing my skin as I'm too weak. I honestly don't care if she sees me naked right now. I need a bath.

Once I'm in my pjs and tucked into bed, Mrs. Blossom brings up a hot chocolate for me to drink before I can nod off to sleep. I turn on my television, not wanting to fall asleep straight away as it's still the middle of the afternoon. I indulge myself in a few films and Mrs. Blossom brings me up some fruit to snack on.

My phone pings a few times, texts coming in from Blaire, Royce, and Zach.

Fucking Zach, the traitorous bastard, checking up on me. I read the texts, and he apologizes for what happened. Apparently, he had no clue what was going to happen, but he will explain everything to me when I feel better. Yeah right. He still owes me an explanation about the Darlington Knights, which he promised on the night of the cocktail party. I don't trust him anymore; the attraction has completely vanished.

I hate them all, and I want them to pay.

I still don't know how I didn't see this all coming. I trusted Miles with my past, my life and my love and he crushed it all in the palm of his hands to be part of some stupid legacy or tradition. Fuck them.

I wake up in the middle of the night, sweating through my satin pajamas from a bad dream. The tears roll down my face, my pillow soaked. I wipe them away as I try to stand up to go to the bathroom. My legs shake, but I seem to get the hang of it quickly, as long as I find objects along the way to balance myself.

Peeling off the soaked dress, I slip on another to make my way downstairs and make another hot chocolate. I need it. I don't bother putting on a dressing gown or slippers, my skin is too hot for the extra layers. I use the polished wooden handrail to steady myself on the steps, taking it one at a time. I saunter towards the kitchen, switching on the lights. It must be late. I look at the time to see it's two in the morning. Great.

Switching on the automatic machine, I insert a hot chocolate pod, waiting for the green light before I can pour it out. I stand there watching the machine until I hear a roar of laughter coming from another room. My father must be back, and he's not alone, the sounds of other voices ring in my ears the closer I get to his study.

My chest tightens, nervous from confronting my father, explaining to him what happened. I'm certain that he isn't on his own right now, but I don't give a shit anymore. My own parent should care about their daughter, protect them with all their life and worth.

Knocking on the door, I receive no answer. I still hear the faint noises of laughter, so I try again, but once again nothing. Fuck it. I'll just go in.

I open the heavy wooden door slightly and call out, "Father," but I don't think he hears me, so I step in further, noticing the backs of three familiar heads facing my father. He's sitting at his desk, looking all smug and way too happy for my liking.

My body shakes, nerves taking over me. "Father!" I call out louder, which helps. He stops talking, the room going silent and he stares me down with a smirk on his face. He takes a sip of his whiskey before pulling a drag of his cigar.

The three heads turn around to find me standing in the doorway.

Hugo, Blake, and Charles face me, their eyes wide and their mouths open in shock.

"Father, what's going on?" My hands clench at my sides, my chest heaving in shock and fear. The image of them laughing as my life was burned away in the fire is still before my eyes. Tears prickle behind my aching eyeballs and my body trembles so much I have to hold onto the door to steady myself. I can't fall again, not in front of them.

"Father?!" all three of the boys say in unison, staring at me blankly, like they've seen a ghost. Well bitches, this ghost is going to haunt you forever.

My father's face wrinkles up as his mouth curls into a maniacal grin, leaning back into his leather upholstered chair.

"That's right, I am Adelaide's father."

To be continued in...

PLAY – DARLINGTON ACADEMY BOOK 2

About the Author

D.V.Eeden is an indie author whose imagination runs wild, constantly day dreaming about new characters and stories. She loves to read and write, devouring books as much as she can. She lives in sunny England after moving from South Africa at a young age, where she works a normal 9-5 job and still finds time to read and write.

For any updates on future releases, insights and anything to do with books join my readers group A D.V.EEDEN readers group on Facebook.

Acknowledgments

I would like to thank everyone who has supported me throughout this journey, my best friend, family, and surrounding friends! I'd also like to say thank you to J Rose, who I met on a Facebook group for reverse harem readers. She has helped me so much throughout this process, not only as my editor but someone who has been there from start to finish, encouraging me not to give up when I have had my mini break downs! I also thank you as the reader, taking your time to read this book and if it weren't for the support from you, I wouldn't be here!

So, THANK YOU!!

Printed in Poland
by Amazon Fulfillment
Poland Sp. z o.o., Wrocław